The
Red Rebel
Extravaganza

A novel by
Angela Kay

To the younger me who felt like writing was something to be embarrassed about.
Never be afraid to share your creativity.
Vulnerability is a strength.
This was worth it.

Contents

Prologue: The Invitation

IT WAS JUST AFTER sunset when the invitation arrived.

In the town square of Cape Solaera, a miniature carousel appeared on a pedestal crafted in twisted wrought iron. Tiny black and white hot air balloons decorated the body of the stand in the absence of color, frozen in their ascent.

The contraption began to rotate, drawing a curious crowd to take in the foreign sight. Rock oxen and birds made of blooming florals joined the traditional horses and jewel-tone unicorns as they galloped in a circular pattern. A haunting melody serenaded their journey.

When the motion became precariously disjointed, the carousel halted without warning. The many lights that framed the structure flashed all at once. Ribbons of crimson and gold spiraled from the top of the carousel as the creatures parted to reveal twin doors crafted in black and white vertical stripes.

A curious child stepped forward, intending to untie the ribbon that held the doors closed. But then it slowly came undone, unassisted. A rush of gasps and grumbles overtook the onlookers as this unexpected event unfolded. The doors parted, and a bound piece of parchment unfurled. In dark lines of fresh ink and swirling penmanship was a message.

Welcome, Wild Rebels!

Congratulations on gaining access to Rovernaum's exclusive shores of Cape Solaera. A new season of The Red Game is about to begin, and it would be my greatest pleasure to invite you to join in alongside our extravagant shows and mind-boggling exhibits to become a Red Rebel. Participating in our grand endeavor will provide you with the chance to gain your heart's greatest desire.

All you have to do...is win.

But beware, if you consign your name to the parchment below and conscript yourself into the event that is about to take place, each player will be bound until the end of the game.

No exceptions. No exclusions.

Come experience each magic—infused event as a new challenge will be presented nightly! The victor crowned on the final day will be the sole Rebel who conquers the night before the night conquers them in turn.

Bring chaos to the stars and cast your fate into the cosmos. Not even the wildest of imaginations can fathom what spectacular wonders await...

Seven will play, one will remain.

And remember, play fearlessly, for only the bravest of souls will win.

Welcome to the Season of Shimmering Souls

The Grand Master of the Red Rebel Extravaganza

Word of the invitation reached every land under the crown of the empress by nightfall. Every kingdom, recognized or not, heard the loudest cries and darkest whispers of what this new game might mean. The kindling to this wildfire wasn't just that the last Red Game had been played more than a decade prior but that the ringmaster had been rumored to be missing. No matter a person's view on the situation, whether it be breathless excitement or callous indifference, one thing was clear. Cassian September, the Grand Master of The Red Rebel Extravaganza, was sending a message.

He was ready to play.

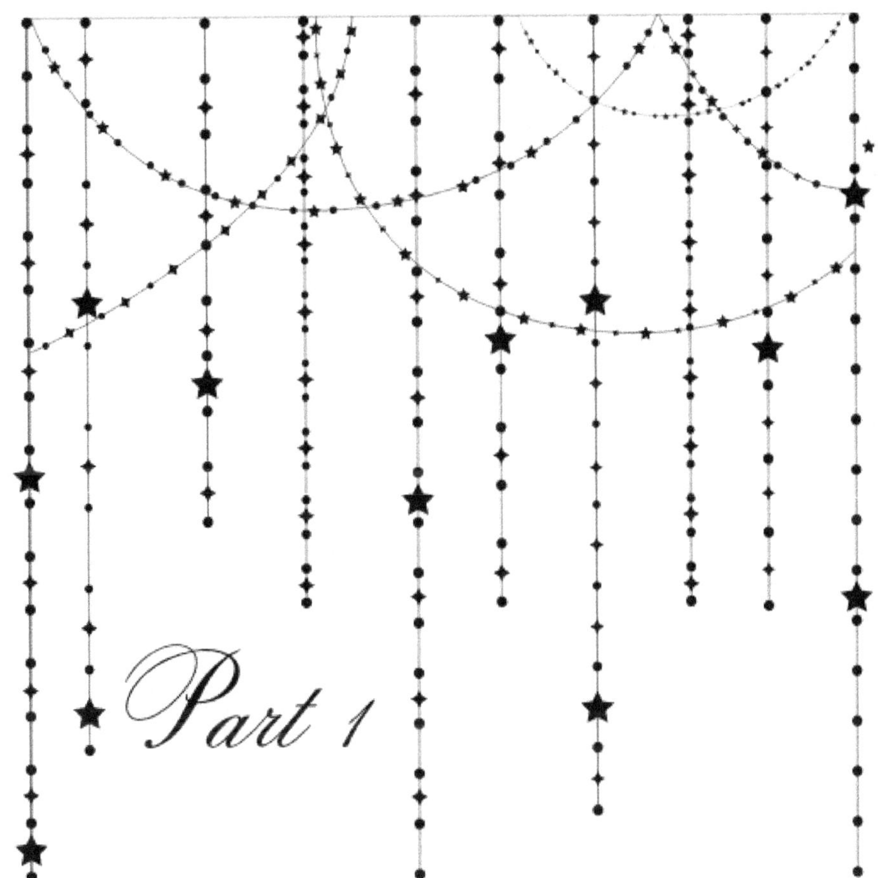

Part 1

CHAPTER ONE

The Tease and the Magician

COPPER JAMES FOUND THE answer to her problems the day the invitation to the Red Game was posted. While others saw a chance to change their fate, she recognized a different opportunity. If the ringmaster wanted to play a new game after such a lengthy hiatus, it meant he *wanted* something, and someone with his status in the world of magic probably knew where other highly coveted things were.

Things she most definitely needed.

Just one more job, and this will all be over, Copper told herself, trying not to think about what it had cost her to get the 'in' for this job. Trusting thieves and smugglers to give her accurate information wasn't her favorite means toward an end goal. She didn't particularly enjoy parting with one of her favorite hideaways to obtain it, either. But it was all she had to work with at the moment.

Copper felt her heart picking up its pace with every few strides she made when crossing into the magic district. The black brick streets and shop windows glowed with the last of the dwindling twilight sun. Every step she took seemed to whisper the same mantra she'd told herself since she had been released from the High Castle dungeon.

One more.

One more.

One more job…

She'd been given a piece of information, regarding the ringmaster, from a not-quite-reputable source. Unfortunately, that was as reliable as it got when she had been out of the loop for an extended period of time. The smuggling world was a fast-paced, fickle beast that fed on the misdeeds of those who thrived within overlapping networks of connections and information that flowed to the tune of profit and ever-changing power struggles. It was a ruthless game that Copper had tried and failed within many times until she'd learned to speak the language of the underground.

Then, she'd succeeded. And done so with a glittering prowess for gaining access to the unknowable about people, places, and things until she was the go-to for high-risk smuggling operations.

That is…until she'd gotten caught.

The air grew rich, a sweet prickling that danced along her skin as she continued into a portion of the city referred to as The Avenue. Copper kept her head low as she waded through tourists and vendors, listening to every transaction she passed on the street: enchanted this and mystical that, she made a mental note of what was requested and sold.

Supply and demand won't help you tonight, she reminded herself when as a weathered piece of paper flapped from where it was fastened to a nearby light post. While magic was not a rare commodity in The Empire of Aerimora, laws still surrounded it. Copper rolled her eyes at the posting that served as a reminder that the laws of the High Castle couldn't touch them there in The Avenue, nor could these magics be used against the empress in return.

Copper squinted when she quickly turned off the main road and approached a cream-colored shop. The last glimmers of the setting sun reflected off the building that lacked a sign or other indication of what was inside. When she reached for the crystal doorknob, her knuckles brushed against the front-facing panel, the gold paint on the doorframe slightly damp.

Copper swiftly withdrew her hand, slowly rubbing the metallic color from her fingers onto the palm of her glove. Her spine straightened, her senses prickling with the early warning bells of something being off. Her eyes widened slightly, her nostrils flared as she became even more aware of her surroundings. The city was always bustling with music or chatter, people buying and selling.

But this street was silent, and that also felt wrong.

"Why are you wet," she asked the doorway, stepping back to eye the storefront. The entire stoop had recently been painted in elegant, reflective lines that drew the eye from every direction. It wasn't that shop owners didn't possess the right to redecorate their historic shops in the capital city, but something about the entire situation had her intuition singing a chorus of warning bells.

*You've fallen for a staged venue before…*a voice said in the back of her head. *What makes this any different?*

Dressed in all black, from her wool scarf and cloak to her glossy boots, Copper paced before the storefront and internally mulled over every scenario. This could be a trap, and she could be entirely out of her depths in making a deal with a man who wielded the power that practically poured from the circus.

She chewed on her lip, her brows furrowing. Would anyone miss her if she walked into that shop and never left?

Cora, Copper told herself, if only to calm the riot of butterflies in her stomach. *Cora would know if I went missing.*

She hadn't visited Copper while she'd been in prison, but that was always a pre-decided agreement. If someone got caught, you stayed away.

It was easier that way.

Planting her hands on her hips, thumbs digging into the belt loops of her black pants, she stared down the shop. Willing the job to go the way she wanted, Copper tied her long, blonde hair up in frustration. She was grateful for the quiet location. The lack of passersby allowed her to breathe her options in and exhale whatever held her back.

"I need this," she told the nagging voice inside her head as though it required an answer. The restless anticipation of this meeting reminded Copper of her early smuggling days when she was in her teens, and everything was new. It wasn't that many years gone by, but she'd seen and done a lot since she'd stepped out of the smuggling game. Somewhere along the way, Copper lost her confidence in her ability to do a job.

"You know, I'm not a terribly patient man, but *oh*, were you worth the wait." The greeting was the equivalent of auditory silk as it drifted out to her through an open window.

Where are you? She hadn't expected to be watched before entering the shop. *You know what he is. So, let's show him who we are.*
Copper was stealth.

She was cunning and planning and disinterested facades.

In her prime, she was an elite mover of items where questions weren't asked, and the right amount of money could even earn a person an acquisitions run.

Thief.

Smuggler.

Shadow of the Night.

But that was then, and as she stood before a threshold of the unknown…she hesitated.

"Please," he continued, "come in."

The door opened smoothly, coming to a silent stop. Staring up at the doorframe, she frowned at the lack of an actual person opening the door.

"Bold use of raw magic…" Copper muttered under her breath. She didn't like that kind of untethered magic. It was too unpredictable and too capable of causing a person actual harm. Copper leaned just a little to her left, peering past the darkened storefront and directly toward the silhouette of a man standing in a back office.

No turning back now, she thought as she stepped over the threshold and toward a decision that could change the course of her life. Copper passed through the part of the shop where regular customers might frequent and between the twin counters that stretched across the width of the space. A beaded curtain brushed itself aside, the parted fabric gathered on either side by unseen fasteners. Lining the path toward the man in the office were vases full of swaying flowers and boxes that rumbled like thunder; the subtle glow of down-lighting warmed shelves and display cases of magical items until the entire room was lit.

Cassian September was so gorgeous; he was practically walking sin. The sharp line of his jaw was offset by a pair of full lips and those charming, deep-set dimples. His warm brown eyes glittered with the promise of granting everything a heart could desire. And maybe even a thing or two that same heart shouldn't admit to wanting.

"Welcome," he said with a grin that verged on dazzling.

Oh…you know you're pretty, don't you? Cassian drew people in with his appearance and demeanor, all languid movements and lovely welcomes that earned him a reputation for leaving people wondering where his words had been their entire life.

"It's not every day I get to be in the company of someone so…accomplished." He gestured toward twin plush chairs placed before the large desk in the middle of the room.

Shining gold accents on the furniture, deep red tapestries on black walls. I know extravagance is commonplace in the magic district, but this room doesn't have any notable signs of wear. Did he stage this place just for our meeting?

"I could say the same, Mr. September." She took a seat, cockily slinging one leg over the other. Copper quickly seeped into the idea of his languid body language, matching his energy and allowing her previous anxiety to all but vanish.

Now that she was engaged in the situation, she had a role to play and an alter ego to summon.

Sitting in front of Cassian September felt oddly similar to being brought before the empress that morning.

Of course, Copper's arrival in that office was by her choosing. Being brought before the council had occurred by use of shackles.

"What brings you here, Ms. James?" Cassian looked at her from under dark lashes, casually surveying her after taking his own seat on the opposite side of the desk.

"Aside from the decor?" She smirked. Even in the dim lighting, Copper noted the mysterious opulence radiating throughout the room.

Cassian chuckled at Copper's quip.

Light laugh, relaxed posture. She noted his open presentation as a cue to continue with her pitch.

"We have a mutual acquaintance who suggested that you might be in search of someone to obtain something for you. I just so happen to be in the business of finding things and ensuring they arrive wherever the highest bidder says they belong."

"Perhaps," Cassian nodded slowly. "When our friend, as you call him, mentioned the potential of this impromptu meeting, he failed to point out that I'd be working with the best." He paused then, making a display of considering their situation. "Your recent incarceration aside, of course."

Copper noted how his eyes lingered on the partially healed split in her lip. A less confident woman might have blanched at his awareness of her departure from the High Castle dungeon. She could have made excuses or padded her proverbial resume as to what had happened that led to her capture. But Copper didn't shy away from his insinuation.

Not in the least.

"How is it that you escaped?" he prodded, a feline grin prowling across his handsome features. "Our fearless leader doesn't seem merciful these days."

"Mr. September, if you expect me to flinch under scrutiny, you're going to be waiting a while."

"I wouldn't say scrutiny."

"You strike me as the sort of person who only seeks the best." Copper cut him off, forcing enough confidence into her words to overshadow the challenge he'd presented. "After all, I escaped, didn't I? I can't imagine you would let a little misunderstanding between myself and the crown keep you from getting whatever it is you want."

She'd made her point, but making him feel he was still in control until they'd struck a deal was essential.

Cassian eyed her for a long moment. "There are few things that I allow to hinder me from getting what I want, Ms. James." With the slightest gesture, he summoned a jeweled tassel to unravel from the ceiling. With a gentle tug, the covering from one of the many windows on the back wall fell away. "You and your past don't happen to be one of them."

A glow of satisfaction burned inside Copper as she lured Cassian to take the bait. *There's the key in the lock…now to just get him to turn it and let me in.*

The silver glow of the rising moon challenged the lantern's glow as it cast shards of mellow light across the map on his desk. This subtle display of magic drew an enchanted paper structure to stand off the page with a residual shimmer of magic. Several stories of windows framed in white stone shot up from the desk, capped by a sprawling roof that resembled more of a small castle than just another business in the city. Tiny dragons stalked the miniature peaks, rolling flames perpetually blackening their rooftop domain. Only one building was so grand and constantly guarded by a pair of dragons.

The Grand Aurora.

Perched on the edge of her crushed velvet seat, Copper's fingertips brushed the lip of the desk as she took in the delicate enchantment. Her heart sped up just a little. The push of fresh magic lingered against her senses.

"It's a hotel." Copper flicked her gaze to his. While she knew precisely what it was and why it was special, she wanted to know why he thought the same.

"This isn't just any hotel." He leaned forward, casting a hand over the map, causing it to seize up before relaxing into a much larger image. "This is The Grand Aurora."

Copper gently stroked the roof of the paper structure, ignoring the insulted cries of the dragons, and found it as sturdy as any other building. "Am I supposed to be impressed?"

Cassian's stare followed the motion of her finger. "Most people are." He sat back to allow her space to take it all in. "Then again, you're not most people, now are you?"

The elaborate hotel was the pinnacle of the city, second only to The High Castle. It was a known hub of magical transactions with doorways to untold places and extensive supernatural trading. If an item existed, and sometimes even if it didn't, anything could be found in one of the many levels. Access to a landmark location like that was a smuggler's dream.

And a death sentence.

"The item you're looking for? It's…inside the hotel?" She took her time and observed the building. There had to be layers of wards protecting the magical happenings within its walls. Copper knew it was almost impossible to infiltrate on her own.

"That isn't an easy question to answer."

"Try." Copper was not amused with the way he was toying with her. "Because I'm not a thief by trade, Mr. September. If the item you're looking for is not somewhere amongst your quite impressive collection, then I'm assuming you're asking for something I don't readily offer."

Copper was surrounded by Cassian's personal collection of the rare, obscure, and legendary. Glowing vials, a single tooth that was bigger than her head, and various gilded weaponry were just a few of the pieces she'd noted in tidy display cases. She'd never laid eyes on some of the more ornate items, staffs of past rulers and tomes probably full of enchantments, but that didn't mean they weren't laying their version of eyes on her in return.

"Let's put it this way." Cassian drew her attention back to him. "The Grand Aurora is currently the easiest way into the shop that has the item I desire."

Copper stared into the eyes of the ringmaster for longer than was socially acceptable. Reflecting back at her was an entirely different world of possibilities and utter madness.

Had she stuttered?

While theft was the early step toward becoming a smuggler, it wasn't exactly her specialty. Copper had cultivated a network of connections over the years to accomplish her smuggling operations, but that usually meant someone else bringing the items to her to move, not her retrieving them herself.

"I imagine there are a lot of shops inside the Grand Aurora."

"That's true. It's a very exclusive invitation when someone gains access to buy, sell or trade inside such an elaborate institution," he agreed. Casually scrawling a name on a small piece of scratch paper, Cassian avoided the decadent letterhead lying bound and blank before him. "The item is an amulet and vial pairing strung together on what is believed to be an unbreakable chain."

Of course, it is, Copper laughed internally, the irony proving too great for her inner voice to stay quiet.

"You don't strike me as the gem-wearing type," Copper said, allowing a measure of annoyance to seep into her tone at his unwillingness to step away from the idea of her taking the job.

"What I do with the item upon delivery is really none of your concern." His words were pointed but still not threatening in her mind's eye. He provided Copper with a sketch of the item in question with the name of a shop written in fresh lines of dark, swirling ink. "Isn't that the point of your services?"

"The point of my services is to survive long enough to get paid," Copper explained cooly. "You're asking for something that I don't…"

"I know why you came here tonight." He cut her off, his voice deepening. "I know of the deal you made."

"A deal?" Copper bluffed.

Does this look like my first negotiation? Her blood heated, her hand clenching into tight fists under the table.

"Do you think I would come here today with plans other than to provide you with my undivided time and attention?" Copper twisted her words into ones of loyal innocence. *Of course,* he was the only one she planned to serve. Who else deserved her best?

"She can't offer you what I can."

Copper dropped her mask and gave him a skeptical look.

You can't offer me my freedom.

"Acquire this small trinket for me, and I'll give you whatever you want. Anything at all." Cassian waved his hand in the air, trying to appear casual. "Sure, you're a smuggler. But don't you have…people who can take care of the acquisitions portion of this job?"

A small trinket? Copper swallowed a laugh before it could leave her throat. Was the man delusional enough to think her network of "people" was still intact after her lengthy stay in the dungeons of The High Castle?

Copper leaned forward, planting her hand on the side of her face and her elbow on the desk, feigning boredom. "I don't make a habit of lining my pockets with promises, Mr. September." She spoke his name as a powerful punctuation.

She made a rule to avoid people or institutions that dealt too closely with her repertoire. But Copper James had known who he was and what he was capable of long before she'd approached him. She also knew, from reputation alone, that if he made a deal, no matter how significant or unimaginable, he would see it through.

She needed a deal like that.

The problem was, he clearly knew that.

Always one step ahead, aren't you?

Cassian circled around to the front of the desk, stopping beside her. Copper sat up straight, lifting her chin to meet his eyes.

"I require your services, Copper." He purred her name. "And in these unique circumstances, you are the only person in your line of work that I would consider hiring for a job this..." He ran a single gloved finger down the length of her arm. "Sensitive."

"Is that so?" Copper wasn't in the business of being touched by people she didn't know, even men as attractive as Cassian. Still, she leaned into his touch, keeping her eyes and mind acutely aware of her surroundings. They had to be when making a deal with a master of deception.

"I know what happened to you outside of Keskairah." Cassian used two fingers to draw a stray lock of hair away from her face. "I'm prepared to make all of that simply go away."

"Don't." Copper left her seat abruptly. She wasn't willing to talk about her time spent outside of the city of Keskairah.

Not with him.

Not with anyone.

"You know, Ms. James." A cool formality seeped into his words when Cassian snapped his fingers, and the map rolled itself shut. "You strike me as the sort of person that needs anything but what they're looking for."

Copper's gaze flattened at the criticism.

"The deal I am offering you would mean you are protected by the treaty between the empire and the old magic of this city. You would be virtually untouchable."

"Untouchable," Copper repeated, incredulous. "That's cute."

There was nowhere she could go, nowhere she could hide from what happened the last day she'd spent in the far east city of Keskairah. No amount of magic could remove the blood from her hands or heal the ache in her soul.

"I'm hosting another game soon," Cassian told her casually. "In fact, I believe the call to play is already posted across the entire empire."

Copper idly pulled at a piece of fuzz on her sleeve. "The Red Game?" Cassian September was notorious for randomly hosting an event called The Red Game within one of his traveling Extravaganza residencies. The Red Rebel Extravaganza was magic incarnate, where a person could gain their life's dreams and greatest desires…while utterly drowning in magic.

"You become a Red Rebel and win the game." He twirled his hand in the air theatrically, producing a smoky silhouette standing proudly before a crowd, victorious, that was clearly Copper participating in the infamous game. "Then, your fate is yours to decide with the kind of magic you would awaken."

Copper was always willing to take her chances with the unknown, but The Red Game was wild magic. She would have to be even more desperate than she was in that moment to agree to play his game.

"Of course, you could always join my troupe." His voice was alluring, husky. "See the entire empire from a front-row seat. You could experience more magic in a single day than you have in your entire lifetime." He traced a lazy pattern into her palm, leaving behind a temporary emblem of the circus.

Copper stared at the depiction of the gemstone hummingbird in her hand and the way the inky stars twinkled above it. She made a fist, and the shimmering gold circle around the images disappeared into smoke and ash.

"You underestimate my exposure to true magic if you think you have that many unseen wonders." Copper retrieved her hand from Cassian's, matching his tone.

"Forgive me." Cassian's smile reached his eyes in what could only be described as genuine amusement.

"What exactly would you have me do?" she asked. "Run away with the circus?"

Cassian straightened, his smile faltering slightly.

"That is what you're offering me, isn't it? Escape from my life, as it is now, to accompany you and your Extravaganza?" She whispered the last word to the tune of his fancy. Wistful and alluring.

"Anything."

"What?"

"I'm offering you anything and everything you could ever want in this life."

Copper snorted, fully freeing her hand from his and planting a palm in the center of his chest. Formality faltered altogether as the gleaming silver buttons of his immaculate vest pressed into the soft flesh of her hand as she pushed him away. "Or, you pay me my going rate, and we'll call it a deal." She winked at him, moving to sit in an overstuffed chair beneath a large painting of the High Castle.

Mr. September's shoulders dropped a little. The moment was shattered.

"Tease," he growled playfully.

"Magician," she struck back.

It was an age-old dance that two attractive, unattached people played, mixed with a business deal that was too good to pass up on either side. Attraction often played a role in getting the upper hand in an agreement, and with Cassian, it came naturally.

I bet your suave demeanor works on just about any woman that possesses something you covet.

But Copper had become a master at parroting behavior. Doing her best to keep on top of rumors and gossip about the biggest names in the game, she had known to come prepared to flirt her way through the entire situation. Cassian liked to play. In fact, she was surprised he hadn't used that charm to obtain the item himself.

"Why do you need my help?" Copper asked, wanting to know as much backstory as possible before entering that shop.

"So many questions…" Cassian breathed, feigning exhaustion.

Copper crooked a brow at him as though to ask, 'Would you prefer to hire someone else?'

"I'm not welcome in that part of the city." He paused, choosing his words carefully. "And the necklace I am after is technically not for sale."

Not for sale? Of course, it wasn't for sale! If Copper's intel was correct, which it usually was, the item he was after was a missing royal jewel!

"Even the Grand Ringmaster himself has limitations?" She feigned surprise. The Avenue had wards crafted against magicians like him, and it was for good reason.

The humor dropped from Cassian's eyes.

"What shop is it in?" Copper snatched the illustration of the amulet off the desk and surveyed it casually.

"Clarke and Wylder." He watched her with an intense focus.

Copper's attention snapped to him from over the lip of the page. "The Oddity Shop?"

Cassian nodded slowly, never breaking their shared gaze.

"The Oddity shop is practically a prison for magical items."

"And people…if you're not careful. I'm told not even The Empress is willing to cross its threshold."

"Or you, for that matter," Copper added dryly.

"Do you want the job or not?"

And there it was. The crack in his mask became a fissure.

All of this told Copper one thing. Whatever value the amulet held in the eyes of the ringmaster, it was worth something—and a lot of somethings, at that—if it was harbored within Clarke and Wylder. Anything worth having, magical or otherwise, could usually be found within the shop that shouldn't exist.

The tricky part was getting out unscathed. Many had tried and failed to take from The Oddity Shop—many were never seen again.

Trying to steal from Clarke and Wylder was near suicide.

But so was continuing on the path Copper had been precariously teetering down for the last few years. There was a murder charge looming over her head.

Death seemed to follow her no matter which decision she made.

This might be my only way out. She told herself, and in that moment, she believed that.

"Yes," she answered him around a slow sigh.

"Yes…what?"

Copper stared at him, savoring the final moments of being the solitary owner of her own soul. "Yes, I will take the job."

"Great!" Cassian leaned forward, a satisfied smirk playing on his lips when he extended his hand. She accepted, sealing their transaction with a magically infused handshake. "It's a deal."

CHAPTER TWO

Sir Raleigh Danger, Supernatural Detective

T HE BIRDS WERE ALMOST never what they seemed.

Pulling the dark, wood door shut behind him, Sebastian Axelson listened to find out if the large bird perched on the crest of the sign had lingered. The sensation of being watched tossed chills of anxious tension up and down his back when he decided to venture into that part of the city. Arriving at his destination didn't ease those concerns either. When he was—well, not quite satisfied—but settled on the fact that he was not being watched, Sebastian slipped a silver-handled cane from the crook of his arm and turned to find an office barren of life. Orange brows knit with tension, and the click of his sophisticated walking stick announced Sebastian's arrival with each step he took. An old injury from a war no one talked about anymore forced him to rely on it for more than just the deteriorated muscle in his thigh.

Sir Raleigh Danger—Supernatural Detective

The wording was painted on the frosted glass facing the street. Reading Raleigh's name left a strong distaste in his mouth. That crow could still be heard swinging on the sign, reminding the hotel owner that it was dangerous for him to be on the dark brick streets of Aerimora. His deepening frown was framed by his red facial hair. He had dire business to attend to, but setting foot inside Raleigh's office went against everything he'd built his business upon.

"Well, if it isn't Mr. Sebastian Axelson," a greeting of sorts came, and, in his mind's eye, the game immediately began.

"Raleigh, I-" he started to say but was cut off by a mocking chuckle. Sebastian moved toward the sound in the far corner. Raising his cane, a warm glow emanated from the base of it, and the wall immediately rippled away with the brief sweeping motion. Removing the guise revealed a corner library tucked away from the rest of the world.

And the Detective inside.

"Of all the names you could have picked…" Raleigh tsked from where he stood on his archival ladder.

Secretly priding himself on seeing through the illusion quickly, Sebastian found the owner of the storefront standing in a nook filled with books, paintings, and other odd objects that were all almost surely illegal. That, or the artifacts, were just so old the very laws themselves had no jurisdiction because no one knew they even existed anymore. There were relatively new laws that attempted to govern the wild magics of the city. Possessing or exercising unregistered items could easily result in a death sentence.

"It's a family name," Sebastian answered wryly. "You, of all people, should know that."

"Oh, I do." Snapping the red book shut, he let it drop into his opposite hand. The blue light illuminating his face still emanated from all edges of the tome. "That's what makes it humorous."

Sebastian did not, in fact, find it humorous. It took everything in him not to shake Raleigh and scream about the impending chaos that was a breath's distance from falling into place if they didn't act quickly.

"I suppose the crown knew about this…collection of yours when you were appointed detective of this district."

"No." He slid down the railings, and his feet hit the floor with a thud. "And you aren't going to enlighten them either."

Raleigh was a tall, lean man with more years of experience tacked on to his relatively mortal existence than anyone truly knew. The cornflower blue of his eyes frequently took on a silver hue due to an unfortunate magical exposure early in his life. Framed in copper-plated spectacles, his gaze was known to pierce those who had the misfortune of being interrogated by him. He raked a hand through his dark curls before giving them a brief shake.

"What can I do for you?" Raleigh presented him with a thin attempt at businesslike civility.

"The magic in the hotel market is becoming…unruly." Sebastian's words were clipped. Primarily because he had to ask for help. But things were changing quickly, and he feared it would shift beyond his control before he knew it.

Even if he wasn't ready to admit that. Not yet, anyway.

He'd spent too many years as guardian of terrible magic inside the Grand Aurora; he wasn't about to wave the white flag now.

"Unruly?" Raleigh repeated an inflection in his tone that Sebastian found hard to place. "You're going to have to be a little more specific. It's not like you haven't dealt with volatile magic in the past."

Sebastian remained silent.

"What's happening in The Grand Aurora that you don't want to tell me?"

Raleigh shelved the book and accidentally disturbed a fluffy chipmoth. It wriggled its way out from the nearest bookshelf. The creature's large, dark eyes surveyed the stranger in his living space. Heaving himself up on wings coated in a delicate layer of hair, the small creature sprang forward to dance with the swinging glass lights in the corner before landing on Raleigh's shoulder with a series of grunts.

"What is that doing in here?" Sebastian sneered at the concept of a domesticated rodent.

Raleigh glanced around, looking past the creature on his shoulder as though his presence wasn't odd in the least. "Oh him." He pointed, and the fuzzy thing licked at his finger. "Don't devour my flesh like that in front of visitors. It's rude," he chastised in a tone of mock scandal.

"Are you insane?" Sebastian sputtered, starting to regret crossing the threshold into this den of madness. The chipmoth pawed its tiny, fleshy feet into Raleigh's shoulder, clearly ruffled by Sebastian's tone.

"No, he followed me home. Nested in my first edition of Aloysius Sylvester's *Study on Grubber Wrangling and Other Unnatural Happenings*, it seemed the right thing to call him."

"Sylvester?"

"Aloysius."

Sebastian blinked. *I don't have words for this…and more importantly, I don't have the time.*

"Copper James is back in Aerimora." He announced as though he'd seen her himself. "She was spotted walking around the city at dusk last night!"

The humor left Raleigh's face as he turned his full attention to the conversation. "What of it?"

What of it? Sebastian thought so loudly he was sure his baffled words were spoken aloud.

"You knew?" The question carried as more of an accusation than an actual inquiry.

Raleigh stared at him a moment too long. "Copper is one of the most successful smugglers in this empire's history." He loosely stifled an incredulous laugh. "Did you expect me not to?"

He didn't know how to answer that, so Sebastian continued on. "There is a rumor circulating that a heist is being planned."

"Don't you have wards against nefarious activities for whatever you think is about to happen?" Raleigh seemed bored with what should have been a startling revelation, spiking Sebastian's temper.

"Wards can be subverted."

"Then you need better magic."

Aloysius squeaked in agreement.

"You mean to protect her." Sebastian gripped one of the two guest chairs that framed the opposite side of Raleigh's desk. His fingers dug into the royal blue fabric as he struggled to maintain composure. "I should have known better than to come to you with something involving her."

Raleigh leaned against the mantle of the fireplace, his foot propped against the leg of his leather desk chair. "Copper James was captured and then brought before the empress and the crown's council to answer for her crimes. Whatever it is that you are implying about my past partnership with her and my ability to do my job now are not only unwelcome, but I suggest you think twice about your next words before your temper gets the better of you, and I respond accordingly."

Sebastian took a moment to soak in that information. *He knew. He knew she'd been freed and intended to do nothing about it to protect us! This is a waste of my time.*

"Who told you of these rumors? That she was back in the capital city?" Raleigh asked.

"The magic is upset. The vendors are getting restless…"

"I see."

"What?"

Raleigh took a step closer, dropping his voice low. "What secrets do you harbor in that glamorous hotel of yours that you fear will get out if anyone looks too closely?"

"Are you going to help me or not?" Sebastian ground out, doing his best not to falter under Raleigh's scrutinizing gaze.

"Probably not, unless you tell me what has you spooked."

"Spooked?" Sebastian laughed at the idea.

"Do you have a better word for it?"

"Guests have been talking…"

"About?"

"About a certain shop making appearances."

Raleigh guffawed. "Hundreds of shops come and go in that hub of yours. The center of the hotel has more magical traffic than the train station has people, and this is a capital city!"

"Is everything a joke to you?" Sebastian snapped.

"What does your brother have to say about all this?"

His face tightened, clearly weary at the very idea. "I haven't spoken to him."

"And you expect me to get involved because…"

Sebastian hobbled over to the door and flung it open so the lettering could be read in the correct order. "Are you not a supernatural detective charged with maintaining the peace between the crown and the keepers of the old magics?"

Raleigh did not respond.

"I want you to stop something before it starts!"

"Do you mean to tell me that you came to inquire about my services because you believe Copper James is going to steal from the hotel, and you need to be…protected?"

Sebastian began to pace.

Raleigh watched him grumble to himself for a long moment before speaking. "I wonder how much damage you'll do to that rug before you divulge the secrets you're so desperate to keep."

"My sources believe Cassian September is involved."

"Look," Raleigh cleared his throat, seeming unfazed by the mention of the ringmaster having returned. "We all played a role in securing this city. We each hid one of the ancient pieces, changed our names, broke up families, and yet…here we are."

"Does she know?"

"Copper? About the amulet?" he grimaced at the idea. "Of course not." Raleigh tucked Aloysius into his nest on the shelf. "Wait here," he instructed the furry rodent. "It's not safe for you where I'm going."

"And where exactly are you going?" Sebastian asked, believing they needed a solution before either left the office.

"If I tell you, it will spoil the fun!" Raleigh slapped him on the shoulder as he walked out of the office.

"Raleigh," Sebastian shouted after him, "Danger!" He tried again, but Raleigh was already too far away to hear.

Or an idea more closely related to the truth. He just didn't care.

CHAPTER THREE

Magic for Hire

THE ROOM OF GOLD and Bone was a cafe in the middle of the city. Copper told herself she'd chosen the outdoor patio because she enjoyed the flowering vines laced through the wide-mouthed opening in the wooden pergola. The reality of the situation was that the ornamental foliage provided a secluded space for her to enjoy the peace of the solitary hour, even as the rush of the early morning breeze chilled her bare arms.

Goosebumps rose on her skin as she heard familiar feet approaching.

Well, it's about time.

"Bold of you to be sitting out in broad daylight," a woman with a cerise braid commented as she sat opposite Copper at the small, round table. Her off-white shirt and gray pants bore a light dusting of flour.

Copper took a long sip of her hot raspberry tea, the steam warming her cheeks and hands. She savored the sweet heat on her tongue and set down the star-speckled mug. "I'd hardly call this daylight, Cora." She gestured up the street at the first slivers of morning light, trying and almost failing to pierce the dense cloud coverage.

"I haven't seen you in over a year, and when you *do* finally come back around, I have to come searching for you?" Cora sounded tired and maybe a little worried. However, the hostility was replaced with familial harassment, even if they weren't blood.

*You're spot on being concerned…*she thought, but her pride wouldn't allow her to say it. "Has it been a year already?"

Cora leaned across the table toward her. "If I hadn't been part of the job we did for the owner of this place, I wouldn't have even known where to look," she hissed, trying not to draw attention to them, though the streets were relatively bare at that hour.

You haven't changed a bit, Copper thought as she took in the angry blush on Cora's olive cheeks and the smile worry line that was there whether she was scolding Copper or fighting with a problematic recipe in her family's bakery.

A smuggling job they had completed resulted in the safe return of the owner's daughter. In an act of gratitude, the man had gifted Copper an entire townhome.

Cora hadn't complained when it had been placed solely in Copper's name. Her family had suffered enough during Cora's younger years; they didn't need their name aligned with that of an infamous smuggler.

Copper simply smirked at her companion. "I missed you too."

Cora slouched back into her chair before gesturing toward the horizon with an exaggerated sigh. "Did you pay someone to do that?"

"What? The clouds?"

Cora nodded.

"No, just pure coincidence." The question hit her a moment later in a way she found funny. "Though I'm flattered that you think I'd go so far as to contact someone to temporarily alter the weather just to suit my needs."

"You've done worse."

"True," Copper stifled a laugh. "But that would have been an expensive ask."

"I'm assuming whatever brought you back is an…expensive job." There was a touch of disapproval in her tone. Cora always had that motherly way about her that just craved to needle Copper about loose ends and inappropriate endeavors.

Copper shrugged and resumed her appraisal of the Grand Aurora's entrance, thanks to a wide roadway perpendicular to the cafe's patio. The hotel was regal in its lavish architecture; it could have been a second palace for the empress.

Such a pretty prison for all those expensive magical things.

Sparkling crystalline windows dazzled in the daylight before turning liquid onyx at night to preserve the privacy of all who entered. The pillars lining the entire front-facing section twisted into iron molding that protected the roof from being breached. Twin dragons heralded the morning sun on their stone backs as they defended a glass dome on the top of the building.

Why are you being so difficult? She mentally chided the hotel.

"Are you okay?" Cora interrupted her thought process.

The pair had survived jobs with incredible odds. Still, Cora always had a way of seeing through her stoic defenses and into the heart of where her mind ventured.

Copper could feel her doing that now, and she hated it. She hated that Cora was a loose end. She was a living, breathing string that Copper could never tie up. But she found Cora's fussing oddly endearing. She embodied a personal weakness when it came to others prying where they didn't belong.

This is why I stayed away...

A server joined them then, offering menus and teas. The single sheet of embossed paper detailed the transition between the warm and cold seasons with nostalgic flavors of spicy goods and hearty meals.

Copper's raspberry tea, with just a citrus twist, was a flavor from the warm season they kept on hand for her year-round. It was a perk she used to think she couldn't live without.

"No, thank you," Cora declined it all until she noticed they were being served by the owner himself. It was before the cafe opened, and Copper was relentlessly spoiled when it came to getting things she wanted when they weren't exactly available. "Although, if you're ready to discuss the cold season menu, I would love to sit down with you later." Cora's family bakery, The Flying Apron, was just around the block, and she often provided the cafe with their particular brand of goods.

Copper hadn't forgotten that when she'd chosen that location to consider her options.

"Of course." The cafe's owner was a warm man with a smile that felt like home. He was as round as he was tall, with only a minor sweep of hair around his head to signal that it had ever been there in the first place.

"Now is fine," Copper gestured to the empty chair between them. The man had brought her a hot breakfast sandwich on a bagel without being asked. He could stay as long as he liked.

Copper lent an ear to their conversation about mint chocolate this and twisted gingerbread that as she watched people start to flow in and out of the hotel. It was still early, and most traffic was vendors making deliveries or people hurrying to early train departures. She spotted an older woman strolling with a fist of treat bags in one hand and a leash hanging idly from her wrist as her fluffy pooch strutted onward.

You would be such an easy target. Copper imagined gaining entry to the hotel by simply knocking into the woman and offering to carry her items for her as compensation for Copper's apparent clumsiness.

There are doormen for that, she reminded herself, knowing she only had one chance to present herself at the entrance. Any other attempts would draw suspicion.

Copper knew the hotel's structure down to the number of floors, windows, and exits. She had researched architectural archives and reviewed tourist information, not that the Grand Aurora allowed many tourists. It was a behemoth of a place with layers of magical guards to keep people like her out. Until now.

Her timing and approach had to be perfect.

Perfectly unremarkable, that is.

The key to a good smuggling job was to be utterly unnoticed.

Her eye caught the shifting emblem on the door even from that distance. The insignia of the crown was plastered on everything with a direct connection to the empress. In this case, it was the hotel bearing her namesake and the colorful, flowering mandala with the etching of a firebird at its heart.

"It's a poor replica," Copper said without context when the owner left.

"Hmm?"

"The emblem of the empress. I saw the original in the Hall of the Phoenix."

"Unbelievable." Cora's eyes visibly prickled in frustration. "They have no idea what actually happened that night."

Copper laughed bitterly. "How could they? I'm still not sure…"

The secrets and lies of Aerimora were almost all closely related to what did and did not pass under the laws of magic. Copper had grown to possess a specific skill set that allowed certain people with the right resources, to attain her services and acquire goods that were no longer sold just *anywhere*. Smuggling was an odd game of give and take that fell into the category of lies and deception. Copper had turned a personal quirk into a lucrative business. At a young age, she realized that magic spoke to her in the way music flowed over a musician or how color and texture spoke to an artist.

Of course, smuggling wasn't as beautiful by comparison.

It had turned downright ugly that night in Keskairah. After all, a man was dead, and that hurt more than any beauty could blot out. The ache in

Copper throbbed, threatening to remain no matter how much time had passed.

"I wasn't sure I would find you here," Cora admitted. "It'd been so long, but I thought maybe–"

"I made a deal." Copper cut her off, not knowing Cora to be the exceptionally sentimental sort, nor was she in the headspace to deal with it now.

"A deal?"

"Two of them, actually."

"Two?"

"For the same item, as it would appear."

And I am in so much trouble because of it…

"Interesting." Cora followed Copper's gaze, and together they watched as one delivery person after another sailed through the front and side doors of the hotel without so much as a second thought from the several doormen poised at each point of entry.

"I'm on furlough, Cora. I didn't escape."

"What?"

"I made a deal with The Empress to retrieve her missing necklace."

"And the second deal?"

Copper pursed her lips, refusing to answer.

"Copper?" Cora pushed. "Who else wants the necklace?"

"It's better if you don't…"

"Tell me," Cora demanded, but Copper still kept quiet.

"I heard you're part of your family's bakery now." Copper shamelessly changed the subject.

"Yeah."

"They took you back after everything then." Copper idly preoccupied herself with a loose stone near her left foot. "That's great."

"We could shelter you for a while. Get you out of the city before…"

"Tell me more about the contracts you have across the city."

"What for?"

"Specifically there." She gestured toward The Grand Aurora.

"I don't have one with them."

"Right. But maybe it's time you sent them some free samples."

Cora stared at her. "This is a joke…right?"

Copper slowly shook her head no.

"We never tried to hit The Grand Aurora because no one ever comes out alive…"

"Because they weren't me," Copper defended.

Cora groaned, tipping her face to the sky in frustration. "This was not why I came here." But it was why she left with Copper in tow.

Their walk was brief. The streets were dimly lit with the first flickers of awakening businesses. The elaborate sign decorating the front of the green bakery did nothing for the side entrance in an alley full of discarded crates. A handful of employees were already there using brooms and a hose to clear the loading area after what appeared to have been a defective sack of flour.

"I don't recall you ever having a death wish." Cora held a pastry box in her upturned palms as Copper rushed around the closed bakery. Under Cora's direction, she hand-picked key lime donuts with powdered sugar and little purple frosting flowers.

Copper's mind flashed to the information she'd tried to scrounge up on the Oddity shop. It wasn't as though there were archival books on a shop that was more alive than some of the people in the city. She'd found scrolls dating back centuries that talked of a shop that was bigger on the inside. One that stored items for safekeeping as well as selling the unimaginable.

What she didn't find was how to get inside.

If the shop even exists at all.

"I don't usually." Copper licked her finger clean after carefully placing a few warm chocolate croissants into the box. A bite of buttery, almond flavoring cradled the sweet chocolate on her tongue; in that moment, it was pure heaven.

"This is suicide." She grabbed Copper's wrist, pointing her toward the sink to wash her hands before touching anything and contaminating her display cases.

"This…is a cornucopia." Copper made a face at Cora as she set the medium-sized baked cone full of tiny baked goods and the sweetest confections into the center of the large box with her clean hand.

Does it count as suicide when a move in any direction might be a death sentence?

The inside of The Flying Apron was a simple storefront with blonde wood floors and two display windows with special glass that kept the treats from melting in the sun. Pastel tables were lined with fresh breads, jars with herb spreads, and rolls filled with cheeses. The cinnamon loaves were lavishly draped in thick caramel and packaged in custom pink boxes. The display cases lined both sides of the floor kept the more delicate items, cream puffs, and hand-decorated donuts in a safe place from temperature changes. The crystal clear glass also protected everything from the little fingers that liked to poke and sample the frosting swirls on any beautiful cakes waiting on the bottom.

Copper dried her freshly washed hands and surveyed the shop for anything else to gain her favor at the hotel's entrance. The number of items sold in the bakery was endless, drawing in customers from all over The Empire as they had goods for every taste.

"This isn't like a job where you risk your skin to get an item from point A to point B," Cora reminded her. "There's plausible deniability in transporting things in a busy city like this. But infiltrating…" Cora glanced around, noting the number of people working in the back rooms.

"This is stupidity wrapped in a dangerous double deal. You can't possibly satisfy both parties."

"I know." Copper swaggered across the shop like she didn't feel a tingling weakness in her knees, preparing for a job she knew she couldn't complete. "But I can try!"

Cora watched as Copper braided and pinned her hair to the back of her head. The fact of the matter was that no amount of blustering could change that not one but two deals had already been struck and that her friend would need all the mental fortitude to accomplish her task.

"Take the custard ones." Cora pointed to the dainty donuts painted in lines of chocolate and raspberry, the latter nearly matching the vibrant hue of Cora's hair. "They're sure to get you at least to the front counter."

Copper gave a sad smile at her acquiescence. There was a weight in the air that settled over them, and it made her skin crawl. Something in her heart raged against the idea of this job, but none of that mattered now. She'd committed, and Copper didn't want to see what happened to people who broke their deals with Cassian September or The Empress.

"I've seen my fair share of magic being raised here in The Avenue," Cora shifted the box to an empty space on the main counter to make some finishing touches. "But we both know that there are bigger and darker sorts of enchantments that could do some real damage when poked by amateur hands."

"Are you calling me an amateur?"

"At your job? No." Cora admitted as she tied the signature bow atop the box and handed it over.

Copper received the box, noting that her friend hadn't fully released it.

"Sebastian Axelson," Cora whispered before Copper turned to leave.

"Who?"

"He's the new owner of the Grand Aurora. You've been gone, and I wasn't sure if you knew. Most people don't. If you get any pushback, maybe knowing his name will help you in a bind? Ownership changed hands while you were in…"

Keskairah. Copper bore the name, the weight, and the pain with every mention and passing thought. It was dark nights, crawling forests, looming shadows, and the kind of cities you didn't go into alone.

"Magic for hire," Cora whispered an old saying from the days when they were stowing away in crates and wearing ridiculous outfits to smuggle any and everything imaginable.

Copper bristled before the front door at the sound of those words. It was bittersweet, the memories that flooded her mind as the clock struck six in the morning. The tittering of the overheard chimes announcing the top of the hour urged Copper forward. Straightening with a sharp inhale, the mask snapped back into place. She was ready to pretend this wasn't the most daunting task she'd taken on in years.

"Magic for hire," she breathed and left the bakery without looking back.

Chapter Four

Old Magic Dies Hard

Detective Raleigh Danger had never doubted himself as much as he did walking into The Avenue that day. There was a point of no return, and he was about to cross it. Once he started investigating his friend in earnest, he would have to see it through. Whatever end that may be.

Shoving his hands into his pockets, Raleigh was too preoccupied to avoid the puddles left by the recent rain. His wet shoes squeaked with each step. A cold dribble ran down the back of his neck, making him shiver with the unwelcome sensation. He sidestepped the rest of the droplets raining from one of the many awnings he passed under.

This season was transitioning into the next, and the weather along with it.

"And where are you now, you sneaky thing?" Raleigh asked under his breath. Stopping in front of a communal posting board, an old wanted poster rippled its corner at him as though taunting him to come and find her.

Because the picture it held was of Copper James.

The likeness was a poor representation of the girl he had known.

"Good to know you leave a lasting impression," he told the weathered piece of paper. Raleigh had taken his time to gather information about whether Copper was loose in the city. He found that if anyone truly knew something, they weren't talking about it. At least they weren't talking to him.

He sighed and snatched the wanted poster off the board.

You knew better than to be wandering around these streets at dusk.

Even the most glittering of cities could become ugly once the daylight faded. This was not a city full of lights to dazzle—no wonders to tantalize the eye. The streets of Aerimora were dangerous at night. When the sun went down, all the dark and questionable magic came out to play. Most were in hidden back rooms and musty taverns, but sometimes these creatures of twisted delight seeped out into the streets.

His days of working smuggling jobs were long gone, but he still kept a mental list of the places he had used. Some were repurposed, changed hands, or were otherwise disconnected from the smuggling world. This left a handful of options as to where Copper could be hiding, and the most likely one was first on his agenda.

You can't deny that things have been different lately, Raleigh told himself as he neared the bakery. Sebastian had made a point when he mentioned how the magical artifacts in the shops all over the city had begun misbehaving. Raleigh knew something was coming; he just hadn't known what.

It was you. The whole city knew you were drawing near, and I somehow missed it…

Raleigh received reports of enchanted jewelry crawling out of their cases. Bottles filled with powder and poultices rattled on their shelves. The magic could sense her, making the animate objects act more alive than some people passing on the street.

"Here we go," Raleigh muttered as he rounded the corner toward a tiny, lime-green building far from the comforts of his office. The knot forming in his stomach felt like a bad omen.

The entrance of the bakery was marked with a frilly sign spelling out The Flying Apron over a periwinkle awning. The shop was famous for the foods it had to offer. Swirls of dark caramel, powdery plumes of sugar dustings, and the fresh herbs of whole bread rounds decorated the display windows. Rich smells of freshly baked things wafted out the open door with each customer that came and went. These mouthwatering goods, crafted from closely guarded family recipes, were unique to The Flying Apron.

After all, magic that produced genuinely good things wasn't something anyone could just stumble across. It had to be refined over time, earning the little shop its prominent place on the most magical street in the empire.

Raleigh reached for the door handle, but two hidden guard dogs chiseled into the panels framing the stoop forced him back.

"Good morning to you too," Raleigh ground out. The swirling gemstone beasts bore their teeth in unison.

Anyone passing might have assumed they were nothing more than life-size decorative wall ornaments until they peeled away from either side of the doorway. The jade-colored dogs growled. Their smooth coats gleamed in the sunlight.

"Danger." A small woman casually wiped flour from her hands on an off-white apron as she exited the shop to greet him.

"Cora." He replied, side-eying the dogs.

"What do you want?"

*I've earned that…*Raleigh thought as her coolness washed over him.

"I received a report." He tried to step forward out of habit, something inside him reaching out to her. The dogs reminded him of his place with a torrent of growls and sneering.

"Hush," she soothed, causing them to sit in unison.

"I cannot investigate a scene if I'm not allowed to cross the threshold." Raleigh slipped a hand into his pocket, palming a packet he didn't want to use unless he had to.

Cora scoffed. "I'm sorry, Detective Danger. Old magic dies hard." The edge to her voice matched the steel in her gaze. "You, of all people, should know that," she added almost flippantly. A piece of raspberry-colored hair fell from the thick braid slung carelessly over her shoulder. "We are protected here in The Avenue, and we're allowed our old magic even under the guidelines of the new laws."

"And you know your bakery is rife with the information someone in my position might need."

Cora stared at him with a dry, unflinching expression.

"Don't think I've forgotten everything we were allowed to do when we were younger."

The dogs sprung to full attention. Their teeth bared, their ears slicked back against their heads, ready to pounce.

Raleigh ripped his hand out of his pocket, bringing forward a tiny pouch of red powder. He tore the bag with his teeth and flung it across the stoop in one sharp motion.

The dogs yelped. Retreating back into the panels on either side of the door, they blended into the decorative embossing they had once been.

A muscle ticked in Cora's jaw as the dust settled. She swept her gaze over him; those pale green eyes curiously matched the lighter shade in the guard dogs' coats.

"I didn't want to do that…I'm just trying to do my job."

"Copper James is not in Aerimora," Cora answered curtly as she turned to walk back into the bakery, hand firmly gripping the handle to ensure he did not follow. "Stop chasing a ghost."

"If I don't find her, someone else will."

The namesake apron of the shop reared its bodiless self out of the door in Cora's place. The piece of enchanted fabric gestured its displeasure about his apparent intrusion with the wild flapping of sweeping, untied strings, punctuated with a slap of Raleigh's hand, forcing him away from the door frame.

Cora crooked a sculpted brow at him, crossing her arms. "How you suffer from the choices you make is none of my concern. Not anymore." She flipped the 'open' sign to 'closed.' "Now get off my stoop."

#

I don't intend on harming her. Raleigh kicked himself for not leading with that. Just because he'd transitioned to the other side of the law didn't mean he didn't still care deeply for his friend. What the three of them had accomplished seemed like a lifetime ago.

I got out before things got ugly.

It wasn't exactly a secret that The Flying Apron was more than it appeared. While it was good to stand in the doorway, for however brief a moment, 'how you suffer from the choices you make' echoed in his mind. Instead of squirreling away goods and slinking around dark alleys in the middle of the night, Raleigh wore three-piece suits and strolled the sidewalks lining the most prestigious districts. He was a man of reputation, his smuggling days all but washed from his record, save for those who knew him both before and after the empress had approached him.

Purchasing a long coat and hat from a street vendor, Raleigh attempted to enter another shop on the Avenue selling scented beads that would roll around a home as long as the sun was up. But, he was immediately met by the window-rattling slam of the enchanted door. He gritted his teeth in response, curbing his frustration with a deep exhale.

Don't you know what I could do to you? Raleigh thought as he stared at his reflection in the pane of glass set into the door.

The jarring effect successfully shoved Aloysius off the sign on the storefront and into Raleigh's wide-mouthed coat pocket.

Surprised, the two just looked at each other, Raleigh over his circular glasses and Aloysius with his giant black eyes and sweet face.

"I thought I told you to wait there for me," Raleigh told him, referring to having left him back at the office.

Slowly and without breaking eye contact, the chipmoth folded his paper-thin wings and large cone-shaped ears inward, using his fat, grubby paws to scoot around in Raleigh's pocket. Finally, Aloysius covered his head with furry, tufted legs and resumed napping.

Raleigh snorted a laugh. *I'll never really get used to that…*

The hostility Raleigh was met with on those streets wasn't unexpected, but it wasn't pleasant either. The shop owners of The Avenue had been split down the middle when he took his current job. Sure, he could fine them for aggression toward the crown. He was an extension of the empress' rule, after all. Many people saw his transition from smuggler to investigator as him going from being one of their own to part of the problem. Slamming the door in his face could result in any punishment the Detective of the Crown saw fit.

He had become the face of supernatural accountability.

But that's why you took the job, now isn't it? Raleigh reminded himself. He'd understood first-hand what life was like for the residents of The Avenue when the corrupt and merciless held his position.

The black stone streets were meticulously maintained, lest the empress look out and see squalor in her streets. The shops ranged from singular little storefronts to large buildings that were practically monuments to commerce. Multi-level shops consumed large portions of real estate on The Avenue. Suspension bridges were knit between the varying levels, allowing easy access to every good and trade.

The capital city eventually outgrew its protective borders set in place by the first empress many generations prior. Expansion swelled toward the seemingly unreachable High Castle carved out of the mountainside. Layers upon layers made up a towering city nestled in the circular valley of a massive mountain range. It was easy to miss the way the people were corralled into that valley. The beauty of the pristine city and the glamor of the various magics in one place was mystifying. But the truth of the matter was that Aerimora's crown jewel of a city was nothing more than a prison for the oldest of magics adorned with a noose of mountains and an empress so removed from her people that even the tallest of buildings didn't crest the sprawling gardens of her residence in the sky.

A dry cackle caught his attention, mocking him from the safety of a nearby alley.

Not now...Raleigh tipped his face toward the sky with a resentful sigh. His patience was being tested.

"I should have known you'd be around here somewhere," he muttered as the old woman shuffled into sight. The hood of her cloak was draped over her head and shoulders, loosely covering her white, scraggly hair.

"You should know better than to come to The Avenue, Detective Danger." Her voice came out as a shrill, sing-songy whine. "We are protected here."

Raleigh frowned. "I was told there was a stranger in this district recently and a young woman who fled on foot?"

Questioning her was a long shot at best, but if anyone knew of any changes in the streets, it was her. Raleigh had residents that he frequently had dealings with. Some caused problems for him, others aided his investigations in exchange for relatively harmless goods.

This woman fell into both those categories, depending on the day.

"No young woman would be caught, dead or alive, in these streets at night," she reminded him. "Not with such heavy foot patrol." She gestured to several guards roaming the outer edge of the boundary between The Avenue and the rest of the city. "We are a rambunctious sort, after all, and we all know The Empress doesn't appreciate unruly magics."

Raleigh took a step closer, looking down into her time-worn face. "Who said anything about it being at night?"

The old woman pursed her lips.

Glancing around, he pulled out a small pouch of red powder. A refined version of the ancient sands was aggressively guarded on the far east of The Empire. He smirked when her eyes locked on his hand. The old woman grabbed for it the way a starving man would a hot meal.

She hissed and grumbled at him when her weathered hands failed to find their mark. "A meeting occurred between a certain smuggler and the King of Magic somewhere along these streets last night."

"You expect me to believe that Copper James and Cassian September are both present in this city?" Raleigh rounded his shoulders. He knew there was a strong likelihood that this was fact, but Raleigh played that down for the sake of his current conversation.

The old woman bristled. "I said no such thing." She sneered, shuffling a little closer. "But if they were, and a deal was struck, she may soon be found outside a certain shop."

"That would be quite the bargain, even for her."

Raleigh opened his mouth to say something more when he made eye contact with a mountain of a man at the other end of the alley. He was there, if only for a moment, but it was long enough for Raleigh to do a double take.

The Oddity Shop. Even his thoughts were a whisper at the realization. He didn't know too many men, in that era, with giant blood coursing through their veins, making Mr. Clarke unmistakable.

It also confirmed the old woman's suggestions.

"What will she take," he asked, still staring down the alley as though the man would reappear.

"I never said she would take anything."

Raleigh's patience wore thin.

"What will she take?" He emphasized every word as he dangled the rare substance before her.

After all, you had to survive the journey to purchase the substance in the first place.

"The scarlet amulet of the Solaera and its matching moonstone vial," she confessed, twisted fingers desperately reaching for the pouch. "The ringmaster would pay a handsome reward to get his hands on a power like that."

"Why now? And what for?"

She shrugged. "Legend has it that it is the heirloom stone crafted from the blood of the first empress and sister stone to the one from which Red Rebel himself was cut."

"The gemstone hummingbird?"

"The very same."

Raleigh's brows furrowed. "Magic like that can't be handled by just anyone."

"Why do you think a magician as powerful as the ringmaster of The Red Rebel Extravaganza sought out her help?"

Raleigh looked down the alley again as he tossed the pouch in the air for her to greedily snatch up. The old woman snickered to herself, inhaling the rich, spicy scent of the red powder cupped in her palms.

Raleigh sighed, knowing how far and quickly magic like that amulet could travel.

If Copper escaped, chances were she'd made a deal to retrieve the amulet for The Empress.

How does the ringmaster come into play? Is something wrong with the circus?

Raleigh started toward his office when a rush of warm air stirred from the alley. He rolled his eyes, knowing exactly what had just happened.

"You should keep him," a young, supple voice called after him.

Raleigh halted, looking over his shoulder at a young albino woman shirking off the ragged clothes of the old woman.

He noted the lack of color in her eyes and hair. *How many times can a person reset their body to a youthful age before they become unable to fully restore their looks?*

How many times had they played this game? How many times did she show up in his path?

"I think it's a him, anyway." The same mischief in her young eyes that had been present in the old worn ones that glared at him moments prior.

Tell me your name. His mind reached out to her, but instead of asking, as he had countless times before, he said: "What do you mean?"

Lady of the Avenue. Consumer of Magics. Nightmare of the Guardian…

She'd had so many names. So many faces.

Raleigh never knew where she would show up. Who she would be.

Sometimes he thought she was his own personal wraith, following him from time to time, place to place. Sometimes he wondered if she was the soul of the Oddity shop, consuming power and rumors to maintain itself.

He also wondered, in darker times, if she existed at all.

"They say a jewel-faced Chipmoth as a pet brings good luck," she told him. "You're going to need all the luck you can get if you don't steer clear of Copper James and her fated path."

Raleigh paused and looked down to where a peach-colored foot dangled from his pocket. The light reflected off the three scarlet jewels on Aloysius' brow. "Fine," he grumbled. Leaving the furry creature to rest peacefully in his pocket was the least complicated decision he'd made all day.

CHAPTER FIVE
A Box of Possibility

COPPER BORROWED A UNIFORM from the back room of The Flying Apron to sell the look she was trying to achieve. Dressed in black slacks and a lime wrap top with the bakery's logo printed over her heart, she approached the hotel with her box. Of course, the treats could be traced back to The Flying Apron after everything was said and done. Then again, the bakery was extremely popular. Anyone could have purchased a box and stolen a uniform to gain access to the landmark hotel. When it came down to it, Cora and her family were protected there in The Avenue.

In that moment, Copper had three goals in mind.

First, get in the door. While she could have found a way to make a reservation at The Grand Aurora, for all she knew, you had to sign the registration book in blood. That wouldn't do well for her anonymity.

Second, find an item to protect me against the wards of Clarke and Wylder. As a seasoned smuggler with a talent for acquisitions, Copper knew this wouldn't be as simple as strolling in, snatching the item out of a case, and walking back out the way she came. Clarke and Wylder was dripping in wards and booby traps, and she couldn't risk getting caught. There was too much at stake.

Third, find the necklace. Getting into the hotel and preparing herself for the job was only half the effort she had to put in. Finding an item that was not meant to be found would be more complicated than getting out with it alive.

The streets had come to life in the time it took her to return to The Room of Gold and Bone. The Avenue was now abuzz with businesses and patrons, carts and vendors. She blended right in with her box of espionage, right up to the whitewashed sidewalk of her mark.

Several floor-length windows framed the front entrance to The Grand Aurora. Blue glass tiles shifting at all hours of the day allowed brief glimpses inside from the street. The panels of the thick double doors were decorated in the pattern of a flowering mandala in shades of lush purples and deep ocean blues. A soft hue of ginger framed image in a large, diamond pattern, reminiscent of the sun setting over a sea of glass. They looked like glittering gems in the large white stone of the absolutely enormous building.

"Watch it!" A woman sneered.

"Carriage for Mrs. Adams!" A man called from the street.

"If I don't have this signed by midday, the deal is off!"

Copper ignored the snide comments and clouds of heavy perfumes as she wove her way through hotel guests with their pampered lifestyles and demands. Her heart pounded as she made her approach. Yet, she strolled up to the front entrance with the ease and purpose of a young woman who had delivered to highly known and influential businesses on numerous occasions.

The doorman did not see it that way.

"I'll have you stop right there, Miss…" He raised his hand. Dressed in the well-known ivory uniform of the Grand Aurora, he had a set to his shoulders that suggested he knew both the place and purpose for everything when it came to the hotel.

"Of course." Copper's smile was broad and innocent.

"What's this?" He eyed the signature periwinkle bow tied elegantly around the pastry box.

"A box of possibility." Copper gently tipped it forward. She did this so the man could read the swirling print stamped on the top. The logo didn't stop there as it arched elegantly over every curl in the elaborate bow.

"The Flying Apron," he scoffed. "We don't have a catering contract with them."

"Consider this an invitation to do just that," Copper answered in her best salesman swagger. "The Flying Apron is interesting in expanding its horizons."

The doorman rocked back on his heels. "Is that so?"

"That's what the boss tells me," she shrugged. "Honestly, I just deliver the goods. I don't know anything about the actual business end of things. I'm just supposed to deliver these to a…Mr. Axelson?"

The doorman's face tightened. He closed the space between them. "Where did you hear that name?" He dropped his voice low.

In the place of this city where good men like you fear to tread.
Copper took a step back. "Like I said, I'm just the messenger."

But the truth was, everyone knew that name. They might not have known he'd returned to the most powerful part of The Avenue. Still, Sebastian Axelson had always had his finger on the pulse of nearly every lucrative venture in Aerimora. He was a modern-day King Midas, so the empress turned a blind eye to the magic that thrived within the Grand Aurora.

The doorman drew a pensive breath and glanced around the busy street as wagons and people passed, paying them no mind. There were frilly skirts and towering hats that the road was coated in more extravagant fabrics and turned-up noses than there were bricks beneath their feet.

"All right." He opened the door for her. "Stop at the front desk and ask for Bea."

"Yes, Sir." Copper ducked under his arm and scurried inside, taking the entryway steps two at a time until she strolled into a large room with high ceilings and gray-speckled tile that stretched on forever.

To her left and right was a typical hotel lobby with patrons and desks, chairs, and brochures. But beyond the grand entrance, another short set of broad steps led into an atrium with a giant, black tree in the center. Its bare limbs reached in every direction.

Copper paused in the middle of the lobby. The light streamed in through the stained glass windows painting her hair in vibrant colors. Tipping her head to the side, she peered under the thick archway that blocked her view of the top of the tree.

She'd had a plan. The enchanted baked goods from Cora supplied her with ample opportunities to lure anyone who ate one into temporary compliance with the person who offered them. From there, she would slip into the heart of the Grand Aurora without anyone noticing. She would go as far as shoving it down the clerk's throat or sweet-talking Mr. Axelson himself if it meant gaining access to the hotel's inner workings.

But then…the building began to sing.

It was a trickling melody at first; the enchanting music swelled and built as she wandered further into the market. The magical items branched into different verses and songs to draw Copper's attention toward this shop or the next.

"The Black Tree Market," she read aloud upon approaching a sign posted between the lobby and the market. "You have a name." She smiled, looking straight up to the very top of the tree. For as long as she'd been smuggling, Copper had heard about the experience of being allowed inside The Grand Aurora. What she didn't know was that the internal market had a name.

Copper recognized the cleaner melody of the pure magic from the racing song of the darker items as they all seemed to herald her arrival, rejoicing in the promise of something different and someone new. She swallowed hard and did as they asked. Initially, no one questioned her presence, let alone glanced in her direction. She was labeled as 'the help' by her uniform, and that was enough for the busy market to pay her no mind.

Stewards of all sizes and colors fretted over insisted patrons. The room was too cold. A meal wasn't rich enough. The color of the sun was just a little too yellow. Regardless of the complaint or desire, the staff of The Grand Aurora bowed and cooed, serving every spoiled demand and selfish whim.

When she was younger, Copper might have looked around to see if others reacted, wondering how those who belonged there could go about their busy days and not be wholly overwhelmed by the power and beauty flowing from the shops built into the hotel. But now, Copper knew better. Others didn't hear the seductive song of magic the way she did, and that was something she'd learned to use to her advantage.

You're everything I thought you would be.

Large chandeliers that hung from the lower ceilings mimicked the inverted shape of the crystal domes above. Just beneath were tall archways that framed the lowest two levels facing the courtyard of the black tree. Each arch was crowned in gold leaf and ocean blue mosaics, leading to elegant white walls. Twisted spindles on a polished black floor faintly reflected the grandeur from above, the images skewed with veins of crackled golden lines.

"Look at you," Copper said to the elegant goods and sweet crafted smells that lined the first level. It was unlike anything she had ever experienced.

It was a smuggler's dream.

One circle around the base of the tree, and several glances into open shop doors, told Copper all she needed to know initially.

"Each shop has a primary color." She planted her free hand on her hip. Aside from the signs and sample racks, the crown of the stained glass decorations appeared to have categorical significance. Red for clothing and personal items, green for literature, and blue for foods, spices, and other edible items. Those with black or white panels had opaque windows, suggesting an even higher level of exclusivity. Or things of questionable intent or origins.

"My kind of people," she said with a sigh.

Questionable magic was always her favorite kind. Once upon a time, magic had been wild and dangerous. But as time passed, people became relatively immune to it as it seeped into bloodlines and worked its way into common use. Magic had been tamed and harnessed until a person need only get their hands on specific objects to wield it. There was little in the way of magic that was unexpected in everyday life. However, raw veins still flowed freely and could produce dangerous consequences if it wasn't filtered through the correct objections or handled by skilled hands.

The many floors were bustling with people of all sizes and colors. A high-end dress code clearly marked the patrons from the staff and vendors. Boxes and bags, carts and wagons cluttered the space between shoppers as they passed by one another, and yet the floors were immaculate.

"It's always a wonder, ain't it?"

Copper turned on her heel, feeling a shocked expression tighten her forehead. "Y-yes," she answered. Her voice sounded too high to her own ears. "I've never seen anything like it."

Situated at one of the ground floor shops, an older man sat at a small stand parked outside a matching shop. Both were decorated in a celestial smattering of paint and shimmer. His eyes were sharp as he beheld her. "And you never will," he agreed. "There's nothing like it in all the king-doms."

"I'm here offering free samples–" she started to say, slowly undoing the ribbon of her box.

"None for me, thanks." The man stroked his bushy mustache.

"No?" Copper chirped and left the bow alone.

"We don't offer edible items here, and the Missus doesn't let me eat sugar these days." He dabbed at the sweat on his bald head before continuing. "She says it's for my health, but I think she just enjoys making my life harder."

Copper made a visual sweep of his cart.

The man sat a little taller on his stool. "Unless you're in the market for something?"

"I could be," Copper gave him a winning smile. "Are you Saul?"

He regarded the storefront behind him. The sign read Saul's Stars and Shimmers. "Some days," he told her. "Some days not. It depends on who's asking…and if the shop shows up."

"Do all of the stores come and go as they please?"

The man looked around, a mischievous twinkle in his eyes. "The ones with real magic do."

"Ah," Copper mused, drawing out the sound. In truth, she couldn't believe her luck. Saul's Stars and Shimmers sold the most sought-after powders in the smuggling community. It was rumored that the invader who overthrew the northeastern kingdom of Swynnhaven had purchased their upper hand from Saul.

Even the sands of time couldn't stand up to one of his enchanted jars.

"As you can see here, I am the real deal." He gestured to his little wooden cart with its broad awning and countless goods. Shining stars and twisted metals comprised most of his cart's hanging portion. The lower shelves bore powders and perfumes in different packages and containers.

"In my experience, the real deal is much easier to impersonate than one would think," Copper told him.

From where he sat on his stool, Saul planted his hands on his knees and leaned toward her. "You want proof, is that it?"

"You can never be too careful."

"What would you be in the market for?"

An amulet, an oddity shop…really anything to get me out of this mess. Copper considered her plans. "I want to not be trapped."

"Trapped…trapped…" he thought aloud, tapping the spot on his upper lip where the two sides of his mustache came together. Pulling a drawer open in the middle of his cart, Saul reached in and pulled out a packet of shimmer from amongst a sea of tiny bottles. "So you want to get out of somewhere *tough.*" He flicked his gaze to hers.

Copper nodded.

Saul gestured for her to come a bit closer. "You take a shimmer like this," he opened the packet and took a small pinch of powder out between his two fingers. "Sprinkle it on the thing that is keeping you trapped and–" Saul showered the ribbon on Copper's pastry box, unfurling on its own.

"Saul," Copper laughed. "Do I look like a child?"

"A child?"

"That was a parlor trick!"

"Bah!" Saul grumbled, shooing her with a swish of his hand. "You asked for proof; there's your proof! You couldn't get this out in The Avenue!"

Copper crooked a brow at him. "Have a good day, Saul."

"Wait, wait." Saul stood, and Copper was surprised to see the man tower over her after appearing relatively small on his stool.

Dumping a tiny bottle of shimmer into his hand, Saul banged his fist on the wooden lip of his cart as though he were angrily knocking on a door.

Bang.
Bang.
BANG.

The shimmer fled his hand and flooded the floor in translucent, billowing plumes. First, it swirled up around every swell and curve of the black tree and then outward in every direction.

"What is it doing," Copper tried to ask.

Saul held up a finger, and in that exact moment, every door in the Grand Aurora ripped open. The sound of a thousand doors opening at once rumbled throughout the entire building.

Cries of surprise and frustration rang out, and all Saul could do was laugh.

The black tree crackled and groaned as it bowed forward just far enough for its lowest branch to swat the back of Saul's head.

"Get outta here!" Saul gave a gravelly growl as the tree stood upright once more. "You can't prove that was me!"

Perfect. "I'll take it."

Saul gave her the white powder in a tiny jar with a cork lid. "Swallow this when you feel trapped, and escape should be yours!"

"Thank you," she said sweetly. "What do I owe you?"

Saul worked his mouth for a moment before winking at the box. "Leave the treats, and we'll call it good."

"Deal," Copper laughed, sliding the box into his hands. "You really are a lifesaver."

#

Copper retrieved a small illustration from her pocket. She'd purchased a lightweight cloak from a vendor on the same floor that enabled her to discard the wrap top that could lead back to Cora if she were caught and disguise her discreet tool belt of items she might need to complete this job. Slinking around in a black undershirt and pants left her much more nondescript should anyone be questioned later about noticing her in passing.

The image in her hands was exactly as she had seen it depicted on the murals when she'd been brought before the empress in the Temple of the Solaera. Most gems were like all the rest in her eyes. But the echo of potential and power she had experienced in the temple made her believe this was something more.

"Why are you so special," she asked, the image of the amulet and bottle pairing sketched on the immaculate paper. Oddly enough, Cassian's drawing remained silent after her question, as a regular page ought to.

A looming presence told her she needed to move on from that space. Though she couldn't see the eyes on her, even with a casual surveying of the area, she could feel them, and that was enough.

Copper knew the history and folklore revolving around the crown jewels. The necklace signified the ruling force behind the throne from the era of The Titans. But that didn't explain why so many influential people were in pursuit of the same necklace.

It did make her wonder who else could know it was what she was after.

And who would follow her to get their hands on it?

The creeping sensation of being watched refused to leave her as she circled around floor after floor on the trunk levels of the seemingly endless shops of the Grand Aurora. It didn't take her long to realize that the odd little community of shop owners indicated direction and time by the tree. The tiles on the ground level acted as a sundial.

"You see if you take a left at the seventh split branch," a shop owner directed a patron, "and then go down two levels to the portion of the tree that has the carvings of The Empire, you'll find what you're looking for in one of the three shops that are directly under the branch with the twisted twigs."

The things she saw in doorways and display windows were interesting. Sometimes it was a purple monkey; other times, it was singing glass figurines or chocolate bars with twinkling, edible gems. Some magic she found to be of the sleight of hand variety, others she wouldn't touch with a ten-foot pole.

When she paused on the fourth level of The Black Tree Market to admire a notch that looked like a face, a rose gold anklet slid up her foot and tied itself around her ankle.

"I learned a long time ago," she started to say, bending to unhook the anklet. "that beautiful things, no matter how charming, tend to be dangerous."

It was beautiful, the way it radiated the natural light pouring in from the crystalline dome ceiling. Still, she knew it to be a sort of tracking magic that held information about each person who wore it.

"No, thank you," she told the shop owner. The bracelet wriggled in her palm like a worm as she handed it back.

The woman with indigo hair and a lip piercing gathered the piece between her gloved fingers and appraised it for a long moment. "Do you make a habit of declining the magic that chooses you?"

"Something like that," Copper said with a wink.

"Then maybe you don't belong here."

Copper did a double take and beheld the woman for a long moment. "Do any of us truly belong here?" she asked, sweeping an appraising gaze over the woman. "If that illegal anklet did what I think it just did–" Copper waited in place until the woman grew visibly hesitant, toying with her piercing.

"Who's to say," she shrugged and turned away to hang up the anklet.

It was true; Copper didn't belong there. But that anklet stole a feelings reading the second it touched Copper's skin. If the vendor drew any more information than that, she didn't let on. It was illegal to draw on the emotions of others, even in The Avenue. Some vendors used it for sales, but there were significant consequences if caught.

I need to find that shop and get out of here. Copper told herself as she moved away from the woman and her soul-sucking jewelry in the most confident stride she could muster. Appearing innocent of any accusation was three-quarters of the battle in her line of work.

Chapter Six

Dumb as a Fox

O n a different floor, Copper rested in the warm glow of a tall window near a twisted root that reached up through the flooring. Instead of reducing it and patching the hole, they'd cleverly molded it into a bench over what must have been years.

"The storefront of The Oddity Shop shifts its shape and location frequently," Cassian had explained before they parted ways. "Some say there's a pattern. Others have told tales of fate and this door that arrives only for those who need it." He'd waved his hand, and a mystical rendition of the door with its starry engravings and crescent twin windows had appeared in a plume of blue smoke. "So, decide that you need this door because it is the key to everything you want and everything you need."

Fate has nothing to do with this.

"I need this." Copper closed her eyes and told the magic that called out to her.

Escape.

Freedom.

I need to find that door.

The sunlight on her face didn't fade so much as it abruptly disappeared, replaced by a looming presence. The enchanting music of the market hushed. Turning, she found a building with windows framed in dark wood dotted with freshly fallen snow, as though the entire store had just been somewhere…else.

"Cute." She crooked a brow.

The intense pull from the shop started as a small kernel of anxious tension low in her stomach. Invisible tendrils of magic caressed her skin and crept up her torso to gently draw at her ribcage, beckoning her to join it.

"Clarke and Wylder." Her words drifted about the busy shopping space as the sounds of the hotel faded into the background.

Grabbing the door handle and stepping inside would be so easy. During her travels, she'd heard that the shop was alive. Others claimed the shopkeepers were older than time itself. There was something significant about seeing the emerald sign reading Clarke & Wylder. What she was about to do was magical sacrilege, even for a smuggler.

You've done worse, she reminded herself before taking hold of the matching, twisted handles.

The enchanted threshold was guarded by twin blue doors. The ornate leaf patterns framing the knobs gleamed like summer leaves after a mid-day rain.

I've seen you somewhere before. Her mind reached out to the doors. Its magic wound around her mind, searching but not invading. Pressing but not harming.

A series of watercolor images swept across the doors almost faster than Copper's eyes could follow. The few images she did pick out were things she'd seen in her past.

Lazy afternoons soaking in a tide pool.

The scarlet coin she'd earned after her first smuggling job in Aerimora.

Then there was a starlit sky she'd watched on an endless night that left her smelling like woodsmoke and a forest outside a city that no one knew the name of any more.

A flash of wind and color wound up over the door panels before circling around the golden handles. A pair of crescent moon windows appeared, fading from opaque to transparent, revealing the shop within.

"Show off," Copper whispered to the door, giving it a feline smile. She'd encountered some unique magic in her time, but there was something so *delicious* about magic with a personality.

As though in response, the bright doors swung open.

Copper half laughed to herself, looking at the threshold to the infamous shop, waiting as though something else should happen.

What? No riddle? Copper glanced around before she took a step inside. A place so exclusive and revered would make a person work for entry more, wouldn't it?

Maybe there is a little bit of fate to this after all…

One moment, Copper was standing on the polished floors of a busy hotel, and the next, her feet were cushioned by a thick welcome rug. The moment was marked by the smell of well-loved books and the immediate recognition that it was closed for business. The storefront was dark, and upon initial inspection, there wasn't a person to be found.

What is that? She wondered when the bite of a different scent came to her, something rich and spicy, with a hint of earthy smoke. Solid and ferocious, it told all who entered that the welcome only extended so far.

Find me, a whisper echoed from inside the shop. *Taste me with all your senses.*

So you *are* more than meets the eye.

She had expected many things, but when the doors closed behind her with an audible click, she stood in the dim light of the small window near the entrance and waited for something to happen. For a moment, the seasoned, skilled deceptionist within her faltered under the weight of every potential mishap before her in the dark.

The Grand Aurora was bustling with life, people buying and selling, eating or carrying towering stacks of packages. The hotel was all soft lines and regal propriety with its brought colors and rules that gave it almost a sterile feeling. Even when it sang to her, it was removed from the here and now.

But the oddity shop? It was alive, regardless of the dormant state it presented. It curled around her senses, welcoming her in with gentle touches and airy, inaudible whispers. That presence in itself was enough to make her skin crawl.

This isn't right.

Or…was it?

Copper took a step or two further inside. Behind the counter, she could make out a few rows of shelving in the dark. A series of tinted glasses and orbs glowed with her proximity. They cast a rainbow of colors across the wooden flooring. It would have been beautiful, even mesmerizing, but then a gentle movement gripped her attention. Copper whipped her gaze to the left, her pulse spiking, but no one was there.

The movement was so brief that when she spotted the hanging cluster of air plants, she huffed a sigh of relief.

The opening and closing of the door must have sent them swinging.

Perched in lofty hanging baskets, the three plants swayed with leaves that were all different from each other. One pointed straight upward in the shape of a tropical bird, the other dropped broad leaves over the sides, nearly bursting at the seams of its tiny home, and the third sprayed thin, red-tipped reeds in every direction.

They looked a little sad like they might need some water, but she was there to find that necklace and get out, not play house sitter to an inattentive shop-owner's plants.

You look like trouble. These plants were young, just babies in their makeshift bassinets. But she'd come in contact with their kind a few times. While they were harmless at this age, the full-grown ones could be lethal.

Cautiously, Copper wandered straight into the open center of the shop, letting her hand idly run along the smooth lip of the wooden counter as she went. Little figurines of flowers, people, and creatures danced in her wake.

One doorway, one window, and a narrow path to them both, she noted, as there was an archway that separated the storefront from the rest of the shop. There was no door there that would keep her from escaping, but there were several pathways that wound their way through the shop, and all of them bottlenecked through that archway. It was less than ideal, but it was a reality she'd have to deal with if the job went south.

Pressing forward on silent feet, Copper pulled the hood of her cloak up and wrapped the thin material around her face. She then secured it with a pin she'd kept in one of the eight pockets on her tool belt, binding her hair and concealing her identity.

This was not somewhere she was meant to be.

The reality of an owner suddenly flicking a switch and revealing her skulking around was enough to make her think twice. Still, the rush of being the mouse slipping around an unsuspecting cat pumped adrenaline through her veins and honed her senses.

She ducked under the broad leaf of another plant, overfilling a nearby shelf. She scanned it briefly for the markers of one of the many dangerous breeds of plants that she had smuggled in the past and found it lacking. Gently brushing it aside, her eyes adjusted to the dim lighting, and the items in the shop took shape. First, it was old and new books alike and signs in languages she didn't yet understand.

Winding her way through rows that went on forever, Copper came across marvelous items that sparked her imagination with burning curiosity. On the varying levels of shelving were rings made of flowing water and cubes that glowed. Even the books seemed to hum songs of their deep inner contents, bearing written portions of the authors' musings. Some of the hidden reading nooks bore the weight of an entire soul as though it was housed within them, sighing nostalgically with each page turned.

There in the dark, Copper slipped around a corner and peeked through a doorway draped with a single curtain where little stars twirled on the ceiling of the tiny room.

How do you trap a sky in glass? she wondered as shards of light fractured from delicate jars tied with decorative ribbons. The crystal clear confinements revealed the heavenly dances of swirling galaxies inside each piece.

More potless plants dangled in lofty woven baskets. Copper didn't recognize any of them, but they started popping up everywhere.

Why are you here? With all those warm lights of the cosmos poured over them in that room, there must be some significance to their presence in the shop?

She let the curtain drift back into place, as beautiful as it was, not wanting the glittering lights to draw unwanted attention. While the music of the magic in the hotel had called to her, the further she explored inside the shop, the more she experienced the pressing weight of whatever lived inside. The sensation of claws taunting, kneading their way out of the dark corners, forced her steps to slow.

She briefly imagined something ancient living inside those walls. The moment she stepped inside the shop, she risked waking whatever slumbered there if she wandered too far. Copper took a deep breath, rolling her shoulders to try to release the tension around her mind and body.

An overactive imagination would get her nowhere but caught. In all her wandering in that shop, she hadn't found another door or window that led out.

She'd seen enough wild magic. Now, if she could just make it out of this building with that necklace and not wake whatever slumbers in the depths of the shop.

She stepped back and heard a strangled yelp. Copper whirled, her eyes wide at the sudden sound. There on the floor was a worn leather book. Crouching down, she touched the silk bookmark, slightly wrinkled from her boot. The book wriggled. Audibly annoyed, it sprouted awkwardly bowed legs.

She gave a tight grimace that said *I'm sorry.* As she didn't dare speak it aloud. Regardless of the purpose of her presence there, she had come into its home and then stepped on it.

Rude.

The surly book slurped the fabric bookmark back into its ruffled pages like an injured tongue as it moved on to a safer place to be left in peace. Its gait reminded her of a hobbling crab but with feet. The sort of tiny feet deserving of tiny shoes.

A familiar creak of weight shifting on old wooden floors drew Copper's attention behind her. She held her breath, waiting for the sound to repeat itself. How far had she wandered?

Was there a quick way out if she was discovered?

Her mind raced with the logistics of escape when the wave of a long tendril caught her attention in the dark as it brushed past her face. Copper turned on her heel and came face to face with a…plant?

Where did you come from? A growing sense of suspicion swelled within her.

It was much bigger than any she'd seen during her time in the southern Kingdom of Sagebrooke Hollow, where they still grew wild but cultivated into manageable resources.

You're wrong. Your existence is…wrong.

A light glowed in the distance, revealing a circular opening in the ceiling that led to an upper level. She could have sworn she felt the exhale of breath on her skin coming from the direction of the plant.

Copper ducked low, hoping the single candle wouldn't reveal her presence.

"What are you doing out of bed?" A man's authoritative voice drew nearer.

Copper scooted backward, her booted foot narrowly missing the halo of light on the floor.

"You know better than to be this far into the shop at night," he told the plant, gathering the large pot and dragging it back to its home with a grunt, the candle simply floating beside him.

Copper couldn't see his face, just his long sleeping gown and the drooping nightcap that kept slipping off his head until he disappeared behind a shelf. Holding her breath, Copper's eyes widened as the light dimmed, and in its wake, the various forms of every plant she had passed and more began to wriggle. She watched from an incredibly dark corner as spiky plant appendages shifted on spindly legs, shuffling in round-bottomed pots, and swinging between the knit hanging planters, she tried to comprehend just how many plants sprang to life when they thought no one was looking.

Carnivorous! Copper's fear rippled through her mind and then out through her limbs as she realized why she could just waltz into the shop.

You are why there was no one around…no one guarding the shop. Her heart raced as she pulled the puzzle pieces together. *You didn't need to guard a shop when there were things inside that could eat people!*

Copper swallowed hard. Palming the hilt of a small dagger hooked into her tool belt, she waited and listened, knowing exactly how to deal with a carnivorous plant from past experience.

Why do there have to be so many? Sweat beaded on her forehead. How many could she deadhead before the sticky sap excuse for saliva corroded her cloak?

And then her skin.

A rolling *tick, tick, tick,* ticking sound broke the silence around her. There in the shadows, she saw an urchin-shaped plant rolling toward her, its hungry mouth salivating with a wet sweep of its tongue.

Out! Her brain screamed, and her body followed. *Out! Out! Out! Out! Out!* It urged with every pounding beat of her heart.

Stumbling through the dark, Copper sacrificed stealth for speed, even if she had lost her bearings when the shopkeeper had wandered by. No necklace was worth being eaten alive. She would come back and try again.

But what if there wasn't another chance?

The thought stopped her in her tracks, her breath coming out in short, frantic pants. It was so dark.

This was a mistake.

She'd sold her soul to the ringmaster, and now there was no going back.

Copper spun in a circle. Every turn she took revealed a new aisle with more books and tokens and nothing that looked familiar.

Why did it have to be dark?

Remembering that she had, in fact, come prepared, Copper unhooked a latch on the right side of her belt and slid out a palm-sized compass. She'd found the enchanted piece at a market clear across the Empire. The red arrow pointed north, and the Emerald pointed toward what the holder needed most. The second arrow swung from one direction, then the opposite.

Show me what I need, she pleaded internally with the compass until its arrow pointed to her right.

She'd only stopped moving momentarily when the prickle of thorns wrapped around her from one shoulder to the other; a damp sensation ran from the base of her neck to the crown of her head.

The urge to vomit forced Copper to press her lips together, subduing the scream about to rip from her soul. Something large enough to bear down on her with considerable height crept up behind her and had been so bold as to *taste* her. The hood of her cloak sagged under the slime it left behind.

Copper ran. Without hesitation. Without a second thought. She shoved the compass into her cloak pocket. Breaking free from the captive web of thorns secured to the back of her cloak, she blindly propelled herself forward down a long hall that ran the width of the shop. A wet snarl followed her, shelves trembling as the creature gave chase. Her ankle was hooked by the tassel of a bound map on a bottom shelf. Copper jerked her leg, trying to get free, when the glimmer from under a door in the alcove to her right illuminated the soft pointing gesture it made.

Light.

The kind of light from a well-lit room.

A light to reveal all the plants that wanted to eat her.

Light that could set her free.

Zigzagging her way through several shorter shelves, Copper ripped a cord from a long sleeve that encircled most of her belt. She secured sections to the shelves in a crisscross pattern as she ran, using self-fastening units to stick them to multiple surfaces. She dropped the tail of it as the monster chasing her became tangled amongst the layers of cording and other magical items. The books reacted in a chorus ranging from outrage to shrieks of thrilled delight. For some of the more dusty books, it was probably the most excitement they'd had in ages.

It gave her just a few feet of extra space, enough to launch herself toward the light. But not before the creature released several wet tendrils slapping after her, one broad leaf sweeping her off her feet. Copper rolled onto her back and came face to face with her pursuer.

A large, carnivorous plant bobbed back and forth, freezing in place when her gaze fell upon it. Eyelessly, this giant plant with dark veins throbbing through its beautifully fluted head watched her every move.

"I see you," she panted the words, not caring if she was found by one of the shopkeepers. The plant appeared frozen under her gaze, as all the others had been.

It's a self-defense mechanism. Copper remembered then why carnivorous plants were always kept in excessively lit greenhouses. The plants had been hunted thousands of years ago for their medicinal properties, as well as their taste for small children and livestock, that they'd learned to become as still as other plants.

She gave it an uneasy glare as she wriggled backward. Counting in her head, Copper gave herself exactly three seconds to muster up the courage to make the move and then scurried toward the light. The second her stare broke from its monstrous body, and it had been free to pursue her.

A short tunnel led to a narrow passage behind a series of bookcases in the nearby alcove. Her head knocked against the wall when the large plant crashed against the false wall separating them. Copper shimmied sideways toward the light, ignoring the way her head spun and the relentless pelting of plants trying and failing to reach her.

Falling out of the secret passage, Copper squinted against the brightness of the well-lit room. Looking around the office, she noticed the latched mechanism that probably slid and swung the bookshelves away from the office door.

Allowing herself a moment to catch her breath, Copper sprawled on the thick rug that covered hardwood floors as she realized the plants could not follow her into the space. Releasing the pin, Copper unbound her head and let her hood drop to the floor.

"What I wouldn't give to be caught by someone who actually knows what's going on in here!" Copper shouted, her words haughty and incredulous. Had the shopkeepers just not heard what had happened, or were they callous enough to let the plants sort out any intruders?

"How do you go about selling things after that?" She made a noise of frustration. "Here's the book you were looking for; sorry about the blood!"

There was a white cuckoo clock hanging on the wall that was shaped like the High Castle of Aerimora at first glance. Framed in a hand-carved map of the Empire, it struck the top of the hour, ejected a small gemstone bird that did a little jig, and then returned inside its home for the rest of the hour. Set in the flat paddle of the pendulum was nestled an amulet and vial pairing; its unbreakable chain was wrapped securely around the neck of the pacing piece.

"You," Copper snarled the word like an accusation, as if the glittering jewel was an offense for simply existing in a place where she'd almost been eaten.

Rolling onto her stomach, Copper beheld the windowless room and the relatively normal office furniture that filled the space: a desk, an old couch, and a series of paintings.

How boring.

But that stupid cuckoo clock?

Pulling herself to her feet, Copper was about to march over to the clock and rip it off the wall if she had to leave with that amulet when her attention was caught by a lonely little shelf built into the wall above a large fish tank. Drawing closer, she found a small set of bottles varying in size, shape, and color. To each side sat multiple tiny herb plants with flickering crystals peeking out from beneath the soil. A series of red-tipped arrows loomed over the shelf and its contents. They were secured to the wall with a cool metal plate behind each one, probably to keep them from burning the shop down.

"I haven't seen a set of these in ages," Copper murmured, holding her hand up to feel the warmth the perpetually heated arrows gave off. The brief change in temperature from her proximity caused the cooling plate to release a puff of frosty air.

The arrows hissed in protest.

*Well, hello…*she thought, recognizing one of the items at the back. The frigid breeze from the cooling plate had disturbed the glamor. Hidden behind bottles, herbs, and gemstones was a stout moonstone vial paired with a crimson amulet. The gem was cradled in swirls of cool silver and shining rose gold brackets.

"So which one of you is the real thing?" she asked as though the genuine article would leap from its resting place and allow her to be on her merry way. "If one of you is a trap," she muttered, a warning. Popping the lid on the bottle of shimmer from Saul, Copper downed the powder in one gulp. She grimaced. The sour aftertaste lingered at the back of her throat.

If Saul's statement was true, this should keep her from being trapped in the Oddity Shop if she chose wrong.

Either that, or I'll spend my days croaking on a lily pad with you guys!
A collection of colorful fish pressed their faces against the glass to see which item she would choose.

She refused to be turned into a fish.

She'd spent enough time in captivity.

A frog wouldn't be so bad…bouncy legs and all.
"You're coming with me," Copper whispered as she plucked the necklace from its perch, ignoring the clock.

Surely the hidden item was the real thing?

Who would put it on display and attached to a clock, of all things?

Lightning struck inside the moonstone vial when her hand passed over the glossy surface of the stone. Copper lurched backward.

You would mock someone else for being this jumpy, she chastised herself. With one last thought about whether or not any of this was worth it, she grabbed the necklace and immediately felt a sharp jolt run up her arm.

"No," she breathed in horror. The striking geometric head of a fox had been seared into her palm in lines of glaring red.

She hissed, not just in pain but in recognition.

The necklace was a fake, and she had been branded a thief.

Copper snatched Saul's empty jar from her pocket. She frantically eyed the label, hoping something would get her out of this mess. Instead, the tiny container shattered in her hand.

I wouldn't risk my spot in The Grand Aurora for my own family, let alone the likes of you, thief. Saul's words hissed from the broken jar.

"Who's there!" The shopkeeper's voice could be heard outside the office.

The ground shook. The shutters crashed against the windows.

Another door appeared on the far wall. Dropping the broken glass and the cursed piece of jewelry, Copper ripped it open and saw the counter in the front of the shop. She looked back and saw the discarded necklace slowly melting into the floor. The other necklace still swayed on the pendulum.

And I suppose you're cursed too...

It had to be.

All of it.

The entire shop.

One branding was enough for a lifetime.

The archway at the front of the shop began to close, the mouth of its opening narrowing swiftly. Copper left the other necklace where it swayed, mocking her stupidity, and chose to escape before the archway sealed her inside. The beautiful twin doors she'd entered through faded to black. The handles blazed with a twin symbol to the one that throbbed on her hand. It unlocked with an audible click. Copper drew a sharp breath. Maybe Saul's shimmer had released her after all.

She grabbed for the handles.

Ignoring the magic.

Ignoring the signs.

She believed she could forego consequences if she could just escape the Oddity Shop.

So, Copper fled through the doorway and into the unknown.

CHAPTER SEVEN

The Evvalorian Era

"**Y**OU FAILED!" SEBASTIAN BIT out when Raleigh returned.

"I did not." Raleigh rolled his eyes. Removing his jacket, he hung it on the coat rack. He then ensured the pocket Aloysius slept in was open enough that the poor thing didn't suffocate.

"Really?" Sebastian leaned against the lip of the desk in Raleigh's office. "Then explain that." He gestured with his cane out the window to the raised dragon wings on top of The Grand Aurora. A red illumination pulsed around their eyes.

"Seems to me you have an intruder," Raleigh mused, a small smile playing along his lips.

A dark cloud had gathered over the city, blocking out most of the mid-afternoon sun. The dragons on the hotel roof weren't real, but the enchantments on them were as true to life as the breath in his lungs. The warning glow and their predatory stance signaled that The Grand Aurora was on lockdown due to a violation inside The Black Tree Market. It was a rare occasion. But it wasn't the first time this had happened.

"I asked one thing of you," Sebastian said.

"This is not my fault. Had you come to me sooner…"

Sebastian cut him off sharply. "Where is your part of the amulet?"

Raleigh settled into an armchair in the corner. "I gave mine to your brother when I took this position. The Crown does thorough checks of your character and personal life, and I couldn't risk them finding it here!"

Sebastian covered his face with his hands, inhaling sharply. "So the amulet pairing is?"

"Together. In The Oddity Shop." Raleigh nodded slowly. "The amulet, chain, and moonstone vial are all under one roof."

"The amulet inside The Oddity Shop is a fake."

Raleigh took a moment to process. "Is it cursed?"

"It is."

"Then, if Copper was sent to retrieve it..."

"No magic in The Empire could protect her from the consequences."

The hair on Raleigh's arms rose. His heart rate quickened as he realized the potential consequences Copper could be facing. His eyes narrowed. "Did you know this would happen?"

Sebastian scoffed. "If I had known, do you think I would have come here?"

"If she got caught–"

"Then she is where she belongs."

"What's that supposed to mean?" Raleigh gritted his teeth, feeling the heat of his temper burning the back of his neck.

"It means that The Oddity Shop is protected, like all the other shops, with an agreement to sell and trade inside The Grand Aurora."

The Obsidian Clause.

Everyone knew what happened to thieves in The Grand Aurora, though no one had experienced it first-hand and lived to talk about it. His stomach sank.

What made you so desperate that you didn't come to me first?

"We have to get her out," Raleigh spoke slowly, sure he was misunderstanding the direction of their conversation.

"What for," Sebastian laughed, and it was a bitter sound that lacked any real humor. "My problem has resolved itself, save a few thousand hinges that need to be replaced."

"You would leave her there to die?"

"Justice has a way of sorting itself out."

The flames in the fireplace swelled on their own accord. "We are not abandoning Copper James to The Obsidian Hall."

"You don't speak for me, Detective."

"It's a prison for magical fiends, not a smuggler!"

"They are one and the same."

Raleigh's anger welled, threatening to boil over. His eyes fell on the way Sebastian protected the cane in his hand as much as he used it for support. His mind leveled, and the way forward unfolded before him.

"It would be a shame if the empress learned of your little walking stick." Raleigh tipped his chin toward the cane. "What is that? A piece from the Evvalorian era? It has to be hundreds of years old."

"You're not going to take away my ability to walk over a common thief."

The stick was magic. The kind of old magic that the empress tried to lock away from those who weren't of noble blood. If she found out the cane was in Aerimora, she would have it confiscated, and Sebastian would suffer the consequences.

"I would take away the very breath from your lungs to protect a single hair on her head. I would stop your beating heart to prevent her from getting a paper cut to her little finger. Do not think yourself so valuable that you make the mistake of believing you are untouchable."

Sebastian stared at him. His face was stoic, but there was a faint glimmer in his brown eyes that Raleigh noted for what it was.

Fear.

Had he truly not known the connection Raleigh, Copper, and Cora had shared? Or had he just assumed that was in the past, along with her smuggling days?

Sebastian sneered. "This is why our friendship ended. You always picked someone else over me."

Raleigh didn't flinch. "Our companionship ended because you could never see beyond yourself. You would let a young girl die for your own convenience. That's all I need to know about your personal character. Now, we're going to pay your brother a visit."

"I'd rather sell my soul to the ringmaster himself than set foot inside that shop again!" Sebastian insisted, not moving from where he stood.

Raleigh stepped closer. "After what you've told me here tonight, I'm not sure you have a soul to sell."

Sebastian's jaw tightened.

"Go!" Raleigh pointed toward the door.

Sebastian left, and when Raleigh followed, he locked the door behind him to ensure Aloysius' safety in his absence.

CHAPTER EIGHT

Cryptic Consequences

THE TRIAL OF COPPER James began at dawn in The Temple of The Solaera.

There had been no judge.

No jury.

Not in the traditional sense, as it had been no ordinary trial.

The cool blue tones of the mosaic tiles swirling across the floor matched the chill seeping into her skin. Copper shivered when she was forced to kneel before The Council of Seven. Three cloaked figures sat on either side of the empress. Their faces were obscured in early morning shadows and ceremonial hoods. The magistrate droned on, doing his duty to present the wrongs she had supposedly committed.

Make it stop… Copper's chest ached with each accusation.

Each use of the dead heir's name.

"Do you grieve so deeply for your own capture?" The empress sneered. Her abrupt question was a hot knife to the magistrate's words, successfully silencing the ancient throne room.

Copper lifted her face toward the empress.

The rest of the council remained still, wordless in their mockery of thrones.

The sun streaming in from the worshipers' balcony illuminated the wild nature of her red hair and the sleek lines of her powerful body. The smoothness of her *pale skin, clad in ivory silk, and the powerful way she held herself gave* the empress *a serene appearance of some ancient goddess. Yet, she sought answers from a smuggler who came from notably lesser origins.*

"I do not enjoy repeating myself."

The empress rose from her place on the dais to loom over her. Most would have trembled in her presence. All Copper could do was marvel at the attainable humanity of the woman before her because they were of similar age and build.

"I grieve for the lives lost, not the trajectory of my own." Copper drew her cloak around her body in response to the continued interrogation. Folding her arms tightly over her abdomen, she turned her face away from the daylight and her own deep-rooted sorrow.

The laugh that came from the empress lacked all sense of joy.

A prickle of a close presence drew Copper's attention. She braced herself, sure a guard had stepped forward to haul her to her feet. But no one was within arm's reach.

The transition between cowering before the Council and opening her eyes to survey her surroundings was blurred. The world tilted, and Copper dug her nails into the thick fabric of the cloak, grasping for some semblance of stability.

Where did this come from?

She would have savored the warmth of a cloak like that during the frigid nights she'd spent in the dungeon.

Escape. An airy whisper filled her ears.

Flee…another urged.

An enchantment in the bones of the temple called out to her, and she wasn't one to ignore magic with intent.

You don't hear it, she thought as she lifted her face and surveyed the council.

Unfortunately, the temple's message was being spoken to a broken soul. Rising again after what she had witnessed involved having the will to live. The truth was, she had not been captured by mistake.

I was tired of running. Tired of hiding.

Of trying.

Little pieces of the Empire's past whispered and sang from the murals depicted on every wall to the glittering stones adorning each of the seven thrones before her. The Temple of The Solaera was practically drowning in ancient magic with all its history and sparkling artifacts.

Copper's eyes lingered on the mural of The Empress for a little too long.

Yes, the magic in the room purred. The amulet.

The world tilted again, and Copper struggled to remember what happened next as the dream faded. The faces of the guards, the magistrate, and the Empress bled from her mind. Their words became distorted and muffled as the memory turned nightmare ended.

A low rumble of thunder drew Copper back to reality. The haze of the trial a few days prior lifted, and her mind tried to understand the dramatic shift in her surroundings. Bathed in pale moonlight, she lay on her side on a floor she didn't recognize.

"This isn't right." She sat up; the foreign room was hollow and out of place.

The blazing image of a fox glowed up from her palm. Copper winced at blood-red lines, bold and ugly and wholly wrong.

"What do we have here?" An unfamiliar voice crooned, muffled and faint.

"Who's there?"

A bedroom. She was in someone's bedroom, which had long since been opened, let alone slept in, with its layers upon layers of dust and thick strings of cobwebs.

How did I get here?

Copper picked herself up off the floor and hesitantly stepped toward the white paneled door. She squinted as she tried to better understand what had happened after she'd fled the Oddity Shop. Her heart pounded wildly when she reached out to grab the doorknob. Everything in her screamed to stay put, given her recent misfortunes with strange doorways.

A sinister growl shook the ground.

"I wouldn't go out there," the same voice taunted on the wind that wafted eerily through the room.

*I'm not in the habit of following disembodied voices…*Copper craned her neck at the warning, eying the out-of-place breeze ruffling the delicate fringe that lined the curtains. She'd never been one to take advice from those she couldn't see.

Was someone watching her?

But what if 'out there' was her only chance of escape from where 'here' was?

Either way, staying here doesn't feel safe.

A dim, sickly glow lit the hall in every direction. Cracked and faded sconces highlighted the distorted paintings and shredded wallpaper. With every step she took, a swirl of air dispersed the thick gloom and shadows covering the floors. The hall's décor suggested it was once a hotel for the rich and elite.

Copper noticed an insignia carved into the wall a short distance down the hall.

"A flowering mandala," she whimpered. The normally beautiful design, bearing the staff and crown in the center and encircled with the cosmic twilight bird herself, was the mark of death.

Bile rose in the back of her throat.

"The Obsidian Hall." Copper recognized the prison as she traced the angry raised edges of thorns woven into the pattern of the Empress. "How?" Her voice was barely a whisper when her hand fell back to her side in defeat.

"This was supposed to be a myth." Copper groaned. Her mind scrambled to make sense of things. At that moment, she couldn't decide where the nightmares stopped and reality began.

Had she ever escaped the High Castle?

What about the Oddity Shop?

The Obsidian Hall housed the most dangerous of magic wielders. Not her.

You knew there would be consequences if you weren't careful.

Copper continued to walk. The floors creaked, and the darkness consumed the halls as the lighting was dim in some spots and wholly absent in others.

She turned a corner and wandered into a corridor with halls going in four different directions. A circle of moonlight white-washed the tiled floors. Unsure of where to go or what to do next, she stood in the safety of the light.

"I didn't take anything!" She called to the powers that be, sure there had to be a guard or warden, someone who kept the place in line.

That stupid amulet.

Howls of anguish battered her from every direction. The doors that lined the hallway rattled in their frames. A prowling growl rolled through the hall from the opposite end, forcing her to retreat into the nearest room. Slamming the door behind her, Copper backed herself into a corner.

Something skittered across her foot. Fingers emerged from the overgrowth of rotted plants and filth that crawled up the wall. Copper shrieked, lurching away from the wall and throwing creeping things from her arms.

Her hands trembled as she moved to the door. She peered out through the keyhole and found the glow of a red eye illuminating it from the other side. She gasped and shoved away from it. A beast made of shadow fractured it off its hinges, barely missing Copper when it crashed into the nearest piece of furniture. The shattered bed frame gave her a temporary weapon to take with her. She palmed it like a bat, ready to swing at anything in her way.

"Stay back!" She dodged the dazed beast as it staggered, shaking its head. Small and large pieces of wood sprayed in every direction. The shadows that swirled around it never fully dispersed, giving this wolf-shaped creature exaggerated features with oversized eyes and lethal fangs.

You shouldn't exist anymore… Copper thought, her stomach working into painful knots.

She stumbled through the halls until she reached a long abandoned grand ballroom. Copper slammed the doors behind her and took a moment to catch her breath. Turning, she looked up and saw exactly why it had been left to rot.

An incoherent gurgle of disgust poured from her lips as her mind faltered to comprehend the next danger ahead. Giant spiders hung from broken chandeliers overhead. She was afraid of the beast in the hall, but it must have known the bigger predator in the ballroom as it did not barrel in after her.

Why this? Why me?

The pearly white spiders beheld her with a smattering of red eyes.

"Oh, oh, why?" She forced a horrified scream down as her whole body went numb.

One giant, curious spider began to descend. The shadow beast stood on all fours in a different doorway not too far from her. It stalked her, slow and methodical, to not be noticed by the spider.

"You can't say you weren't warned," the female voice from the bedroom cooed as the spider descended.

White knuckling the sharp piece of broken bed frame, Copper panted through the panic building in her chest. The soft clicking of the spider's appendages as it made its way down a web as thick as rope was enough to make her knees quake.

"Such a pity–such a beauty," the male spider crooned. His voice was deep and more heavily accented than the larger female's.

"This is no mistake," the female answered. "She bears the mark of The Vagabond."

Copper glanced at the fox head on her hand but returned her gaze to the creatures just as quickly. The slightest movement caused her to jump and wave her weapon back and forth. "What are you?"

"We're spiders, love," the female answered.

"I would think that quite obvious," the male added, his onyx striping a twin to her scarlet ones as the two shared a chuckle.

"What do you want?" Copper took another step back. The push and pull of her instincts wanted to retreat from the spiders and not back right into the waiting jaws of the beast.

"I would think that would also be obvious." The female gave a wet hiss and snap of her fangs.

Copper had heard of giant creatures in the deep woods of several kingdoms that drew even the bravest of warriors to madness if they survived.

No one ever said anything about them talking.

"Wait," the female halted. "This one seems…familiar."

"Familiar," her mate repeated, craning his head.

"Yes," she leaned a little closer, legs arching. "We've seen this face in the homeland."

"Ahh, yes. Beautiful Keskairah."

Copper's ears pricked at this. "What of Keskairah?"

"Our kind can see through all eyes from the colony we were born of," the female explained, blinking more eyes than Copper cared to count. "We saw you with the heir." At the mention of his title, the entire ceiling rumbled as many smaller spiders made their presence known. They all answered in reverence to the title of the future king from their home country.

"Then you know I'm not at fault," Copper called back.

Her stomach lurched.

His blood is not on my hands.

She remembered his blood pooling under the sea of tears released by the clouds. The way his chest had stilled under her hands. How her own ears had gone deaf to the world around her. The taste of his name on her lips.

Rogan.

"A tragedy," the female hissed. "And yet, you still do the bidding of his murderer!"

Bidding? Copper wrinkled her brow, her mouth twisting in disgust. Her mind scrambled for all the jobs she had done since that night. Her heart thundered as she tried to wrap her thoughts around when, where, how…

"Who?" Copper demanded. "Who did it? Who killed The Heir of Keskairah?"

"Don't pretend you don't know," the female boomed.

"Who!" Copper screamed so hard that her body trembled from the force of it.

The male chuckled, a wicked glint in his many eyes. "The ringmaster, of course."

Copper's world spun on its axis.

The meeting.

The Oddity Shop. It all led here.

"He set me up," she murmured. "He wanted me trapped here. That way, I couldn't find out what he had done."

"Your kind is always prone to that sort of thing. Betrayal, blasphemy, disgusting human traits, really."

"It's too bad you won't live to seek out your revenge," the female threatened.

Copper knew she should be afraid.

Knew she should run, beg, cry out for help.

*The ringmaster, of course…*was all she could hear.

Everything she'd been through since Keskairah, all the experiences, mistakes, hours, and all of the agony in between, had been because of Cassian September.

You strike me as the sort of person that needs anything but what they're looking for.

He'd mocked her. Hired her and then expected her to just *die?* All for his agenda?

"What did he get out of killing him," she murmured, eyes clouding with angry tears.

The spiders swarmed her then, their giant bodies surging forward. These massive creatures might have won her as their next meal if they had learned to not toy with their food. They'd given Copper a reason to live.

Vengeance was a compelling motivator.

Copper gripped her makeshift bat with trembling hands as a single tear slipped from her eyes.

Cassian September had killed the man she loved, then set her up to take a fall that should have ended her life.

And he would pay for that mistake.

If she could escape The Obsidian Hall alive.

CHAPTER NINE

Unwanted Reunions

THE SCENT WAS DIFFERENT for each person who set foot inside Clark & Wylder. For Sebastian, it was rich coffee and the tang of foreign citrus crops. The lights inside swelled from a dull, calming glow to a blazing illumination. Objects rattled in their cases at his presence.

I remember you. He recognized the firebirds in the painted glass on the opposite wall that peeled away, soaring around the place for the first time in years.

"Hel…oh…" Mr. Wylder's face went from welcoming to gravely confused at the sight of Raleigh Danger and Sebastian Axelson standing before him. He was a tall, lanky man with a youthful face that made him look too young for his silver business suit. He ran a nervous hand through his shaggy blond hair.

Pull yourself together, Sebastian thought. It took everything in him not to roll his eyes at Mr. Wylder's lack of professionalism.

"Jonah?" Raleigh sputtered with wild fascination. "Jonah, is Mr. Wylder of Clarke & Wylder?"

A child, he surveyed Jonah. *My brother chose a child to care for this place instead of me!*

Sebastian gripped his walking stick a little tighter when they walked through a back door of The Grand Aurora. The threat of losing his mobility had been enough to allow Raleigh inside, and the entrance to The Oddity Shop had simply presented itself to them in a secluded hallway as though it had been waiting for them.

The Oddity Shop had always liked Raleigh.

He hadn't needed the key Sebastian kept on his person at all times.

"Seb…ah…Mr. Axelson," Mr. Wylder chirped, confusion on his face. When they arrived, a tiny jumping bean he'd been attempting to coax into doing its namesake activity leaped into his front pocket.

Sebastian walked right up to the counter. "Jonah, where is he?"

"I don't think you want to bother him right now. He's with a customer."

"You and I both know I couldn't care less about his preoccupations." Sebastian pointed out with a languid arrogance. "Where is he?"

#

Raleigh wandered around the shop. There were several items on the shelves, but it was their reactions that gave him pause. A perpetual ring of flowing water evaporated, and the whispering souls in the windowed reading nooks drew silent. Raleigh eyed each shelf as he slowly passed by. Many books that growled or gasped in his presence could do real damage if left unchecked.

"Cowards," Raleigh whispered. His reputation of being a magic wrangler clearly preceded him. "Didn't you miss me?" He cast his gaze about the heart of the shop as he stroked a hand-carved engraving on the wall.

Lifting the corner of a red curtain, Raleigh peered into a dark, narrow hall that opened into a small room where he heard Mr. Clarke and a female customer.

"You take this, and you mix it into the waters. It'll take a few days, but you must follow the steps exactly as they are written." Mr. Clarke's back was to Raleigh, but his low voice was unmistakable as he explained instructions to the woman beside him.

Mr. Clarke was in every way Mr. Wylder's opposite. Where Jonah was an utter delight, the greatest cruelties of the world had soured Mr. Clarke's disposition. There was rumored to be some giant blood in his lineage. It showed in the broad sweep of Mr. Clarke's shoulders and the imposing way he filled a room.

So, that was you in the alley. Raleigh gritted his teeth. *If this plan backfires, you might very well kill me.*

"But will it work?" The woman's sleeve shifted to reveal a familiar symbol that was unmistakable.

Raleigh's attention was piqued.

Ophelia. Her ebony skin was decorated with a loosely drawn circular emblem and the gemstone hummingbird flying under a shower of stars. His mind flashed to warm summer nights dancing around bonfires in the city square during the celebration of the new empress.

They had swindled the very players of the last red game out of their own prizes.

She had taught him how to master illusive magics from her home kingdom.

She had cursed his name when they'd been caught, and she'd nearly lost her position.

"The Extravaganza…" He couldn't believe his luck.

That's why you were following me in the alley… Raleigh flashed the curtain a brilliant smile, letting it glide from his fingers. The fabric drooped back into place without notice. *You think I've teamed up with Cassian and his troupe to cause trouble with the Empire's magic!*

This? This he could work with.

An oversized grandfather clock bellowed, drawing Raleigh back to the task at hand. He slipped on a pair of thick, black gloves from his pocket and rubbed his hands together. He then held them out before the wood and glass panels of the clock the way a person might warm themselves before a fire. Heat radiated from within, but there was no visible flame.

The little firebirds overhead squawked and dove dangerously close to his head. Ignoring them, Raleigh waited until the clock finished its tolling. He had once watched a man awaken the magic inside the clock without the proper knowledge or protection. The results were a living burn that would slowly consume him over time.

Raleigh wasn't interested in experiencing that sort of agony.

Luckily, he had learned from the best. When the lantern-shaped amulet under the collar of his shirt rose up off his chest, he gripped the twisted spindles of the grandfather clock, forcing a surge of power that pulsed jarring booms that echoed into every corner of the shop. Dust, books, and valuable objects rattled free from their shelves. The clock and amulet spoke a language of illumination, snuffing out all light in the place.

"Don't!" Mr. Clarke called out, but he was too late.

Clang. A final, warped bellow rang out.

Crack. The clock rose to a staggering height.

Just before he moved, Raleigh made eye contact with Ophelia. A brief wink, and he did exactly what Sebastian had told him not to before their arrival. She shook her head at him as Raleigh swung his entire body through the spindles. Before anything else could be done, he was swallowed by the massive clock, and the shop was left quaking in the aftermath.

#

"I… didn't know it could do that," Jonah stuttered in the dark, breaking the stunned silence that had fallen over them.

"It shouldn't," Mr. Clarke answered. His brown eyes darkened in a wave of anger barely contained. "That is, it wasn't made for that."

"Where did he go?" Ophelia asked as the clock awkwardly reclaimed its original shape.

"I think it's time you leave," said Mr. Clarke as he struck a match and held it before him. As the firebirds bathed in the match's flame, they lit a series of candles around all the visible parts of the shop, both on the main floor and the overhead balconies.

"You let him in; you clean up this mess." He barked at Mr. Wylder before going behind the curtain to finish dealing with Ophelia.

"Them," Jonah corrected. His eyes fell on Sebastian as the room slowly came into view with each candle lit.

"Them?" Mr. Clarke bristled.

The firebirds rejoined the other stained glass pieces. When everything returned as it was, Sebastian sat sideways in a crushed red velvet armchair atop a raised platform with all the confidence and mischievousness of a wicked cat who had just eaten the family's pet canary. In a salacious voice, he leaned forward, making striking eye contact with someone he got along with even less than Detective Raleigh Danger.

"Hello, brother."

CHAPTER TEN

The Denial of Death

DISTORTED CLANGING ECHOED IN Raleigh's wake when the magic grandfather clock spit him out through an elevator door in The Grand Aurora Hotel. Ominous shadows spilled over the prison floor. The forbidden level thirteen harbored evil beings and enchanted items that could not be trusted in the real world. After years of confinement, what resided there consumed what was once a pristine wing of suites.

"Copper! Copper James," he shouted, trying to ignore the images and smells that surged around him. Wicked memories rose up with the scents explicitly crafted for him to recall and then witness them happening again.

The things that lived there, ancient and creeping, toyed with Raleigh's mind, projecting his worst fears into a warped reality as he called out Copper's name. In one hall, wild magic ravaged the Empire until there was nothing but rubble, ruins, and death everywhere he turned.

It was why he had taken the role of Supernatural Detective in the first place.

Someone had to keep the magical capital in line.

"Raleigh," an ethereal female voice called out to him. Her seductive words enraptured him and caused his stomach to lurch simultaneously. "Raleigh Danger."

She was his other fear.

"Tirzah." He breathed her name in utter misery. Floor thirteen was the realm of death to him, and the woman before him was proof of that.

"You've come back to me." She floated toward him, only to become disjointed and malformed when she took a step forward.

Raleigh tried to edge past her. Tirzah's feet slowly lifted until her toes were caressing the ground. The hem of her dark plum dress flirted with the floor as she hovered dangerously close to his face.

"Don't do this," Raleigh kept his face passive, his voice cold. "You're not real, not here." Inside, he ached for her, but she was a thing now, not the woman he knew. What she had become was so foreign and off-putting that it was hard to maintain the indifferent mask he wore. But if he let it slip, even for a moment, The Obsidian Hall would win, and he would never get out of there.

Both he and Copper James would be doomed. It was so easy to get trapped by one's own emotions in that place.

"You don't think she's still alive, do you?" Tirzah smiled. Her breath was cold against his skin. Lifting a gloved hand, she tipped her head to the side, bringing her palm up to feel the heat from his face.

"What have you done?"

Tirzah gave him her most brilliant smile.

She would not make it that easy for him.

She never had.

"Look at you," Raleigh muttered.

He remembered the warmth of summer glowing in her vibrant skin. The way her dark hair was liquid onyx in the sun. He remembered the love they had for one another.

Not this pale gray flesh speckled with scars and forever unhealed bruises. Her long, dark hair had begun swaying about her. Her hollow eyes, thickly lined in sooty smudges, hungrily drank him in, and her once full lips were near colorless. Red lip stain streaked downward on her face, marring the left side of her jaw.

Tirzah arched her back, bringing her a little higher than eye level. "I am what you made me." Her crackled laughter caused Raleigh physical pain. "Empress of the Shadows of Skyecross, descendant of Keskairah…"

"Whatever you've become, you've done to yourself," Raleigh said as he passed through her.

Because Tirzah was gone, and the figment before him was nothing more than that.

A memory.

#

"S–stay back!" Copper waved the broken spindle of the bed frame between the monsters.

The shadow beast moved first. The urgency of another predator moving in was too great a risk.

"Oh, how hard you've worked for me." Copper taunted. "You can't relinquish your claim on me now!"

The beast twisted at a weird angle when Copper swung at it, causing it to crash into one of the spiders closest to her.

A rumble emanating from the beast closing in at her back formed a familiar pattern.

Are you laughing at me?

It was enough for Copper to sneer as she tucked her chin. "I. Will. Not. Die. Here," she shouted with each swing. The beast attacked, a hungry snarl rippling against her back. Copper swung hard, forcing the beast to land closer to the spiders.

"That's good to hear." Raleigh's voice came from across the room, and the echo bounced off the glistening walls before reaching her on the icy floor. "None of your new friends seem terribly keen on that plan."

Copper shifted her grip on the stick. "Raleigh?"

It was hard to believe her own eyes. She'd seen so many bizarre horrors, and did Raleigh look…older? It had been a few years, but there was something different about the man who stood there compared to her memory of when she saw him last.

"Detective Danger," the spiders growled in unison; the playfulness left their voices. "You don't belong here."

It is you. Copper thought, the tension in her jaw loosening just a little.

"At your service." Raleigh pulled a device from his pocket and wound the end of it. "Really, I'm hurt! Not even a 'Welcome Back' card?"

In one languid move, he threw the object, and it exploded in front of the shadow beast with a brilliant flash. The creature howled as the shadows evaporated under the spray of light until the beast was no more.

The powder lining the device ignited the crusty webs separating them. The flames seared up the web at blinding speed, engulfing the two spiders dangling from the chandeliers before working their way up to the smaller hoard on the high ceilings.

"Copper James," he announced over the death cries of the opal spiders. "You couldn't have written?" He casually moved toward her from the opposite side of the space as if the room wasn't being set on fire.

"I've been busy," she gestured upward with her stick, watching as the largest spider in the group glowed like a burning ember, stumbling around as she died overhead.

"Come on!" He gestured toward the direction from which he had arrived.

Copper climbed over broken furniture and the debris of dead things that she tried not to consider. The room was heating fast with the rapidly spreading flames. Sticky webs burned away and revealed old weapons from those who had tried and failed to defeat the spiders.

"If we die, then so do you!" A crackling screech flooded the room. Copper's mouth fell open, watching as the legs of the opal spider crumpled and fell straight toward her.

It took the span of a heartbeat for Raleigh to realize that Copper wasn't going to move in time. Closing the space between them, he wound through thick webs, watching when the crispy spider got caught in its web, breaking through one layer at a time.

"Move," Raleigh boomed, tackling Copper out of the way and rolling them into the hall. The spider hit the once elegant marble floor with a plume of ash, embers, and fractured webbing sections.

Quickly separating, Raleigh gaped at her as he stood.

"What?" Copper asked him, sitting up with a slight waver, her head spinning.

"You know, I understand how you got stuck. I always assumed that you were as good at getting out of trouble as you were at hiding and moving things that weren't yours!"

"Are you mocking me?" Copper climbed to her feet, ignoring the helping hand he'd extended to her.

"No," Raleigh shook his head, then grimaced. "Well, maybe a little. How did you manage to survive for this long and then not think, 'Hey maybe I should move before the dying five-hundred-pound spider falls on my pretty little head?'"

"I can't believe you're making fun of me in the middle of The Obsidian Hall!" She hissed the last portion.

"Let's find a way out of here, and we can discuss my personality flaws later."

"Why would you come for me," she narrowed her eyes, not following him when he moved to walk down a foreign hall. "Why would you come to this place?" She surveyed walls and doorways she must have seen a hundred times, or maybe never at all. At that point, everything looked the same, and nothing made much sense.

"After what you did for me in Keskairah? Did you expect otherwise?"

Copper whirled on him. "I didn't think anyone would be stupid enough to enter this place willingly!"

A ripple of a growl, broken and hungry, spread through the dark halls in the brief moments of silence following their tense exchange. Raleigh and Copper stopped moving, listening carefully to gauge how close the beast was and from which direction it was approaching.

"Where there's one shadow beast," Raleigh began.

"There's bound to be more?" Copper finished his thought.

He nodded. "They always travel in packs."

"I thought they were extinct!"

"Whatever you do, don't…"

"Run!" Copper grabbed his arm and jerked him down the nearest side hall upon seeing a glowing pair of red eyes.

"You can't run from these things!" Raleigh shouted as he kept pace with her. "You have to face them head-on, or they just get–"

The cursed maze of the floor produced obstacles of fake walls and lurching creatures that sprung up around every corner. For every sprint Copper took in one direction, Raleigh corrected by pulling her in the other. Her instincts regarding magic might have saved them from more than one trap door or precariously perched creature on the ceiling. Still, Raleigh's uncanny familiarity with the floor drew them near the exit.

Relief washed over Copper as an iron door, untouched by time or creeping thing, came into view. But as soon as she saw it, a beast sauntered out at the end of the hall. Copper shrieked, skidding to a stop until she fell flat on her back and disappeared beneath the dense layer of fog that coated the floors.

Raleigh blindly reached for her, grabbing her shirt and dragging her backward into an open foyer.

"Come with me." He tucked them behind a patch of overgrown ivy lining the wall and threw an unseen item further down the hall.

Breathlessly, they waited as the beast tore after the item and missed them entirely. A desperate need to escape urged them both down the hall and away from the beast that did not give chase. Pulling the hourglass amulet from around his neck, Raleigh unlocked the heavy metal door with its cogs and wheels.

A chorus of groans and shrieks protested from the other side when Raleigh and Copper swiftly pushed the bulging door until the iron safeguards hissed and popped, signaling that it had been sealed.

Peeling away from Raleigh, Copper laughed through a hysterical moment of relief. But, as the adrenaline faded, she slumped against the wall and slid down it until she was seated on the floor.

"Honestly," Raleigh panted as he sprawled out beside her. "We've survived worse."

Copper hid her face in her hands, feeling the blood rushing through her body. She desperately tried to find her peace, but a sudden stillness washed over her.

"He killed him," Copper told him.

"What?" Raleigh lifted his head.

"The ringmaster. He was in Keskairah when we were," Copper slowly lowered her hands.

"What of it?"

"The spiders! They said—"

"They'd say anything to corner their prey!"

"He sent me after a cursed piece, Raleigh. He wanted me to land here so I wouldn't discover what he'd done!" She held up her branded palm to him.

"How long have you been in here?" He tried to change the subject.

"I'm not sure." Copper gulped, the smell of burning spider reaching her. She looked into his eyes. Those familiar steel blue eyes with their unnatural silver lining to the iris. She remembered a time when they were more like deep oceans. She remembered a time when he was all she wanted.

Raleigh took her hand in his, running his thumb over the mark. "We're not assassins, Copper. What exactly are you going to do even if you did find Cassian?"

Copper jerked her hand away from him. "Revenge, Raleigh. I want revenge." she pulled her hand away from his. "He has ruined everything I have ever had," she pushed to her feet and glared at him, biting into each word as though it were an oath. "If the ringmaster wants to play a game, then so be it."

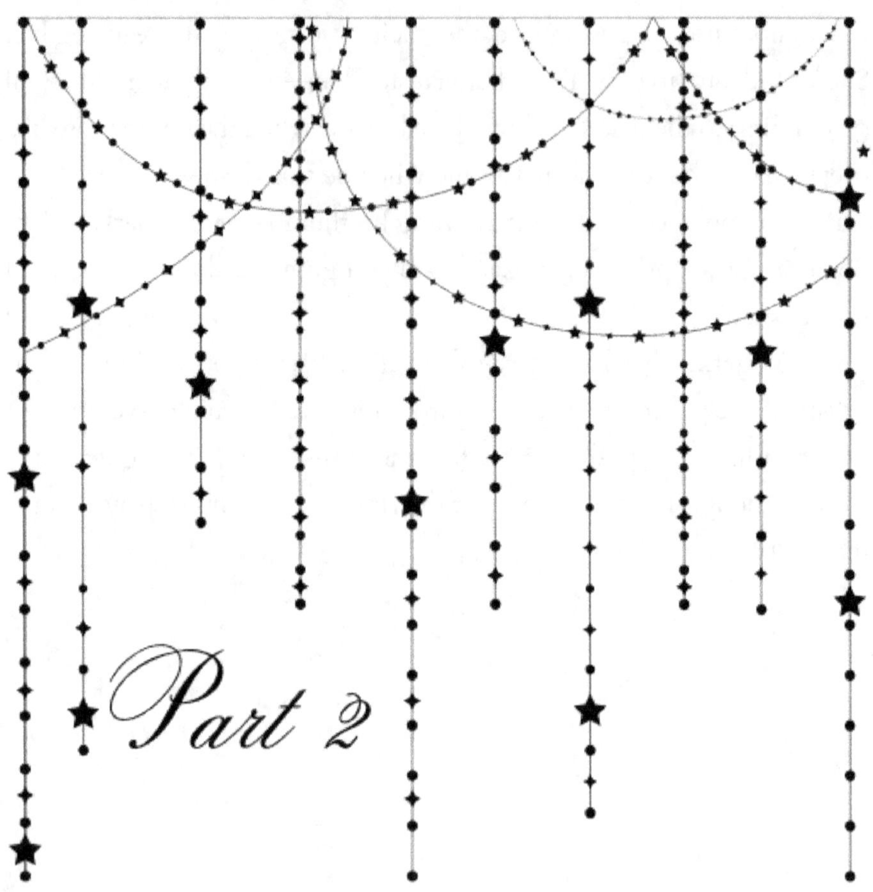

Part 2

CHAPTER ELEVEN

The Scarlet Tether

EZLYN'S DEBUT ON THE tightrope was anything but ordinary.

In the heart of the circus, a particular tent rose high above the rest. It was covered by a crimson fabric fluttering like a skirt in the breeze. Inside, the material was painted in bleeding watercolors depicting elegant designs and abstract artwork of flame eaters, contortionists, magicians and many others who had performed in the main arena in past seasons. The funnel of fabric that made up the top of the room was framed in numerous strings of round bulbs secured from the highest points, sweeping down to each outer support beam.

One by one, the lights snuffed out in a spray of swirling embers, fading until the only one was left in a series of small spotlights focused on a platform high in the air, revealing a series of lemon and emerald bottles that drank in the light like glowing fireflies.

A colorless wonder in a sea of vibrant pigments, a short young woman was dressed from neckline to ankle in a sleek white body suit adorned with dazzling crystals that caught the light from every angle. A dreamy masquerade mask decorated the upper part of her face in a delicate lace pattern of pale ivory and shining rose gold. From it, a series of beaded crystals dangled down to dance about her jawline, providing a unique disguise under her striking crop of lavender hair.

No longer the doe-eyed child of the past, Ezlyn waited for Akos' backing before she mounted her final platform that towered high over the ground floor.

"The show doesn't start until you allow yourself to fall!" Akos' voice was little more than a cajoling comment that intermingled with the roar of a crowd enraptured with anticipation upon seeing her.

"What a show that would be," Ezlyn's warm reply was flirty, catlike, and smooth in the way it wound its way over her dark, strawberry colored lips.

"Be careful," Akos shook his head, unable to hide his smile.

Ezlyn could hear the grin in his voice even as she turned away from him to take her place. She smirked at him over her shoulder, her gaze caught on the half crescent of the sun shaped scar under his amber colored eye, a stark contrast to its teal twin.

The air was tinged with the smell of sweat, sawdust, and the layer of hot, sticky caramel the vendors were drizzling over tangy, crisp apple slices. Ezlyn inhaled the savory scent of buttered popcorn wafting up from the main floor as she took her first step forward and out of Akos' broad arms. Her toes teetered off the edge, causing the wild cries and joyful bantering to dim to a flurry of hushed whispers. Her first few steps drew surprised gasps as she floated on air, the tightrope rising up to meet her.

Akos watched, his mismatched eyes surveying every detail to ensure her safety. "This is going to kill you," his voice was thick with antagonistic qualities, fully expecting a shocked response.

"Demon to some, angel to others." Ezlyn softly tsked, gripping the charms that dangled around her neck, she superstitiously gave each one a kiss before turning to beam a wide smile out to the crowd. "Will your charms never cease?"

With a sharp jerk of her wrist, Ezlyn produced a white staff that glittered under the spotlight. Gripping it horizontally in both hands, she used it as a balancing mechanism until she drew near to the first bottle and rotated the staff. With each turn, the staff sliced through the tightrope, emerging on the other side as though it were little more than air. One by one, she broke the bottles set out before her, showering the floor in riotous sprays of harmless sparks.

Ezlyn tumbled forward, cartwheeling toward the center bottle, and cracked it with ease, igniting the staff in a flame that roared outward toward both ends, leaving her hand grip untouched. The lights extinguished all together then, allowing the whirling of the staff and the cracking of the bottle to be showcased in a breathtaking display.

When the last bottle ruptured, Ezlyn was found by the scouring spotlight to be standing on the opposite platform. A sound of triumphant music sounded, cueing the crowd to cheer.

"But wait," Ezlyn said breathlessly, "there's more!" Squatting down like a bound spring, Ezlyn surged forward as a final bottle appeared in the center of the rope.

"What are you?" Akos muttered to himself, knowing this was not a usual part of the act.

Loosing a breath, Ezlyn ran across the tightrope with her flaming staff and leapt, the sudden jerking sending the bottle flying in the air, allowing her to hit it like a piñata and send a circle of light bursting through the air. Landing in the center of the rope, Ezlyn bathed in the applause brought forward by her efforts, even under the displeased gaze of her spotting team.

What was that? She wondered as her heart raced.

Ezlyn turned on her heel to face Akos, showing off in a way she had not practiced, and when she abruptly fell at an awkward angle even Akos lurched forward in surprise. Ezlyn's sudden plunge from her seemingly gravity defying perch elicited more than a few shrieks from the crowd.

She grabbed at open air, eyes wide as a yelp tore from her lips.

Not like this, she pleaded with whoever was listening. Falls like that weren't just career ending.

They were life ending as well.

She met Akos' gaze as gravity swiftly pulled her down toward her apparent doom. In the span of a single breath, she remembered something she had been previously taught by the head aerialist.

"Don't fall," he had said. "But if you do, use this."

Ezlyn shifted the packed bracelet on her wrist. Throwing her right arm upward, a gathering of three wide ribbons dyed scarlet shot out from a cuff around her wrist, securing themselves to two beams, and a suspension cord. Ezlyn spun in a tight spiral descending swiftly until she was mere feet above the ground. A wide skirt of onyx fabric bloomed around her waist reaching down to the floor simultaneously with her feet. A triangular cut out at the front of the skirt revealed broad black stripes bleeding down the legs of her body suit as she effortlessly freed herself from the wrist cuff that had just saved her from colliding with the floor. She'd narrowly escaped a situation that would have had lethal consequences.

As the amulet around her neck whirled to a halt on her chest, Ezlyn seamlessly found her bearings and gracefully spread her arms outward in a grand display as the crowd cheered.

"Welcome to The Red Rebel Extravaganza!"

#

"You ruined my act!" Xerxes, a woman with hair the color of pale moonlight, charged after Ezlyn the moment she passed behind a heavy flap out of view of the circus goers.

Ezlyn tipped her head to the side as she continued to walk, knowing full well Xerxes would continue to hobble after her. "It wasn't on purpose," she muttered begrudgingly, pushing through another series of canvas halls and into the one that led to the many hidden dressing rooms.

"You climb up the ladder, tiptoe across the bottles, do a simple tumble forward just enough to startle the audience and then you finish the act on the opposite side," Xerxes shouted, ignoring the sudden increase in swelling under the bandage tucked around her ankle. "But oh, no! Not bold, talented, cherished Ezlyn," she sneered, more upset that she did not complete the act herself, but Xerxes's temper had a way of mingling with her words in a way that frequently got her in trouble.

"That," Ezlyn jutted a finger in the direction of the main tent. "was me almost losing my life in front of the biggest crowd of the year."

A moment of silence passed between them in which Xerxes, the taller of the two, stared at Ezlyn, her face a mix of melting fury and conflicted disgust. Her jaw working as she inwardly processed the logistics of what had just happened.

"Your act could never match what I did tonight," Ezlyn sneered, clearly breathless from her ordeal. "I did not plan that. I did not lose my balance," she continued in clipped sentences. "It was…" she huffed, unsure how to explain it.

"What was that?" Akos presented from an inter-sectioned portion of the back hall, having made his way after her the moment Ezlyn had set foot on the ground. His broad presence took up significantly more space than that of the waif of Xerxes standing next to him.

"That's what I would like to know," Xerxes crossed her arms with enough attitude to rival a spoiled toddler.

"I–" Ezlyn toyed with the delicate chain of gold around her neck that held her lucky charms and paced a bit before she could muster the will to admit what she had experienced. "It was like I was…pushed?" Her face wrinkled in confusion when she voiced it aloud. It sounded ridiculous, even to her own ears.

"Pushed?" Xerxes arched a skeptical brow.

"No," Akos shook his head. "I was there."

"As were hundreds of guests!" Xerxes pursed her lips. "I think we would have seen if someone had made their way out to you and given a good shove!" Venom swirled around her words.

"How dare you?" Ezlyn erupted, one hand on the drape over her dressing tent when she'd whirled around to face Xerxes.

"How dare I?" Xerxes lunged forward. "How dare *you!*"

A cloaked figure shot out from the darkness of her dressing room when she wasn't looking and a foreign hand reached out and clutched the paired necklace, ripping it free from her neck.

"No!" Ezlyn jerked forward with the force of the assault.

"Hey!" Akos roared, springing into action as Ezlyn tumbled to the floor.

A flash of blue light blinded Ezlyn as the removal of her necklace pulled her forward by her chest and then snapped her head backward when the chain broke. It was as though her very soul had been snatched alongside the necklace and was spirited away with the thief.

"Stop!" Ezlyn croaked, pressing a hand to the base of her throat.

The chaos that followed slowed time down to an echo of a single heartbeat. The roar of Akos' pursuit, paired with the surprised sound from Xerxes that would have caught Ezlyn off guard had she not been battling to stay upright.

Had the thief been in there the whole time, waiting for her? She hadn't noticed anyone upon her entrance. But the performers hall was always poorly lit save for the vanity lights framing her mirror. Xerxes' words came across to her in muffled, warped spurts as though they were spoken over the rush of a wild waterfall.

Hunching forward, Ezlyn rested her elbows on her knees and dipped her head as she rubbed the bleeding fabric burn on the wrist where her safety cuff had been. The soft skin of her arm had already begun to bruise where the silks had wrapped tightly around her during the length of her spin. Her head throbbed in a way she didn't understand, and could not remedy on her own.

"What is going on back here?" Ophelia burst into the tent without warning.

"A thief." Xerxes managed to say, though she was noticeably distracted by Ezlyn's sudden shift in demeanor. "They took Ezlyn's charms!"

Ophelia, the former mechanical elephant trainer, had long since traded in her geared top hat for a much different role. Cassian had set a game in motion, but when he failed to arrive, the magic had summoned her forward as a replacement.

She stood before Ezlyn, and raked her tight curls to one side of her head. She braced one hand against the counter and leaned forward over Ezlyn. Ophelia was dressed in fabrics of tangerine, ocean blue and aloe green that hugged her like a second skin. A wide slit ran down each arm, as well as both sides of her skirt, revealing sculpted limbs that went on for days. Her dark skin was dusted in a fine shimmering powder that reflected the light around her, giving her the effervescent glow a Ring Master needed to draw the attention of the crowd without seeming to put forward too much effort.

"Did you see who it was? Where they went?" Ophelia grabbed a stool and sat almost knee to knee with Ezlyn who was wilting with each moment that passed them by.

Ezlyn failed to meet Ophelia's gaze. "It was all I had left of my mother."

"They're gone." Akos pushed past Xerxes and knelt down behind Ezlyn, looking between the two women.

Akos gingerly slid a large hand over the base of Ezlyn's neck, bringing her attention to him. "When I say things like that, about you dying? You're not supposed to prove me right." He said with a pitiful laugh as he examined her for injuries.

"It was all I had left," she whispered.

And the only thing that let her perform at the level she did.

Free from falling. Free from getting hurt.

The charms had usurped power from her mother's years of performing and was Ezlyn's only chance to find her again if the circus every broke free of where Cassian had left them.

"Ezlyn?" In his haste to rejoin her backstage, some of Akos' long, coffee colored hair had slipped from the thick braid he hastily wove it into for shows. The round lights posted above the vanity mirror shone brightly around them, revealing the lighter streaks in his hair and the true extent of Ezlyn's injuries.

"I can't replace them," Ezlyn sniffled. "The charms were tokens she'd collected over years. I can't, they were special."

"We'll find them," Ophelia promised. "Magic like that isn't easily displaced."

CHAPTER TWELVE

The Opening Ceremony

LIKE AMBITIOUS MOTHS HEEDING the call of a seductive flame, those accepted into The Red Game were summoned to the city square of Cape Solaera for the Opening Ceremony. Of course, many had tried to sign their name to the enchanted paper upon which the call to play had been displayed. Only seven names blazed across the page with a crackle and glow that raised the ink off the parchment because the signatures had been sealed with magic.

The crowds of onlookers waited as several men in red and black uniforms escorted each player past the corded barricades and into the center of the square.

There, a woman framed in shadows stood alone. The lamps lining that portion of the street had been snuffed out, and only the light from the shop windows remained. She wore a pair of fitted trousers, striped from hip to heel in alternating sections of black and ivory. Behind the curls of her coattails was a golden fountain barren of water. With her gloved hands overlapping, the statuesque woman was utterly; still, her head bowed and face hidden by shadow.

When all seven players had been presented to her, she lifted her face in time with the nearest streetlamp as it clattered on with a broad sound that echoed over the crowd. Her scarlet lips parted into a devastating grin. Her ebony skin glowed in the single shard of light. Tight coils of dark hair framed her face and stopped just below her jawline.

"Step forward." Her melodic voice beckoned like a siren from beneath her top hat.

One by one, each of the seven players ducked under or stepped over the velvet barrier ropes. Of the seven players, there were four women and three men. A set of instructions had been delivered to their temporary lodgings in the city and an outfit for the night. Those in the crowd who had heard rumors of this dress code arrived in the blended retro-futuristic style of both luxurious Victorian fabrics and clunky metal technologies. Bowler caps and walking sticks were a stark contrast to the gears and flowing electricity conduits that decorated tightly laced corsets and oddly shaped accessories. Yet somehow, it all worked and was truly a sight to behold, each outfit more creative than the next.

Seven place markers circled the fountain. Each player chose a spot to stand on while it was still nondescript, their backs to the fountain. The fountain began to hum when the last Rebel put both feet on their circle. Power surged up from a deep, untapped well.

"Welcome," the woman greeted them, a note of mischief playing along the sultry curve of her lips. "My name is Ophelia."

"Listen closely because she will only be saying this once!" A small man wove in and out of the crowds wearing a colorful costume.

"Each of you will be given a role in the game we are about to play. Every move you make, each item you take, and location you explore will be keyed to your specific role. Embrace it, and your game will be that much easier. Shirk it, and there will be consequences."

Ophelia strolled past each player, noting the wordless marker at each of their feet. As she did, two women dressed similarly to her bestowed upon each Rebel two pieces that varied significantly.

Ophelia moved forward to a woman dressed in all black. Her raven locks blended into the flowing layers of her obsidian gown. A single silver band restricted her hair from flowing freely into her face. Ophelia beheld the cool set of the woman's face and the way the stone under her feet bled from the inside out.

"Huntress," she said.

The woman gave a curt nod as she was handed a black spray of fur to sling around her shoulders. A dozen or more weapons dangled in sheaths from its reinforced hem, and an ornate silver collar was added to secure it.

The next player was a tall and robust man with a crop of short blonde hair. He was given the title of 'Knight' with a large piece of armor and a gleaming sword to brandish. There was an incredibly enthusiastic outcry from several female portions of the crowd. It wasn't unusual for players to bring guests to cheer them on.

After all, this was a game for the ages.

When Ophelia came to the next man, she noted how he already wore a magic coat and a spark of mischief. The brown leather jacket had wide shreds in the fabric across his back and chest. Both were lined with a gray brocade fabric decorated with silver blossoms. His charcoal pants bore heavy leather straps around his waist and thighs, peppered with pockets and hoops perfect for harboring weapons of all sorts.

"Raleigh Danger," she muttered incredulously, having just seen him in the Oddity shop the week before. She eyed the critter that observed her from his shoulder. Chipmoths were not native to that part of The Empire. "Rogue," Ophelia announced in a dismissive tone. Raleigh was gifted a bow and a sheath of arrows, tipped a gleaming red. A few whistles pierced the crowd. He smirked, basking in, knowing some onlookers witnessed his skills during the last game he played.

When Copper had signed up for The Red Game, Raleigh had been next in line to do the same. It wasn't that he'd wanted to play the game again, but there was something dangerously hollow in Copper when she swore revenge on Cassian that compelled him to join in if only to keep an eye on her.

The young woman after him in the circle had short hair the color of freshly bloomed lilac petals and a gleaming sheen to her skin. She was notably younger than the rest. Her name had been accepted on the invitation, so there was no questioning its presence in the opening ceremony. But there were rumbles of surprise and curiosity when attention was drawn to her.

"Ezlyn. Fae," Ophelia spit out, and a surge of silver sprung up from where she stood. It coated her arms in silver brackets as a sharp gasp tore from her throat. A pair of nearly transparent wings ripped through the shoulder of her tunic before unfurling nearly down to her knees.

The crowd gasped; whispers of dark magic and shape-shifting surrounded such an unexpected gift.

Even for the Extravaganza, this was something else.

Rounding to the next two rebels, Ophelia found a husband and wife pair dressed impeccably. Him, with his full beard and smart suit bearing gleaming buttons. Her in fitted pants, a long white coat, and a high-necked lace collar of pearl silk.

"Nobility," Ophelia crooned, amused by their gall to even set foot into a game that might otherwise be considered beneath their station. The woman lifted her chin at the scrutinizing tone. The man puffed out his chest.

"Lady Illuminae and Lord Hypnos," she mockingly bowed before them, only rising back to her full height when the man had been given a thin black walking stick and whirling top hat. Then, Ophelia handed the woman a pair of black leather gloves and a circular pendant with visibly moving fluid inside.

Almost coming full circle, Ophelia stopped with a loud clatter of her feet on stone, coming to attention. For a long, agonizing moment, she stood before another young woman a handful of years older than Ezlyn. She looked her over, a blend of amusement and challenge dancing in Ophelia's eyes.

The woman had dressed in a cream-colored corset with a wide curve of chocolate brocade fabric stitched into the center. Brass brackets held the front together in intricate clasps. The same brown material covered her thighs in pants with shreds on the sides, revealing opaque lace blooms against her skin. It reached down to her knees before cascading into layers of creamy fabrics and other sheer laces.

"Copper James, Vagabond," Ophelia let her teeth tear into the word with an audible snap, leaning in a little too close, her eyes wild with power.

Word had spread fast that Copper had been marked by the Oddity Shop of Clarke & Wylder.

It only seemed fitting that she played the role she was clearly born to bear.

Copper did not flinch. The split in her lip was healed now, and not a single person could make her feel like she deserved to return to that dungeon.

Not even when the crowd gasped at her name. Raleigh had tried all kinds of different magic to light the curse, but so far, he had failed. The brand was always there, even laughing at Copper in her sleep.

The stone at Copper's feet burned with gold and silver sparks quietly sputtering from under her tightly laced boots. A folded cloak of midnight sky with tiny luminescent stars hand stitched into various constellations was placed at her feet. On top was a rose-shaped vial on a long chain, a small amount of semi-opaque fluid sloshing inside.

A necklace, how fitting. Copper thought. Clearly, the ringmaster had a sick sense of humor to give her a necklace in this game of his after what he'd sent her to do.

Realizing she had waited too long to receive the gifts if they could be called that, Copper took both, slinging the pendant over her slender neck, but when she reached for the cloak, it vanished. Copper hesitated, meeting the woman's eyes before her with a note of confusion.

"It's enchanted," the sweet woman with her magenta hair murmured. "It's still there; go ahead and take it."

Copper nodded subtly; her fingers glossed over the fabric, and it came back into view. Tucking it under her arm, she resumed her stance and waited for further instruction.

Together they stood, the seven brave players of The Red Game. The next generation of Rebels.

Huntress.

Knight.

Rogue.

Fae.

Lord Hypnos.

Lady Illuminae.

And, The Vagabond.

"As you can all see, these seven have officially embarked upon the journey of a lifetime to not only win The Red Game but to seek out the solution to unlocking the greatest desires of their hearts," Ophelia announced to the observing crowd. "As I have bestowed upon them the gifts of their role for the next several days, I will now set them free to seek out their guide items in preparation for tomorrow's festivities." She turned back to The Rebels. "And remember: Play Fearlessly, for only the bravest of souls will win," she reminded them with a dazzling grin.

Ophelia turned away from the players, feeling their attention planted firmly on her and her alone. "Act I: The Invitation is complete."

#

Copper looked to Raleigh as the crowds lobbied for one Rebel's or the other's attention. A wave of uncertainty washed over her as they had little instruction about what to expect or even what to do next.

"What happens now," she asked him when they met between their two place markers around the fountain.

Raliegh's eyes narrowed as he surveyed the area as though he was still trying to wrap his head around what had just happened. "We wait for another letter," he surmised. "Just because Cassian didn't show his face here tonight doesn't mean he isn't still running this game from the shadows."

"Why doesn't that make me feel any better," Copper groaned under her breath.

"Because it shouldn't," he looked down at her. Copper was about a head shorter than Raleigh, and it never really stood out to her until they were standing in close proximity. "Something is wrong here, Copper. Don't trust anything until we get a better idea of what this game wants to do with us."

"*Do* with us," Copper repeated. "You act like the game itself is going to swallow us whole." She tried to give levity to the last part with a strangled laugh, but it fell flat when he just looked at her.

"Thinking that this is just a game was your first mistake," Raleigh's mouth slashed into a firm line. "There's a reason I tried to avoid you coming here and starting this in the first place."

Copper leaned back from him. It was subtle, but the reprimand was there, and her revenge-focused mind didn't take well to the idea of being told no.

"You know why I came here," she snarled. "You know what he did…"

"And I know what can happen when someone's judgment is clouded by anger and hurt and…"

Copper felt the sting swell in her eyes, and her temper surged in her chest, up her neck, filling her ears with the unwillingness to hear another word of what he had to say. "Don't think I can't do this by myself. You and your *logic* aren't welcome here so long as that *murderer* still draws breath."

"That's not what I meant…" Raleigh tried, but Copper had already gathered her things and disappeared into the crowd.

CHAPTER THIRTEEN

Disdain

A RUMBLE OF THUNDER rolled in on dark waves, carried from a far-off strike of lightning that briefly illuminated the horizon as the residues of sunset faded into the night. It was humid in Cape Solaera but still dry enough, even with a pending storm, that patrons paid little mind and carried on with the festivities.

Pharaoh stood alone on one of the private, opalescent balconies that overlooked the city. His long, dark hair hung freely in curling, wet tendrils over his back and shoulders. The golden earth tones of his skin were highlighted by the warm glow of the evening lights and framed by the rippling of his open tunic with jeweled accents. His fists tightened over the railing as his intense gaze shifted from a far off place to the street below. While all the other roadways wound back into the city in one way or another, one extended directly into the gloom of the cavernous fissure that split the massive cliff right down the middle. This broad expanse of stone acted as a barrier between Caper Solaera and the rest of Rovernaum. It was on the cusp of the constant night where only persons of questionable moral character and those looking for trouble could be found.

This is where he had observed the night's event, wholly removed and full of disdain for what would occur. He ranked high enough in the hierarchy of the Extravaganza that if he did not wish to participate in certain activities, the opening ceremony being one of them, he did not have to.

The moment Ophelia left the square, the entire city burst to life. Rides, bonfires, elaborate costumes, and glowing orbs illuminated the city in bright pops of color and light that revealed all.

Pharaoh's brown eyes surveyed the square as the rebels were left to roam for the night. He tried not to grimace as he watched Ezlyn, one of their own, stumble away unassisted and faltering. None of them interfered as the game was about to begin, and the will wouldn't truly be their own. Little did any of the rebels know that tonight would be their last hours of freedom for the rest of their stay.

As though he could see the rush of magic swelling toward them like a raging tsunami, Pharaoh had stoically bore the weight of what was about to happen on his shoulders mere hours before the opening ceremony. The large clock tower in the city's center loomed over him as the minutes passed with a sort of slowness that was almost painful.

Pharaoh could taste the twisted wave of magic filling the air.

Ellis, his partner in performing, among other things, joined him on the balcony. Her tight blond curls and slight frame were in juxtaposition to his large form and dark complexion as she slunk around his side, her fingers toying with the beads dangling from the hem of his tunic.

"What is it?" Her cherry-red lips curled around the words innocently.

"What have we done?" Pharaoh's hand absently wound around her waist, possessively drawing her against him.

"Our jobs," Ophelia bit out from the mouth of the doorway. "Don't you have a performance scheduled soon?" She left them then to slip into one of the many back halls running throughout the residential cliffs' inner portion. All sense of bravado and glamor had bled from her voice when she left the spotlight.

"This isn't a normal game…" Pharaoh ground out.

No one knew what to expect because no one had seen Cassian in quite some time. They'd felt the summons of the magic written into their contracts. They arrived in time to prepare for a new season without actually ever laying eyes on the ringmaster.

Then Ophelia had taken his place, much to her own surprise, and the whole world stopped making sense.

But that was the twisted part about how Cassian engaged his employees in his little game. They all knew the binding of the Extravaganza magic would ensure that everyone was in their places at all times.

Not a single cue would be missed.

"Don't be too long," Ellis murmured, her long lashes brushing against his cheek when she stood on her tiptoes to brush a kiss to his jaw.

Pharaoh closed his eyes at the contact but didn't reply when she left his side to go and prepare for their first show of the season.

The city stretched out before him, the fates of many dangling on shrinking threads of puppetry and a false sense that nothing bad could happen at the circus.

"Before we arrived, Cape Solaera was nothing more than a sloping, sand-ladened city. Just a tiny little trading post and really just a whole lot of nothing," Pharaoh uttered, as though he wasn't standing there alone. Now, it was dotted with street after street of brick-and-mortar shops, a market of tent and wagon vendors that covered a fair portion of the shoreline, and the tall trio of performing tents that were quite literally calling his name.

There was just one thing missing, and it was not something easily overlooked.

Cassian never was.

"What are you doing? Where are you?" The words slipped from Pharaoh's lips and into the open air. He knew Cassian had to be close. Though he didn't know when or how he had re-entered the circus or why he hid, Pharaoh knew with cruel certainty that they were about to be swept away into the most bizarre season of the Red Game yet.

And there was nothing he could do about it.

The surge of Red Rebel's magic prickled in his veins when the clock struck midnight. With each minute that passed, the undeniable urge to fulfill the contract he had signed drew him to action.

He was bound to the circus, body and soul; as the saying went, the show must go on.

CHAPTER FOURTEEN

Fishes and Stones

CLOTHED IN BRILLIANT RED and glimmering with an age-old song of power and elegance, The Red Rebel Extravaganza started another season. Far from the Oddity Shop and undetected by the beasts of Aerimora, a series of spectacular tents, varying in both height and color, stood in unison along the shoreline.

"Hold…still!" The young Hollis Roux grumbled as she tiptoed her way to the circus. She stretched her short legs to near capacity in broad, sweeping steps as she crossed stones and the backs of large fish surfacing to drink in the moonlight on her mission to reach the shoreline.

If I fall into this water, you're all going to be fried for dinner! She mentally cursed the fish.

Her cherry red braid whipped back and forth between her shoulders. Her fitted, seaworthy clothing made her movements light. When she reached the rock wall that circled the harbor, Hollis Roux scampered over it to the sandy shore. She wanted to see so many things; her young heart nearly burst with excitement.

And oh, was she ready to see the circus from her bedtime stories.

Hollis looked back at the ship that had acted as the only home she had ever known over the last decade. A sense of guilt swept over her as she disobeyed a direct order.

"I want to go ashore," Hollis had insisted. "I want to see the Extravaganza."

"No," Captain Eliza Rhozyn had dismissed the idea immediately.

"But I-"Hollis had argued in the privacy of the Captain's quarters.

"Captain," A prominent crew member had barged in.

Captain Rhozyn had raised a brow at the way he paused. "Did you need formal announcing or…" She didn't miss a beat. The annoyance in her voice carried over from the attitude she'd received from Hollis.

Who was already out the window before the crewmember saw her.

*She's not going to like this…*But Hollis had seen an opportunity, and she'd taken it.

Hollis Roux was the Captain's secret. Having a child meant having a weakness; for a female Captain, that just wouldn't do. Hollis was a ghost of a child in the way she was raised on the ship, and not one member of the crew was aware of her presence.

She intended to keep it that way.

Hollis could imagine the twisted way her lips settled into a frown when she realized what had happened. But, Captain Rhozyn had taught the child to be as the shadows, skirting the corners of a room.

To be seen but not perceived.

She was the Captain's eyes and ears throughout their travels and was utterly invaluable because she was not known.

Well, either way, I'm already in trouble. There would be consequences, but that was unavoidable at this point. So, Hollis Roux pressed on.

The entire cove of Cape Solaera was littered with a vast market densely packed with people that Hollis Roux imagined she would have to wade through them with intent in order to not get swallowed up by the crowd.

"Hey! Look out!" She cried, and people bowed outward from her tiny path until she arrived at a place where the sand and rock blended into an established road. From there, she saw the whole of The Extravaganza's silhouette.

"It's a real town," she marveled aloud, having assumed that it would be more of a caravan of vendor tents and the Extravaganza structures blending with the established city.

A wind whipped through the city, there and gone before more than a few disgruntled shop owners noticed as they picked up overturned baskets and stray paper items. But that wind blew at the hood of a woman in passing and revealed a pale face framed in flyaway blonde curls. Her eyes were sharp, focused on the crowd in a way Hollis recognized. But it was not the beautiful face nor the piercing gaze, but the fact that she was there one moment and gone the next, wholly swallowed up by her cloak as she and the garment became invisible in the night.

"Wow," Hollis whispered, following in her wake the best she could, seeing the path forward clearly.

Hollis had wandered alone amongst many cities, both large and small, but there was something about this place. The way the air sang and crackled around her, it was as though the night had come alive, and she could dance through it completely unnoticed for an eternity. She lost the invisible woman soon enough, but Hollis didn't care at that point.

Pathways along the shore turned into roads that led into paved walkways. Lofty grass and sand turned into an increasing number of buildings until Hollis found herself in the sparkling middle of the city. There, she saw street lamps made up of golden cranes holding sea glass shaped like ornate shells and exotic fish. Pale buildings of cream-colored bricks created numerous city blocks in a way Hollis had not expected.

Staring at a row of shops, Hollis sighed at her lack of money to buy anything. Stumbling backward and out of the way of a group of amorous tourists, Hollis saw a tent flap slightly glowing in a dark, narrow alley.

And the invisible woman slipping inside.

Looking around to see if anyone would notice, she slipped between the gates that guarded the entrance and wandered inside, hoping she would find a secret nugget of magic.

'Don't Look Behind the Curtain'

The simple instruction painted on a sign in black paint and block lettering was tempting to some but a concrete rule for others. The white tarp that covered it was average at best. Still, the layer of shimmering tulle encasing the tent was where the magic began.

At least from the outside looking in.

"A tent flap isn't exactly a curtain…" Hollis thought aloud, fully prepared to bend the rules in her favor. In her mind, that discrepancy in itself was an invitation into the unknown.

CHAPTER FIFTEEN

Magic in Her Bones

T HE AFTER-PARTY TO THE Opening Ceremony was a wild celebration. Colorfully painted people, food, beads, and glowing lights erupted in the streets. The town square had been all bated breath and tense onlookers watching for a rush of wonder and magic. But the party that overtook the city as the crowds steadily flowed outward was everything The Extravaganza promised and more.

The heat swelled, causing the stench of warm bodies to mingle with the aromas of cooking foods and dizzying scented bubbles that wafted in an endless curtain of temptation.

Raleigh felt the buzz of magic and excitement coursing through him. He made his way through one section of town after another, laying eyes on the various landmarks to see what, if anything, had changed.

The Rebels were always housed in a private location to avoid crowds interfering with gameplay. When he'd rounded the corner after exiting the cliffside housing wing, Raleigh came across the three signature tents of The Red Rebel Extravaganza. To the left and right were two smaller tents, one made of pale seafoam glass, the other appeared to be cloaked in woven tapestries. The center tent was crafted in pure shimmering gold.

Golden tents.

Raging parties.

Mysterious missives.

It was just what the leader of The Red Rebel Extravaganza lived for.

But, one question had been circulating Cape Solaera from the beginning of the night.

Where is Cassian September?

The ringmaster had made the announcement of the new game by sending out the original invitation, yet he was nowhere to be found.

The last time the game was played, nearly ten years ago, the circus had set up shop on vacant ground next to the harbor. He could see the lights of rides and games on the far side of the beach, which meant that all the vendors had weaseled their tents and carts amongst the shops throughout the heart of the city once more.

It's like no time has passed...

But he was there ten years ago.

He saw Cassian confined and barely escaped before the ringmaster's vengeful curse took hold.

Raleigh knew that Cassian hadn't escaped but didn't have the heart to tell Copper. There was a fair chance her circumstances had still been his doing.

He just didn't know why.

The music pulsed, and the revelry grew as Raleigh slipped through the crowd, untouched. His ability to wander purposefully had always helped him escape tricky situations. The Extravaganza crowds were no different as he made his way into the throng of people that filled the streets further than the eye could see. Stopping to sign a few items and smile at enamored fans, Raleigh adjusted quickly to the notoriety of being famous again.

"How does it feel to be a walking legend?" A young woman tittered as he signed things she'd thrust into his hands. The way she looked at him, he half expected herself to be the next thing she put in his grasp.

"A legend?" Raleigh humored her. "Is that what they're calling me now?"

She giggled, her cheeks reddening to the same shade as her painted lips. "Well, of course! How many people can say they've actually played in The Red Game, let alone twice?"

Aloysius squeaked and stampeded across Raleigh's shoulders in a territorial display. Having people adore him as a Rebel of The Red Game was much more preferable to spitting on him as Detective Raleigh Danger. *Magic changed when the ringmaster went away... I'm just here to make sure it stays that way.* It's what he'd wanted to say. To tell them to run for their lives.

If the shores of Cape Solaera had been reopened for a new Red Game, then there was something very wrong.

"It's not like you to get jealous," Raleigh lifted his chin and gave Aloysius a soothing pat.

However, the chipmoth thought differently and was not impressed with the press of people all around them. Aloysius leaned into the curve of his finger, making sure to get a good scratch behind the ears.

He wasn't the only one getting attention. A number of the headline performers were out putting on minor displays and signing autographs. Some had been with the circus from the beginning, refusing to age in favor of more than a lifetime of lavish praise and exquisite performing.

There are so many new performers. He made a mental note to introduce himself to each and every one of them.

"It's a strategy of mine." He told his furry friend. "To familiarize myself with every performer I came across. You never know when favor or familiarity will pay off in a game like this. You better get used to us being around more strangers than usual."

Aloysius gave a grunt and squeal that told Raleigh he had received an eye roll in response.

Lifting his face, Raleigh noted The King of the Circus in his shirtless glory brooding from his perch. The opal balconies peppering the cliffside led inward to the tunnels that lined the cliff with chiseled internal housing networks.

So, you are here...

Raleigh nodded in greeting, and Pharaoh immediately took his leave from his palace in the sky. There was a conversation to be had there at some point.

Primarily why he'd left his friend in a cursed city for the last decade.

#

In the golden light cast on the street outside the mask shop display window was where Raleigh found Copper James and the crowd that was interested in the supposed felon. The music was enticing as it drew the soul into play. People flooded the area, the allure of trouble proving too great to keep away. The rhythmic beat pounded on, and people danced and laughed, living the night to the fullest with beverages of all types as they watched and waited for anything to happen.

Copper didn't seem to care in the least. Or at least, that's the way she made it seem. The drink in her hand sloshed as she waved it around in the air, her hips swaying to the music.

She didn't care if they considered her a thief.

A traitor.

A Murderer? *That one is debatable.*

Because tonight, she was free.

Free to wander and party and nonchalantly gather as much information as possible.

Raleigh had tried to dissuade her from signing up for The Red Game, going so far as to follow her across the empire on a train. He'd pleaded, reasoned, harassed, and even physically tried to haul her away at one point. Ultimately, she'd still arrived in Rovernaum, signing her name to the original invitation. When it was sealed with magic, officially accepting her into the game, Raleigh had done the same.

The odds of both being chosen amongst everyone who had signed up were nearly impossible. There never were any hard and fast criteria as to who was chosen or why. The number of Rebels selected tended to vary as well.

Yet, there they were.

"You don't have to do this," Copper griped when she felt the guilt from the weight of his glare.

"You are a reckless, foolish child." Raleigh had ground out, slamming the pen down, not questioning whether he would also be accepted into the game. "I didn't save you from that…place." He hesitated to say the name with so many people surging around them in the town square of Cape Solaera. "Just so you could turn around and put yourself in more danger!"

"I was protected," Copped said over her shoulder through gritted teeth.

"Clearly," Raleigh snatched her wrist and raised her hand to shove the fox-shaped brand from Clark and Wylder on her palm into her face. "I know you think signing up for the game is a way to get revenge, but you don't know how difficult it is to get the upper hand on someone as powerful as Cassian September."

"Leave me be." She jerked her hand free of his grasp. "I didn't ask you to come here."

He raked a frustrated hand through his hair. "And yet here we are."

The look he had given her still lingered in her mind. She hadn't seen Raleigh for years, and when she had, he'd been older. Copper didn't want to know what took the boy she knew and molded him into a man in such a short amount of time.

You always were more reckless with magic than I was…

She'd donned one of the hand-crafted masks, and the shop owner, who had set up an external display of their work, was elated to have a Rebel wearing one of his pieces.

When Copper saw Raleigh coming her way, she turned and waved. But, her stomach betrayed her, doing an unexpected somersault.

Don't do that. Don't feel…that.

Why did he always have that effect on her? It wasn't exactly butterflies like when they were younger; everything was new and exciting. It was different this time around. Raleigh was adventure wrapped in secrets and a laugh that could warm the coldest hearts. He was infectious, dangerous with a side of obnoxious optimism.

I could turn around and fade into this crowd and avoid him. It wouldn't be nice…but it's an option.

Then again, what better way to spend the evening than a Rogue and a Vagabond lighting up the town? The gold filigree of the mask twisted around the upper portion of her face in the depiction of a fox. The nod to her recent branding wasn't lost on him.

"Cute," Raleigh yelled over the noise. "You know, it's a shame you're not more outgoing," he gestured to the glimmering mask.

Copper took his hand in her own and spun herself around in a winding circle as though they were in the middle of a ballroom. "Haven't you heard?"

Raleigh raised his brows at her, clearly amused with tipsy Copper.

"I've got magic in my bones!"

The rumors that had swirled around Copper since her arrival that morning were near laughable. She was a high priestess, a love child of the King of Keskairah, or maybe even a plant from the empress herself!

Everything but what she actually was.

Ready to win the game and kill the ringmaster.

They shared a laugh before Copper looked around and realized how little she really knew about Cape Solaera.

"You said you'd been here before?" she ducked her head a little when Aloysius moved from Raleigh's shoulder to her own, where he poked and snuffled at the wiry fox ears that stood off her mask.

Raleigh nodded, keeping a watchful eye on the chipmoth. "It's a little different now," he gestured to an Extravaganza sign. "But the geography is essentially the same."

"Give me the rundown," Copper made a broad gesture with her cup before gently shooing Aloysius.

In the week Copper and Raleigh had spent preparing for The Red Game, she'd become familiar with the rodent. While she didn't mind him, grubby feet pawing at her scalp didn't help her focus on the task. Especially with a wash of fizzy bubbles rushing through her system from one cup after another of whatever was passed to her.

What they'd also done was an awkward shuffle around their past grievances while laying out a game plan for their arrival.

Raleigh scoped out the circus for things he hadn't seen before, and Copper made the rounds socially for as much information as possible.

Of course, they hadn't expected the invisible cloak, which had made her job that much easier.

"A rundown of the town," Raleigh mused as he took a drink off of one of many trays that floated around the central portion of the city.

The beauty of temporarily residing in an enchanted city was using the magic that allowed trays to carry themselves, serving cups of all shapes and sizes that filled themselves with whatever a person desired.

Copper nodded, taking another sip of the sweet nectar.

"Ah, this is the central part of town. North is the fairway, south is where the street vendors seemed to have started lining the roadways, west by the shoreline is where most of the circus is set up, and here is the actual town where all your brick and mortar shops are."

"And–" Copper coaxed.

"And?" Raleigh couldn't help but laugh when she shimmied at his side.

"East?" She gestured toward the fissure.

Raleigh's smile faded. "You don't need to go there."

"That," she playfully poked at him. "is not what I asked."

"It's one of the largest ruins of the old kingdom you'll ever see."

Copper paused her gyrating as a dense fog spilled out the top of the cleft in the cliffside. It was illuminated with pulsing light just beneath its mysterious surface as it flowed up and out of the fissure, suggesting there was quite the nightlife inside.

"Do you think they really existed?" Copper tipped her head, seeing the fissure as an ugly wound in a beautiful landscape. Winding roads and towering homes lined the cliff face in its deeper landings. Flowering trees and swinging vines dangled at precarious angles, perfectly at home within a breath's distance of tumbling to their doom.

"Who?"

"The Titans," Copper's voice took on a wistful quality. "There are some landmarks, but I just–" she shook her head. "If they were so great, why aren't they still here? Those ageless, powerful, untamable creatures."

Raleigh admired Copper's profile with a warmth he didn't know he possessed. "I don't know," was all he managed to say.

Copper spared him a glance and then bled back into the crowd. "And what about here?"

"Here is where all the magic happens," Raleigh answered as she took his hand and pulled him into the crush of bodies.

"I thought you'd be scouting the town by now," he didn't have to shout like before, thanks to their proximity.

"As it turns out, my guide item gifted to me by our generous host has a lot to say."

"Oh?" Raleigh didn't miss a beat as he danced alongside her.

"According to the cloak, Cassian is dead." Copper's face twisted a little as though the conversation as a whole left a bad taste in her mouth.

"You don't believe that, do you?"

Copper mouthed the word 'no' with a subtle shake.

"So, he doesn't want to be found," Raleigh mused, his eyes going glassy, his gaze distant.

"I'm not sure yet," she answered nonchalantly. "But I intend to find out! And then...I intend on finding him."

A torrent of activity suddenly rushed through the crowd like a rising tide. A flurry of information spread from one group of people to the next until the music started to die.

The rumor of the ringmaster's untimely death had circulated.

And now, the whole circus knew.

CHAPTER SIXTEEN

A Court of Silks and Rings

R ADIANT EMBERS OF STARLIGHT cascaded from the sky. These little
pieces of glittering paper were cast at the pinnacle of a street performance involving bubble manipulation of ethereal constellations.

"What a disaster this whole week has been," Copper sighed.

"The only disaster you're going to attract is shortening your own life if
you don't start taking this game seriously," an angry voice breathed over
her shoulder.

"Hush, you," Copper griped, shoving the hood off her head and giving
herself a reprieve from the magic of the items she'd been given. "Whoever
gave you to me must think I need some twisted punishment. Guide item
my foot."

She hadn't bothered to explain how the cloak had made its sentience
known when she'd spoken with Raleigh, but it had caught her entirely off
guard.

*Immediately after the opening ceremony, Copper brushed the twinkling
pieces of luminescent confetti from her hood to conceal her otherwise invisible
movements. She paid little attention to whether she bumped into patrons here
or accidentally knocked an elbow there as she picked pockets and snatched items
from stalls. Her new cloak was a smuggler's dream, with an enchanted fabric to
disguise the wearer, not to mention the enormous pockets stitched into the inner*

lining. The bewildered looks of those who couldn't see her were nearly lost on her as she ruminated on how she was to proceed in the game. It wasn't that she needed anything that she'd taken that night, but there was a piece of her that found comfort in the rush of having something that wasn't hers.

The first time the cloak had spoken to Copper James was immediately after the opening ceremony. As people crowded the Rebels, Copper swiftly donned her cloak and disappeared, much to her surprise and the crowd's amusement. It was an airy, seamless existence, similar to floating through the circus with almost no one to get in her way.

"Oh, not this again," the cloak had groaned mere paces from the town square.

It was anything but subtle how the cloak made his sentience known. If anyone had seen Copper in those first few moments, she might have appeared to passersby as a hyper-realistic statue. Looking left, then right, she waited for someone to snake around her, twisting dreadful yarns about the dangers of magic and the consequences of the game.

But no one appeared.

Breaking the emotional cast that held her in place, Copper turned in a full circle and found no ominous presence lurking.

"Stop twirling like an idiot," the mysterious voice had snarled.

It was at that moment that Copper James realized two things.

One, the voice was not coming from beside her but around her.

And two, she was far over her head with the magic of The Extravaganza.

"It's you," she pushed at the inner lining of the cloak. "You're talking?" she asked under her breath, waiting and listening to see if the cloak would speak again or if it would do something different.

Something more…malicious?

"And apparently, you can hear me." He had crooned the last word with a sticky sweet inflection. "How blessed you are."

"Can't everyone?"

"No."

Copper had taken a few ridged steps forward.

"So, they let common thieves and criminals play the game now. Isn't that right, Copper James?"

"What would you know about–" Copper had straightened at his pompous words. "How do you know my name?"

"You insult me."

A week after she'd escaped from the Obsidian Hall, Copper, and the other Rebels, had entered through the corridor of Cape Solaera on the very north end of the city and had been heralded as royalty. People cheered, and music played as they walked through the roadway lined with people. The street lamps had been strung one to the next with flowering garlands. If they weren't truly aware of the kind of game they each had consigned their names to, then this display of excitement only moved to cover the dangerous quality of the event a little more. Being the center of that kind of attention, to the extent the fans of the game were going, was almost off-putting.

Copper had thrown her feelers out in order to get a sense of where the largest source of magic might be to pinpoint Cassian's location. Still, something about crossing the threshold of the city dampened the way she could hear or feel magic.

"Oh, they should have left me locked in that trunk." Clearly, that hadn't stopped the cloak she was wearing, though.

"Smuggler," he had told her. "Imposter," it had hissed in one ear. "Murderer."

"Stop it," she'd breathed, clamping her eyes shut.

"The ringmaster is dead," the cloak's words had drifted into airy echoes that encompassed her the way its fabric did. "He's dead, and you have come here in vain."

"No!" Copper shouted, bursting from her cocoon of invisibility with both hands. She refused the idea that he was gone, and she'd exposed herself to a wicked sort of magic for nothing.

Believing she might be able to find out more in the passing conversations of unaware guests and partiers than she could in drowning her sorrows, Copper had dropped that little nugget of supposed truth about Cassian with Raleigh. She knew when she was ready to interact with him again, he would have investigated the validity of the idea of Cassian genuinely being alive.

Her mind repeatedly drifted back to the night when she'd made a deal with a man in a back office to obtain her freedom. Then again, deception was the name of the game when it came to her line of work. Convenience was a tool to trick the unassuming, and she would not be so easily swayed.

"Are you asking me a question, or do you always habitually speak your uninhibited thoughts aloud?" The cloak grumbled for the first time since she'd redonned the garment.

"I don't intend on spending the duration of my game listening to lies, *Cloak*," Copper warned. "Whether or not Cassian is dead is none of my concern."

Lies.

"So, you have a choice. Either you can aid me in this game, or you can spend the rest of your time locked away or maybe even as a decorative floor piece for one of the animal pens I'm sure is around here somewhere."

The cloak scoffed in her ear, but before he could answer, there was a shift in his tone as it drew her back into the shadow with unseen hands. "Be more mindful of your surroundings, Copper James." His words were grave. "You have more foes than friends in this place."

Copper rolled her eyes. "Didn't you call me a murderer earlier tonight? Now you're giving me tips to win the game? Pick a side, you overgrown washcloth."

"Washcloth!" The cloak fumed at the insult.

There was a subtle movement on the crowd's edge, prowling around in the shadows. He was such a spectacle; Copper was surprised he wasn't getting the attention of the other performers as they played and paraded about the streets. The man was a tall, broad, wild-looking thing. He moved with the kind of purpose and swagger reminiscent of a lion that had decided to get up off all fours and simply walk around the circus.

He passed through the open circle between observers and a performer wholly unnoticed. Copper watched as not a single eye fell on him. She followed this creature of a man as he scoped out the scene, not appearing to single one person out from another.

Pulled by the seductive allure of unbridled things, she wandered away from the city's heart and toward the performance tents.

"Who is that?" Copper finally asked.

"Sylvaine," The cloak breathed the name like a love song. "The cloak he is wearing is called Sylvaine. Some know her as the Cloak of Shiloh Anora, but I knew her as Sylvaine."

Copper's brows rose. "Is she…a friend of yours?"

"In another life." He answered with a tone of regret. "You must know that there are many items of incredible value at any Red Game. The man wearing Sylvaine has no business being here."

The man they spoke of stopped suddenly, his gaze falling on her, prominent and accusing. Copper felt the weight of his stare, realizing that not only could she see him when she clearly wasn't supposed to, but that he could see her as well. She bristled, stopping mid-step, her fingers gripping the cloak a little tighter.

"She is special," the cloak continued. "The cloak of Shiloh Anora is nearly as old as I am and just as powerful."

The swirling lights of a passing fire display caught in the center stone of the circlet that wrapped around the man's head. The shimmering gold fabric reached over both shoulders and tucked into the black gathering of cloth tied around his waist. He was beautiful and feral as he gave her a wicked grin. When the fire display passed, he was nowhere to be found.

"What about him?" Copper looked left and right, sure that he couldn't have just disappeared. But there she was, standing before the iconic tents of The Extravaganza.

You had too much to drink. Copper wondered if he had truly been there or if the fizzy bubbles still flooded her mind.

"He is unimportant to your game just now."

"A Court of Silks and Rings," Copper read the sign above the opening of the largest tent on the shoreline. The cool whistle of chilled air rushed up to greet her as she entered was a welcome reprieve in contrast to the tropical climate.

Standing off to the side, she watched a prominent figure, twisted and angled, magically shredding a rope into a set of aerial silks. The long bolts of fabric were the only thing keeping him suspended high above the deep purple circle of the performance floor.

"Pharaoh." The cloak said the name in a tone halfway between reverence and absolute dread.

Anyone who heard of the circus had undoubtedly heard of the man who had become one of the main attractions. Pharaoh, The King of the Circus, had come out to play, and he'd set his sights on dazzling the crowd.

Obviously, he was succeeding.

The man's muscles were taut with practiced exertion as the music continued to beat. The drums rumbled as he floated through the air. Copper's eyes wandered to the people, with their pensive expressions of awe and complete enrapturement in him. The tent was shrouded in darkness, allowing the event's magic to slip about like a thief in the night.

That, and his sculpted body, was a magic all on its own.

"It never hurts to be pretty, does it?" Copper raised her brows, surprised that someone could look effortlessly perfect.

The cloak scoffed but didn't comment.

Copper rolled her eyes at him, dropping her hood to avoid his commentary briefly. Ruefully, her gaze drifted over the seated crowd, all twinkling eyes and awed expressions with their attention lifted toward the spectacle. None of them noticed those moving in the dim lighting, busily prepping the next act or shooting the breeze while they waited. With their dark clothing, they were the unspoken creatures that skirted around at night, building sets and raising platforms to bridge the gaps where magic bore a distaste for the mundane.

After a few minutes, Copper saw a small girl clad in baggy trousers and a fitted, sleeveless shirt who watched from the shadows. She was utterly enchanted, eyes glued to every twist and drop Pharaoh made. Her red hair swayed as she stretched and moved her body, tasting the magic of performance through imitation.

"Look at you." Copper smiled, enjoying this little hidden show much more than the strapping man suspended high in the air. Though he performed with robust accuracy, there was something so entertaining and endearing about the fascination of a child pretending she could soar on little more than a few swaths of silk and lofty circus dreams.

Copper tucked herself behind the barrier a little more, forgetting for a moment that she was near invisible to most, purely because she didn't want to ruin the child's experience.

"Innocent wonder is always more magical than any showcase of The Extravaganza," the cloak said.

Copper hummed in agreement. "I wonder if she's part of the troupe or if she wandered off from her parents?"

A sudden drop elicited shrieks and gasps of terror from the crowd. Turning her attention back to the show, Copper joined the rest in amazement as

Pharaoh flipped end over end. His legs were tucked in close as several feet of fabric unfurled from his heavily wrapped, outstretched arms. Whirling through the air, he approached the ground too quickly. Some in the crowd stood, alarm painted across stunned faces.

Until Pharaoh halted.

Suspended just above the glittering floor, he was a mere breath from his face breaking the fall. Every muscle visible to the naked eye was drawn taut under his brown skin.

The gasps and absolute rupture of applause from the crowd made Copper jump.

Pharaoh paused for a long moment before moving his legs around the two pieces of silk. He whipped himself up, sideways and over until he stood in the center of the circle, feet coming elegantly to the floor. The two black bands of fabric waved freely around him.

The performance music broke over the audience's applause. The drums gave the stage a much softer sound reminiscent of a mountain valley and the unique hum of forests teaming with life. There was a light to this sweeping echo of sound as it rose up to meet each ear. Enchantingly hollow and yet somehow completely full, it ignited an entirely different sensation as the room was bathed in soft, low lighting.

"Wow," the child whispered, clapping along with the crowd.

Pharaoh's wide pair of black silks began to move independently, shredding and dividing into hundreds of rotating ribbons. Whirling with an unfelt wind, the pieces encircled a pouch that descended from the ceiling. There, Copper and the rest of the audience could make out the shape of the fabric cocoon that looked to be made of silken cotton candy, hanging still and lifeless. The upper edges were a soft, early sunrise blue that faded into a color of shattered eggshells before bleeding down into a baby pink that exploded into an electric shade of violet.

A gentle shifting took hold. A seam appeared in one of the outer curves. Sharp edges of wings unfurled slowly, only to snap open with an audible crack similar to a whip's. Arching a delicate leg outward, a beautiful woman with short blond curls spun out and around the cocoon, wrapping her lower half in a thin drape of fabric that started at her waist and revealed a gleaming hoop suspended in the open air.

She floated there as murmurs swept through the crowd. A set of translucent wings caught the light; thin golden bands outlined each curve and section of the full-length wings. She spun so quickly that Copper could have sworn there were two of them. Then, just as fast as she had begun, her hoop stopped and dropped to the ground. Her entire being shattered into a thousand pastel butterflies that burst into flight around the metallic circle on the floor.

"Oh!" the little girl across the tent cupped her mouth, a surprise rippling through her entire stance.

In the stunned silence of the room, Pharaoh strode out with a broom, sweeping up the gold flecks left on the floor from his partner's sudden disappearance. Batting at the butterflies that got in his way, Pharaoh casually whistled as he walked onto the glossy platform. Bending over, he set the broom aside, examining the hoop before picking it up and bringing it back to a three-dimensional form with a snap of his wrist.

Pharaoh continued to whirl the hoop around one arm and then the next until he bounced it off his shoulder, the top of his head, and finally flung it in the air only to catch it over his other shoulder. He slung the broadest part of it over his back, where the young blonde reappeared, arms and wings spread wide.

The crowd roared.

She waved a hand triumphantly, one leg and arm laced through the hoop as Pharaoh bowed to the crowd, enjoying the fanfare before carrying her off stage.

Copper raised her hood and watched as the two paraded by.

"Oh! Am I welcome to rejoin observing the show?"

"I didn't want your bitter disposition to ruin the moment," Copper answered, not paying him much mind.

"Ellis?" The cloak gasped.

That caught Copper's attention.

"She seems to be one of the headlining acts," Copper noted.

"She seems awfully alive for being dead," the cloak snapped back.

How the woman bent reality was startling. Even more shocking was the furrow of confusion that lined the other woman's brow when they moved past Copper. Though she knew she was hidden under her cloak, Copper could have sworn they'd made eye contact.

"It would appear you assume a lot of people in this circus to be dead," Copper said as she watched the mystified child she'd noticed earlier look past her with star-struck wonder, framed in innocence and a hunger she recognized all too well. What she didn't like was watching a large, bald man follow her around the corner, and she decided it would be best to follow as well.

Nothing good ever came from a strange man following a distracted child.

"I *assume* nothing. I was there the night her neck snapped center stage."

Copper grimaced at the idea. Turning to exit through a side flap, when she came face to face with the wild man that had led her to the tent minutes prior. He looked down on her in what could only be described as smoldering amusement. His cat eyes beheld her, the distance between them far too little.

"Oh," Copper made a move to step back.

"August." The cloak ground out. His tone reflected both disgust and a minor note of 'I knew this was coming.'

August grinned, revealing a dazzling white smile and slightly elongated incisors. They weren't full-on fangs, but they looked sharp enough to hurt. Her chest flushed, and her heart picked up its pace at his proximity and appraising gaze.

I wonder what it would feel like to be bitten by that grin. Would that ring in your nose feel warm or cool against my skin?

Copper blinked rapidly at the surprising heat blooming in her thoughts.

He took her right hand in his own, never breaking eye contact as he bowed to kiss it before purring the word "Majesty."

Copper's mouth parted a little as she watched, completely at a loss. He rose to his full height, still taking her in as he did.

"I'm not–" she tried. "I mean, I'm no one."

August tipped his head at her in a catlike motion when she scooted around him, stumbling backward over crates and tent stakes.

"Aren't you?" His deep voice rumbled where only a shard of light illuminated the ground, painting the thin grass between them in the silhouette of her shadow.

"What?" Copper hesitated, poising herself to run if necessary.

"Someone. Aren't you someone?" He sauntered forward. "Smuggler, Rebel, Vagabond?" The last word was breathed over her as he had claimed all the space between them.

"I am," she hesitated, snapping her gaze up to his face. "A lot of things, I suppose. But I just…how can you see me?"

He chuckled. The moment was shattered. "I could ask you the same thing." He nudged a cloak resting over his shoulders that was made of the brightest parts of the night sky, a shimmering twin to her own. "If you ever want to learn how to really use that thing."

"Hardly," Copper's cloak rebuked the idea.

A woman's voice folded around them, all-consuming and warm. "*Addy,*" she purred, and Copper could have sworn the hem of her cloak curled in on itself.

"Sylvaine." He murmured back.

"They seem to know one another." Copper gestured between herself and August, where their woven strings that dangled from the mouth of the hoods reached for one another.

August appeared unsurprised by this. "Do they speak to you?"

A torrent of screams and chaos rippled through the city at the conclusion of a street show. It momentarily drew Copper's attention away, reminding her of the child she saw during the performance.

When she turned from where she had left him, Copper's wild stranger was nowhere to be found.

Him, nor the Cloak of Shiloh Anora.

I know the feeling. Copper James noted the familiar tremble of loss shudder over her back. Only this time, it was not her own, but the cloak being separated from Sylvaine once more.

As Copper made to find the girl, she wondered how old the cloak was and how many times he had been parted from Sylvaine.

CHAPTER SEVENTEEN

Momma Lou's Magics and Mischiefs

To Raleigh, death was one thing he knew about only in reference to others. He'd seen it happen, probably even caused it in a third person, misfortune on their part.

The point was that Raleigh had witnessed death in many formats, but to consider the Grand Ringmaster himself dead was somehow impossible.

"What is Cassian after…" Raleigh squinted as he surveyed the different parties going on around each corner. He shook his head, unsure what to believe. "How did he have enough power to start a new game?" He lifted his chin to ask Aloysius.

Aloysius stared stoically forward and chipped a string of coos as chipping was their namesake sound.

Apparently, it was very profound as Raleigh nodded slowly in agreement.

After Detective Raleigh Danger parted ways with Copper James, he continued to scope out the rows upon rows of market stalls. Using his years of sleuthing experience, he wove in and out of glamorous tents and lantern-lit wagons. Exploring The Extravaganza to better understand who and what had taken up residence there, he purchased small magical knickknacks for later use. Raleigh knew the best way to discover what was happening was to immerse himself in the local culture.

He ran a hand through the dark hellions of hair springing up from his scalp, having long since given up trying to tame them in that tropical humidity.

There isn't enough gel in the world.

From the sound of it, Aloysius enjoyed the view from atop Raleigh's head by the sound of his sporadic squeaks and chirps. He was mesmerized by the glass beads and billowing folds of various fabrics fluttering in the evening breeze. He'd always had an affinity for things he could burrow into. It was all Raleigh could do to keep from laughing when Aloysius' hairless, chubby feet bounced from bustles to top hats in search of his next prized discovery.

That is until he ran out of places to land and collided with a woman dressed in a glossy, white silk corset decorated with delicate lace embroidery. More than a dozen silk flowers with black chains vertically lined her corset. She had several layers of ruching around her hips until nothing but rose lace tights covered her legs.

"Drop something?" The woman taunted, holding Aloysius' round gut in the palm of her hand.

Aloysius' antennae sprang forward at the sight of the delicate folds of winter white fabric, and rumbling coo emanated from him. The sound resonated through his body until the woman made a sound of disgust and tossed him back into the air.

"You're cute and all, but I know your kind." She pointed at him, even as Raleigh tried to restrain his amorous friend. "Don't even think about nesting in my dress."

"Sorry, he's easily excitable." Raleigh gave her a charming grin as he stuffed the chip moth into his coat. The magical garment opened its awaiting pocket to an exaggerated size to swallow the chipmoth whole.

And keep him there.

"Aren't you all?" The woman's pile of elegantly twisted hair tilted a little. Her pale silver eyes took him in for a long moment.

Raleigh chuckled awkwardly, knowing she'd seen the spectacle of his hungry jacket. "Have we met before?" There was something so daringly familiar about this woman, but he couldn't put his finger on it.

I see what you think you're hiding. There was a faint shimmer outlining her entire being that told him she had glamoured her appearance. Who she was and who she presented herself to be could be very different people.

"My name is Xerxes." She offered her hand to him. Her pale lips parted in an enchanting smile that leaned more toward icy mischief than dazzling seduction.

"Raleigh." He cupped her hand with his own, shaking it briefly.

"Just…Raleigh?" Xerxes gave him a speculative once over, flirting with a suggestive curl to her lips.

"Isn't that enough?" He crooked a brow at her with the addition of his own alluring grin. She appeared to be one of the circus performers. His name had been announced at The Opening Ceremony, meaning his identity wasn't exactly a secret.

Xerxes gave him a knowing, sideways look. "He's very territorial for a chipmoth."

"You have no idea," Raleigh muttered. "Are you sure we haven't crossed paths before?"

"I've been in every city of this empire," Xerxes said. "I'm sure anything is possible." She gave him a wink before wiggling her finger at Aloysius and sauntering away. "You should come to see one of my shows later this week, 'Just Raleigh.'" She smiled, "You might see something you like." Her hips swayed purposefully as she left them, a ruched train of fabric following her.

Raleigh couldn't help but smile. *You've gotten involved with a performer before. It didn't end well.* He reminded himself. Shaking his head, he moved forward. He tucked the idea of following her into the back of his mind, knowing as tempting as it was, he had more important things to do.

"Nice choice." Raleigh applauded a befuddled Aloysius. "Let's try for subtlety next time around."

Moving forward into the portion of the market, Raleigh was bombarded with street vendors showcasing all kinds of wearable goods.

"A unique gift for anyone," a peddler shouted from his booth.

"Fabrics from Swynnhaven," another cried. A slew of forever-frozen icicles swayed from the hem of a garment they held high overhead.

"Get your ears, gears, and toy cannons!"

Ears? Raleigh wondered about that offer, but his furry friend decided to tuck into a quiet awning where an old woman sat waiting for her next customer. Raleigh followed, never knowing what trouble Aloysius would get into on his own.

Inside the tent, a woman's pale eyes rose to meet his. A tired smile boosted layers of wrinkled skin as she tried to rise from her stool. It was a slow, disjointed movement that Raleigh felt in his bones.

"It's all right," he assured her.

"You're not from here," she answered quietly, a grateful smile on her face.

"No, not quite." He answered with a nod, running a hand along an entire rack of clothing to his right.

"For someone not from this place, you walk these roads with a sort of purpose." She observed rifling through a wicker basket with a set of twisted handles. She crooked a skeptical brow at Aloysius when he landed inside.

"You don't miss much," Raleigh answered. With two fingers, he shooed Aloysius away for his own safety.

"I might be half blind and near crippled with this old back of mine, but your essence screams of something different," the woman mused. Her right eye was magnified significantly when she looked at him through an orb the size of an orange. She then rolled it in the dip of her twisted palm. A blue flame emanated around it, licking up over its smooth surface before she tossed it into the air, and it disappeared.

"I thought this was a clothing vendor?" Raleigh watched her work effortlessly with the object and recognized its magic.

The woman ensnared him in a look that glittered with mischief. "It is what you need it to be." Pulling on a rod, using her walking stick as leverage, she caused the canopy to drop a hidden layer of fabric over the opening of her stall.

Raleigh pulled back the extra layer, intending to leave. He found on the other side that they were now on the edge of The Extravaganza near the docks. "Momma Lou." He turned back to face her with an exasperated sigh. "Why have you brought me here?"

"Are you actually a Rebel this season, Detective Danger," she asked in a tone that was both young and old but blatantly confident in her accusation.

"What else would I be?" Raleigh stared at her for a long moment. *How long have you been watching me?*

Momma Lou was…persuasive.

Sometimes, wickedly so.

He had a feeling that if she had a vested interest in The Red Game, he would not walk out of that tent the same way he had arrived.

"I'm here to play the game if that's what you're asking?"

Oh, feel that. The magic this woman wielded was a heavy blanket masking the air. As much as he wanted to depart from her stall, something about it kept his feet planted on the ground. He knew what it was; he knew it by name, but at that moment, a mental fog fell over him, and Raleigh forgot why he had wanted to leave in the first place.

"If you really are here to just play the game," she began.

"Of course I—" Raleigh's attention drifted to the jeweled birds flitting around the makeshift ceiling. They were an imitation of the iconic circus emblem, the Red Rebel. The wicked hummingbird had been the mascot for as long as The Extravaganza had traveled.

The wind chimes sang a warning melody. The mystical items hanging in pouches along a piece of twine strung between the canopy support beams jumped in response. The pot over a flameless pit boiled when Momma Lou inhaled sharply at being interrupted. "I will not repeat myself, Detective Danger."

Raleigh pressed his lips into a thin line.

"Now." Momma Lou cleared her throat, bringing her walking stick down against the ground. The tent lifted its skirt, revealing their dealings to the whole market. The clothing on her racks came together in a collage of styles, floating in the air at her will. "You have a choice to make. Either you remain the rebel that has garnered you such a nefarious reputation within the game, or you can do some good for a change." She muttered, bending over into a large trunk. "The powers that be want to know that you're here for the right reasons."

The powers that be? Raleigh couldn't decide if she meant the empress herself or Ophelia in her interim ringmaster position. He rubbed at the back of his neck. There, an old symbol still clung to his skin in the form of a scar. "I'm more curious as to why you allowed yourself to be trapped in this city for the last decade. If anyone were able to break Cassian's curse… it's you."

"Not all of us wish to be free, boy."

A disembodied pirate shirt threw items at Raleigh, one after another. He could dodge the first few items, but a heavy gold pirate bracelet nailed him on the upper left part of his forehead and sent him stumbling.

"Ow!" Raleigh shouted, startling several patrons and drawing the protective attention of several neighboring vendors.

The old woman waved them off before they had much chance to intervene. "You're fine, you're fine," the woman soothed. "Are you bleeding? No? See? Yes. You're just fine." Her head wrap shifted when she nodded in quick succession.

"I came here to change the course of my life, but in case you haven't noticed, I am marked," Raleigh said through gritted teeth. Pulling on his lower eyelid to emphasize the liquid metal of his silver eyes. "No matter what I do, I will always be marked by the decisions I have made."

Momma Lou stopped short. Her colorful kaftan tried to continue on without her, the hem straining to keep moving until she slapped it in reprimand. "We all make mistakes." She pursed her lips in annoyance. "This is your chance to remedy that. Maybe your beloved Avenue will accept you with open arms when this game is through."

Raleigh pressed a hand against his forehead to ensure he wasn't bleeding and winced as a cool compress floated over to him. "How do you do that?"

"Magic." The old woman shrugged, finding herself funny when the tassels on the awning and everything in between wriggled with life.

Raleigh looked around, noticeably conflicted.

Momma Lou rolled her eyes, "I am utterly exasperated with your inability to take an opportunity that is directly in front of you!"

Raleigh narrowed his eyes at her. "What opportunity?" She'd made a few flowery statements but hadn't actually presented him with anything tangible. "Cassian is either dead or still imprisoned, and I don't see either of those things changing as a benefit to me."

"Then why did you follow her here?" Momma Lou's words were careful, almost reserved, as she speared him with a look that nearly laid him bare.

Raleigh saw the diversion for what it was. "Tell me what you know about this game and Cassian's role in it."

"Were it that easy…" Momma Lou cackled, mocking him for even asking. She then floated a short list on yellowed paper.

"What's this for?" Raleigh's brows knit together when he read the list of impossible items.

"Collect those things for me, and when you return, perhaps those items will clear my aging mind for the answers you seek." She waved her hands around in the air. "It's hard for the old bones, you know, to shuffle around the market these days with all its changing magic and unkempt doorways…"

"Don't," Raleigh pointed at the ornery magic in the corner when it moved to throw something else at him. "You want to sponsor me in The Red Game?"

Momma Lou settled back in her stool. "Now you're paying attention."

Raleigh eyed the list once more, mentally noting what he would have to go through to fulfill it. "This won't be easy."

"Good," Momma Lou smiled a wide, toothy grin. "Then, it's a deal."

Raleigh rolled his eyes as he left. Perched on her tent, a wickedly scrawled sign read *Momma Lou's Magics and Mischiefs.*

Never has a sign been more fitting.

Collecting Aloysius, he shoved the list in his pocket. Raleigh knew that old crone was trouble. From the beginning, she'd been with the circus and learned more about Cassian, Red Rebel, and everything in between. It was dangerous to be in possession of that kind of knowledge, but she'd made herself essential to the inner workings that she was almost as famous as the gemstone hummingbird mascot.

The fact that she had turned her eye on him left Raleigh with mixed feelings as he ventured back out into the chaos of the circus.

CHAPTER EIGHTEEN

The Color of Enchantment

THE COLOR OF ENCHANTMENT manifested as a delicate gold and silver shimmer that coated Hollis Roux from head to toe in an exquisite layer of wonder and excitement. She'd spent no more than an hour ashore, and already she felt her very soul being immersed in an effervescent form of pure joy. Returning to the area where the shops blended with the vendor tents, she leaped and twirled, imagining herself weightlessly bound in aerial silks. Her heart soared as it did when she swung from The Blue Giraffe's rope bridges, finding a kindred spirit within the troupe of aerialists.

A sea of lights painted the buildings a cliffside in a wave of dusky blue shimmers and green auroras when they struck the globes of the sea glass street lamps. Blending into the crowd of sporadic street dancers, Hollis laughed and joined in as people of all ages, colors, and sizes partied on into the night. The number of costumes and mysterious stories harbored behind painted masks and under tall decorative hats was fascinating. Hollis paused on the sidelines to take it all in. She had seen and smelled so many different kinds of magic in a single night, but now she wanted to taste it.

The only question was, how?

I don't want to see magicians and sleight of hand! Hollis thought as she slipped past street shows. *That's not real magic!*

She'd seen hats that changed with the color of the wearer's mood, circlets made of starlight, glowing serums locked behind thorny cages, and weapons made from parts of the most dangerous creatures known to the empire.

"I thought those were just stories!" Hollis gaped at the sign through the shop window that labeled the rare, monster-born weapons. She didn't dare speak any of the creatures' names aloud for fear of accidentally summoning them. She moved on quickly, giving the weapons several disturbed side eyes as she went.

Beyond that, there was a ring that whispered secret memories of the previous owners, echoing of lifetimes in the past, and a bag that seemed to jump and lurch as though it were alive. There wasn't any magic in the latter, just a vendor's disgruntled cat knocking over tiny vials of magic oils labeled 'Luna's Lanterns' that were marketed for candle making.

"That smells amazing." Hollis was suddenly struck with the sweet smell of molten butterscotch. Following her nose, she found a whole wagon shelf full of hand-sized cauldrons bubbling with frothy melted marshmallows and tiny star-shaped sprinkles. A few tents down were clear bowls of unicorn noodles that moved like no food ever should. There were roasted legs of animals she'd never heard of, seasoned to perfection and emanating an aroma that would make even the pickiest of eaters salivate.

"All right, Little Red," Hollis said to herself. Planting a hand on either hip, she struck a miniature power pose and surveyed the area. "Use the old thinkety think." Leaning against an awning pole, Hollis shook her head at the audacity of the place for being just as incredible as she imagined it to be.

And more.

A woman across the way noticed her, waving Hollis over when there was a brief break in the crowd.

"Me?"

The woman nodded in response, her smile growing.

Hollis strode up to a lemonade stand under a three-point tent made from draped black canvas. It looked like a haunted hat from the outside, but it was pure springtime on the inside. The sweet scent of lilacs hugged the air. Numerous shelves painted a vibrant teal, glowed with tiny vials. Each one was filled with different add-ons one could pour into the beverage of their choice.

"Hello," the woman with long chestnut greeted Hollis. Her grin brought a genuine kindness to her eyes.

"Hi," Hollis answered from the edge of the tent. She never entered strange places without scoping the place out first, and it was too easy to get snatched up when you were pint-sized.

"Come in, come in," the woman urged. "My name is Ms. Lorna. What's yours?"

"I… don't have any money," Hollis warned her.

"That's ok, I've been working on a little something, and I need someone to pass out samples." She turned to pull a round tray from an upper shelf with tiny glasses made of every color and odd consistency.

"You want me to give these away?" Hollis asked carefully, her doe eyes wary as she waited for the woman's response.

"Yes, and if you do it well, there's a prize for you at the end." Ms. Lorna whispered enticingly, handing the tray to Hollis.

Not seeing the harm in it, Hollis took the tray that read Lorna's Luscious Lemonades, the "L's" having a pretty cursive swirl, and began passing the little beverages around, announcing to people that they were the best in town, that they would cure whatever ailed them, or at the very least, quench their thirst as she had heard other vendors promise of their goods during the evening. Before she realized how far she'd actually gone, Hollis had made it nearly to the opposite end of the lane, all the beverages gone, when the cry of a loud voice caught her attention.

"Mr. Brawn is my name and elusive magic is my game!"

Mr. Brawn wore a padded leather vest dotted with gold bezels set in a diamond patterned across his entire torso. His white hair was streaked with charcoal accents, and his long overcoat gave him the impression of a sea captain, at least in her eyes.

She'd seen many men who looked like him and couldn't help but wander a bit closer. The large, older captains were always the most interesting, with the best stories and nastiest scars. Hollis watched as he fished a large coin from his burgundy pants, flipping it between his fingers.

She missed what he was saying at first as he shouted over the bustle of patrons. Some gathered to watch him work, and others paid him little more than a passing glance. Setting his bowler cap on the ground before him, the man enchanted those around him with several sleight-of-hand tricks.

"I've seen all this before," Hollis griped, quickly growing bored. When he drew the observers' attention to one side, Hollis ignored the misdirect and followed his other hand. She saw the coin where it wasn't supposed to be before it returned to where he had drawn their focus.

Hollis rolled her eyes.

This was not the sort of magic she'd ventured out to see.

As though sensing her skepticism, Mr. Brawn pulled out all the stops.

"Have any of you seen my trusty sidekick?" He bent forward and asked the children seated on the ground. When he was nowhere to be found, Mr. Brawn folded his thumb over his fist and flipped the coin into the air. It bounced over several objects before it rolled down the upper slope of a canopy. Finally, the coin circled around the fountain before bouncing once, then twice back toward him. On the third bounce, the coin flipped forward, and from it sprung a whole man dressed in a similar style to the old man, though he seemed quite a bit younger.

"At your service, Mr. Brawn!" He announced, landing on bended knee. He tipped his rounded hat forward and grinned at the cheering crowd.

"Did you see?"

"Where did he come from?"

"How did he get in the coin?"

Mr. Brawn moved to pick up the plain piece of gold. The face of the other man, now in full form beside him, left the coin's face smooth and empty.

Hollis stood in wide-eyed amazement. "Now that's a treasure worth having," she said. Her mind was already whirling. She had to get her hands on one!

Hollis watched in wonder as the crowd dumped all kinds of currency into the twin bowler hats.

"Did you like that," Mr. Brawn knelt down to her eye level. A rosiness to his cheeks gave him a warm, grandfatherly feel. Or, at least, what she assumed was a grandfatherly feel.

Hollis had never had a grandfather.

"It was spectacular," Hollis nearly burst with elation.

"Big word for a little girl." He chuckled, twisting the coin between his two fingers. He fanned out both hands, palms facing her, and the coin disappeared. "If you enjoyed it so much, maybe I'll tell you the secret of where you can buy one if Mom and Dad see fit to purchase it for you."

Hollis watched as he pointed to a storefront on the end of the block. Warm light spilled out from large windows framed in black molding. She turned to look at him, only to see a pair of coins spinning. When she tried to grab for them, both coins rolled away, disappearing into the cracks of the street.

With a disgruntled huff, she crossed her arms over her chest and eyed the shop he had gestured toward. Having tracked down the souvenir she coveted most, Hollis Roux noted the placement of the stars overhead and knew it was almost time to return to the ship.

But not without that coin.

"Now, all I need is money."

#

Running as fast as she could, dodging between patrons, and sliding under moving carts, Hollis wound her way back to the tent with the glowing sign framed in large buzzing bulbs that read 'Lorna's Luscious Lemonades' and returned the empty tray.

"My sales doubled because of your efforts, my little good luck charm!" Ms. Lorna congratulated Hollis. "Did you want to pass more samples?"

By then, Hollis was doing an excited jig, her gaze repeatedly flicking back toward the shop Mr. Brawn had pointed her toward, "I…uh…" Hollis hesitated.

Lorna laughed, "That's all right," she said gently. Digging in a small pouch from the shelf behind her, she pulled out a sort of coin Hollis had never seen before. The large coin was heavier than it looked and crafted of rose-colored gold. One side was decorated with a twisted dragon, and a mountain range on the other.

"It's pretty," Hollis eyed it, unsure what to make of the coin she held.

"Don't spend that just anywhere," Lorna warned, "It's what some might consider…special."

Hollis nodded, still looking at the piece when she walked away. Standing in the middle of the street, she was puzzled over how much it could be worth and if it was something she could trade for a coin like Mr. Brawn's.

"Or, I take both back to the ship." She grinned as a wicked plot formed in her devious little mind. Depositing the coin in her pocket, Hollis knew there was another way she could have her cake and eat it too.

Carefully, she eyed those who passed by. Waiting and watching, she found a mark that would be easy enough to relieve of their money. She spotted a man she knew to be part of the ship's crew; she watched him purchase a meal while he walked around and slipped a fair amount of change back into his wide-mouthed pocket.

"You've always been the dull sort." She said to the wrinkled skin on the back of his head.

Hollis was used to being unseen. When she slipped a hand into the man's pocket, as she had more times than she could count, she had expected to find gold, money, or whatever currency they used in that city. In her mind, she was already wandering down to the shop where she would find a magic coin, buy something tasty or maybe something pretty, and return to The Blue Giraffe unnoticed.

What she didn't expect was to get caught.

CHAPTER NINETEEN

Little Thief, Little Thief

"**L**OOKING FOR SOMETHING SPECIFIC?" A sultry voice with a bite of an accent crooned over Raleigh's shoulder on one of the main streets. The scent of black pepper and bergamot heralded her approach. "I hear that old hag reveals secrets if you know what to ask."

Aloysius gave a grunt of disapproval.

The arrows Raleigh had been gifted during the opening ceremony clattered to a stop when he came face to face with the piercing, cat-like eyes of The Huntress. "If your game plan is to follow me around, then you're missing the point." It wasn't that he was opposed to forming an alliance in the game, but something about that woman made him want to hide Aloysius before he ended up a trophy on her wall.

The way you're looking at me, I could end up right there next to him!

She huffed a laugh. "I like to get a feel for my opponents. Scope out the landscape to really get a feel–" She lightly drug long fingernails against the exposed skin on the back of Raleigh's hand. "for the competition."

That is not the kind of feels I'm looking for, Ma'am…

"My, my, just Raleigh, don't we have a taste for the eclectic." Xerxes taunted as she sauntered up on him and The Huntress. The word eclectic, the way she eyed the other woman, was not a compliment.

"You could say that," Raleigh answered casually, casting his gaze between both women. In his unusual life, Raleigh had been caught between women in a plethora of questionable situations.

The Huntress drank in Xerxes for a long moment, unfazed by her arrival. "You parade around like a pretty peacock, but I wonder what would happen if someone tugged on that invisible leash your precious ringmaster keeps so tightly wound around your neck?"

"You'd have to buy me dinner first," she purred. "I've been contracted into this circus on and off for years, but don't think I'm anything but my own person."

"Now, ladies," Raleigh put his hands up defensively. His coat strained to remove him from the situation by pulling backward when several patrons pushed past them. While it didn't really have a mind of its own, the coat enhanced his game by building off his unfiltered emotions.

A scream rang out at the end of the lane, and most of the street turned toward the sound.

"Busy night," Xerxes murmured absentmindedly as she watched for some sign of what was happening.

"It could be part of the game," Raleigh said to The Huntress, but she was already gone.

Whether out of morbid curiosity or simply because Raleigh wanted to further survey the peculiar woman, he followed Xerxes around the corner just in time to witness a girl break free from her assailant's grasp by planting a foot on his chest and shoving backward. Her wild red hair whipped around as she tumbled in the air, somehow managing to land on her feet.

Xerxes continued to wander cautiously through the crowd, watching with a cat-like focus as the child looped up and over canopies and wagons to escape the sailor.

"Look at you go," Xerxes commended.

The girl moved effortlessly over severely varying terrain until one misstep had her reaching for a handhold that was too far away, and she fell.

"Get back here, you little thief!" The man got another solid hold of her, digging his hands into her hair and gripping as close to her scalp as possible.

"Stop!" a young woman in the street cried at the burly man.

Raleigh noticed how Xerxes reacted with visible signs of tension, and she didn't move from where they'd stopped on the street corner.

"She's just a child!" A shout came from the crowd.

"A child who needs to be taught a lesson," the pirate barreled on.

Raleigh stepped forward to see what the situation was about. "Now, Ladies and Gentlemen," he cast his voice in a broad circle to gain as much attention as possible, "if the man feels the need to discipline his daughter…"

The crew member sized Raleigh up, nostrils flaring as he barked a laugh. "No spawn of mine would ever be found a thief."

"Then I suggest you take what's yours." He opened his palm to Hollis, who reluctantly returned the small change she'd taken off the pirate. "Be on your way."

Raleigh saw the savage gleam in her emerald eyes. When he realized the whole issue was over no more than pocket change, he turned his attention back to her. "Why would you risk stealing this little from something that big." He tipped his head back toward the pirate.

The red-headed girl stood just behind him, mouth vacant of words as she could not come up with a reason for her actions.

"Move," the pirate loomed over them both.

"Leave," Raleigh ground out. "Because you won't be touching her."

"Around or through you, glasses," the pirate flicked Raleigh's round spectacles, missing the charge of magic running through him. "Makes no difference to me."

"Goliath, meet David." Xerxes shook her head in disbelief from the cusp of the crowd.

"Well, in that case." Raleigh took a swing at the sailor, and the man went down.

Hard.

"Run!" Hollis grabbed Raleigh's hand and pulled, knowing what had happened to a man who attacked one of Captain Rhozyn's crew.

\#

Copper's mind kept wandering back to the man she'd met outside the tent. The way his circlet had gleamed, the amused way he'd beheld her, and the way his hair shone like firelight. A wildfire. She'd met men like him before. All liquid heat and raging desire, but no matter how many pretty promises he made, the object of his desires always got burned.

But she still felt the caress of his mouth on her skin when he'd kissed her hand. And the way he'd called her Majesty?

Distracting.

All of it was so…distracting.

"No," Copper James groaned as she watched the child from the tent target the largest man in the market. It had snapped her back to reality, but not for a good reason. "No, you did not." She added when the girl casually reached into his pocket to fish out the few spare coins he'd just deposited inside.

"Feisty little thing." The cloak seemed to almost admire her.

The bald man turned. The rings in his ear jingled at the sharp angle of the movement in time for him to snatch the child's hand from his pocket.

"What do you think you're doing?" He bellowed, his face reddened.

Instinctively, Copper moved forward to get a better view of the situation. Something in her stirred at a fellow thief getting caught.

"Do you see the brand on his arm," the cloak pointed out. "You don't get that from braiding hair and petting puppies."

Copper hummed in agreement. The pirate brand, a crusty, blackened symbol framed in distorted flesh, was earned from doing some of the darkest things in places ordinary people didn't go. It told Copper all she needed to know.

She doesn't stand a chance.

"Why did it have to be a pirate?" Copper hissed, remembering a time in her young life when she'd learned a similar lesson the hard way. Turning to learn more about the game she was supposed to play, Copper didn't get more than a step or two in the opposite direction when that pesky twang of conscience nagged at her.

"No," Copper argued with herself. "She's fine, and getting involved gets you killed." Looking over her shoulder, she weighed her options. "I mean, she's gotta learn how to be better somehow."

"It will be a hard lesson learned," the cloaked chimed in. His words were neither intentionally inspiring nor condemning.

A loud crash and squeal erupted one street over. Copper's lips drew thin in frustration when she tried to walk away. Her head said to go in one direction, even as her feet carried her in another.

"You were a lot cuter when you were pretending to be an aerialist," Copper grumbled and, with no small amount of annoyance, turned back to help.

In a flash of limbs and color, Copper watched as Raleigh and the child in question escaped down the street. They only made it a few steps when Raleigh turned back to the pirate, who let out a strangled gasp as he clawed at an invisible vice around his throat.

"What did you do to him?" The girl gaped, eyes flicking to Raleigh, who had been fully prepared to continue the retreat.

Raleigh turned sharply. The man tried to climb to his feet only to drop to his knees, eyes bulging. "Nothing that would make something like that happen." He shook his head slowly, unable to look away.

A man with wiry arms and a twisted mustache came into view then, his balled fists the only visible suggestion that there was anything restricting the man's airway.

"What is that?" Copper grimaced at the way the pirate continued to struggle.

"It would appear, Archie, the invisible man, has taken issue with the pirate creating a scene," the cloak observed.

"Yield," Archie huffed. His sharp, coastal accent bit into his words as he glowered at the bald man. "We do not take kindly to bullies." He pulled harder until the large man bowed backward to meet Archie's narrow form.

Copper watched the people passing by. Some observed others cheered for one side or the other.

They think it's a show!

"Archie!" Xerxes warned a little too late.

The sudden prick of a blade at his back gave the invisible man pause.

"And I don't take kindly to members of my crew being strangled," Captain Eliza Rhozyn announced. The crowd parted to allow her a wide berth as she and a group of rough-looking crew members filtered into the market.

The symbol of a skull draped in pearls in the heart of a sun was boldly emblazoned on the broad sweep of the Captain's hat for everyone to see.

"It's not often that one sees a pirate queen on land," the cloak mused. Because Captain Rhozyn wasn't just the Captain of an enchanted ship.

Eliza, Copper's heart lurched. "She's one of the Royal Seven?" Copper asked him, knowing Rhozyn from a different time and place.

He nodded. "And she's surrounded by one of the most menacing crews this empire has seen in over a century."

"Well done!" Ophelia cheered, spurring on a round of applause echoed by the crowd around them. "Welcome, welcome one and all to our first attraction of the night!" she announced, joining the group from the opposing side. She gave a slight wave of her hand, and Archie released the pirate.

"Your…what?" Captain Rhozyn's mismatched eyes widened, not believing her ears. An influx of performers filtered in through the crowd looking much less mystified than the pirates as they gathered to watch with the rest of the crowd.

"Tonight, we have a special treat for those of you patroning our street vendors, and it is an event you will not want to miss!"

As the tension in the situation built, onlookers in the street gathered more and more by the second; sure, this was some sort of unscheduled pop-up show in the streets.

Pirates vs. The Rebels. Copper thought. It was a spectacle, to be sure, especially with the familiar faces of some of the star acts present.

"Where's Pharaoh," one guest shouted.

"Get her! Save the child from the stinking pirates!"

"Show the girl who's boss," a man shouted.

"Well, if it isn't the Grand ringmaster herself," Captain Rhozyn's voice was inky black in the sultry way her mouth curled around each word.

"It's been some time, Captain Rhozyn," Ophelia said in her light, role-playing tone. But it was the rage in her eyes that betrayed her true feelings. "Call off your dogs," she ordered under her breath.

"My 'dogs,'" Captain Rhozyn clutched at an imaginary string of pearls around her neck, "it seems to me that your people are the ones attacking innocent patrons!"

Ophelia scoffed at the word innocent.

The crowd booed in the direction of the pirate, who had ceased his tirade upon her arrival.

"Ladies and Gentlemen, it's my understanding that this group of rough and tumble pirates have come here trying to cause trouble. We can't have that, now, can we?" She goaded the crowd, once again confirming that this was nothing more than a show for their pleasure and entertainment.

"No!" The crowd booed.

When Ophelia and Rhozyn came almost toe to toe, Copper crept closer under the guise of her cloak.

"You really think making a show out of this is the best idea?" The Captain sneered.

"I know why you're here," Ophelia lowered her voice. "My people have had their eyes on that child since she left your boat." She looked at Hollis and noticed how she tried to blend into the crowd of pirates gathered behind Rhozyn. "You dare bring a slave from the isles to this place?"

Copper watched as the girl shimmied away from Raleigh and disappeared into the crowd. *Eliza Rhozyn.* Copper thought, confused at the idea of her possessing a slave of any kind, especially a child. *I know you. I knew you. None of this makes sense.*

"I answer only to the rules of the sea, and my word is law," Captain Rhozyn shouted for all to hear, ignoring Ophelia's accusation. "I am not bound by the rules of the Extravaganza!"

"I won't warn you again," Ophelia instructed calmly, projecting her voice again in true ringmaster style. "Leave now or subject yourself to the mercy of the circus."

The crowd of people watched with bated breath.

"You accuse me of possessing a slave," Rhozyn dropped her voice. "Yet you're harboring a fugitive right here in the heart of your beloved Red Game?"

"This isn't a battle you'll win." Ophelia took a long look at Rhozyn. "You have no power here."

"Bring me Copper James, and I'll vacate your little game without another word." Rhozyn traced a finger along the crisp surface of an apple sitting in a basket beside her.

What? Copper stepped back, remembering an old debt and a wrong that had never been righted. *You can't still be holding on to that…*

"Have it your way," Ophelia lifted her chin, unwilling to admit to Copper's presence or her status as a wanted person.

"Is that a challenge?" Captain Rhozyn's eyes glimmered with mischief, her words almost lyrical with delight.

"It is whatever you perceive it to be."

Captain Rhozyn ducked her head, eyes darkening, her stare never breaking from Ophelia's. "You want me to participate in your little game?"

No. Copper narrowed her eyes at Rhozyn's profile.

"Bring me Copper James, and we'll settle this by Cassian's rules!" Rhozyn shouted.

The crowd roared in excitement.

"Oh dear," the cloak sounded genuinely surprised.

"What does that mean?"

"You're not going to like it."

Ophelia waved her hand and a series of smaller tents sprung up along the shoreline. "Rebels, pick your tent, and prepare for a duel!"

CHAPTER TWENTY

Dueling it Out

WORD OF THE DUELS along the inky shoreline spread quickly, and all Rebels were present within minutes. The head of wardrobe quickly dressed them in dueling costumes fit for warriors.

"What exactly are you going to have us do?" Lord Hypnos toyed with his bushy mustache as he and the other Rebels stood before Ophelia on the shoreline.

"What part of a duel is difficult for you to understand?" The Huntress snapped there in the dark.

"I didn't know this would be part of the game. Not all of us are…vagabonds." Lady Illuminae adjusted the maroon silk scarf around her neck while looking down her nose at Copper James.

"Because I'm such a bloodthirsty monster?" Copper laughed incredulously.

"Don't act like you've never killed a man. We all know what happened to the heir of Keskairah," Lady Illuminae delivered the insult in an airy tone.

"From the sound of it, we all have reputations for one thing or another." The Knight sauntered up, and several women screamed his name from the crowd. He planted himself between Lady Illuminae and Copper James. "In my opinion, whatever the heir got, it was well deserved." He told Copper under his breath, a winning smile on his handsome face.

Raleigh snorted a laugh. "Pal, you are barking up the *wrong* tree..."

"So nice of you to join us," Ophelia crooned, her face tight.

Standing with her back to a row of six tents, she clasped her hands together and greeted the rebels.

"This is going to be quite the event," Copper's cloak mused. She'd learned that leaving the cloak open while raising the hood allowed her to converse with the magic inside without making her invisible.

"Because of the pirates?" Copper asked.

"Yes, but also, that is The Black Gate." The garment shifted toward the numerous charcoal and scarlet uniforms casually filtering in from all directions.

"The what?"

"The Black Gate is The Extravaganza's personal security. Although mercenaries is probably a better descriptor in terms of the lengths they are willing to go to keep the peace and, above all else, protect the performers."

"This isn't your run-of-the-mill act, then."

"Not in the least. For now, they'll act as a buffer between the crowd and the players, but their presence will become much more...prominent if things turn ugly."

The rules of the game had been lax, even upon their arrival, but the itinerary had been laid out clearly for each of the Rebels and those who had journeyed from far and wide to watch the historic return of the Red Game. Every night, there would be an 'act' to observe. Complete the night's task, and the player continued, fail and you lost the Red Game. The Opening Ceremony was supposed to be the only event for night one. The awe and wonder drew crowds to see who they wanted to root for and what 'character' they wanted to support by buying merchandise and cheering them on.

Because it was just a game.

But Captain Rhozyn's arrival had clearly changed those plans, and in true stage fashion, the show must go on, and the circus adapted.

"What we have here is a duel for the ages," Ophelia announced as the crowd hushed, the smell of salty sea air mixed with the earthy scent of freshly poured of sand and sawdust. "In each of these tents is an opponent of epic proportions!"

The crowd cheered, the excitement pulsing all around them. Whispers among the Rebels revealed that Ezlyn hadn't arrived. In fact, she hadn't been seen since the start of the night.

"Pick a tent and prepare to watch one of our brave rebels duel for the right to continue on to night two of the Red Game!" Ophelia gestured toward the crowd and then back to the six standing before her. "Rebels, pick your tent and prepare to meet your opponent!"

"They all look the same," Copper said to Raleigh, her arms crossed as she tried to get a feel for what might lay behind them.

"Nothing ever makes sense in these games." Raleigh shook his head.

Part of her smuggling craft meant Copper tried to anticipate more than a few steps ahead at a time. But that was under controlled situations and with an entire team at her disposal.

She wasn't used to working alone.

Feeling out of control of the situations had become her norm since Keskairah, but that didn't mean she liked it.

"So we're going in blind?" Copper frowned.

"Completely."

"Lovely," the sarcasm rolled off her lips like it was her native language. Her feet moved before she overthought it further. The crunch of sand flying from under her boot followed her as she sprung.

How can I trust my own intuition after everything that's happened?

She'd walked into Clarke & Wylder with a tool belt of tricks and years of experience in the theft and smuggling world, not to mention an insider's insight from Cassian, and still got caught.

But maybe that was the point all along.

Copper picked a tent of black canvas striped with metallic, golden paint. She didn't look back at Raleigh before she strolled the canvas doorway and into an arena encircled by eager rows of onlookers.

Strolling past a rack of weapons, her eyes widened a bit. *Oh, this is not the comedic sort of dueling you've associated with the circus in the past.*

This wouldn't be a magical duel but one of brute strength and hand-to-hand skill mixed with a little footwork strategy.

Brute strength, and strained reunions.

Because her opponent was ready and waiting, her mismatched eye honed in on Copper's every move.

Eliza. Copper noted the proud stance, the sharp jawline and subtle scars from past adventures. *I knew you'd find me eventually…just not like this.*

Scanning Captain Rhozyn dropped her arms and looked at her crew in the stands. Wordlessly, she gestured toward Copper in an expression of disbelief. They laughed at her, loud and boisterous. Captain Rhozyn smirked. Shirking her heavy jacket, she handed it over to her first mate, a tall, broad man who was clearly displeased with the entire ordeal.

"You want us to–" He trailed off with a nod, suggesting that the crew take care of Copper instead of the Captain herself.

"No," Captain Rhozyn geared up. "This one's mine."

Exchanging some of her heavy items for lighter ones would allow her more agility fighting in the arena. Her boots displaced the sand with every calm, collected step she took toward the center of the ring.

"Come on, Poppet," Captain Rhozyn coaxed languidly. "You're not prepared for this. Let's try this again once I've collected my price. You can fight all you want once the capital has their hands on you."

Copper paused. "Price?"

"I think she means a bounty on your head," the cloak said.

Rhozyn laughed. "You didn't know?"

"Who put a price on my head?"

"The empress, of course." She slowly drew a sword from her belt. "Seems you skipped town without fulfilling your end of some deal."

"The amulet," Copper groaned under her breath. She knew there was a chance that the empress would grow tired of waiting, but to put a price on her head? "As if this game wasn't going to be hard enough."

"Did you think Cassian September would save you from the *empress*," her cloak audibly sneered.

"Not. Helping," Copper hissed through her teeth.

She'd escaped the High Castle by accepting the task of returning the necklace to the empress.

She'd made the same deal with Cassian that evening.

You're not above double-crossing people, but did we really have to make such lethal deals back to back? Even then, Copper didn't know who she would have given the necklace to had her failed heist succeeded. It probably would have come down to who she believed to be more powerful.

Until Cassian betrayed her.

That made the decision a little easier in hindsight.

The week between being rescued by Raleigh and preparing for the game had been a blur of research and preparations.

A week too long, maybe.

Royalty wasn't known for their patience.

"I'll even give you another chance with the weapons I have on my ship."

"Not something I'm interested in," Copper answered, casually choosing a blade from the rack, her hand brushing the edge of her cloak.

"Now, now," Captain Rhozyn gestured toward Copper cloak. "No magic; that would be cheating."

"I imagine she would know all about cheating in a duel." Copper's cloak spoke up.

"We both know I don't need magic to beat you. I never have."

Rhozyn's face darkened, her brows lowering, her eyes narrowed. "Seal the arena!"

#

Copper stood on one side of the arena where a few dozen patrons peppered the multiple rows of event seating. The opposite side was filled with what looked like a fair amount of Captain Rhozyn's crew.

A small woman arrived in her ceremonial Kaftan and turban crafted in emerald fabric with gold embroidery. She hobbled as she poured a magic neutralizing sand on the rocks encircling the inside of the tent. Tiny, breathy screams could be heard on contact, giving it an eerie touch, but it ensured a fair battle.

"Welcome one and all to a truly unique event!" Ophelia began. "On one hand, we have Copper James, The Vagabond. On the other, we have Captain Rhozyn, the infamous Pirate Queen."

The crowd booed or cheered for each name, depending on their alliances.

"The rules are simple. Should Copper James win, she earns her item for night two of the game, and the Captain is rejected from these shores *forever*. But, should the Captain win…"

The crowd booed.

"Copper James would be at the mercy of the bounty placed upon her head. First to yield, or die, loses! Place your bets, shield the eyes of the innocent, and away we go!" She held a gun straight up in the air, firing once to signal the beginning of the duel before moving on to the next tent.

#

Raleigh had spent more time in the last week worrying about Copper than he had the entire time he'd known her. Getting caught in the Obsidian Hall wasn't the woman he knew. The time and consideration she put into her jobs was an artwork.

Or at least it used to be.

Getting caught and being painfully unprepared for Clarke & Wylder had been beyond reckless.

It's almost like you want to get caught, he thought as he watched her stroll into her tent with the casual swagger of a woman shopping in a market, not someone in the headspace of survival.

I did what I could to prepare her, he told himself, but uneasiness still settled over his skin as he walked into his own duel. He surveyed the arena and saw an obstacle course.

"Not exactly what I expected," Raleigh grumbled, putting on a fake smile and wave for the cheering crowd as a handful of crew members swarmed around him. They quickly equipped him with the items he'd left in his room. He slung his bow, quivered over his shoulder, and waited for further instruction.

"We all know the circus is known for its death-defying stunts, but let's take a journey a step further into the realm of mental acuity and self-reflection that comes with overpowering your opponent." A voice came from overhead speakers, rich and charming but clearly prerecorded.

Self…reflection?

"The goal of the duel is to reach the top before your opponent. Win, and you move on to night two. Lose, and you die." The last part was a little more chipper than it should have been.

By design, only one of them would leave the tent alive.

Is this how they'll dwindle down the number of players? By turning us against each other?

"Death when magic is involved releases its own kind of power. That's how you're going to recover so quickly…how you're going to escape," Raleigh thought out loud, connecting some of the dots.

Each Rebel was saturated in magic, having signed Cassian's binding contract.

Each death would bring him closer to regaining enough power to break free.

What lines won't you cross?

Twin platforms led to two ramps that would launch them into the tangled web of beams, ropes, and platforms that made up the tangled web of the obstacle course before them.

Raleigh watched his opponent step onto the far platform as he did the same. He didn't recognize the man as another rebel. In fact, he couldn't make out any of his features at all. Cloaked in shadow and a dark hood, his opponent could have been anyone.

Fisting his hands, Raleigh stared at the silhouette of a man and waited. A single gunshot rang out over them, and they were catapulted into the race of their lives.

Raleigh broke a sweat in less than three minutes.

He swung across the arena on a single black rope with a small wooden foot and handholds. He fired his arrows at three targets, and the magical projectiles met their mark each time.

My archery skills haven't gotten that rusty, but these enchanted arrows don't exactly hurt.

Surging up the makeshift bridge, he ducked as his opponent shot an arrow at his head, piercing a balloon full of paint behind him instead. Leaping forward, Raleigh carried himself across the open air by swinging from one circular, dangling hoop to the next. He left a trail of paint droplets in his wake. Whenever he looked over, his opponent was neck and neck with him.

A cry rang out in the next tent. A splash of blood smeared against the outside panel, stopping both men in their tracks. Raleigh reached for one of the enchanted arrows but then hesitated.

"Dragon?" Raleigh grimaced.

His opponent slowly nodded, cringing away from the sight.

Who are you? Raleigh wondered. Copper's opponent was clearly to be Rhozyn from the confrontation earlier, but the shadowed figure across the way was an utter mystery to him.

The scarlet stain slid down the canvas and away from the halo of a spotlight. "Oh. Oh yeah. Definitely a dragon." Raleigh swallowed his first 'oh' as the bile rose in his throat.

Climbing up a crude rope ladder, Raleigh swung his whole body around to reach a single beam between him and the next set of targets.

Of course, you're already here.

He secured the bow over his shoulder when he noted the hanging balloons overhead. Three red, three black. One burst and Raleigh's side of the beam tilted. Immediately, he took aim at the black balloons over the other man's head and shot it down.

His opponent did the same.

Raleigh's last balloon burst, coating him in sticky paste. Instead of going down with his side of the beam, Raleigh ran forward, grabbed the residual rope from the balloons, and pulled himself onto the furthest platform. The other man faltered but held onto the remaining portion of the beam.

Raleigh arrived at the final target. Winded and bleeding, he frowned. His opponent was face to face with him, arrow drawn. Raleigh shook his head, looking back at the beam and then at the man before him.

"That's...impossible." There was no way for him to have gained on Raleigh.

There was nowhere else to go. Nothing else to shoot.

He was the final target.

Drawing an arrow, Raleigh aimed at the other man and waited. The room fell utterly silent as they waited to see which body would collapse. Both arrows were loosed. Raleigh caught his opponent's arrow in his left hand as his arrow split around his opponent's head and then came back together to ring the bell hidden on the very top of the course.

"I don't kill." Raleigh ground out. He stared at the hooded figure only to realize his shocked expression mirrored back at him as the man's hood fell away.

"Welcome to the circus." The formerly hooded man smirked and tossed a card at Raleigh's feet.

Raleigh stooped to pick it up, an image of a silver compass on it. The mirror image of himself was gone when he stood up, card in hand.

The hooded cloak was nothing more than a pool of fabric fluttering to the ground.

#

Copper James and Captain Rhozyn squared off. In the breath before the cool edges of their blades pointed at each other, Copper was grateful for her time aboard the smuggling ships.

Why are you doing this? Copper thought. *Everything I learned about fighting was by your side!* She'd spent many months at sea learning invaluable fighting skills. How to hone her body, the extra balance it took to explode as her opponent, and the flexibility of motion to correct herself mid-motion. Eliza had been part of her informal class when the sea raged, and Copper had taught never to drop a blade, even under the worst conditions. Together, they learned how to dig deep for those hard-earned inner reserves when the wind was wild, and the freezing rain pelted their bodies.

But even then, Copper knew Eliza would be a wicked opponent if they ever crossed paths after the bitter way they had parted some years ago.

"You always squint like that when you fight," Rhozyn huffed. She was unmoved by any of Copper's attacks. For every swing Copper carried through, Captain Rhozyn quickly countered. It was child's play for her and a simple act of humoring her prey before she devoured her whole.

Oh, so you do remember me.

Copper heard Raleigh's bellow from the next tent over. It was a slight shift but enough for the Captain to notice.

"Mm, he really is something, isn't he?" She grinned knowingly. Rhozyn leaned in as her sword struck Copper's. The move brought enough tension between the two blades to briefly hold them in place.

"I don't know what you mean," Copper panted, shoving hard enough to send Rhozyn backward. She circled around to give herself a safe distance between them.

"You fight like him," she wrinkled her nose when she hissed, "cowardly."

"You talk too much." Copper sneered.

"I bet he taught you how to do more than just fight on that ship." Captain Rhozyn lunged at Copper to startle her but didn't follow through with the motion.

Copper scoffed. "What would you know about my time spent onboard? You were too busy making 'deals' with every man there." She lashed forward with a grunt and near miss. "In fact, I think I see a lot of them in your crew. Was that your recruiting technique?"

Captain Rhozyn stopped, smirking as she narrowed her eyes. "I've yet to meet a smuggler who hasn't had to persuade her way out of one situation or another."

"Consider me a novelty then." Copper arrogantly spread her arms out wide.

Captain Rhozyn grimaced. "My men will fix that for you when you join us as my prisoner." She flicked her blade and freed the necklace from

Copper's throat. "They've been itching for companionship all those lonely nights at sea. They'll break you in nicely for the jailers in the capital."

For every lunge, there was an evasion; for every block, another blow. The two women traveled around in a twisted dance of blood and metal until Copper said something that struck a chord.

"Is that what you let them do with your little thief?" Copper panted. "Is that why she's so desperate to escape her master?"

Enraged, Captain Rhozyn brought the pommel of her sword down on Copper's shoulders and swept her legs out from under her. She spit on her once she was down and let out a savage snarl of curses.

Copper sat back on her forearms, shocked by the sudden shift in Rhozyn's fighting and temperament. She'd always been a loose cannon, but she had portrayed a cool confidence in her skills and a brazen approach to every strike. But, when Rhozyn brought the blade down, her anger fueled her moves instead of her decades of skill. Copper shoved backward, kicking out one of Rhozyn's knees in the process.

"Oh," Copper regained her footing quickly, realizing her comment had hit home. Stopping short, she watched as Rhozyn tried to grit her teeth through the agony of her injured knee and regain her footing. "She means something to you."

For the first time since they had engaged, Rhozyn faltered. There was a brief pause in their battle, imperceptible to those watching from the outskirts of their makeshift arena, but a shift in Rhozyn's face promised a gruesome death. "Say that again, and I'll cut your throat right here where everyone can watch you bleed!"

Dropping her own blade, Captain Rhozyn pulled out a hidden knife. She gripped it hard in a downward swing that Copper could see her knuckles pale. She dodged the knife twice with her sword, almost freeing it from her grasp, before crouching and lurching to the side.

Rhozyn's blade stuck into one of the tent's support beams with a groan.

Jumping up onto the barrier between the arena and the crowd, Copper shook her head as she watched Rhozyn struggle." You're not going to kill me," she reasoned. "There's a price on my head; you said so yourself."

"I might," Captain Rhozyn swung broad, missing narrowly. It was a sloppy move. "No one said you had to be alive for me to collect the bounty," she panted, clearly out of breath. "Your head would talk a lot less if I removed it from your body!"

She lunged again, but Copper countered her swing. This time, the blade flew, but not before Rhozyn got on the inside curve of Copper's dominant hand and ripped her off the barrier by her hair.

"You think I can't beat you because you have a legacy?" She snarled into Copper's face, one arm paralyzing her fighting arm, while she dug the nails of her free hand painfully deep into Copper's scalp. "Do you think that you are so Shepard blessed that I wouldn't be able to find and kill you for what you did?"

Copper choked when Rhozyn smashed her head against the barrier. She struggled at the awkward bend of her spine, completely at Rhozyn's mercy.

If you're going to play dirty, so am I!

Wrenching her whole body, Copper brought her face around and sunk her teeth into the soft, exposed flesh of Rhozyn's arm at the exact moment she looped her leg around and jerked the weakest part of Rhozyn's knee.

Captain Rhozyn cried out in pain.

"I have nothing!" Copper spit the fresh blood into Rhozyn's face, the metallic tang still coating her mouth as she shot up to her feet, knocking the pirate Captain backward into the sand.

Rhozyn took a knee, eyes wide as she gripped her arm.

Copper spit more blood, stalking over to Rhozyn's displaced sword. She bent to pick it up and felt a presence settle over her.

"Behind you!" Someone in the crowd pointed, but she was not unprepared.

A fluid quarter circle was all it took to end the duel.

With the careful, upward jerk of her bare foot, Copper flipped the sword up into the air and challenged Rhozyn's stance with her own. Catching her off guard, Copper punched Rhozyn's face and kicked her diaphragm, which sent her flat on her back. Struggling for breath, she watched Copper loom over her. The edge of her blade pricked Rhozyn's flesh, her sword nowhere within reach.

In the diminishing grandeur of her poor temper and arrogance, Captain Rhozyn lay still, the vacancy of shock haunting her face.

She had lost the duel.

"We have a winner!" Ophelia shouted in the pensive silence.

As the crowd voiced the cheers or displeasure, Copper held Rhozyn's gaze, speaking where only the two could hear.

"Something you love is mine now," Copper said bitterly, the heat of adrenaline searing across her chest and shoulders as she backed off Rhozyn, and the crowd erupted in applause. "Remember that the next time you try to come at me like that." Sticking the blade to the ground, Copper James stormed toward the tent's entrance, wiping her mouth with her sleeve.

Under the heavy watch of her crew, Captain Rhozyn stood, fuming with shame and fury. "You think it's that easy?" She shouted after Copper. "You think…" Her words were cut short when she tried to cross the stone barrier and failed due to the Extravaganza magic.

As the patrons dispersed, paying their due applause, their attention flicked to other street shows and vendors. The performers made pointed eye contact with each other when Captain Rhozyn still stood on the shore as the tent faded in the early morning light, panting like a wild animal as she eyed Copper disappearing into the crowd.

"You'll regret this," Rhozyn promised before returning to the little boat she'd arrived in.

Copper James ignored her as she knelt down, picking up a card with a picture of a book and an invitation to come and find it on the back.

Night one of The Red Game was complete.

Chapter Twenty-One

If a Wildflower Were a Person

THE PAIN DIDN'T SET in until the opening ceremony had finished.

When it did, the whole of Ezlyn's back felt like one gaping wound. Her tattered skin had bled for hours in the places where her bone structure had shifted, and the wings had sprouted. Laying curled up in absolute misery, Ezlyn watched as the night blossomed into morning.

Her only real company had been the wind chimes hanging over her balcony, singing out their hollow tin melody with every brush of the breeze. Something inside her urged her toward the game, telling her she should worry about how much time had passed and what her absence would mean. But the pain was consuming.

Tanith, the head of the costume department, finally arrived with food and the next day's costume. "Ezlyn!" She'd gasped at the sorry state she'd found Ezlyn in, quickly sent for help, and got to work. "Let's get you cleaned up."

"Stop!" Ezlyn sobbed as Tanith and two others bathed her in hot water.

"I know it hurts, but the heat helps set them properly. You can't be walking around here with crooked wings."

It took two to care for the wings and one just to hold her upright until, finally, Ezlyn passed out. When she woke, her wounds were healed, and the trembling had stopped. Someone helped her out into the sitting room that faced the balcony. There she found some of her favorite food: seasoned fries with cool green sauce, chocolate banana sushi, fresh dragon, and peach fruit tarts.

And, of course, there sat Ophelia.

How did I know you would be here, Ezlyn thought as she struggled to get comfortable.

Ophelia was an ebony statue of grace, power, and the biggest unspoken 'I told you so' Ezlyn had ever seen.

"I don't regret doing it." Ezlyn took small bites and drank slowly from the steaming mug of berry tea set before her. The day's trauma had left her mind and body raw, but she knew it would only worsen if she didn't fortify herself.

"You are a child of the circus. Did you honestly believe you would get away with consigning your name to the game and not suffer some kind of consequence?"

Ezlyn observed her in measured silence. Her mother had been a performer, and when she'd disappeared, Ophelia had taken her place and done her best with what she had. That didn't mean she didn't have to face the consequences of her actions.

"I am not, nor have I ever been, contracted into the Extravaganza."

"Correction. You weren't contracted into the circus." Ophelia's voice was stark and harrowing. "But you were raised by it." There was no apology or empathy in her voice. She was a stone-cold, statuesque ringmaster. The magic of The Red Game had changed her from a motherly figure to the master of The Red Game, and Ezlyn didn't know what else she expected.

After all, she'd been warned of the cruelties of Red Rebel's magic.

Time and time again, she'd been warned.

But still, she'd signed her name to the invitation, and here they were.

"Is this my punishment for disobeying you," Ezlyn challenged, doing her best to hide her wince when she sat back too abruptly.

Ophelia stared at her for a long moment. "I would never bestow upon you the sort of fate you have decided for yourself purely to make a point. Your actions have brought you into the eye of the Rebel. What happens now is up to you."

"The eye of the rebel," Ezlyn scoffed. "Red Rebel is a bedtime story to keep naughty children in line." She stood with as much bravado as her aching body would allow. "I am not a child and will no longer sit by while my mother remains missing."

Ophelia squinted out the window, her face stricken. It was a valiant effort to maintain her composure. She murmured a string of words under her breath in a tongue Ezlyn knew her to slip into in times of frustration.

Ezlyn stood by her words. *Nothing you've come here to say will change my mind. I will play, and I will win, and there's nothing you can do to stop me!*

Ophelia rose to her feet in one languid movement. "I won't stand in your way. You have made your decision, and as acting ringmaster, I cannot be seen showing favor to one Rebel over another." Cupping Ezlyn's face in her hands, Ophelia drank her in.

"What are you doing?" Ezlyn pulled away.

"I want to remember you as you were, not who you will become."

Before she left, Ophelia made Ezlyn aware that she'd missed night one and would not be compensated for the task she had missed.

"Compensated?"

"You consigned your name to the game 'no exceptions, no exclusions.' Did you think you could simply miss the first night of events and not be punished?" Ophelia asked incredulously.

"What happens now?"

Ophelia's hand was on the doorknob. "The magic decides. Not me."

Ezlyn didn't so much as flinch until the latch on her door clicked into place. The weight of her own words mixed with those of Ophelia bore down on her heavily with the knowledge that life had forever changed, once again, the night Cassian's invitation had arrived.

Bathed in the warm glow of sunset, Ezlyn stood before the oval, floor-length mirror as she had with her mother a decade prior. She turned and observed the unexpected modification to her own body. Dressed in an open-back gown that accommodated the delicate folds of her wings, a slit in the front revealed fitted pants framed in a sheer skirt.

"This balance thing is something else," Ezlyn muttered as her muscles tried to accommodate the additional weight on her upper body.

If a wildflower were a person, it would be Ezlyn. Not because she had lavender hair or wings shaped like broad, cascading petals. Despite it all, she would continue to rise untamed. In an unruly forest of thorns, she would thrive.

As the afternoon sky bruised into dusk, she strengthened her resolve because she knew what was coming when she looked at the only photograph she had of her mother. "I will play fearlessly. And I will find you."

It was almost time to face another evening at the circus.

And she would be ready.

"You could kill in that dress," Akos said from the shadows.

Ezlyn side-eyed him over her shoulder. "Maybe that's the point."

He laughed. The low sound made her toes curl.

"Do you make a habit of sneaking into young girls' rooms at night?" She turned, arms open, when he came for her, his arms wrapping around her, low and tight to avoid crushing her new wings.

"I can't believe you did this," he breathed into her neck.

Ezlyn's head was at an odd angle; their height and size difference was almost laughable.

"I've missed you," she whispered.

Akos pulled away to study her face; his mismatched eyes danced between admiration and concern. "You must be careful; the Black Gate is saying this isn't a normal game."

Ezlyn's warmth toward him soured. "And I'm not a normal person."

Akos lovingly pinched her chin between two fingers. "You don't have to tell me twice."

A rush of heat spread over Ezlyn's chest and crept up her neck.

She knew young love didn't usually last, but when Akos had joined the Black Gate the previous year as one of their youngest recruits, they'd juggled their responsibilities while meeting each other in secret. It was a deliciously deceitful romance, but that's what made it all the more fun.

He kissed her then. Just a playful peck at first, his fingers still gripping her chin. Then his hand slowly slid down the column of her throat, wrapping around one side of her neck, front to back. He pulled her to him. His mouth claimed hers the way it had countless times before.

His eyes slashed into lustful lines. "You show them how this game is played, Princess." His firm mouth murmured against the delicate curve of her lips. "Or there will be consequences."

Ezlyn slid her hands up his arms. "Mm, sounds like positive reinforcement to me."

He scoffed a laugh, sweeping her into his arms.

"Are you sure you want me to win?" She teased.

"I want you to live," his words took on a serious note.

"Me too." Ezlyn stared solemnly at him. "And I will, Akos. I will win. I will find my mother, and I will live the life I was supposed to before this curse took hold of the circus. We will live the life we've always wanted."

Akos hefted a sigh that tossed the hair swept across her forehead. "Promise?"

"It's a guarantee."

CHAPTER TWENTY-TWO

Truce

"**R**EADY FOR NIGHT TWO, Miss James?" Tanith asked, her earthy skin a striking contrast to her pink curls when she came up the stairs to the main living area, her racks, and storage carts magically appearing beside her.

Copper didn't speak; she just wearily gestured at the person in the middle of her living space. Her 'prize' for defeating Captain Rhozyn was the child everyone believed had been a slave aboard the pirate ship, The Blue Giraffe.

"This is it?" Hollis asked from where she sat cross-legged on a rug.

"This isn't enough for you?" Tanith asked lightly from just behind Copper's overstuffed chair. She made a show of setting up a rack for clothing for night two, but her attention was sharply aware of Hollis Roux. "When I was your age, I couldn't *dream* of something this nice."

"Then you had a boring childhood," Hollis said matter-of-factly as she took in the plush rug and pillowed seats lining both sides of the a-line room. Then the balcony windows, and finally, the tent door at the bottom of the stairs.

Copper snorted at the retort, covering her mouth and nose with her palm when Tanith turned a mildly insulted eye to her.

"Is this a tent or a people-sized birdhouse?" Hollis stood and planted hands on her almost non-existent hips.

"It's…both, I suppose." Tanith hesitated to explain such a complicated concept to a child who'd never experienced spacial magic.

"That depends. Do you consider yourself a bird?" Copped challenged playfully.

A child is the last thing I need right now.

Hollis ran from the stone doors behind them, one that led to the hall in the cliffside caverns, to the balcony windows that overlooked the city, and then down the spiral staircase that opened a tent flap on the other side of the city. "It's…"

"Magic," Copper called before Hollis trudged back up the stairs.

"Has she been like this all day?" Tanith murmured.

"All. Day." Copper gave her a tight, fake smile to go along with her words' false note of pleasantry. "Of course, that was after her utter melt-down when the pirates left without her."

"So…not a slave then?"

Copper spread her arms wide. "Your guess is as good as mine. She's practically feral, though."

On the outside, the tent was a small, residential dwelling. But, inside, it was an A-line loft complete with fairy lights and oversized pillows.

"Look at it!" Hollis threw her arms up and outward. She repeatedly stepped outside and returned, trying to wrap her mind around the significant size difference.

"Make it stop," Copper groaned. Exhaustion didn't begin to describe the feelings screaming through her limbs.

Tanith huffed a laugh. "The novelty wears off soon enough."

"Do you have children," Copper asked.

The amusement slipped from Tanith's face. "Once upon a time, I suppose."

Copper didn't press for more after she saw the pain in the woman's face.

"I saw you," Hollis said too loudly, walking right into Copper's personal space, probably annoyed that they were talking about her; she ignored Tanith altogether.

"What?" Copper leaned back.

"In the streets. Your head was just…floating there." She made an awkward hovering gesture with her hands. "Is it this?" Hollis ran her hand over the cloak loosely slung over Copper's shoulders. "Is it…magic? Or just…ya know. An illusion?"

Tanith was suspiciously silent as though she, too, questioned the cloak's enchanted nature.

Isn't it your job to know all the clothes in this place?

"That…tickles," the cloak ground out, swatting her hand away with a sleeve that wasn't there before.

"Probably magic," Copper shrugged, crossing her arms to show that it was not her that had taken a swing at Hollis.

"You know, we *wash* salty garments on the ship," Hollis harassed the cloak, pointing her stubby finger at the stars on the fabric. "Do think I won't run you through the wringer…"

"Keep that little heathen away from me!" He snarled.

"Right." Tanith clapped her hands together, attempting to exit the awkward situation. "Well, I've set out your costumes for night two, and a team will be back to dress you closer to this evening."

"Do we stay here now?" Hollis hopped to yet another topic. "I mean. Me and you? You won, right? So I have to be here with you now?"

They both watched her go, then looked at each other. Copper met her gaze a little reluctantly and nodded in response.

It was only a few hours past sunrise when they'd arrived at their temporary home. When the excitement wore off, the fact that Hollis Roux hadn't slept in close to twenty-four hours presented in the way she slumped suddenly against the nearest cushion that lined either wall of the living space.

"It's–" she yawned. "So pretty."

"So, you're just…ok with all of this?" Copper sat back, crossing her legs and slinging an arm over the back of her chair.

"It's cute that you think they won't be back for me." Hollis put on a show rife with casual bravado. "The magic of the game can't last forever, right?"

"That's not what I asked." Copper narrowed her eyes. She recognized a kindred spirit in the way the little girl played along in order to survive and gave Hollis a small smile. "I'm aware that Eliza will be back for you; she's never been one to give up easily."

Hollis sat up a little. "You…you know her?"

Copper nodded, pressing her lips together at the idea of explaining further.

"So you know," Hollis slid forward to sit on her knees on the floor. "You know this isn't…forever. Me being here?"

Copper watched her for a long moment. *I forgot what it was like to be so young and full of confusing emotions.*

Not that Copper still didn't feel too much too fast, but she liked to think she'd mastered her face enough to not let it do the talking for her anymore.

"Do you want to go back?"

Hollis pulled a loose fiber in the rub. "Maybe."

"They left you here," Copper probed. "What makes you think they'd want a slave like you back?"

Hollis shot to her feet. "You don't know anything! The Blue Giraffe was my home and…"

"Was?" Copper caught the word as quickly as Hollis had spewed it. "Don't you mean…is?"

Hollis blinked once, then twice.

"The rest of the crew doesn't know you exist...do they?"

Hollis shook her head no.

"But you were happy there? You were...treated well?"

Hollis Roux's eyes took on a glassy sheen when she nodded.

"What is it that you want then..."

"Hollis," she told Copper, a small crack in her voice. "She called me Hollis Roux because when I was a baby, she said I was as pretty as the Holly Berry trees from her home lands..."

A baby? Copper marveled as she recognized the green of the tree in her eyes and the red of the berries in her hair. *Did Eliza have a secret baby?* All the aggression, the draining of color from her face...it hadn't just been Rhozyn's pride that had been bruised. Copper had taken her *child.*

*Oh, I definitely haven't seen the last of you...*she thought, already mentally planning how to get Hollis back to Captain Rhozyn when the game was over without getting herself killed.

"You want to win the game," Hollis presented her palms to Copper, tension evident in her shoulders. "And I'm in this for a little more adventure. You let me see the circus. I'll help you play the game, and then you can just...give me back."

"Give you back." Copper gave a surprised laugh. "You realize she's going to try and kill me for taking you?"

Hollis Roux's face dropped a little. "I'm not a slave to be traded. I never have been, and I never will be. Either way, if you don't give me back..."

"She'll try and kill me regardless." Copper rolled her shoulders and leaned forward, resting her forearms on her thighs. "Look, I don't have any plans on raising a child any more than you plan on sticking around."

"What's in it for you?" Hollis sniffed.

"Keeping you here or playing the game?" Copper rose from her chair when the jade kettle on the little kitchenette stove whistled. Pouring two cups of steaming tea, she handed Hollis one of the ornate sapphire mugs and sat on the floor cushions near her new little companion.

"The original ringmaster owes me a debt, and I plan on winning to draw him out of hiding and collect what's mine." Copper blew on her tea before sipping the steaming citrus-flavored drink.

"I heard he was dead," Hollis muttered.

Her comment was ignored.

Cassian dying was too convenient. It was too easy of a way out for what she had planned for him.

Cassian being dead meant she didn't have a reason to live.

He had to be alive.

"That's what everyone's been saying anyway." Hollis stared down into her cup. "What about me? What happens to me when this is over?"

"Once upon a time, I was you," Copper said simply.

"Is that why Captain wants your head on a stake?" Hollis asked, swirling the liquid in the cup without splashing any over the rim. "Because she's afraid you'll win?"

Copper snorted. "No, that…is a story for another time. But, if I can teach you a few things to keep you from the trouble I experienced before you move on, then maybe we can agree to a truce. Just for this week. I teach you what I know, and you stop trying to get yourself killed."

"And then you'll take me back?"

Copper's brow rose in surprise. "I can make sure you get close enough to get yourself there. But you'll understand if I don't make false pleasantries with your Captain, all things considered."

"That would be ok." Hollis took a sip of her tea and reeled backward, an expression of disgust on her face

"Too hot?" Copper leaned over to look into the cup when Hollis stared into it with utter mortification.

"No! I think it just bit me?" Hollis grimaced and dropped it without warning.

Act II: The Hunt

Wild Rebels,

Congratulations on proving your merit by succeeding in overcoming your dueling opponent. My, what an unconventional start to a new season of The Red Game. Consider last night as a trial run in terms of what lies ahead.

We will not be veering off course again.

All Rebels are expected to participate from here on out or will suffer the consequences of Red Rebel himself. Our enchanted mascot may be small, but the wrath of the gemstone hummingbirds from the crystal caverns is not just legendary but lethal.

It's been said that some of you felt that last night's event was too easy, but never fear, The Red Game will resume its course in tonight's pursuit of the item on the card you received upon completing last night's event.

Enter The Rebel Market if you dare, and seek the item that will guide you through the rest of the events.

Let the Hunt begin.

Welcome to the Season of Shimmering Souls

Act IX

The Grand Master of the Red Rebel Extravaganza

P.S. As to the rumors of my death, there are far greater things to worry about than whether or not I am writing these missives from beyond the grave.

CHAPTER TWENTY-THREE

The Rebel Market

CLOAKED IN A GARB of obsidian silk, Ophelia stood at the mouth of the fissure between the cliffs. All roads ended at a large gate that led into The Rebel Market. Patrons were not allowed in this area of Cape Solaera for their own safety. However, every available opalescent balcony was packed with those who had paid for exclusive access to watch that part of the game.

"Akos." Ophelia nodded to one of the largest guards who flanked her on either side. His long hair was partially braided away from his face, and the rest flowed freely over the weapons strapped to his muscular back. His mismatched eyes fell upon each of the Rebels as he withdrew a set of keys from his uniform pocket. The small amount of light from the lanterns they all carried reflected on the sun-shaped scar under his golden left eye. Its twin was as blue as the early morning sky.

All seven Rebels arrived at the gate. Standing a fair distance apart, no one talked, which was just fine by everyone involved.

Ezlyn lifted her eyes from the ground, her wings unfurling as Akos crossed before her. As severe as the moment was, a slight curve to her lips forced him to turn his head to mask his own grin while he unlocked the gate.

"Welcome to night two," Ophelia said in a grave tone. "As the directions from the Grand ringmaster pointed out, you are to seek out your guide item from within the Rebel Market."

Copper absent-mindedly ran her thumb over her card, the picture of the book slightly raised on its surface burned in her mind's eye as they waited.

"What's the Rebel Market?" Hollis whispered up at Copper.

Copper raised a finger to her lips to hush her before pointing toward Ophelia, who was still talking.

"The Rebel Market is one of the few wild magics still alive and well within The Empire. Guard yourself closely because The Extravaganza will not be able to intervene on anyone's behalf if you find yourself in a questionable situation."

An uncharacteristically cool wind ripped through their numbers, making everyone grateful for the various coats and cloaks provided in their wardrobes for the evening. Each Rebel was dressed in dark fabrics to blend in with the low lighting of the enchanted fissure.

Copper's cloak had faded into obsidian velvet and laid over her dark blue corset, covering the capped sleeves. Dark gray knee-high boots covered her skin-tight pants and gave her the look of a hooded assassin.

Raleigh's jacket had bled into black leather to match the strips of leather over the tears in the dark denim of his pants. The Huntress slunk soundlessly under her fur cloak, tugging it tighter around her shoulders as her charcoal-lined eyes darted over the rough walls of the entrance.

Does your coat talk to you too? Copper couldn't help but wonder. Raleigh didn't seem as distracted as she felt with her cloak's consistent commentary, but maybe that meant it was a reactive sort of magic instead of...sentient?

Or I'm going crazy.

Both were valid options at that point.

"Children, weapons, and pets are not advised in the Rebel Market," Akos said as he unlocked the gate. "Leave your items at the table with the stewards to your left. You can reclaim them upon your departure from the market."

Hollis stood at Copper's side, her dark boots squeaking under the frilly black dress Tanith had picked for her. She looked up at Copper, unsure of what to do.

"No one has died who has played the game right," Lord Hypnos could be overheard, soothing his wife's whispered concerns.

It was true. But the stakes of the game weren't apparent either. After Ezlyn's reappearance with seemingly little consequence, the same questions danced around everyone's minds. What were the ramifications of failing a task from the ringmaster and the cursed Red Rebel?

Ezlyn surveyed them all, a curiosity in her eyes as she tucked her wings in tight and stepped forward when the gates groaned open.

"Be safe." Akos' fingers trailed along the tips of her own in passing.

They were officially entering the unknown and beyond the safety of the circus.

"Stay close." Copper said to Hollis at the same time Lord Hypnos said the same to his wife, clutching his walking stick to one side and Lady Illuminae to the other.

"Here we go." The Knight grinned fearlessly, minor cuts freshly scabbed on his face from the night before. Undoing a few of the brackets on his suit vest, he placed some of his bigger weapons down on the table.

"Round two," Raleigh said as he deposited Aloysius into the hands of a waiting Extravaganza steward. "It's best you stay here," he whispered to the indignant chipmoth. Reaching behind him, he gently gripped Hollis Roux's shoulder. "You too."

Hollis jerked out of his grasp, a wicked sneer on her face. "Don't touch me."

Raleigh lifted his gaze to Copper. "This isn't a place for kids. Not even one like her."

Copper stared at him for a long moment. Then, she blinked, nodding as she guided Hollis to a kind woman waiting at the table. "Keep an eye on him," she pointed at Aloysius. "I'll be back."

Hollis didn't object, but the confused expression she gave Copper over her shoulder stuck with Copper longer than she expected.

"If everyone is ready," Ophelia stepped to the side. "You may now enter at your own risk."

Chapter Twenty-Four
Branded for Confrontation

A SIGH OF WIND from the sea exhaled against Copper's back, replacing the balmy air as though mourning the presence of the wicked market. The sensation drew her attention to the cliff base, and the second she laid her eyes on it, Copper knew why a chill ran up her spine.

"The Solaera Valley Market," the cloak's words were bleak.

"Solaera Valley?" Copper murmured.

"The Extravaganza refers to it as the Rebel Market," Raleigh answered, clearly believing she was talking to him.

"Oh?" Copper raised her brows, forcing herself to be more present. She hadn't revealed the voice she heard when wearing the hooded garment to him.

Part of her didn't intend to.

"The rest of us know it as the Solaera Valley Market," he continued. "It's drawn to the circus. It seems to pop up in back alleys and abandoned avenues wherever The Red Rebel Extravaganza goes."

"So much of this place sounds like bedtime stories and old wives' tales," Copper half laughed. "Then you see it for yourself, and it's–"

"Real." Raleigh nodded, finishing her sentence as he fell in line beside her.

"I feel like I've taken a lot of time over the years to familiarize myself with the various artifacts I've come in contact with. All the different circles we've run in. But this?" When she stood before the gray gate with broad stone pillars bearing chiseled imagery of large gargoyles guarding the entrance, Copper shivered in anticipation.

"We prepared for this," Raleigh reminded her under his breath, running a contemplative hand along his jaw. "But to be fair, I think the stakes are slightly higher than anticipated."

"How perceptive he is," her cloak mocked.

Copper gave him a side eye that said *what is that supposed to mean?* It was a big statement, even for him. They'd spent the week prior reading all they could on previous games and preparing for a lot of hypotheticals.

"Something is off. The game feels…" He wriggled his shoulders as he tried to find the words.

"Different?"

"I guess. The market rests outside the protective barrier of magic that keeps the game from going too far," Raleigh explained quietly. "It is its own entity."

"We're on our own the second we cross that threshold." Copper gave a heavy sigh, starting to realize the game wasn't just a game after all.

"I think we have been the whole time."

"Did you think you came here to be fluffed and coddled? Idiots…foolish, mortal idiots." Another gem from her cloak.

Shepherd, take me now. Copper groaned her prayer for relief internally.

"Why not," she muttered, wrapping her arms around herself to try and maintain her focus with each barb from her cloak. "We survived the Obsidian Hall…what's a little questionable shopping?"

"You survived *what?*" Her cloak cackled.

Raleigh snorted. "That's your reasoning?"

"Whatever gets me through the day." Copper shrugged, moving forward.

The narrow lane made of stone and shadows swallowed all light and sound behind them until no sign of The Extravaganza appeared. With The Knight at the forefront, the rest walked in twos until the eerie tunnel opened into the market.

"How high of stakes are we talking?" Copper leaned into Raleigh somewhere in the dark.

"When I signed up for my first game, a safety clause was written into the fine print. It essentially protected the players from lethal means."

Copper rolled her eyes. "Even Cassian September isn't beyond death."

"No, but you gather enough magic-infused tokens, and it wards against situations that cause it."

"I thought The Extravaganza was about glitz and wonder?" Where was the fun? The effortless excitement?

"It was remarkable," her cloak sighed. "Nothing like these cowards the other items have talked about so far."

Are there more talking items? Copper knew the Extravaganza was full of magic, but no one had hinted at hearing their gifts speaking to them.

"It is," Raleigh noted. "But knowing you couldn't die emboldened the players. The shows became bigger, the risks they took unhindered by self-preservation."

"You signed up for a game without a protection clause?" The cloak nearly gasped. "Did you come here to die, Copper James? Put me back!" he strained against her; thankfully, no one could see them there in the dark.

"Now, who's a coward," Copper reminded him under her breath.

"Hmm?" Raleigh asked.

Copper covered quickly. "There wasn't clear terminology toward what to expect at all if you think about it."

The sounds of busy streets and the scent of wet stone and wood smoke washed over them. The fissure was as tall as it was wide. Burning fire pits lit the streets, the colors of the smoke and flames changing in unison. The illuminated signs and displays from the endless shops and dens lit up the forever night. Halos of fog distorted crackling lights of neons and gold. Level after level was carved into the fissure walls, all seeming to bear down on the arena of the ground floor.

"Be safe," Raleigh gripped her arm briefly.

Copper gave him a tight smile in response.

One by one, they snuffed out their lanterns and set them in a dark alcove. Then, each rebel went their separate ways, exiting the dark sporadically to avoid appearing to be in a group. Extravaganza magic was highly coveted, and if word got out that they were one of the seven rebels from this year's season, there was no telling what could happen.

I've heard stories about you, Copper marveled as she took in the push and pull of that forbidden place.

Taking a sharp series of turns, she was met with a large, multistoried shop. The endless rows of windows were similar to a greenhouse in that it bore pale, geometric panels of crystal blue glass. The carnivorous plants housed within heralded her proximity when dozens of them leaned in her direction.

"Too soon." She grimaced. Pausing briefly, Copper took a long look at the structure.

Why do you swallow light? Not a single piece reflected even the smallest portion of light for an entire building crafted in glass panels. Her eyes tracked to the ceiling where a singular black orb hung.

"That is a very old piece of magic." Her cloak pointed out in a stern voice.

"An old type of magic that we are going to stay far away from," Copper replied, slowly moving away from the building as all the plants lifted their attention to the orb once more.

*Though it's something worth coming back to…*Her mind wandered into the area of the price it would bring.

Magic-subverting objects were almost as sought after as ones that gave the wielder power.

As Copper made her way further into the market, the streets were littered with packs of people, and only those who traveled by themselves kept to the sides. Slinking along in the shadows, they were less likely to be singled out.

Copper walked about the market with a swagger that said she belonged there. *This really isn't a Sunday stroll, window shopping sort of place,* she told herself as she watched large gangs prowling the streets. Only those who wandered around by themselves looking lost garnered their attention.

"Can you see behind us?" Copper asked the cloak quietly.

"Like a second pair of eyes?" He pondered. "Not quite. I see in whatever direction you are looking. But it wouldn't be a bad idea in this place."

Copper peered over her shoulder through the shining plate of a stationary cart and saw a figure hovering in the distance.

"What do you make of that?"

"Keep moving."

The overwhelming feeling of being followed continued to build as Copper ducked in one tent and out the other. She'd circled behind a wagon and eventually wound her way back into the main street again, this time in front of a loud nightclub. The Fallen Star Tavern was decorated in black and honeycomb stars that twisted and burned all on their own. Music filtered out through the scarlet double doors, where two men dressed in black guarded the entrance.

"Poisoned Potions Apothecary" had an alluring aroma flowing from oval windows. The whole building was cheekily shaped like a potion vial, with dark purple fluid constantly circling around the outside in a transparent tube system.

"Celestials and potions, now that's a brand of magic I haven't seen in eons," the cloak waxed nostalgic.

"Is there anything in the place that isn't going to try and kill me?"

"No."

None of these places look like somewhere I would find a book. Copper sighed as she peeked down at her card from night one. *I could spend all night here.* While that might have seemed daunting, she felt more at home in the hidden places than in the spotlight of the Extravaganza. There in the comfort of the night, she could slip around, investigating and exploring all the things she might need someday.

But none of them was the item she was there to look for.

Copper skipped over Coffin Coiffures, Matilda's Boils and Brews, and a little hut shaped like a teapot with steam coming out of the spout. The latter had a sign stuck in the ground, and a shop name scrawled in a language she didn't quite recognize. Still, there was something about the symbols embossed into the sign. She couldn't decide if it meant a fermented poisoned tea bag or a possible volcano eruption.

"Death, death, and more death," Copper shook her head. "It's a wonder they don't advertise this along with The Extravaganza. Come for the show; stay for the extremely lethal ugly stepchild of a back alley."

The cloak snorted a laugh.

Scooting out of the way of two racing carts, Copper entered an alcove and was swiftly in awe of what lay before her. The unique markings on the sign overhead told her this particular vendor was part of The Red Game itself.

"What are you waiting for?" The cloak urged. "Go inside!"

Copper found a narrow, red door with panels of glass windows that had appeared on her left. "I don't think you grasp my luck with strange doors lately."

"Do you want us to keep being followed or not?" The cloak shoved her arm forward. Copper took the handle begrudgingly and stepped inside.

#

"Welcome to the Rebel Market," a bodiless voice greeted her in an automated clip that made Copper wonder if the greeting was pre-recorded. "Are you a Rebel, a guide merchant, or a performer?"

"Maybe I don't fall into any of those categories." Copper answered, casually peering out the window; she didn't see anyone waiting around outside for her. She surveyed the dimly lit rows of shelving before her, unwilling to reveal who or what she was too readily. "Am I still permitted to shop?"

The aisles shifted and spun. Three circular lights hummed to life overhead, revealing a wall of shelves full of dozens of magical items.

"Oh…wow." Copper's eyes widened. "I'll take that as a yes," she added, unable to stop herself from cautiously perusing the shelves.

"Here at the Rebel Market, we pride ourselves on preparing all Rebels of the Extravaganza with everything they might need to win The Red Game, whether it's event merchandise." A wall of weapons and tactical gear revealed itself. "Poisons for the upper hand." A glass case of potions and herbs slid down the wall until it rested at eye level. "And, of course, an outfit for every day of the game."

Copper paused. "Good to know being poisoned is something I need to watch out for," she grumbled, gently pushing aside the glass case.

A strained sound came from the back corner then. Believing she was alone in the room, Copper wandered past all the sparkling objects and found a war-scorned book on a tattered shred of fabric atop a barrel.

The tome was bound in black scaled leather, charred and smoky as though it had been fastened out of the hide of a dragon. The face of its cover was twisted and distorted in a pattern that reminded her of a sinking whirlpool. Purple silk bookmarks hung out of its hundreds of pages in several shreds of fabric. A series of silver brackets lined its spine, chains reaching from each and looping into a hoop secured to a corner piece.

A small piece of her hurt for the item. The wounds speckling its cover looked sore where it had been discarded in an unvisited corner of the shop.

"Shackles? For a book?" Copper murmured, running her hand over the tiny gem laid into the flat panel where a heavy padlock had been closed around it. Pulling the card she had won from the previous night's event, she compared the picture on it to the one before her, but it kept shifting between two images like some twisted, holographic playing card.

Are you why I'm here?

The book drew a ragged breath as she gently ran a finger down its spine. She failed to find any identifying lettering or markings for what kind of book it had been. With careful attention, Copper leaned against the wooden ledge of the barrel and tried to coax the pages open. It squirmed under her touch but didn't open.

For the first time since she entered the shop, Copper was met with a physical person, not just an incorporeal voice.

"He's in rough condition." The shop owner stepped out from one of the many nooks in her dark purple tunic and smooth scalp. "But if he called out to you…then maybe I can help?"

"This is…quite the place." She was unable to stop staring at the woman who matched the voice she'd previously heard overhead perfectly. She appeared sweet, like a walking violet, with her kind eyes and gentle build. This was not the kind of shop owner she expected to host a business inside the shadow market.

"It's a family heirloom of sorts, this shop." The woman answered sheepishly under a thick fringe of lofty lashes. "I can come and go as I please from a back room. I don't like to go out into the actual market…reputation and all."

Who are you? Copper's perception of the Rebel Market shifted as she searched for an explanation why such an elegant flower of a person was carrying on in such a loathsome valley.

They had met before.

Somewhere.

Sometime.

For the life of me, I just can't place you…

The brand on Copper's hand glowed red hot. She gripped her fist, trying not to wince at the pain, but a nearly imperceptible shift on the shop owner's face told Copper that her presence there had shifted in the other woman's eyes.

Thief.

Marked.

Branded.

The fox there shifted, twisting and curling on her skin until it looked like it was laughing up at her with a wide grin and eyes slashed into narrow lines.

A shadow shifted in the corner of her eye. It was brief but enough to draw Copper's attention away, toward the front of the shop, for just a moment.

The woman's hand lashed out, snatching Copper's wrist and pulling it across the barrel. "Your kind is all over this filthy place," she hissed, a touch of an accent slipping into her words. "Taking and breaking and thinking you're owed everything in this forsaken empire!"

"Let me go!" Copper pulled, but the woman held tight.

A glint of metal and Copper's eyes widened.

Knife!

"We do not tolerate thieves!" The woman roared, lashing out with a small blade with its obsidian handle.

We? The word stood out to Copper, who wondered who else she could expect in the shop.

Surely they would have come to see what was going on?

"I said let go!" Copper reared backward, quickly bringing her foot up and planting it against the shopkeeper's abdomen, breaking her hold on her wrist and sending her and the knife flying.

Copper braced herself against the nearby wall, scanning the place for something to defend herself as the owner scrambled for the knife when it slid under a deep shelf.

Giving up on the blade, the woman grabbed a staff behind the counter and lunged toward Copper. She dodged the blow, diving behind a display case and scurrying toward the front door.

The shop owner cried in a language she didn't understand, followed by a wet snarl. Copper stumbled to her feet, looking over her shoulder at where the shackles of the worn book latched onto the shop owner's arm and freshly torn flesh.

The woman wrenched her arm around and sent the book flying across the shop, only to land with a small slide at Copper's feet.

"You're coming with me." Copper told it, sweeping the book under her arm and into the safety of her cloak.

The book sighed a huff of relief. The air warmed her side, and for just a second, she wondered if it would try to take a bite out of her next.

"Stay where you are," Copper held her hand up as the shopkeeper stalked toward her, the jade staff raised. She knew if she turned her back and ran out the door, the woman would strike before she could escape.

"You should have died in the shop that branded you." The woman snarled.

You should have died. It was a curse that pierced Copper through. It wasn't the worst thing said to her in her life, nor was that moment the most challenging thing she'd experienced in the last few weeks.

But it did something to her.

Something inside Copper snapped as everything that had happened recently rushed through her.

"The Heir of Keskairah is dead!" A man's voice echoed in the distance. "And he's dead because of you!"

"Do you grieve so deeply for your own capture?" The empress had accused, believing her grief to be turned inward instead of the weight bearing down on her from the grief of love won and then lost.

"You strike me as the sort of person that needs anything but what they're looking for." Cassian had said when she didn't jump at his offer.

"I wouldn't risk my spot in The Grand Aurora for my own family, let alone the likes of you."

"It's too bad you won't live to seek out your revenge…" the female spider had threatened.

"I want to live," Copper admitted, a riot of anger and fierce indignation surged within her.

"So live," her cloak whispered.

Heat coursed through her veins, subduing the icy pit in her heart where the hurt, pain, and loss had burrowed into, attempting to stay for good. The fire that rose within her burned it out, and in its place was the raw realization that it was enough.

All the suffering.

All the agony.

Every decision she'd made since she'd watched Rogan take his last breath.

Enough. Enough. Enough!

No longer the victim.

No longer at fault.

Pulling herself back into the moment, Copper planted her feet firmly against the shop floors. "I'm warning you," she said calmly as she slowly set the book on the floor. "If you come at me with that thing, I will hurt you with it."

I will survive.

Freedom from the mental prison of guilt and strain she'd put herself under, released in a tingling sensation that framed her mind and soul, clearing away the sting that kept her in a chokehold for so long.

Her fight had returned.

The shopkeeper scoffed a laugh. "I come from generations of keepers. If you think you can..."

Before the woman could finish, before she could bluster and taunt Copper with her presumably impressive lineage, Copper struck, moving faster than the woman could react.

Copper seized the staff with one hand, smashing the woman in the nose with her other hand before bending her backward over her own counter and pinning her to it with the jade staff by her exposed throat.

"You know," Copper pressed harder with the staff when the owner tried to get free. "I've been in a bad place for quite some time...even turned myself over to," she bobbed her head side to side, "*questionable* authority believing I was the problem."

The woman struggled again, and Copper pinned her legs with her own, pressing the forked head of the staff harder against the counter.

The shopkeeper stopped, her charcoal-lined eyes wide as her chest heaved under the effort she'd put forward.

"I think I'm done making myself suffer," she twisted the staff, and the shopkeeper screeched her rage. "I think I'm done handing myself over to people like you to pay for crimes I haven't committed!" She bore her teeth at the woman. "Grief is funny like that…but I've done nothing to you or your shop. So, let me leave this place the way I came, and I won't show you exactly how I earned this brand."

"And the book?" More angry panting from the shop owner.

Copper didn't break her stare. "A parting gift for your inhospitality toward me and your poor bookkeeping skills."

"You'll die in that game," The woman spit, but there was an acquiescence in her face that signaled Copper to let go.

"Then I expect you to dance on my grave," Copper shoved backward. "But until then…" she kept a wary eye on the livid shopkeeper as she picked up the book and closed the door behind her.

CHAPTER TWENTY-FIVE
Carnivorous Instruments

"YOU ARE BOUND TO the circus with a contract stronger than the ones the Rebels signed before the start of the game, Pharaoh." Ophelia tried to remind him, following along as he stalked through the hidden tunnels that connected the performer's living quarters from the rest of the circus. "You are compelled to do as the ringmaster bids."

In exchange for signing up to work for the circus, the cursed magic of the gemstone hummingbird heightened his natural performing abilities and extended his lifespan. But there were loopholes, small spaces of time between performances, and his duties as senior staff in the Extravaganza that allowed him a little more free will than during peak performing periods.

"Are you going to try and stop me," Pharaoh challenged as he wiped the overdone stage makeup from his face and neck.

When his first show of the night ended, he'd traded his flashy costume for a dark pair of pants and shirt in the wardrobe tent, then shrouded himself in a charcoal cloak. Binding his long hair at the back of his head, Pharaoh eyed Ophelia through the mirror.

"You know I'm only saying this for your safety." Ophelia crossed her arms in the doorway, clearly uncomfortable.

"You're the current ringmaster. Technically, I'm supposed to do your bidding now." He turned to face her when he discarded the makeup-removing wipe. "Plus, none of us have been safe since long before this game started."

"Interim ringmaster," she corrected.

Pharaoh scoffed at the note of loyalty in her voice. "You still think he's coming back?"

Ophelia just stared at him.

You look as tired as I feel, he thought when he noted a weariness to her face and a slump to her shoulders that spoke volumes.

"Something has been wrong for a long time, O." The nickname was one that few got away with using. "We all knew something was wrong when Cassian didn't return before the start of the game. In fact, we should have known something was wrong when the protection clause had been dropped from the invitation to play."

Ophelia dropped her gaze to the floor. "I didn't want to believe it. When *Captain* Eliza Rhozyn breached the circus, Copper James drew blood during their duel…"

Pharaoh had been in the crowd during Copper's duel. Each drop of the Captain's blood that hit the sand was another reminder of how bad things had gotten. Spilled blood would have never happened in one of the past games. The magic wouldn't have allowed it.

"That's why I need to get out there and see things with my own eyes." Pharaoh moved past her and out into the hall that led to the main exit. Inside the cliffside dwellings, there were only so many ways a person could leave, being that the opulent residence had been carved out of stone.

Ophelia put out an arm, not physically restraining him, but just halting him long enough for her to not have to raise her voice.

"What good will any of that do? Are you going to go out and find Cassian lurking in the shadows, waiting to be found, and…what?" The color drained from her face at the very idea. "Bring him to his senses?"

"Something is wrong," he repeated, over-enunciating each word, his breath tossing the springing curls standing several inches off Ophelia's head. "Hiding inside these mountains or an arena isn't going to do any of us any good. We've been trapped inside this city for too long, and I don't know about you, but having an extended life span means nothing if we're stuck here forever."

Her stacked bracelets jangled as she waved him off, a sour twist to her mouth. "Go on and do whatever it is you need to do. But don't think I can save you from the consequences because of my position."

"No," Pharaoh started down the hall. "We all saw exactly how far your mercy goes with Ezlyn."

Ophelia turned on her heel, ready to snarl a slew of insults at him, but when she peered down the polished stone hallway, Pharaoh was nowhere to be found.

#

"Why did you risk us both in that shop for that…*thing*?" Her cloak audibly sneered.

"Well, I didn't hear you being any help!" Copper answered.

"The shop was coated in some kind of ward. I couldn't see, let alone speak."

"Is that really an excuse?" Copper smiled to herself, taunting the enchanted garment before suddenly dropping herself behind a cart.

A group of men, shop owners, and patrons alike stormed by, grumbling about a thief.

"I wonder who they could be looking for," he matched her taunting tone.

"Hush you," Copper peered around the corner of the cart.

"You could always…give it back?" He suggested casually.

"Give it back?" Copper shifted the book from one arm to the other.

Returning a stolen item wasn't always as easy as simply putting it back. Copper had learned this the hard way many times over the years. But it didn't teach her not to move things that weren't hers. Instead, she knew to make sure the connection she'd made the smuggling deal with was valid and that the item was worth taking in the first place.

The artistry of smuggling lay both in knowing the value of an object and understanding how to get the item somewhere it would truly shine. It wasn't worth taking if it didn't hold more value than what it cost to move. In the case of the book, she would make sure it was repaired to its former glory and then decide what to do with it next.

"I think I was supposed to find it," she told him quietly. Looking at the card she'd won from the night before, it still shifted the image back and forth, and she couldn't decide if that was a good or bad thing.

Copper had made an immediate effort to make herself scarce the moment she left that shop, knowing her semi-truce with the shopkeeper would only hold until she was outside the building. That woman had screamed "thief!" at the top of her lungs, sending a torrent of others after her.

Copper had hooked a sharp left, snatched a pale scarf, and slowed her pace.

"This might help," the cloak had said, shifting the texture and color of his fabric from the night sky to a silky amethyst.

The men had blown right past her, but Copper knew she was pushing her luck every moment she remained in the market.

"Let's get out of here," she told the cloak, accepting that she'd accomplished her task and needed to return to Cape Solaera.

Stopping sharply, Copper saw a dark shadow on the ground beside her. There was a heated, prickling sensation that ran over her skin.

Magic.

Not the kind that flowed all around them from one booth to the next, tangling from the carts and arms of vendors.

This was the kind that reached out to taste her.

To get a feel for who or what she was.

Whirling, Copper grabbed the man behind her and pinned him to the inner wall of the alley to her left. Coming face to face with him, she was very near to cutting his throat with a broken piece of glass from the discarded waste when she recognized the deeply amused expression before her.

"Raleigh." She frowned, a note of both relief and chastisement in her voice.

His eyes were wild with amusement as a bouquet of flowers sprang forward from his lapel. "Ms. James."

Copper took the flowers and released her hold on his jacket. "So, you're a clown now?"

"I can be whatever you want me to be…" He looked her over, clearly enthralled by her sudden show of force. "Anyone ever tell you how attractive it is when you play rough?"

"Oh, stop," Copper groaned, stepping away from him. "Did you complete your task?"

"Did you?" Raleigh continued to be amused. "Seems like you've garnered quite the following after your little stunt in the Rebel Market."

"What of it?" Copper couldn't help but wonder how he'd found out so quickly.

"Copper, this is a game. Did you think everything wasn't on display in one way or another?"

Copper closed her eyes against the realization. "Because this place is too dangerous for the crowds to physically attend."

"It's not as widely captured as, say, the opening ceremony…but there was enough that it reminded me not to get on your bad side."

*Of course…*Copper reminded herself. *Because this is all just a game.*

Copper opened her mouth to tell Raleigh about the book she found when a slurping, gnawing sound drew their attention. Feeling a gentle tug on the hem of her cloak, she looked down to see an ordinary-looking concertina. But where its hexagon-shaped face should have had buttons, a mouth of razor-sharp teeth was there instead, all chewing on Copper's hem.

"Copper James! Get this abomination off me!" Her cloak roared.

"Hey!" Copper snarled, trying to snatch the cloak away from the tiny beast. "Quit that, or the only thing you'll be tasting is my shoe!"

Raleigh took hold of Copper and lifted a booted foot to the tiny accordion, sending it flying down the alleyway.

"Why is everything in this place alive?" She groaned through clenched teeth in disgust when she peered over his shoulder to watch as the enchanted instrument scooted away like a caterpillar. A disgruntled grumble tumbled from the mouth near the handle as it left them with a haunted song carried from each move of its body.

"Magic, I suppose."

"Shepherd, help the poor soul who tries to play that instrument."

"You're welcome." He told her in a sultry tone that immediately brought her back to herself.

Copper dropped her arms to her side, not realizing she'd taken hold of him in the first place, and stepped back. "You're stupid if you think I'm going to thank you for that."

"Okay, but that," He looked to see if the creature was still scooting along the street when another squeal of shock rang out in the distance. "Was not my fault."

"That one sounded like a chicken," Copper whispered. "And I wouldn't have even stopped here if you hadn't been following me!"

"You're not bored, right?" Raleigh stifled another laugh, but his grin was unmistakable.

"I would love to be bored," Copper answered with aggressive, over pronounced words.

"I know things have been weird." His words took on a gentle lilt.

"That's an understatement."

He waited patiently, observing her with an interest and mild admiration that she pretended not to notice.

Copper fell silent. *You're so much different than I remember.*
Raleigh rubbed the back of his neck. "Look—"

"How old are you now, Raleigh?" There was an accusation in her tone.

"Old enough," he answered.

While his personality was still relatively the same, there was a depth to the boy she knew. She'd seen it during the week they'd spent holed up in his place of work before entering the game. The way he spent his time and how he handled magic was with much less reverence and far more intention. He carried himself better. He didn't swagger with the bravado of a young man but commanded his body to move the way men who knew themselves and the world did.

"I did some digging, and my understanding is that Cassian had been in hiding for a long time, and the point of the game is to win something magical." He changed the subject back to Cassian, and for the time being, Copper allowed it because she saw it then. The tiny tell he made with his mouth when he lied to her was there at the end of his words. The gentle twitch allowed a dimple to peek out and then disappear as the tell dangled there like a red light indicator that something was wrong.

But where was the lie?

"And what's more magical than the ringmaster himself," Copper added, frustrated. "You're not telling me something new…"

"I lost something the last time this game was played," Raleigh explained. "While I'd rather not discuss it, especially not here, you winning would help me get that back."

Why did you lie?

"He gambled something valuable and failed at winning," her cloak snarked. "He acts like it was just…taken!"

Copper schooled her face, not allowing the torrent of emotions to surface.

You lied.

Right to my face.

Liar. Liar. Liar.

"But what happens if you lose," Copper wrinkled her brow in concern. "All this talk about the wrath of Red Rebel like the magic of that little bird will come after us? The contract is only for the week, but what happens to the person who loses each night? Seven will play, one will remain, remember?"

"I don't know," Raleigh shook his head. "The game has never been played like this before."

But there's still something you're not telling me…

A pregnant silence fell between them.

"Raleigh?"

"Hm?"

"If Cassian chose to go into hiding…who or what was he hiding from?"

"And more importantly," Raleigh challenged another twitch of his mouth. "What was worth coming out of hiding long enough to make contact with you and start a new game?"

CHAPTER TWENTY-SIX

Shadow of the King

Long after the Rebels had entered the market, Pharaoh stalked up the incline to the stone gate. As he went, a shadow crept along the ground beside him. Large and pensive, it manifested from the conflicting nature of his actions against the magic that bound him to the circus.

"You know not to bother me here," he warned the shadow, noting the fraying outlines of it the closer he drew to the fissure.

The shadow paid him little mind as it and a number of others slinking along the edge of his sanity.

*You promised you were done with this game…*a voice whispered at the back of his head as he walked the dark path between the circus and the market, guided by a small glowing light in his hand.

The Red Game was no longer an entity he recognized. Not to mention the need to intervene in events was becoming too strong, and he knew that sooner or later, consequences would catch up with him if he didn't take a step back.

The more you get involved, the harder the magic of the Extravaganza will push back, Pharaoh reminded himself as he tried to ignore the early signs.

"I have to know what's going on," he insisted under his breath as the weight of the guards of magic set in place pushed against him. From a rooftop balcony, he'd watched as the Rebels had passed through the enchanted gate that kept unsuspecting tourists from treading somewhere even the most experienced of the Extravaganza didn't dare go.

And they'd simply walked right in.

*So much for all of our air-tight barrier magic…*Pharaoh thought as he came to the threshold, and the familiar warning spark forced him a few steps back. It was a clear sign that he was about to go somewhere he didn't belong.

Pulling a broken chain from his pocket, he gathered the two ends in his fist and ran a thumb over each charm. Together, when touched in the right order, the charms expressed small bursts of magic. The right sequence allowed him to pass into the fissure without notice. His shadow, and the warped magic intertwining with it, faded under the sunless presence of the market.

This is a mistake; he breathed in the rush of tainted magic the moment he stepped into the fissure. The pulse of the different twisted kinds of magic danced along his skin. Still, it failed to fully sear its way into the layer coating him from the Extravaganza.

Out of all the sources pouring out vile forms of magic, there was one place he intended to start. The Rebel Market was a notorious shop with its enchanted items of the past that he was drawn to. The shop was where all the things from previous games were required to be deposited at the conclusion of each event. The magic that flowed through them was too powerful to be allowed out in the real world.

If any of the Rebels were educated in the history of the Extravaganza, that shop is where they would find their guide items for that evening's event.

Pharaoh ignored the pull and flavors of other magics, making a beeline to the shop where he found the keeper ranting about a stolen book and cursing the name of a rebel who took it.

Copper James.

"She was here." The bald shop owner gestured to an empty spot at the back of the shop. A book-shaped clearing amongst the dust.

Frowning, Pharaoh noted that the shadow behind him was getting stronger faster than usual. He needed to get out of the market, and soon.

"And what do you make of that?"

"I wouldn't have sold it to just anyone." The keeper weighed her words carefully. "The Tome of Fable is special."

*Of course, it was The Tome of Fable…*Pharaoh groaned internally.

"I thought that book was lost?" He eyed her with open suspicion.

In those long spans of silence, the shop owner grew anxious.

"What is brought to me after each game is not my choosing," she tried to defend herself. It was no secret who Pharaoh was there in the market. "Your kind doesn't venture often here."

Pharaoh noted that her gaze kept flicking over his shoulder. The airy tendrils crept around his feet. It was the first breath of trouble that he should've seen coming.

"How long?" Pharaoh asked under his breath, a looming presence prickling at his back.

"It followed her in," the shop owner tracked the enchanted shadow with her eyes, giving him an idea of where it stood.

Pharaoh planted his hands on the counter and rounded his shoulders. "Let's play then," he said darkly, inviting the creature to do its worst.

"What?" The shop owner struggled to meet his gaze.

"Run," he breathed just before he swung around, his extended arm sending the shadow flying across the room.

It rebounded faster than he expected, prompting Pharaoh to shatter the display case under the window and spear the creature straight through its middle with the oversized sword.

An enraged shriek tore through the place as the shadow creature, more wraith than beast, warped around the blade to launch at Pharaoh.

Together, they fell into one of the many rows of shelving; cracking bottles and quaking things littered the floor as Pharaoh threw the creature into an adjoining shelf.

The spear fell right through it as though it were no more than smoke and air. Still, he had felt the sturdiness of its presence when he'd tackled it against the glass cases on the side wall where helmets and glasses alike sat in orb-shaped protections.

I wonder what a blinding orb would do to a wraith?

Amid the scuffle, the shopkeeper calmly lowered the shades over the windows that framed either side of the front door. "I think this calls for a little more privacy…" If there was one thing the market enjoyed most, it was a good fight, and drawing a crowd to a shop full of volatile magic was the last thing she needed.

Pharaoh struggled to keep the shadow pinned as he freed a hand to reach into his cloak, only to find it empty.

Where is that necklace…

The shadow gave a wicked, airy chuckle as the dark items in the back corner rattled against their chains. It then hauled Pharaoh backward, knocking him into several small shelves of vials and pouches. He felt the crack of glass and the sizzle of wretched fluid soaking his cloak.

Twisting, he slammed the shadow to the ground and loosed the fasten of his cloak, freeing it from his body. When he threw the cloak off, Pharaoh looked at the back wall, as he dodged a blow from the shadow.

Weapons?

He knew people had turned to questionable means in the past to win the Red Game, but full-on weapons? In the shop that held the guide items, it was more of an oversized display than it was an actual store.

The shop owner stepped in then, but not in the way he expected. The bald woman, all elegant lines and demure presence, charged at him, a dark slash of paint across her eyes as she swung a large axe dangerously close to him.

Pharaoh's gaze flicked to the broken potion bottles overhead. At the front counter, he was sure she'd been doused in something that changed her into the angry warrior before him.

Pharaoh dodged one sweep of the axe, and it split the shelf to his left in half. A few steps backward and another swing. This time, she cracked a glowing orb; the light seeping out illuminated the hiding spot of the necklace that had slid out of his pocket and under one of the far shelves.

"There you are," Pharaoh grunted, planting a kick to the woman's chest after her third failed swing, sending her crashing against the counter, the axe clattering to the floor.

Brushing his thumb across a different series of charms, Pharaoh called his cloak forward, causing it to spring to life. Seizing up off the floor, it wrapped itself around the shop owner's head and kept her scrambling to remove the determined fabric.

He then ran toward the necklace but was buffered by the shadow, shoving him against a side window that didn't crack even under the immense force of them both. Pharaoh grabbed onto whatever he could and swung the shadow into a stack littered with more tomes and paper artifacts than he knew existed.

A red book, centered on the shelf, spread its pages wide and let out a deafening wail that had everyone present covering their ears. The shadow raised a transparent foot and kicked the book shut. Rolling to its feet, it came face to face with Pharaoh, who was ready and waiting, a dark, satisfied smirk on his face.

"Come here," he said with a crook of his finger.

The shadow wasn't looking at him. No, its dark and hollow unblinking gaze was set on the young woman in the street; her blonde hair draped under a thin, ornate scarf was a beacon in the nearly sunless avenue when an errant breeze ripped it off her head.

Something the shop owner said just before their fight broke out sparked in his mind.

It followed her in.

Pharaoh pushed off the shelf, leaving jars and bottles rattling as both he and the shadow bolted for the door. Leaping, Pharaoh tackled the shadow headlong into the doorway. The panel in the sole door of the shop rattled as they collided against the narrow frame, but again, the glass didn't shatter.

All of the external glass must be enchanted not to break.

"Why were you following her?" Pharaoh boomed as he wrapped the necklace around the hilt of the discarded sword, transforming the saber into a weapon crafted in pure light and using it to pin the shadow down against a tabletop display case. "What do you want with this year's Rebels?"

The creature screeched unintelligible fractures of sound in response.

Her face wiped clean from Pharaoh's temporarily animate cloak, the shop owner pulled out her emergency efforts and moved to subdue them both.

"Don't!" Pharaoh shouted too late. The shop owner's normally securing magic was deflected from the wraith, sending them both flying back-ward.

The shadow was ripped from Pharaoh's grasp as he was sent careening through the air. He landed with an awkward roll, sliding to a miserable stop at the feet of none other than Copper James.

"No!" Pharaoh growled.

The shadow was nowhere to be seen.

Climbing to his feet, he made a mental note to talk to Akos about the event, but he had to first decide if he was going to incriminate himself by admitting his own presence in the shadow market.

"I'm going to regret you someday," he told the necklace as he quickly deposited it back into his cloak.

Chapter Twenty-Seven

Solaera in the Market

THE FURTHER COPPER WALKED through the market, the more she saw how the entire place was made of shadows. For every glowing sign and raging club, a dozen shadows were cast in every direction until the walls themselves crawled with their presence. Rounding a corner toward the tunnel they had entered, the shop appeared. But something different about the front-facing shop windows made her hesitate.

Are those…panels over the windows?

A piercing, fractured sound erupted from inside the shop. Copper covered her ears and dropped to her knees.

"Copper James. Do not go in that establishment!" The cloak warned, cocooning her in his invisibility.

"Don't!" A man could be heard shouting from inside the building.

The door flew off its hinges, and with it, a man. He was sent careening through the air and landed with an awkward roll. The door carried further, crashing into a stand on the other side of the street. The man, however, slid to a miserable stop at her feet.

"What are you doing?" Copper gasped as she burst from the cloak and appeared over him.

"Probably paying that off for a while." He grunted, pushing up on his elbows.

Copper instinctively touched his arm to assist him as he climbed to his feet. "It's just a door." She looked between him and the shop, realizing it was the same place of business that she'd come from earlier. "How much could it really cost?"

His face slackened as magical items slithered, crawled, and flew out of the open doorway. "Well, I'm gonna say it was pretty spendy if it kept all of those inside…"

"Oh." Copper realized what he meant. "It was enchanted."

"It was enchanted," he confirmed.

"Lovely," she chirped.

Palming a necklace, the man towered over her. All broad shoulders and golden skin, Copper realized then where she'd seen him before.

The performer from the tent…Pharaoh, she remembered the show he'd put on her first night in The Extravaganza.

And the partner her cloak insisted was dead.

He stared up at the stone pillars on either side of the shop and ran a thumb over something in his fist to the broken ends of a chain dangling from either side.

"If those items get free…" Copper started.

"Are you prepared to catch them?" He gave her a skeptical look before he ran back toward the shop to try and stop as many items as he could from escaping.

"You think I can't?" Copper ran right behind him, her cloak billowing in her wake. Numerous little items had escaped from the shop, all shimmying upward.

"Fine." His hair had broken free from its tether, forcing him to stop and retie it, revealing the shaved sides of his head once again. "How do you feel about heights?"

Copper laughed as she kicked off her shoes. "I once scaled a clock tower to steal the gem hidden in the face."

Pharaoh's crooked a skeptical brow at her as he planted a foot on the base of the first pedestal and watched her gently tuck a book behind a sign that leaned against the shop. "I thought you were supposed to be some infamous smuggler."

"Smuggler, thief. We all start in the same place." She hesitated with her cloak, unsure if someone would take him while she ascended the side of the building.

"Wait," the cloak told her, and before she understood why, he'd shifted into a short cape, freeing her to climb at will.

"Sometimes I find the items, and sometimes I move them for sale," Copper found footholds easily in the stone grooves. With each heave of her body upward, she collected wriggling feathers as they inched their way up the pillar and shoved them into her pocket.

Pharaoh leaned over the arch of the eaves, snatching a metal beetle with an aqua marina stone set in its back. "And you're proud of that?"

Copper crouched on the top of the second pedestal and made a show of considering his judgmental tone. "Should I not be?"

A winged scepter flew past Copper's head. It moved so quickly that she felt the brush of wind against her cheek but failed to grab hold of it.

Pharaoh leaped forward and snatched the royal piece out of the air before grabbing onto the ledge of the overhead sign. He swung there, item in hand, as his feet scrambled to find support.

"Stop flirting and get out of here," her cloak growled. "You're drawing too much attention to yourself!"

Copper glanced over her shoulder and noticed the crowd that was starting to gather. "Who do you think is drawing more attention, me or you?"

Pharaoh arched backward and curled forwards a few times until he got enough momentum to pull himself up and over onto the tip of the roof. "Me," he answered, a satisfied grin on his face.

Copper climbed up onto the roof and looked outward. In the time it took them to scale the front of the store, more items had escaped, and others had been taken.

"There's too many," Pharaoh growled.

"Stop!" Copper shouted at the people who began helping themselves, and while none of them paid her any mind, all of the items did as they were told.

Pharaoh squinted at Copper over his shoulder. "How did you…"

I don't know, was what she wanted to say. However, she looked at him, and something else took hold of her. "Not all of us can be the King of the Circus," she started to climb down. "But that doesn't mean I don't know how to chase what I want."

Pharaoh laughed, loud and genuine, then followed her down, his one arm full of the various items he'd gathered along the way.

#

The keeper stood inside the shop, scowling as she wielded a tiny, scarlet whistle. It made no audible sound to the human ear, but the whole market stirred. Every enchanted item strained against the pull of the sound, and those that belonged in the shop fled to the owner. This included the items Pharaoh and Copper collected.

Light seeped from Pharaoh's pocket, just a tiny amount at first, as it dripped into a puddle at their feet. It then swelled into an airy form that leaped and turned in a playful manner around Copper as she collected the book she'd set aside.

"Oh." She murmured her surprise. "Well, hello…" She winced a little when it wove in and around her hair before it pooled in the hollow of her collarbone.

"It won't hurt you." Pharaoh's lofty eyes betrayed his rigid stance. His voice was quiet as he watched the fractal of light thin and spread until it reached the book, healing it on contact.

"Oh…feel that," her cloak purred.

"I've never seen light magic up close before." Copper marveled at the little bud of light and the spread of warmth that heated her skin.

"It likes you." Pharaoh pointed out.

"It has good taste." She pretended to puff her chest out at him.

A small eruption of fireworks sprung up from the book's cover as it shifted into the image from Copper's card.

"My guide item," she inhaled the sweet scent of restorative magic.

"You," a large man with a dirty apron exited a nearby establishment and stared with the others who had gathered. He took several steps backward as though part of him couldn't believe his eyes, and the other part wanted to run.

The whole market began whispering.

Solaera.

Solaera.

Solaera.

"Don't," Pharaoh warned, putting his hand out, but it was too late.

"Solaera in the market!" The man cried, and the announcement halted everything in the shadow market.

People ran.

Windows slammed shut.

Vendors dropped drapes over their displays.

Copper stood there in disbelief. "What just happened?" she murmured, looking to Pharaoh. "Why did they call me a Solaera?"

That name was a position of reverence. A priestess to govern all magics.

Copper was a thief.

A smuggler.

The reason a man was dead.

She was not a Solaera.

Pharaoh bristled, his face darkening. "Look, kid. Whatever you're here to do…I can't help you."

"Then it's a good thing no one asked you," Copper retorted, shocked by his sudden change in demeanor.

Pharaoh sighed heavily through his nose. "Just be careful."

Then, he left her standing in the ghost town of the street, fog swirling around her legs and a book of magic in her hands.

"Copper James," her cloak finally spoke up. "I think it's time we take our leave."

Chapter Twenty-Eight

An Exchanging of Secrets

Raleigh spent his time in the fissure buying a few blades and various other weapons, as well as sticking his detective nose where it didn't belong. Finding his guide item, a compass of all things made him grateful he'd stocked up on weapons. Reviewing his card from night one, he recognized the emblem of a shady trading spot where he'd then navigated through an entire den of questionable individuals to steal the compass.

What does it say about me that everything I look for is always hidden in the worst parts of the Empire?

Raleigh then set out to collect items for Momma Lou that were fit more for a fairytale witch living in a stone cottage from some haunted wood, not a peddler woman in the market. What it came down to, though, was that he didn't ask questions when he handed over the suspicious shopping list to Momma Lou.

Spooky things for a spooky woman.

"Incredible!" She stuck her nose in the bag, eyeing each item with exuberance. "How?" She asked him with a note of wonder. "I've been trying to acquire some of these objects for decades, and you did this in one evening?"

Raleigh drew a breath through his teeth. "I can't tell you that."

The truth was that he simply had more valuable things to bargain with than she did.

Secrets.

Time.

Really, anything but a piece of his body or soul.

I didn't earn the title of Detective by sitting behind a desk. He'd been to more places and experienced more cultures than the average traveler. What he had to offer was of higher value than even the rarer objects she'd asked for.

She crooked a pencil-thin brow at him. "So what is it you want to know?"

"How is Cassian able to do all of this?" He held out a hand, referring to the circus as a whole.

Maybe a little too broad...

"Ask me a better question," she told him as she settled on a stool with a grunt, resting her cane over her lap.

Fair.

He tried again. "Are the wards on Cassian holding?"

"No."

Not a huge surprise, I guess. But why are you being so tight-lipped...

Raleigh drew a deep breath, the jasmine flowers in the corner almost overpowering the area. *Are you the reason I associate that smell with magic?*

"Is he at risk of escaping?"

"Isn't he always? Just how many questions do you think the list earned you?"

Oh, so I've struck a nerve. How close am I to one of your dirty secrets?

"More than you're willing to give, I'm sure."

Momma Lou pursed her lips. "Cassian is as confined as he was the day we jailed him. That being said, he has always had *tethers* to the outside world that enable him to accomplish certain things."

"Tethers that could allow him to host meetings with people?"

How would your knowing about Copper's meeting with Cassian hurt us? He weighed his options even after the words had come out of his mouth.

"Perhaps. If not in body, then maybe in spirit. Illusions of sorts?"

"He can't be at his full power yet, or he would have presented at the beginning of the game." Raleigh thought aloud.

"Or…he has a much flashier idea as to how to resurface to his adoring fans."

A Grand entrance would be his style.

Raleigh's stomach ached at the implications of it all. Not for himself, but at the lengths they all went to that might have been for nothing.

After all, confining the devil took more than petty parlor tricks.

And it had cost some of their group absolutely everything.

"I imagine it took quite a bit of power to pull back the curse enough to let us all in." Raleigh had hesitated at each border crossed, knowing there was a chance that if he set foot too close to the kingdom, the city, the circus, he might never leave.

"Rejoining the game was a stupid endeavor on your part if you value your freedom."

"Revenge?" Raleigh toyed with a plant using its stem to sword fight with his finger. "Seems like a difficult task to complete when you're not physically present, and the winner could…"

"Could…what?" Momma Lou taunted.

Raleigh blinked. "Nothing, because there is no prize that would stop him."

"Win your heart's greatest desire…" Momma Lou fanned out her hands, wiggling her fingers in mock enthusiasm.

"No one's greatest desire would be to stop him…"

"Except?" She led him to the finish line.

"Except Copper James."

But he presented himself to her. Practically dared her to play the game.

"None of us truly know the mind of the ringmaster. But he wants her here for a purpose. That you can be sure of."

Raleigh focused his stare on her then. "You know more than you're telling me."

"Don't I always? It's what keeps me *interesting*."

"Tell me, or you'll find yourself lacking the items you were so eager to receive." He gestured to the bag of goods he'd brought her.

"You wouldn't dare." She warned, and a wave of her cane had the bag leaping into a nearby trunk that sealed itself.

"Wouldn't I?" Raleigh felt the silver in his eyes flare. "Isn't that why you asked so much of me in the first place?" He whispered her proper name in her ear, and the old woman's wrinkled face fell, her eyes widening.

She gripped his arm, stumbling to her feet as she searched his eyes for some unspoken marker. "*How?*"

"You sent me into the fissure of the ancients. Did you think your secrets would be kept for eternity?" He purred back at her.

Momma Lou took a full step back, looking him over with disgust. "Leave this place at once!" She flicked two fingers, and the curtain opened. "Out!"

"Always a pleasure, Lou." Raleigh tipped an imaginary hat in her direction.

"Oh, how you pride yourself, knowing the business of others," the old woman griped. Her deepest secret had been stripped bare for the light of day in the exchange of a single breath. "You'll keep what you know to yourself if you know what's good for you, boy."

"Doesn't bother you," Raleigh asked. "Stealing the souls of the young? Knowing what you do. Knowing their fate?"

"You are not what I would consider young."

"I was speaking of Copper James and her ward."

"No," Momma Lou snapped, her eyes lit up with the molten light of mischief that had witnessed the troubles of a thousand lifetimes. "I do not regret much, especially not that," she admitted with a wicked, haggard smile. "But, I would not tempt fate so blatantly, Mr. Danger, as to tell anyone my secret."

"Detective Danger, Ma'am," he corrected, giving her a mocking, two-finger salute, before pulling the hood over his unruly curls and blending seamlessly into the crowd. "Now, if you don't mind…I have a show to catch."

CHAPTER TWENTY-NINE

The Unquenched Soul

"Back so soon?" Ophelia remarked from the doorway of Ezlyn's suite.

Ezlyn hugged her knees. There, she soaked in the glamorous light of the circus as it washed over her from where she sat on her balcony floor. She did not bother to look at Ophelia when she entered. "Where else would I be?"

"Out playing your part in the game."

"To what…find my guide item?" Ezlyn raised her hand, clutching her broken necklace.

"Where did you get that?" Ophelia frowned and took a few steps closer to get a better look. "And what makes you think that's your guide item?"

Ezlyn fished a card out of her pocket and flicked it at Ophelia's feet. "See for yourself…"

Ophelia read the card. The image painted there melted into a picture of the necklace. The ink burned her fingers, forcing her to drop it with a hiss.

"It's cute that you think you have any control over this city and its events." Ezlyn tucked her chin into the fold over her elbow. "Your game is flawed."

"Just because your first few days have been easy doesn't mean…"

"Pharaoh brought that to me." Ezlyn glared over the upper curve of her right wing. "He found me in the market and sent me back here. I don't know where he found it, but he protected me from the market."

Ophelia clenched her jaw.

Ezlyn rose to her feet in a fluid movement; her wings effortlessly lifted her until her feet touched the floor. The sapphire tones in her silk tank top and matching pants caught the lights of the city in waves of lemon and orange that shimmered across the material. "Even your performers are having issues following the rules this year."

"He shouldn't have done that," Ophelia stated, her words as calm as she could manage.

"I thought the ringmaster wasn't supposed to meet privately with Rebels?" Ezlyn crossed her arms, her wings flared with her words. "You should probably leave."

Ophelia stared at Ezlyn. On one hand, she was right. The rules were clear regarding interference, but this wasn't a normal game either.

And Ezlyn wasn't a normal Rebel.

"You're…dismissing me?" Ophelia chirped at the teenager's audacity.

"It's for the good of the company," Ezlyn repeated Ophelia's excuse of choice back at her. Every decision she made, especially when it came to Ezlyn and the limitations she put on her, was 'for the good of the company.'

"Be careful, Ezlyn," Ophelia warned. "The other powers at play will not be so forgiving of your attitude as I am."

"I'm counting on it," Ezlyn sneered.

Playing the game, she was taking control of her life for the first time since she experienced the curse of the circus firsthand.

"We've been stuck here for ten years," Ezlyn spoke up when Ophelia moved to leave. "I'm playing this game to break the curse keeping us here since the rest of you have done little more than sit on your hands."

Her mother was missing.

Cassian had abandoned them.

It was time to figure out how to escape Cape Solaera for good.

CHAPTER THIRTY

Saucy Serenades

I t was two hours from sunset by the time Copper woke. As the city lights illuminated the open windows on the opposite end of the open-concept living space, she walked down the narrow spiral steps from the upper level of the loft.

Not yet, she thought as she averted her eyes from the cloak. She needed a few minutes of waking peace before resuming her game.

On the lower level, she found a buffet had been soundlessly delivered.

That or I slept like the dead.

"Oh, you're still warm," she groaned at the cardamom roll in her hand.

Copper took a long moment to watch in silent deliberation as Hollis slept strewn across a series of cushions.

She should probably start waking up to eat.

But there was a warming plate keeping everything from growing cold. And there was something about studying her guide item without a million questions being asked drew Copper towards letting Hollis sleep.

But first, she grabbed her cloak.

Copper had tried and failed to access the book's magic upon completing last night's event. So, she'd temporarily tucked it into a trunk on the lower level and gone to sleep. Situated amongst the hand-stitched folds of a patchwork quilt, the large book was so heavy it created a temporary dent in the folds of fabric. Even though the magic in the market had healed the tome, it still echoed with the voices of a thousand lifetimes.

Copper grimaced, and that was the first time she had noticed that she didn't miss being able to hear magical items.

But why can I hear you now when everything else has been silent these last few days?

"Good evening, Copper James." The cloak greeted her.

"Good evening," she answered. Something about their time in the Rebel Market had subdued the surly attitude from the cloak. She wasn't sure how long that would last. For the time being, she capitalized on his helpfulness.

"The Tome of Fable is a myth." She told the cloak. "Isn't it?"

"In some ways, yes. The book existed long before the Red Game started, and it was rumored to be enchanted with the soul of a past lover of the Grand ringmaster himself."

"Is Cassian's lover really trapped inside?"

"No."

"So it's just a book?" Copper asked as she laid it out on a low table.

The book growled in response.

Drawing her legs underneath her, Copper sat straight-backed and wide-eyed as she stared at the book.

I miss the good old days when books were just books and plants didn't try to eat me.

"It is not *just* anything." The cloak corrected.

"Well, what am I supposed to do with it?"

The words on the cover shifted before her eyes, spelling out the greeting: *Hello, Addy.*

"I remember you," he answered. This time, his words were directed at the book.

"Addy," Copper read the word aloud. "That's what the cloak of Shiloh Anora called you too. Is that your name?"

"My name is not one easily spoken in your language. I was called Adrastos by the mortals of my more…corporeal era."

"Where did you come from?" Copper asked quietly.

"That is not important." He answered, a stern clip to his words.

"Well then, what should I call you?"

A hefty sigh followed that question. "Addy will do."

"All right, Addy. How does this guide item work?" Using the same finger as before to trace the curvature of the book's spine, Copper admired each glossy fastener and glimmering bracket that kept the lid shut.

"Wait!" He warned.

When she finally released the last shackle, the book lifted into the air, black and white pages sprawling sharp edges as golden lettering arched off the pages.

Adrastos let out a savage growl, and the book fell dormant onto the table once more.

"You know," Copper sat back, unphased. "I can't say I wouldn't react the same way after what you've clearly been through."

"Wild magic does as it pleases," her cloak muttered. "There should be a bracelet of sorts. Gently try to remove one of the brackets encasing the spine."

Copper did as she was told until one of the many brackets finally peeled away. The book shimmied with the sensation, and Copper slipped the silver cuff over her right wrist. There was a bite of magic as it adhered to her skin.

Bracing a hand on either side of the small table, she frowned. "Well?" Copper asked expectantly, but the tome didn't move.

"Do you expect it to hop on one leg?"

"No, but I mean…it greeted you?" Copper reasoned.

"Try again," Addy coaxed.

Copper took a fortifying breath and turned the book over on the table to see if she'd missed another hidden mechanism. It was still a heavy book when she turned it back, but the cover had changed once again. This time it was the color of burnt auburn and deep rose with various gears and raised cursive text all jumbled together.

Oh. Well, that's different…

A few pops and clicks reverberated under the cover. Copper leaned forward as each letter tumbled down the left side of the cover.

Play fearlessly, it spelled out in gear-shaped letters as chains roped their way across from the top left of the book, swirling around into an old time-piece before slipping under the fasten that held it in place. The text on her bracelet warmed, glowing with a blue light.

She peeled the front cover open. Luscious pages fluttered under her touch. The first page was blank. As was the second, but on the third, flourishes seeped onto the page as though they were freshly inked in that moment.

Welcome.

It greeted her with a delicate, swirling font.

Play fearlessly.

It continued.

For only the bravest of souls will win…

"I've read all this before…"

"Turn the page," Addy told her.

"Oh." She was intensely focused on the page before her.

Are you ready to play?

The words scrawled themselves across the center of the next page.

"Yes." Copper felt breathless as she engaged with yet another sort of strange magic.

Her palms were clammy as dozens of pages flipped themselves sequentially until the tome fell halfway open and a map was presented to them.

Cape Solaera was drawn on yellowing paper with dark ink and splashes of vibrant colors. Every tent stood with its own raised peaks outlined in the color they were crafted. One by one, small sets of footprints led from their tent to somewhere she had not been before.

"I don't mean to interrupt…" Tanith's voice came from the doorway.

"Wait…" Addy tried, but Copper flipped the hood off her head and shut the book.

"No…no, come in." Copper drug a trunk half full of her own items over with her foot and shoved the book inside.

Copper rubbed the back of her neck, unable to stop her mind from wondering, if her guide was a magical book, what had everyone else discovered upon seeking out their own item?

"Oh, smell that!" Hollis Roux appeared and immediately stuffed her face with the first food she saw.

"Hello, hello!" Tanith began her usual setup. Her bright magenta hair was tied atop her head in a giant messy bun that leaned this way and that with her every move.

Copper hadn't paid much attention to Tanith the first few times she'd seen her, but the woman's lilting accent brought a sense of calm to their fitting sessions. There was something so disarming about Tanith and how her freckles dotting her cheeks and nose rose to line her eyes in dots of cinnamon and butterscotch. Her waif-like build and gentle demeanor made Copper feel almost foolish for being guarded.

"So, should we get your fitting started?" Tanith clapped her hands together in excitement.

Copper looked down at Hollis Roux's dirty hands and feet. "Maybe you should bathe first."

"But, I had a bath last week," Hollis protested.

"This…is going to be fun," Tanith said in a light, airy way.

Copped just shook her head, "You need to bathe."

"But I don't want to!" Hollis jumped to her feet.

"Tough," Tanith chirped, and without warning, she shoved Hollis into the bathing room to the right of the door and slammed it shut. She then refused to let go of the door knob until she heard the shower turn on before stepping aside.

"That…works." Copper shrugged with a laugh, but her mind kept returning to what the book held and the metal band dangling from her wrist.

It hadn't taken Hollis long, but once she was in the shower, several questionable sailing songs came echoing from the bathing room, making Copper cringe.

"IN THE OLD SHUDDERED HUBBARD'S WHERE I FOUND MY LOVER, THE MOST CURIOUS PIRATE AROUND!"

"You're *joking*," Copper whispered in pure mortification as Tanith measured her for future outfits.

"IN THE DEAD OF THE NIGHT, HE FOUND SUCH A FRIGHT, BOLD AND BRIGHT!"

"I heard she came from the Blue Giraffe," Tanith whispered. "Is that true?"

"WHEN MY OLD MAN SHOT HIM DEAD TO THE GROUND…"

Obviously. Copper thought, staring at the ceiling, her face heated in embarrassment.

During the third song, when she'd burst into a lyric about a busty barmaid and sweet summer nights turning into fall, Copper finally moved to put a stop to the serenades.

"I heard you had a run-in with The King of the Circus," Tanith mentioned Pharaoh with a wiggle of her fingers.

Copper halted. "What of it?"

"Nothing," Tanith cast her nosy gaze down at the rack of clothing, clearly pretending to still be working.

"How do you know about that?"

"Oh, girl…" Tanith swatted at Copper's knee. "There are viewing crystals everywhere! How do you think patrons watch the more dangerous parts of the game?"

Copper swallowed hard. "You're going to have to point these cameras out to me."

"Yep!" Tanith climbed to her feet in one fluid motion when she heard the water in the bathroom turn off. "I mean…you don't have to worry about changing. There aren't any in the living spaces…but pretty much everywhere else!"

Well, that would have been good to know a lot sooner…

Hollis came out in a towel, hair soaking wet, but the satisfied smirk on her face told Copper all she needed to know.

*You did that on purpose…*Copper marveled.

Every lewd lyric had been punishment for forcing her to shower.

When Tanith guided her to a private corner with a changing partition and a fresh stack of clothing, Hollis loudly announced from behind the striped room divider, "You're not going to make me wear outdoor feet, are you?"

"What?" Tanith laughed, craning her neck to listen, sure she'd misunderstood.

"What are outdoor feet?" Copper asked from where she stood on a circular platform before a mirror.

"Shoes," Hollis Roux spat out the word with a pretend gag.

Tanith quickly smothered a laugh with her hand.

"Yes, child," Copper answered dryly with a shake of her head. "You have to wear outside feet."

Hollis Roux was expressing her displeasure when a series of bells rang out over the city, drawing all of their attention and bringing her whine to an abrupt end.

It was rhythmic, yet haunting, the way the melody chimed in the distance. It immediately drew their evening to a close.

"What is that?" Hollis asked, coming out from behind the divider wearing the dress Tanith had brought, a small golden top hat decorated with red ruched fabric, and a round watch nestled on the inner curve of the brim.

Copper was immediately impressed when Hollis slipped on the matching boots without complaint.

"The ceremonial bells," Tanith said solemnly as she braided Hollis Roux's hair and secured it under her top hat. "The Red Game is about to start."

CHAPTER THIRTY-ONE

"Are You Ready for a Show?"

R ALEIGH'S CURIOSITY FREQUENTLY GOT the better of him.

Did he necessarily need to uncover the secrets within what he knew to be a cursed circus? Probably not. But the detective in him was dying to know how the Extravaganza continued on without the infusion of magic from Cassian September and his enchanted gemstone hummingbird.

Raleigh found his way back to the tourist strip of the Extravaganza. Remembering Xerxes strutting her way down the main fairway earlier that day and how she had encouraged him to take in one of her shows, he took her up on her offer.

The leading performers' dressing rooms were tucked away in secret alcoves and tent passages hidden in plain sight. Thanks to those canvas tunnels, a person could wander from one show to the next without ever setting foot outside. While they weren't easily found by those who were just passing through, if you knew where to look, the private sectors could be easily found.

Or, in Raleigh's case, if you knew who to follow.

Finding Xerxes wasn't hard. He followed the opulent line of partygoers dressed in a similar white-washed fashion of fabrics and jewels. The doorway was covered in a dense canopy of pearls and opal beads paired with little trinkets like feathers and other glittering objects. Parting the thick strands, he looked inside to find soft tulle draped from the top of the ceiling lining each wall only to pool on the floor.

Many intoxicated partygoers laughed and swayed as they carried on in the way those who take to the Extravaganza as a lifestyle often did. At the center of it, all was Xerxes perched atop an oversized, wingback chair.

Aloysius blinked briefly. The white fur from the chair was too similar to his own.

A pair of tipsy partygoers dressed in vibrant-colored outfits clung to either side of Raleigh.

"Detective Danger," one of them purred. "So nice of you to visit us!"

"Careful," the other interjected with a broad smile. "He might arrest us."

This is not what I came here for…but I'm not mad, Raleigh thought as they cooed and petted him, all while giggling at each other. This eventually drew Xerxes' attention, causing her to rise from her stool and invite him in.

"I thought I was the life of the party?" She announced a little too loudly, matching the tone of the group. There was a slight flush to her throat from whatever was in her silver cup.

"I thought I might find you in here somewhere," Raleigh walked over to her. "Is that a chipmoth chair?"

A crash and clatter in the corner, followed by more riotous laughter, distracted her momentarily. "It is!" she petted it lovingly. "But don't worry, your furry friend isn't one of them." She winked.

Aloysius tucked closely in the curve of Raleigh's neck.

"What brings you to my corner of the circus…'just' Raleigh," she teased him.

It hit him between the eyes then, glamor or no. The albino and the chipmoth.

"They say a jewel-faced Chipmoth as a pet brings good luck," she told him. "You're going to need all the luck you can get if you don't steer clear of Copper James and her fated path."

Raleigh faltered. The crone from The Avenue…the red powder…the luck of the jewel-faced chipmoth.

You… he gritted his teeth to keep from saying too much.

"I guess I didn't realize I needed a reason to come and say hello."

No matter where I go, there you are…even inside a cursed city?

"You liked something you saw then?" One of the girls who'd fawned over him crowed. "Is that it?"

Raleigh crooked a brow at Xerxes, ignoring the tittering of the others entirely. "How could I not?"

Xerxes playfully tipped her head to the side, her smile bright. "Go on."

Ever in need of reminding of your beauty? Is it because you know how fleeting your youth is?

"It's so effortless for you, being the star of the show, I mean. I'd love to watch if you're performing again soon?"

"Why not," Xerxes sauntered before him, looping a finger under the fabric of his vest to lead him forward.

Don't do that.

Without blinking, she removed her entire corset and tossed it aside. The smooth curves of her exposed torso taunted him with every movement.

"What?" Xerxes gave him a coy smile. "This is what you came here for, isn't it?" she asked him in an airy, almost innocent voice.

Raleigh looked away, back, then away again, unable to harness his surprised smile. "Honestly, it's really not."

That's right, play right into my hand. Tell me all your secrets.

Xerxes laughed, bright and bubbly. She'd abandoned the corset in favor of a high-collared blue tailcoat with Neon white stripes down the arms and a triangular arch across her lower back. A dozen or more white buttons lined the arch, her cuffs, and the deep V lined with sheer laces that closed just above her navel.

Raleigh blinked slowly, swallowing carefully before he met her gaze again. If she wanted to put on a show, so could he.

"Are you ready for a show?" She beamed under his attention.

"I think I just got one." Raleigh was still trying to pry his eyebrows from his hairline when she instructed him to go wait in the audience for the actual event to begin.

#

"Where are you going?" Raleigh half laughed when Aloysius soared up, and away the second he saw a cut in the canvas halls that led out to the open sky. "Coward!"

It's not like she would add you to her chair collection.

Raleigh was a little dazed when he wandered through the back halls, forgetting himself.

That was…unexpected.

It wasn't that he was disgusted by her presence, but that woman had been popping up his whole life; he almost always saw her coming.

Xerxes was new and exciting, old and familiar. He had better things to do, but there was something about her he just couldn't avoid.

Something disturbingly acute in the way that he knew better but just couldn't help himself.

"And where did you come from?" When Raleigh started paying attention to his surroundings a little closer, he realized that his chosen path should have led him to the main arena, not another tent door. He suspiciously eyed his surroundings, waiting for anything to spark recognition, but it was as though he'd walked into a completely different circus area.

"I'm getting too old for this," Raleigh grumbled.

Although his hair still had a luxurious sheen and his face bore no sign of the passage of time, he'd been around far longer than he cared to think about. The fact that magic was getting the upper hand on him simply by the distraction of a bare-breasted young woman was telltale enough that he needed to wrap things up before he made a mistake he couldn't easily undo.

Again.

"Come in." A voice called to him when Raleigh turned around to walk back the way he'd come.

Raleigh's eyes drew wide; the deep resonance of that voice was familiar in a way that made his bones feel brittle. Turning on his heel, Raleigh unthinkingly tightened his hands into fists as the curtain parted on its own to reveal a dark room.

"And if I don't?" Raleigh challenged, watching a glowing orb defy gravity, bopping up and down in the dark as though running back and forth over the same five knuckles.

The orb stopped, abruptly caged within the confines of a large fist, the overlapping fingers blocking out its light.

"It wasn't a request."

A floor light raised upward, casting Pharaoh in a dim backlighting. It didn't fully illuminate the isolated room, but it was enough for Raleigh to see that Pharaoh was seated behind a circular table.

"I thought you'd sworn off gambling," Raleigh stated idly, eyes sweeping the room as he tried to gauge how much trouble he was in.

Pharaoh leaned forward, resting his elbows on the green carpet of the table. "It's hard to pass up a sure thing," he spoke slowly, deliberately, watching Raleigh with a predator's gaze.

"Well, I'll let you get to that." Raleigh attempted to excuse himself, but when he turned his back on Pharaoh, he knew he'd made a mistake.

Pharaoh raised his hand, and the jacket Raleigh wore seized up. Stopping him midstep, it flung him back into one of the several chairs lining the outer ring of the table.

"Come, sit." Pharaoh leaned over Raleigh's chair, shoving him uncomfortably close to the edge, "Why don't you stay a while?"

Raleigh closed his eyes and bowed his head. "You know, I figured we'd cross paths eventually. You being a part of the show and all." He gestured blindly around the room.

"How did you end up in this game again, Detective Danger?"

"Call it morbid curiosity."

"I distinctly remember you being banished from these shores."

Raleigh's eyes flashed open. "Now, wait–"

Pharaoh dug his fists into Raleigh's collar. Pulling him up out of the chair, he slammed his back onto the table.

"What're you doing?" Raleigh protested until he was face to face with an amulet crafted in glowing sunstone and Pharaoh spreading one of Raleigh's eyes wide to stare into it, unblinking, as though waiting for a reaction.

"I'm not him." Raleigh shoved him.

By him, he meant Cassian, stealing faces and wandering among them without notice.

Pharaoh waited a few moments longer, but when Raleigh's eyes didn't react, he released him, albeit begrudgingly.

"You can understand why I…"

"Yeah," Raleigh dusted himself off.

"What're you doing here, Danger?"

Raleigh tucked the knowledge of the necklace into the back of his mind to potentially use as leverage later. "It's a long story," he weighed his following words carefully. "I could ask you the same question. I thought the Extravaganza was sealed?"

"Time's funny like that," Pharaoh glared at him. "You turn your back for a second, and the whole empire is in jeopardy."

"Look," Raleigh held up his hands when the jacket stiffened, keeping him from retreating further. "I tried to fix my mistakes."

None of your tricks are going to save you now. A miserable reality swept over him. Not with a magical powerhouse like Pharaoh standing before him.

"And where has that gotten any of us?" Pharaoh spread his arms out wide. "I've been trapped in this place for ten years along with the rest of the troupe, not knowing what's happened or who's even still alive!"

"They are," Raleigh cut in. "The ones who got out. They're alive. I made sure of it."

Pharaoh stopped talking, taking a long moment to process that. "How many?"

"Everyone. Last time I checked."

"How?" Pharaoh's voice took on a lethal calm. "I want answers."

"And I don't have them," Raleigh threw his hands up. "I have been everywhere and done everything I can to remedy this, and I just..." he shrugged. "I can't. Not without her."

Pharaoh began to pace. "Did she ever mention being here to you?"

"No." Raleigh rested his elbows on his knees, rubbing the back of his head.

"She's young, right?" Pharaoh copped a small smile, allowing a brief moment of weakness before an expression of uncertainty settled across his face.

"Very," Raleigh sighed, focusing on the far wall. "They both are."

"Almost too young for all of this. Everything that's about to happen."

"She's already survived worse," Raleigh pointed out. "So let's make sure the event is as painless as possible."

"I saw a shadow in the rebel market," Pharaoh confessed.

"When?"

"When you were there with her."

Raleigh opened his mouth to answer but paused, narrowing his eyes. "You're already following her," his voice held a hint of scandal. "The event doesn't even start for another–"

"I know when it starts," Pharaoh spoke over him. "You had your time, Danger. It's come and gone, and where you are now is a product of the decisions you made in days past. I refuse to lose any more of what I have because of you!"

Raleigh chose to remain silent.

"Fix this," Pharaoh urged. "Or I will hold you personally responsible if the entire empire burns."

Act III
Splendor & Vanity

Six little rebels all playing in a game...

What a successful hunt most of you enjoyed last evening! As I'm sure you noticed, there's much more than meets the eye when it comes to the treacherous Rebel Market and the rumors that surround it. Magic always requires a balance. Darkness comes with the light, and beauty shines through the most unexpected of resources.

Books, compasses, jewelry, weapons, and items of trickery. The show each of you put on in hunting down your guide items was reminiscent of any act within the circus. Such whimsy, such...splendor.

But too much of a good thing can ruin a show before it even begins. Arrogance and vanity have a way of tarnishing what would otherwise be a glittering display of suspense and wonder.

The so-called "King of the Circus" should know this well.

In order to advance to the next station in the game, a little self-reflection may be just what the ringmaster ordered.

Today's task holds a special place in Red Rebel's glass heart.

It's a shame that one of you won't get a chance to witness it.

Welcome to the Season of Shimmering Souls

Act III

The Grand Master of the Red Rebel Extravaganza

CHAPTER THIRTY-TWO

The Crystal Caverns

THE KNIGHT DID NOT arrive for night three of the game.

In the wake of Cassian's most recent letter, curious eyes scanned the arena for the seventh player as, one by one, the rebels lined up for Ophelia's instructions.

Why was it different for her? Copper noticed the one Ophelia had dubbed Fae and wondered what The Knights' absence meant. If the young woman with the lavender hair had been allowed to participate in night two, did that mean that a player could earn their way back into the game?

"The Knight is gone," Copper said to Addy.

"Indeed," his voice rumbled in response.

"What does that mean?" She squinted at the crystal cavern before them. "Does he watch from the sidelines? Was he expelled from the circus altogether, like some potential retaliation, sore loser clause?"

"I fear the consequences may be of a more malicious variety," Addy told her. "Do you not hear the magic of this place? The way they cry out in regards to the danger that waits here?"

No, she thought but didn't actually answer as the reality of her situation settled over her in a cruel realization. The magic of the Extravaganza *didn't* speak to her the way others did. *I wonder if Cassian did this or if it's just a trait of the Extravaganza?*

Blue hour struck with blinding force. The surge of magic could be seen from every angle of the shore. A shimmering wave started the second the sun was swallowed by the sea, and the sky took on a dusky hue between late afternoon and evening. The crystal cavern shone with fractals of residual light as, one by one, the Rebels arrived.

"It's hardly a national monument." Lady Illuminae sniffed.

"Be silent, you prissy buffoon," The Huntress, in her leather pants and near-transparent corset, growled.

"Tonight's event must be undertaken with the strictest of consideration." Ophelia waved her hand toward the blinding wall of stone behind her. "This hallowed cavern is where the millennium mirrors were crafted."

"Copper James," Addy spoke up. "The Millennium mirrors are not a toy to be played with. If they have brought you to this place, then you have traveled far beyond the shores of Cape Solaera...."

"Hmm?" Copper didn't dare speak where all her fellow Rebels could hear.

"When they had you pass through the canvass halls of the tent to access this place, it must have transported you to a different part of the Kingdom of Rovernaum. Listen. Do you hear the sea?"

Copper blinked, and the stony shore behind them faded away into a valley of lemon grass and purple mountainscapes. She blinked again, and the coast of Cape Solaera returned.

A devilish smirk parted Raleigh's lips when his gaze followed Copper's. Had he noticed the illusion as well? Or maybe it was the mention of what lurked behind the mirrors.

"Your reflection protects you from the shadows beyond," Ophelia explained.

I've seen a lot of shadow magic...but is that where they come from? The other side of the mirror? Copper looked beyond Ophelia to the glacial formation of crystalline walls before them.

"As the letter read, self-reflection will be key in advancing to tomorrow night." Pulling aside a curtain of hanging ivy, a glistening cavern of white crystal shone before them. "Advance through the crystal maze, find your markers from the guide item you retrieved from the Rebel Market, and navigate toward the exit."

Every Rebel visibly steeled themselves.

"But before you enter, we of the Extravaganza have provided you a grounding item of sorts." Ophelia held up a hand, and six flowers bloomed before their eyes. Giant petals unfolded before each player, and from them, their guide items sat on pedestals crafted from large stems. For Copper, a surprised Hollis Roux blinked at the light as she held tightly to The Tome of Fable.

"Now that's what I call a ride!" Hollis Roux hopped down and strolled toward Copper.

"Something is not right here," Addy grumbled, but even he couldn't pinpoint the cause of his suspicions.

"How did you get here?" Copper asked her quietly, her eyes wide.

Aloysius grunted and squealed as he flitted over to Raleigh with a silver compass clutched in his hands.

"No idea," Hollis shrugged, turning to face the others as they collected their items; she dusted off her hands. "Well, let's get started!"

One by one, the Rebels entered the white crystal caverns with their companions or items.

"What good is that book going to do? It didn't work last night." Hollis waited impatiently as she handed over the book. "I mean… I'm good at mazes, but this is probably magic so…"

"Ask The Tome of Fable specific questions," Addy suggested. "Now that you wear the binding bracelet, it should be much more agreeable."

"Let's…try again." Copper palmed the heavy tome. "Show me the white crystal caverns of Rovernaum."

A glittering, luminescent page unfurled before them, spilling a map off the page. Straining to see, Hollis read the inscription aloud.

"The white crystal cavern harbors many ancient artifacts and is the birthplace of the millennium mirrors. This maze of mirrors can hold great riches for those brave enough to enter. Avoid being tempted by your own magic-enriched reflection, or suffer the consequences."

"Lovely," Copper muttered, having had her fill of magical mirrors to last a lifetime.

Hollis fell off her tippy toes with a brief stumble. "I don't get it. How is this supposed to be hard?"

"I'm sure we'll find out," Copper answered with a false note of levity. "Stay close."

Hollis walked ahead of Copper anyway and right into the nearest pane of glass. "Ow," she rubbed her smarting face.

"I've never liked children," Addy said with an exasperated sigh.

"You've never been in a maze of mirrors at a carnival before have you?"

Hollis rapidly blinked, clearing the tears that stung her eyes. "No."

The glittering cavern reflected everything and nothing at the same time. It was a natural hall of mirrors, and for some unspeakable reason, Copper felt her skin crawl at every turn.

"The pirates used to tell all kinds of stories, you know…back when I was little…"

Copper smiled to herself. "Because you're old now?"

Hollis Roux rolled her eyes. "One was a legend that said if you looked long enough at your own reflection in the right mirror, it would turn into something else."

"I've heard that one before. I've just never come across a millennium mirror before, so I didn't put much thought into it." Copper grabbed Hollis Roux's forehead just before she walked right into a crystal panel.

"What? I saw it!"

"Mm," Copper hummed in disbelief. "Keep your eyes down, and you should be able to see the edges of each turn better."

Copper glanced up, and for the briefest of moments, she saw what the warnings meant. There was a haziness in the foreground of her reflection. It wasn't the reflection itself that would cause them harm, but the shadows behind the mirror.

The things that lived between.

"This way!" Hollis charged forward without warning, only to collide face-first into another thin crystal panel, this time with a resounding thud.

Copper stifled a laugh as the Tome of Fable flew up on its haunches, expressing its annoyance over Hollis repeatedly running blindly into her reflection. Judging by the distant rattle of the glass walls, many others were doing the same.

"Concussions," Copper shook her head. "Concussions everywhere…"

"Copper James, you need to…" A choked sound came from the cloak. "Focus…" he ground out.

Then, he went silent.

And Copper made the mistake of looking at herself in the glassy surface of the cavern. Her face was the same, but she was older, with a muscular build to her body that she knew took years of work. Instead of her warm brown eyes, golden irises stared back at her.

"Who are you?" The reflection mouthed, the soundless question resonated so profoundly with her that for a brief moment, Copper's hand slowly came to her mouth as though the taste of the words were still on her lips.

The hoop in Copper's ear burned red hot, having slowly heated since her eyes settled on the panel, but it took an advanced level of heat for Copper to be pulled from the enchantment. With a hiss of pain, Copper's head jerked to the side, her hand instinctively coming to her ear, only to burn the upper swell of her palm.

Copper was startled to find Hollis Roux missing.

"Hollis?" Copper's voice echoed, even as she drew nearer by the second.

"Here," Hollis waved when Copper came into view.

"We enter a cavern marked with warnings, and you wandered off that quickly?"

Hollis looked at her like she was stupid. "You wandered away from me." She pointed at the painted pebbles that lined their path, and the darker stone one Copper had just exited.

"No…I," Copper hesitated. "I didn't move?"

"Yeah, you did," Hollis said. "All right, Mr. Book, where to now?"

Copper glanced over her shoulder then, a sickly hue gathering in the crystal panels in a way that made her stomach churn. "Let's keep moving."

Which would you prefer?

The book asked, presenting a decision map with three options. The first was splendor, decorated with a top hat and glittering stars. The second was cut paired with a sharp edges gem, and the third was clarity surrounded by a dozen or more arrows.

Copper blinked slowly, perpetually looking backward as the light from the entrance succumbed to blackness. "Hollis," she murmured as the girl prattled on about what the options could mean. "Just…pick one," she added breathlessly, knowing that sort of darkness all too well.

"Why?" Hollis snapped around, seeing nothing wrong with where they were.

"Clarity," Copper half shouted at the book, and a colored stone formation was presented on the following pages.

"Why are you?" Hollis tried to ask, but Copper suddenly urged her forward.

"Go." The whispers of the shadows begin to rake at her mind. "Go!" she shouted and ran toward the periwinkle stones.

The horror of the prison floor flooded the crystal cavern as they ran. Hollis, wide-eyed and confused, tripped over an unseen obstacle, dropping the book. Copper stooped to pick her up.

Beware Cassian's doorway…Blood red ink warned in bold lettering.

A haunting howl, long and foreboding, echoed through the cavern then and for all the individual paths the rebels had taken, their voices raised in unison as the sound of shadow beasts filled the cavern.

"Run!" Copper screamed with a genuine tint of fear.

Hollis took off without question. "Come on!"

The dome pathways were lined with distorted versions of themselves. The further they went, winding around and over the crystal projections, the more warped the reflections became.

A jagged, crystal hand reached for Hollis Roux's ankle. Copper gasped, bringing her foot down; she shattered it. Hollis leaped backward, but Copper immediately urged her on, feeling the prickles of icy proximity at her neck.

The book fell open then; a picture of the vial Copper had been gifted at the ceremony.

"My necklace?" Copper gasped, quickly lifting Hollis over a high barrier.

Turning back, she instantly wished she hadn't when distorted glass figures came forward.

Copper snapped the cork off the vial around her throat with her teeth and flung the contents behind her in an arching motion. The tangle of screaming intermingled with the sound of acidic fluid popping and melting everything it touched.

Bounding over the barrier, Copper collided with Hollis, who stood on the ledge of a steep decline in the halls.

"Don't!" Hollis tried to warn, but it was too late.

Copper tripping over Hollis sent them all sliding down the winding glass slide. They landed in a dark antechamber. Their screams followed them when they slid to a stop on a dusty stone floor. The grating sound of the cavern shutting behind them without warning was nearly lost on them. Copper lay flat on the floor, panting with the rush of it all, watching Hollis scoot away with giant eyes and trembling hands.

"That would've been the best slide ever if we didn't almost die just now." Hollis said matter-of-factly.

Copper folded her arms over her head, trying to catch her breath as the cuts on her body from the rough crystal descent began to ooze through her clothing. "Where are we?"

"I've…seen this before," Hollis did a quick circle around the room.

"You have?"

"Well, sort of?" Hollis answered. "There's a painting like this near the exit in the hall of mirrors in the fairway."

Copper opened the tome after climbing to her feet. Every item had a name and a dedicated page of images and descriptions. The book repeatedly flipped between a black stone with golden symbols and a green stone with a key in the middle. "One of these should be the item to bring us back?"

Copper felt a sting in her palm. The brand from the Oddity Shop glowed red hot. She hissed in response to the sudden pain as a single drop of her blood hit the floor.

The Oddity Shop? Here?

"Right," Hollis planted her hands on her nearly non-existent hips and frowned at the ancient-looking items. "Eenie, meanie, minie…this one!" Hollis jumped forward and grabbed the gem with the key.

"No!" Copper grabbed her arm just as the wall opened up and swallowed them whole.

Chapter Thirty-Three

Sinister Designs

THE CAVERN CONSUMED ALL.

And it happened faster than any of the remaining Rebels could have imagined.

One moment, Copper and Hollis stood in fractured images adjacent to Raleigh's, and the next, they were gone.

This is...bad. Raleigh's muscles tensed as a looming presence closed in around him.

A hand gripped his collar. Jerking forward, he failed to break free and was hauled into a side cavern.

"Still afraid of the dark, Raleigh?" A male voice breathed against the shell of his ear. "That's what you call yourself these days, isn't it?"

Raleigh shoved the oversized hands off him and whirled on a face he didn't think he'd ever have the misfortune of seeing again.

"August?" Raleigh grimaced.

The King of Rovernaum stood before him with a wicked sneer, his body shimmering with the outline of a magic Raleigh had only mastered once. The pain had been unbearable, and it wasn't something he'd ever wanted to try again. A silver circlet placed over his scarlet hair, the strong lines of August's body prowled forward until Raleigh realized that August wasn't *in* the crystal, but part of it? Moving, breathing crystal shards, a projection of himself there, but also not.

Why are you here?

Raleigh reached his hand out and felt the crystal wall between them.

"You…brought her…here," August accused, tan leather gloves wrapped around his trembling fists.

The walls began to bleed, and August shuddered. The emerald garment, a piece Raleigh recognized as The Cloak of Shiloh Anora, hung freely over his shoulders and wrapped around his chest, manifesting silver brackets over his breastbone as though it could hold him together—keep him from breaking under the weight of the magic in the cavern.

"Stop this," Raleigh's eyes widened. "You'll kill yourself over something you can't change. I'm here. Let me figure this out!"

Bolts of red spider-webbed across the ground and then quickly outward.

Darkness had swarmed the tunnels, forcing each Rebel further into the crystalline cavern.

That's when the screaming started.

"The council…called me forward," August tried to explain, but the pain wracked his body; losing his footing, he staggered.

"Magnificent, isn't it?" Tirzah's voice echoed off the walls.

Both men turned their attention to the darkness taking the shape of a woman. One that both, unfortunately, knew too well.

Tirzah was what happened when Raleigh had subverted death. She was the ghost of his past that he couldn't shake. She was the last twisted peace of magic that haunted him in his weakest moments.

Some people had personal demons; Raleigh had Tirzah.

"Leave us, witch," August snarled, his form fracturing across the different cuts in the crystal wall until he was one panel away from her.

Tirzah moved just as fast, if not faster, liquid night staining the glistening cavern walls. "Where's the fun in that, Majesty?" she purred, and the snarl that ripped from August's throat told Raleigh she'd referenced something important. Something personal that even he didn't know about.

"You know, I was just thinking, 'What would make this awful situation worse?' And there you are." Raleigh drew her attention toward himself.

"What do you fear, Detective Danger?" she asked, slinking toward him even as August brought forward a wooden staff. The polished wood shone with forest charms and other tokens from his kingdom.

Powerful. He's so powerful, and even his magic couldn't keep Cassian at bay. Raleigh's skin crawled with the reminder of just how much trouble they were in.

"What do I fear?" Raleigh gave a bitter laugh as he eyed the spot where Copper had been, not bothering to look when August cast Tirzah and her shadows out of the cavern with the blinding sort of sunlight that peeked through the canopy of thick tree covers. The kind of light that warmed streams and dotted well-worn hiking paths. The scent of rain-washed pine and bonfires left in his wake, blotting out the rotting death Tirzah always seemed to summon.

When Raleigh sat up, having been thrown by the burst of power, he was alone. But her question still remained. "Not a lot," he answered. Because it was true. He had fought and lived and loved, and there were only a handful of fears he could not overcome.

But losing Copper again? Potentially for good?

That was very near the top of his list.

Chapter Thirty-Four

Child of the Void

Ezlyn could taste the tang of magic when she walked up to the crystal cavern. She'd mistakenly believed she could avoid touching the cursed stone by gently flapping her new wings. She hadn't mastered actually flying with them, but she could muster a few minutes of hovering.

Come on, work with me.

Her secondary guide item, a ring on her finger, burned hot with each turn she took. At first, she thought it was bringing her closer to the end of the maze. She found her strength faltering and her mind growing cloudy.

Then, the darkness consumed her.

Ezlyn's head lolled when she woke amongst the clouds.

Weightless and burning, her whole body felt drugged. Arching her back, she struggled to pull herself upright. Coming to the realization that she'd been propped up, Ezlyn opened her eyes, lazy and unfocused, and saw the gleaming palace from her dreams.

The cold stones from the northern Kingdom of Swynnhaven.

"You're awake," a feminine voice echoed, both near and far.

Ezlyn rubbed the soft tips of her fingers over the side of her scalp, creating tiny texture waves in her short, lavender hair when her hand retreated, needing it for balance, as she quickly found out.

"Where am I?" Her words came out hoarse.

"Nowhere in particular." The voice sounded much closer this time.

Ezlyn lifted her head and was met with the vision of someone that could only be described as the physical embodiment of time. Standing beneath a white-flowered tree that had been strung with pieces of colored glass and ornate timepieces hanging from its branches, the woman beheld her with a worn sort of reverence.

She was absolutely radiant. Her entire presence was so fluid, with platinum hair that also shone like the purest beam of the sun. Her contemplative, crystal eyes were as blue as the sky. Air flowed through the billowing folds of her gown. There was an illusion of an hourglass set against the curves of her torso, with a fringe of clock hands lining the scoop of her neckline and trailing down the cinched circle of her waist.

"You have…wings." Ezlyn gulped, the familiar silhouette gliding along her back.

"Time flies." Her words were light, airy.

"How did I get h—" Ezlyn tried to stand. "Is this…some kind of test?

"Unfortunately, you don't have any time left, child of the void." The woman's face turned stony, like the cruel mistress that she was. "Everything will fall into ruin if you don't *wake up*."

The brilliant aesthetic collapsed with jarring force into absolute chaos. Before her, the once glittering stone palace was set ablaze; atop it was a woman with dark cherry hair. Birds of fire burned overhead and rained destruction wherever they went.

"Ezlyn!" Her mother's voice rang out clear and grieved, trapped in the capital city's foothills. "You have to wake up! You have to find—"

"No!" Ezlyn found herself alone then, her mother and her warning swallowed up as the world burned up.

Ezlyn screamed her way into consciousness and woke to a strong arm holding her tight. Her wings flared as her need to escape overpowered any other senses.

Her mother's face had melted.

The scent of burning flesh still lingered as Ezlyn kicked and screamed.

"It *burns*!" Ezlyn sobbed. "Everything…oh, it burns!"

"Stop, Ezlyn!" A familiar voice tried to reason with her. "It's ok. It's over!"

Her hands shook, and her back arched as she struggled away from the crystal that had made up the stone palace. It was everywhere all at once.

The walls were closing in around her.

"Look. At. Me!"

Ezlyn let out another panicked scream. Sweat beaded on her brow as she tried to understand what had happened.

"Ezlyn!" Akos forced her to face him. "It's all right. I'm here. It's only me."

"I need to get out!" She pushed away from him and rolled to her feet.

"Then let's get out," Akos gently guided her toward the lights shining into the tunnels.

Emerging from the path she had taken into the cavern, Ezlyn stepped out into the night and found most of the Rebels scattered about the entrance.

What…happened?

Some cried, others rocked, and even Detective Danger sat off to the side, staring into the abyss.

One thing was clear.

No one had been left untouched by the wicked magic inside the cavern.

"It was so real." She stumbled a little, and Akos was there to support her in more ways than one. "My mother," she gripped the front of his shirt with both fists as sweat dribbled down her neck. "It was real."

CHAPTER THIRTY-FIVE

The Silent Partner

"The heir of Keskairah is dead." The empress had spoken from her elevated throne, giving her a note of superiority amongst the council. Her scarlet hair had flowed over silk-robed shoulders as her piercing emerald eyes had searched Copper's face for something; whether that was guilt or truth had yet to be seen.

Six cloaked figures of the council bore witness to the event, three sitting to both the left and right of the empress in their respective thrones of notably lesser status. Each one had cast their judging, unseen glares over Copper because the heir of Keskairah had been murdered.

"Your necklace," Copper murmured absentmindedly.

The empress bristled, her hand going to her covered neckline, failing to land upon a crucial item to her reign. "What of it?"

Copper sat back on her legs, the shackles binding her wrists clanking as her back straightened. "What happened to it?"

A rage lit in the eyes of the empress that caused a palpable shift in the room. Maybe it was the reckless abandon that came with Copper James repeatedly telling herself that she didn't care where her life landed next or if it ended right there, but that fiery gaze burning a proverbial hole right through her stirred something in Copper that should have silenced all others.

Then again, she wasn't all others.

But she was in trouble.

And this was her way out.

"Oh. You lost it," Copper accused the empress in a scandalized whisper. A look of wild abandon illuminated her gaunt features as she tipped her head back and laughed at the ruler's shocked silence.

The room drew pin-drop silent as Copper laughed and laughed, one lung full after another, tears streaming down her face. Part of it was an act. A simple tactic to unnerve the council, but part of her needed the release. The trauma of what she had experienced during the murder of the heir had swelled in her, drawing an invisible, emotional cord taut until finally, somewhere deep inside, it snapped because she'd found her way out.

She could escape and live to see another day.

All she had to do was wait.

So, Copper planted her palms on the cool floor as she leaned forward, squinting against the sunlight as she did. "Can you even rule without it?"

"End her then and let's be done with this," The empress said flatly, preparing to exit the temple without another word.

Copper sat back in surprise, drawing her bound hands against her chest. "You would kill me over…" She looked at the mural and back to the empress, her eyes skimming over all the different colored robes of the council in between. "I didn't kill the heir of Keskairah any more than you did," Copper blurted when the gravity of the situation settled over her.

The empress stood with her back to Copper, the sharp line of her jaw visible when she craned her head to speak. "I would kill you to satisfy a blood debt that you left in your wake when you abandoned the body of the heir of Keskairah in the capital city of Skyecross."

"Never mind the fact that you just laughed in the face of the empress," a smooth male voice came from under one of the hooded figures.

"For what purpose should I let you live?" the empress challenged.

Copper blinked slowly.

Her gaze settled on a random design in the floor before her.

What reason did you give a supreme ruler to allow you to live when any one of your valuable accomplishments was undoubtedly against the law. The laws the empress herself had set and expected all upstanding citizens of the empire to uphold.

Admitting to them would certainly earn her an equal death sentence to the one she was already facing.

"The imperial ruler of the greatest empire the world has ever seen would never be so irresponsible as to lose such a sacred artifact," A fourth council member snarled. "The very idea that this…this unsanctimonious rabble would even propose such a thing if it were truly missing not only shows her true character but also reveals…" he blustered on long after Copper stopped listening.

There was a flash of something on the empress' face, just for a moment, but the way she gripped the ornate ends of either armrest of her throne told Copper everything she needed to know.

"Leave us," the empress snapped, cutting off the ranting council member, and punctuated the order by flinging her hand in the air in dismissal.

Every council member turned in unison to face her then, and it was this wordless accusation that undid the gravity of their brief reign over the direction of the life of Copper James.

"I will not tolerate this sort of insolence in the sacred temple of the Solaera," she instructed through grit teeth. "Shepherd blessed or not, you will not survive such reckless accusations."

With the implication that gruesome punishment was about to be executed, the six council members exited the room, the large double doors echoing in the silence left in their wake.

It wasn't that they didn't need to bear witness to what was supposedly about to happen; it was for their own safety that they vacated the ancient, makeshift throne room, speaking to the raw power that lived inside the young empress.

"Scream," she ordered in a low voice when it was just the two of them.

Copper straightened in confusion, her face asking the question her words did not.

"If you want to leave this room alive…then my council needs to believe that you are in fear of losing your life in their absence," she explained very slowly.

"Should I be afraid?" Copper verbally taunted, even as she glanced over her shoulder at the sealed door, realizing then that the empress was not above a shady deal.

"Tell me, Ms. James…" The empress made a show of pondering her words carefully. "Are you as good at what you do as the rumors suggest?"

Copper straightened, "I suppose that depends on who you ask."

"Can you find my amulet?" The empress challenged.

Copper looked over her shoulder at the giant door standing between her and the council who would have her dead before the sun crested the majestic mountains of old. Glancing at the mural and the famous amulet, she inclined her head toward the empress in recognition.

"I can," she assured her.

The empress nodded slowly. "Then let's play a game of sorts."

"A…game," Copper repeated, not hiding her hesitance.

The empress leaned forward then, looking straight into Copper's face. "Find my amulet, discreetly return it to me, and we'll see what we can do about this little situation of yours."

Copper chuffed a laugh. "You're going to have to be much more specific about that deal you're offering."

The empress drummed her fingers against the armrest of her throne, weighing the implications of her essentially freeing the smuggler in contrast with someone eventually discovering that she no longer had her sacred amulet.

"What is it that you want?"

Copper stared flatly at her, raising her bound hands. "Take a guess."

"Your freedom?"

"I want to be left alone. I didn't kill the heir." She swallowed hard. "And I don't want to be looking over my shoulder for the rest of my life."

"That's a tall order, making someone as known as you simply disappear.

"So is finding your amulet," Copper answered sharply. "I'm sure you can figure something out. Your amulet in exchange for my slate being wiped clean."

The empress idly picked an imaginary piece of lint from her robes as she considered the deal. "I suppose neither of us have any choice, do we?"

Copper raised her shackles again. "Seems to me that the ball is in your court, Majesty."

"Good," The empress nodded slowly, her unfocused gaze pinned to the far wall. "It's a deal, then."

Copper nodded her agreement, a wild glint in her eyes.

And then?

Copper screamed.

#

Copper woke with that same scream on her lips, but instead of kneeling before the empress, she was laid out in the middle of the Oddity Shop.

That tumble through the panel must've been harder than I thought… she told herself as she struggled to sit up. Putting a hand to her forehead, Copper was relieved to see a normal-looking, well-lit room around them. Watching Hollis lay flat out like a child-sized starfish. Rubbing her own knees as she looked around for any sign of the carnivorous plants that had plagued her during her last visit.

We need to get out of here…

"Why do we keep falling?" Hollis groaned as she slowly pushed up to a sitting position.

"Why would you do that?" From where she sat on the floor, Copper squinted at Hollis Roux and her ridiculously impulsive behavior.

"The wall ate us!" Hollis Roux's voice pitched a little higher in exasperation. "What was I supposed to do, say 'Hey Mr. Wall, could you not eat me the second I grabbed the…'"

Hollis paused.

Copper's gaze flattened.

"Oh. You meant, why did I grab the…"

"Yes," Copper covered her face with her hands. "I meant, why did you grab the item off the pedestal?"

Hollis scooted to a kneeling position. "You take so *long* to make decisions." She gave a spirited defense, drawing out the word 'long.'

"Because decisions have consequences," Copper argued in a harsh whisper, her gaze darting around the seemingly empty room.

Hollis climbed to her feet with a nonchalant shrug. "I mean, we're alive."

Copper gave a frustrated grunt, dragging Hollis across the wood floor to a chair in the middle of the room. "Just…stay…here."

"But where are you—" Hollis tried to argue.

"This?" Copper held up a finger. "This is a very old, very magical shop that. I don't know how we got here, and I don't know how we get back, but I need you to stay here and stay quiet while I go find out. Can you do that for me?"

Hollis crossed her arms and legs, angling away from Copper. "I'm not a baby," she mouthed off to her.

"Great." Copper gave her a rueful smile. "Prove that to me by staying put."

As much time as Copper had spent wandering the rooms of the Oddity shop the first time she'd been there, none of her surroundings seemed familiar.

"Addy, what can you tell me about…" she started to ask the surly cloak when she realized something.

It's gone. A cool prickle of anxiety rushed over her exposed skin when the cloak usually brushed against her arms.

"You won't find an Addy here, I'm afraid," a male voice called to her.

When she rounded the corner lined with stacks of history and folklore books and was surprised to find herself not near the front of the store but in a nook with an average-looking table and a man buried amongst them.

He wore silver-gray slacks and a light blue button-up with the sleeves rolled to his elbows. His brown hair was softly quaffed in front, appearing to fade into shorter lengths the closer it got to his neck. It was an insignificant fact, but his hair was the only visible part of his head as he was disguised by the craning of his neck and the unusually late books set in piles before him. He was tall, judging by the awkward set of his legs under the table and how he hunched over it.

"Hello?" Copper asked, and his handsome face immediately lifted to take her in, though it was partially shadowed by the imposing books.

"Hello," his greeting was much warmer, though there was a note of surprise.

Then, a flash of instances flooded Copper's mind, all of these unfamiliar faces in a dozen or more situations and places she hadn't seen or experienced before. Times and places, colors and smells blinded her for only a second, passing too fast for her to really hold onto any of them, but nevertheless, they had been there and gone, and she was left with a voracious sense of…longing?

In that brief distracting experience, the man had come to his feet and circled around the table. This lanky man with his broad shoulders stood before her, frowning as he beheld her torn clothing and series of slivers and cuts.

"What happened here?" he asked, taking her hand.

"You wouldn't believe me if I told you," she answered, watching his long fingers pull a small piece of crystal from her skin.

Moving to a shelf near the window to her left, the man pulled out a small, handheld chest and opened it on the table, retrieving a swatch of ivory bandage.

Copper's brows knit as she tried to place the man, watching as he hunched forward to examine the cut before placing the bandage. His hands stopped when he reached for her sleeve.

"May I?" he gestured toward the torn fabric.

"Oh, yes," she answered, a little surprised he'd asked.

Gingerly, he rolled up her sleeve to reveal her bleeding arm. "Are you in danger of something?" he asked gently, centering the bandage perfectly over the wound before securing it in place.

Copper raised her brows at the unexpected question. "No, it's just…" she cleared her throat, having decided to not mention how she knew a face she'd never seen, "the owners of this place don't exactly…care for me."

"Is that so?" he asked, carefully bandaging her arm, his warm brown eyes flicking up to her face every now and then.

"It's a long story," Copper groaned, noticing the soft shadow growing along his jawline.

"Well, I think we can ignore whatever they find wrong with you."

"If only it were that easy," Copper half laughed, watching as the bandage melted into her skin with a welcome warmth that rushed through her system, healing the rest of her wounds just as quickly. "Oh…wow. Thank you," she sighed gratefully.

"You're welcome, of course," he crossed his arms and leaned against the table. "And it is that easy. I own the biggest share in the Oddity Shop, so if I say your grievances are forgiven, it goes."

Copper gave him a skeptical look. "Oh? Are you Clarke or Wylder?" she asked, knowing from experience that he was neither.

The man chuckled, "Neither," he answered with a slight shake of his head. "Think of me as more of a…silent partner."

So silent that I've never heard of you? Copper eyed him, wondering if anything could truly be trusted in that place.

"Do you have a name?"

"I do."

Copper beheld him expectantly, but he didn't readily offer it.

"What do you know about Cassian's doorway?"

Copper blinked. *Beware Cassian's doorway…*It had been scrawled across the book in the cavern, and now…

"Nothing," She shook her head. "Should I?"

He made a soft humming sound.

"That's an interesting tattoo."

Copper tucked her hands behind her back. "It's not a tattoo."

Judah set his cup down quietly and looked up at her. "Do you make a habit of telling others of your sins?"

"No." Copper shook her head. "Not at all."

"And yet here you are, telling me about the brand I gave you."

The brand you…what?

"Is she with you?"

Copper turned to see Hollis awkwardly standing in the doorway.

"You were taking a long time," she offered as an excuse for leaving the chair she'd been planted in, with an awkward twisting of her hands.

"Yes, she is," Copper murmured, moving toward her, though there was something in her, a tingle in her fingertips that gave her the urge to reach out for this stranger.

"The door…it doesn't lead out. Not where we were anyway." Hollis whispered, her eyes flicking to the man in the background.

"How far did you go this time?" Copper whispered back.

"Just there," Hollis pointed to the room to Copper's left, which hadn't been there when she'd passed that space minutes before.

Copper glanced at the man, who had returned to leaning against the table, "One sec," she held up a finger with a fake smile.

"By all means," he welcomed her to explore.

"Where are we?" Hollis Roux's voice was full of wonder, practically dangling from the doorway.

They were far enough away from the harbor that the air smelled sweet and clean, like fresh-cut watermelon. Hollis had only opened the Oddity Shop's door for just a second, but it was long enough for the scent of the city streets to flow into the place. When Copper opened it again, the light outside was a little more faded, but the scent was still there.

"This is the Kingdom of Wellwick," a different man announced brashly behind the counter. He was startling in size, his dark hair cropped and his light eyes piercing.

Copper whirled sharply, slamming the door behind them.

"And I don't think you belong here." He frowned, but then his eyes fell on Hollis Roux, and a note of alarm crossed his features.

Mr. Clarke, Copper watched him, careful not to betray her guilt from her last visit in her actions. She knew him by rumor alone, having heard that the man was descended from giants. While he wasn't obscenely large, his sheer size was intimidating.

A third man casually strolled in, looking through a few papers in his hands before placing one on the counter. "If you need these books by tomorrow, I'll have to put a rush on them." Mr. Wylder was the younger of the two, his sandy-colored hair swept under a hat.

"Judah," Mr. Clarke directed his question to the man at the table, while gesturing toward Hollis. "Is that?"

"Yes." His answer was clipped, his focus on the papers.

Hollis took a step closer to Copper, clearly unsettled by the turn in their conversation.

Mr. Wylder looked up from the catalog, gazing between their unexpected guests and the other two men. Whatever they were cautiously discussing did not seem to land as solidly in his mind as it had in theirs.

"She's young," the man called Judah commented, flicking his gaze up with a mischievous circle around his eyes.

"Yes." Mr. Clarke looked at Hollis and then back at Copper. "You're playing the Red Game with a child," he ground out. "*That* child?"

"I'm almost twelve," Hollis sneered.

All eyes fell on her, and it visibly deflated her bravado a bit.

Mr. Clarke rolled his eyes. Mr. Wylder casually laughed, still sorting through the other papers.

"Yes, of course," Mr. Clarke answered in an exasperated, sarcastic tone. "Forgive me."

Do you not know me? Copper thought as she tried to get a feel for the room. Where she expected to find accusations and menacing frowns, she found more surprise and wonder.

You were there, Copper glanced at Mr. Wylder, recognizing the sharp line of his jaw as the shopkeeper who chastised the plants that night.

"We came here by mistake, and we just need to get back to Cape Solaera," Copper explained in the most disarming way she knew how.

"How has your game been proceeding?" Mr. Clarke asked, his question too pointed to be considered casual.

"What game?" Copper bluffed.

Mr. Clarke's gaze flattened.

"Oh boy," Mr. Wylder muttered under his breath and quickly excused himself from the room.

"As you can imagine, quite a bit of information passes through all the doorways in this place," Judah pointed out. "We know who you are, Ms. James."

"And what of Raleigh Danger?" Mr. Clarke went on.

"What about him?" Copper asked, feeling laid bare before them.

I don't like that you know me, but I don't know a thing about you.

"There are three things you should be concerned with above all else." Mr. Clarke took a few steps, his long strides bringing him before her surpassingly fast.

"Caius," Jonah stood, saying the name of Mr. Clarke in a warning voice.

Copper craned her neck, never feeling so short in her life.

"How Pharaoh projects that level of magic in a dying circus, what exactly is behind Cassian's doorway, and knowing that Raleigh Danger is not who he says he is."

"What?" Copper scrambled to keep up.

"That's enough," Judah rose from his table.

Mr. Clarke ignored him, "That doorway was shackled for a reason, and if you…"

The shop shuddered as though in warning before the light faded from the windows and the colored light from the Extravaganza poured in through the windows.

"Here's your stop!" Mr. Wylder appeared once more, jumping the counter to quickly escort them out.

"Wait," Copper argued, looking back at the men who clearly knew more about what was going on than she did.

"Sorry, busy schedule," Mr. Wylder chattered, handing Copper the green stone with the iron key as he all but shoved them out the doorway.

Mr. Wylder knelt down briefly, taking Hollis Roux's hand. "It was an honor to meet you."

Copper turned around and recognized the Solaera Valley Market instantly. "There's a lot of new being thrown around tonight," Copper muttered, frustrated that she could not know more of Mr. Clarke's warning.

"That shopkeeper, he knew me," Hollis said quietly, still looking at the hand he'd taken.

"Have you met him before?" Copper was only half listening as she tried to wrap her head around what had just happened.

"No," Hollis shook her head, sounding distant and thoughtful. "I've never been allowed to meet anyone."

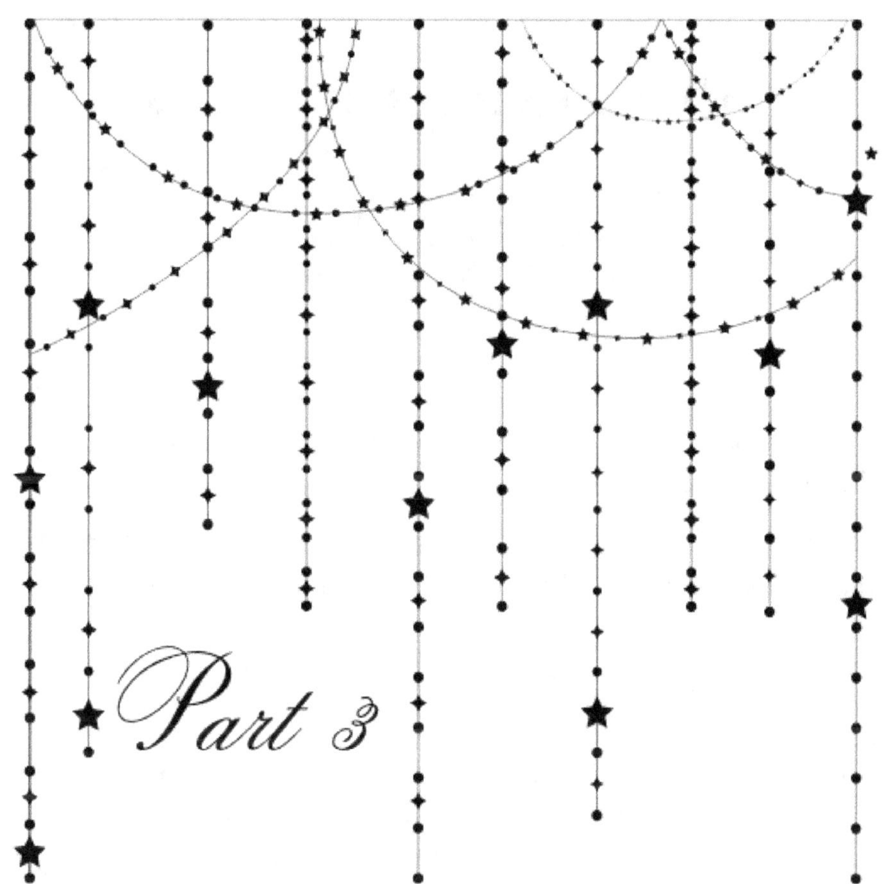

Part 3

CHAPTER THIRTY-SIX

Cassian's Doorway

MAYBE TRUSTING A POSSESSED *book wasn't my best idea.*

After Clarke & Wylder spat them back out into Cape Solaera, Copper drug Hollis back to their living quarters to grab her game items and descended into dimly lit, sloping tunnels, she'd discovered on a previous night.

"I think we're here?" Copper popped the book open again, following the path with her finger as they hooked a sharp "s" curve and walked directly into a room with a tall ceiling and crescent moon-shaped floor.

While the book and bracelet had served as a light during their stretch of dark pathway, there was no need for the latter here because there appeared to be a system of ever-burning lanterns and glowing walls surrounding the place.

"Is it safe?" Hollis whispered, poking her head out from the cloak.

"I suppose?" Copper dropped her hood to peer around. There had been a few people milling about in the central gathering place, but she didn't see a single rebel in the tunnels, and Copper couldn't help but wonder if they were ahead of the competition or, worse, if they were on some kind of wild goose chase.

"Wow," Hollis Roux's voice echoed from the other side of the chamber. "That's a lot of doors!"

Ducking under heavy, hanging vines, Copper emerged on the other side to see a tall wall that was different from the others. Covered in spreading ivy, the wall was littered in whitewashed doors of all shapes and sizes. Some were small, set several feet above Copper's head, and some were large, standing flush against the cavern floor. Some had symbols, and others bore barely visible decorations, but one door stood out from all the others.

A scarlet doorway stood tall, set back into a stone archway in black, gray, and ivory brick.

"This one seems special," Hollis planted her hands on her hips as she observed it.

"Was it the chains that told you that?" Copper commented sarcastically.

A dark symbol sat over the door in a red panel that came to a point at the top. It looked like a clock's blank face, similar to the door without the handle. But the heavy iron chains and locks, seven to be exact, drew the eye and gave it an ominous presence.

"Why do you suppose it's locked?" Hollis asked, looking at all the other doors that hadn't been covered in moss or ivy. "All the others look…open?"

Copper noticed the tiny symbol of Red Rebel in the center of the clock face and frowned. "I'm sure they have their reasons."

Pulling out the tome, a swirling, black and gold emblem bounced off the wall. Copper stepped forward, cleared a hole in the ivy, and revealed the tiniest of doors, not much larger than the palm of her hand.

The tome's pages flipped once more until it showed a flower-shaped key.

"Is that," Hollis looked at the tiny key, "supposed to open…that?" she questioned, looking back up at the enormous door.

"I don't think so," Copper answered pensively, plucking the key from the book.

While the book didn't give any other information, Copper surveyed the wall of doors, then the pattern and symbol on the key. Setting the tome down, the key atop it, Copper used her bare hands to clear away the ivy coating the wall in heavy foliage, revealing a tiny wildflower door that sat flush with the floor. But when Copper did clear it away, it was as though the key and lock called out to each other, the key straining on the cover of the tome.

"Could it really be that easy," Copper asked thoughtfully as she slid the key into the lock and turned it with ease. A series of unseen happenings inside the wall gave way, freeing one of the seven locks on the large door. However, the chains were too tightly bound, and unfastening a single lock did very little.

"One down," Copper stated, sitting cross-legged on the floor.

"What's inside?" Hollis got down on the floor with Copper, reaching toward the little flower door and turning the tiny handle.

The heavy scent of fresh wildflowers filled the air immediately. There was a tiny room on the other side, one that held a small, misshapen piece of metal.

"What do you suppose it is?" Hollis carefully retrieved it, flipping it over in her hands several times.

"I'm not sure," Copper took it when Hollis handed it over. It didn't look significant in the least, but there was a cutout in the top of it, the same as a key might have for a hook. "Best to hang onto it for now."

Hollis agreed, her fingers toying unthinkingly with her jeweled hat pin tucking into the front pocket of her vest.

Copper stood there and watched for a short while. She glanced down at the tome, noticing a new set of lettering on its spine shining clear under the dull blue lighting of the winged glow bugs that harmlessly flitted about.

The Tome of Fable.

Fable. Copper thought. *Who were you?*

#

Raleigh had to work to remove the feeling of Tirzah on his skin. The night of Splendor had been anything but. The effects of the cavern had done little but traumatize most of the Rebels.

Maybe that was the point?

Taking his guide item out of his pocket, the silver compass gleamed in the overhead light of his temporary living quarters. Seeing it reminded him to gather up the cloak he found when exiting the cavern.

The same cavern that Hollis and Copper had yet to return from.

"Take me to Copper James," he told the compass. With a soft click, the cover of the compass was unlatched, and the arrow spun and spun until it finally pointed him in the direction he wanted to go.

He'd found her in tunnels that even he hadn't known existed. Sitting amongst glowing bugs and a sleeping ward, Copper stared at the book in her lap, and Hollis slept under a dark cloak in the corner.

"Something of an odd choice in the way of reading locations," Raleigh said as he swaggered into her line of sight.

Copper didn't bother to look up.

"What did you win from tonight's events?" She asked, surprisingly cool even for their current strained relations.

"We didn't win anything. It was just a way to entertain the crowd and thin out our numbers. Where did you go? I'm happy you were spared the worst of it...they had to bring in senior members of the circus to sort of the aftermath of the cavern." He stared off for a beat too long.

"Are you ok?"

"Don't worry about me," Raleigh shrugged.

Copper returned to the book. "Was Pharaoh there?"

"Yeah," Raleigh groaned as he took a seat on the floor next to her. "That ghost of his too."

"Ellis?"

Raleigh nodded.

"Is she really not alive?"

"Not alive?"

Copper shrugged. "I've heard things."

"Ellis supposedly died at Pharaoh's hand years ago in some performing accident...I don't know if it's true."

"Then why did you call her a ghost?" Copper's skin flushed hot. "I mean, I see her... she's right there."

Raleigh leaned in to murmur against her hair. "Do you always believe what you see in a circus?"

Copper unthinkingly arched into him a little as though pressing closer would hinder others from hearing, the raised embroidery of his vest gently scratching at her bare back. "She's an illusion."

"The best of them all." Raleigh chuckled, the noise sounding slightly darker than she would have liked, but she tipped her chin down, casting a side-eye in his direction.

Copper squinted at him. "Why are you here?"

She looked tired. Beautiful, but tired.

Raleigh felt the question like an icicle to the heart. "I came to check on you."

Copper dwelled on that for a few heartbeats.

Raleigh took in the series of ancient doors. "They're beautiful."

"And probably cursed. I think this is what's keeping Cassian locked away somewhere."

"So what does that tell you?" Raleigh wrapped an arm around her shoulders.

Copper sat back and looked at the largest door. "If I win the game, I free the beast."

"Isn't that what you want?"

Copper rested her head on his shoulder and stared toward Hollis Roux. "I want him dead, but who do I become if I do that?"

"Who says you have to kill him?" Raleigh angled his face toward hers.

"He killed Rogan," Copper murmured the name of the dead Heir of Keskairah for the first time in a very long time. "Cassian doesn't just get away with that."

"You know my views on revenge…but the right answer will come to you." Drawing her closer, he planted a kiss on her forehead. "Either way, I'm here, whatever you decide."

Chapter Thirty-Seven

Agony

L**ONG AFTER MOST OF** the city had gone to sleep, the lights of the circus still glowed under the heavy observation of the stars in the sky. There was always an unspoken competition between the constellations and the thousands of tiny lights that lit up the Extravaganza on the far side of the shore where it wouldn't disturb those who resided there year-round.

Beyond the city structures and the tents was a portion of land where carnival rides carried on, powered by electricity. It was an exclusive section that wasn't readily available to just anyone. Mostly because while the glowing lights were electric, the rides were powered by something much more.

Unfortunately, even enchantments fail sometimes.

On that particular night, there were no stars in the sky due to the dense covering of the darkest clouds anyone had seen in some time.

To those who played the game, it was still nighttime as they slept soundly in their arranged housing. And as it approached waking time, some hours before sunset, the rebel's night was split by the whir and boom of a failing power grid.

A storm was brewing.

Just not the sort those who resided in the Extravaganza had come to expect of their tropical climate.

"And you're sure he's not…him," Akos asked in the shadows of the street. He followed Pharaoh into a small tent and right into an office buried somewhere in the cliff dwellings, lit by a dozen or more candles.

"Raleigh?" Pharaoh clarified. "No, not unless Cassian has figured out how to mask his eyes while shifting."

"He reeks of the Capital," Akos grumbled, sitting in one of the wing-backed chairs before the desk. "It doesn't seem right having them here. They all feel…wrong?"

"Don't get close then." Pharaoh half laughed as he grabbed two glasses out of a small cupboard on the far wall. "The game will sort them out one way or another."

Akos frowned, "What's your plan then?"

"My plan?" Pharaoh asked, handing his companion a short, crystal glass of amber liquid before sliding into a leather desk chair opposite him. "Isn't security *your* job?"

"Most of my men weren't trained with those kinds of magical tactics in mind," Akos took a sip from his glass and grimaced. "Where'd you get this?"

Pharaoh gave Akos a wry expression. "So what you're telling me is that the black gate is currently stationed in a magical setting and isn't prepared to actually deal with magical happenings?"

"We've been trained for most things, but they're still not ready for the chaos Cassian is capable of. We know how to repel certain magic, and they can deal with just about any form of hand-to-hand combat, but…" Akos sighed in frustration; leaning forward, he rested his forearms on his thighs. "None of us truly stand a chance against his brand of illusions."

Pharaoh crooked a skeptical brow at him.

"Ok, maybe you could." Akos hung his head. "But I'm worried about people getting caught in the crossfire."

"You mean you're worried about Ezlyn getting hurt."

"That too."

"Ophelia has blinders on when it comes to Cassian." Pharaoh stretched his arms upward, releasing the tension in his shoulders before folding them over his head while he thought.

Akos stopped. "You want to circumvent her?"

"If possible."

"So… what'd you have in mind?"

"He's going to slip up, sooner or later, and that's when we'll figure out what angle he's playing."

Akos remained in his chair as he watched Pharaoh begin to pace, nodding as he thought it over. "We could add more observation during the game."

"That's not enough," Pharaoh stopped in the middle of the room. Scanning the stacks of dark wood shelving built into the walls of the square room, he strode over to the middle shelf behind the desk and pulled out a gray book with silver lettering.

"What's this?" Akos moved to the edge of his chair when Pharaoh flipped to a page in the middle of the book and turned it to face him when he set it down on the desk.

"An option."

Akos reviewed it, nodding slowly. "And when would you want to do this?"

"She's bound until the end of the game," Pharaoh remarked. "I'm hoping I won't have to use it."

"But, if Cassian truly has returned…"

"I'd like to have a backup plan."

"Do you have the items?" Akos eyed the book.

"I have one of them," Pharaoh rubbed his forehead.

"And you need my help to get the other?" Akos asked pensively, not quite sure where Pharaoh was leading.

"No," Pharaoh shook his head. "I need your help with this," he pointed to a different section on the page.

Akos stared for a long moment before looking back to Pharaoh. "You could die doing this."

"I'm aware."

Akos sat back in his chair, slumped down with his arms propped up on both armrests. "If this goes wrong…"

"Do you have another plan?"

"No."

"Then this can't go wrong. Now can it?"

Akos shoved himself up to a standing position. "I'll start briefing my inner circle now…but the ring and the staff should be in the rebel market…good luck finding that necklace, though. That's the one Ezlyn wore until recently."

"I'm aware." Pharaoh stared blankly at the book on his desk as he mentally prepared for the reality of what could happen very shortly.

As Akos moved to leave, something Pharaoh said came full circle in his mind. "How did you confirm that Raleigh's eyes weren't Cassian's?"

"What do you mean?" Pharaoh bristled, remembering how he used Ezlyn's necklace to examine Raleigh's eyes.

"It takes a special kind of magic to lift that guise… doesn't it?"

Pharaoh stared at his reflection in the pane of a framed photograph. "Don't ask questions if you're not ready to deal with the answers."

"I know we're in a tough situation, but Ezlyn didn't deserve…"

"It's not like I took it off her neck myself…" Pharaoh rolled his neck, not wanting to get into the ethics of doing what he had to to prepare them for what was coming.

"Well, someone did," Akos ground out. "And if I find out you…"

"You'll what?"

Akos stared at him, a rage kindling in his eyes.

"Go on," Pharaoh gestured. "Say it."

A muscle feathered in Akos' jaw. "If you played a role in hurting her when this is all over, you'll pay for it."

He smirked at Akos, his voice carrying a note of false pleasantries. "I wouldn't expect anything else."

A tense moment of silence passed between them in which Akos turned to storm out when he halted to look at Pharaoh over his shoulder.

"What is it like? To be the brother of the devil?"

"Agony," Pharaoh took a swig from his class. "Absolute agony."

Act IV. Peril

Rebels,

Congratulations on making it to night four.

Each time a performer sets foot on stage, there is a willing element of endangerment that one must take on to perform on the exquisite level expected of The Extravaganza. In order to obtain your heart's desire, you must first prove that you are willing to master the death-defying peril of a performer's will. Only then can you face your next challenge.

Assuming you advance to night four.

So, play fearlessly, and you will succeed.

Choose the coward's method to proceed, and you simply...will not.

Five will play, one will win.

Welcome to the Season of Shimmering Souls

Act IV

The Grand Master of the Red Rebel Extravaganza

CHAPTER THIRTY-EIGHT

Cataclysm

A DAMP FOG ROLLED in on an airy whisper of wind on the eve of night four. The abnormal haze drove a majority of patrons indoors for their evening meal, making the fairway a ghost town as the Rebels arrived. It was as though the whole of The Red Rebel Extravaganza was grieving, and the weather acted accordingly.

As the Rebels had filtered into the town square one by one, there'd been a noticeably ominous change in the air. Not just because of the relatively practical outfits they had all been dressed in, form-fitting clothing and jumpsuits paired with climbing shoes, but there was an unexpected melancholy effect in the simple form of silence when they were funneled toward the carnival district.

The area of the circus that was constantly filled with the hum, whir, and elated squeals that came from the partakers in the carnival rides was barren of all sound. The temporary clearing gave it such an eerie vibe that Copper felt the weight of an absence she didn't yet understand.

Something feels…wrong. Copper's skin crawled in a way she couldn't shake.

They were on the brink of something dangerous.

As though an ancient awareness had awakened the night before when they'd entered the crystal caverns.

And it had followed them out.

The death of joy hovered among them when only the pop and sizzle of the carnival lights could be heard amongst the fog that slowly seeped across the gravel. The sun had long since set, leaving the outskirts of the carnival feeling dark and dangerous.

"Where is everybody?" Raleigh thought aloud, casting a wary gaze toward Copper.

There weren't any onlookers for the game that evening, but also because Cassian's next letter had appeared in the same manner as the prior two letters, and it was clear that another member had left the game.

Who would not be arriving was the question on everyone's mind.

"Tonight is a race to the top to see how deserving each of you is of claiming a coveted spot as an Extravaganza performer…if only for one night." Ophelia's voice sounded hollow in the open fairway.

No flair.

No showmanship.

"While one might expect to audition for such a role in an empty performance tent, your potential initiation begins here." Even Ophelia was dressed in something far less flashy with her scarlet ringmaster coat, thigh-high boots, and black leather pants paired with a dark lace corset. As though she and the costume creators knew there would be no one else present to witness the night's events or any potentially elaborately decorated outfits.

When Copper saw Raleigh dressed in dark, fitted clothing and the way he idly laced his thumbs under his decorative suspenders, it reminded her of another time when dressing for a job meant arriving as unnoticeable as possible. She was dressed similarly in a charcoal jumpsuit with twin lines of buttons dotting her abdomen. Wide straps reached over her shoulders and crisscrossed across her back. A vertically striped shirt reached up from where the jumpsuit halted below her bust line. Stopping at a half sleeve, it clung to her pleasing figure.

What she wasn't wearing was Addy.

Leaving him behind had been a requirement for night four. In fact, it appeared that everyone had arrived without the items they'd been gifted at the beginning of the game.

"Are we supposed to be…mimes?" She quietly wondered aloud when she looked at her gloved hands.

Raleigh snorted a laugh at the idea, giving the interim ringmaster a saucy wink when she speared them both with a look.

"In this sea of cogs and machinery," Ophelia paced before them, her hands clasped behind her back. "It is your job to prove your worth in the various performing arts by finding and securing your entry pass into an event."

Hollis Roux had been dressed in a romper that mirrored Copper's outfit, with a long stretch of mismatching striped tights covering her legs from the hem of her shorts to her clunky boots as she stood off to the side with Tanith.

Copper quickly finished her braid and gave Hollis Roux a wink when she noticed the pensive attitude that gave the girl a bristled posture. Hollis Roux wiggled her pigtails at her in response, a small, genuine smile on her face.

"Before you are a series of carnival rides," Ophelia explained the task at hand.

The Rebels watched her closely as they stood on their markers.

The Huntress.

The Rogue.

Lord Hypnos.

Lady Illuminae.

The Vagabond.

Ezlyn, The Fae, was missing along with The Knight.

The Rebels all shifted in their costumes, everyone fully aware of the kind of magic it took to pull off many of the stunts showcased in the circus.

A kind of magic that none of them possessed.

"This entire area relies on a steady, blended current of magic-infused electricity," Ophelia pointed out.

For a few startling seconds, the carnival rides surged to life without warning. Lights twinkled, and mechanical extensions spun in time with what was supposed to be merry music.

It didn't infuse the area with joy.

The haunting melody rattled on with no patrons in the streets or passengers on the rides.

"I'm sure you've noticed the dozens of envelopes stashed about the fairway," Ophelia walked to a hidden stand and pulled out five different colored pieces of folded paper. "Inside each of these is a different item. Some hold treasure, others bear unfortunate tortures," she flicked one away at a time, and they vanished into thin air. "Some will give you an advantage in the game…"

"And others will hinder you," Hollis grumbled under her breath beside Tanith. "Can't she just get on with it?"

Tanith choked back a laugh, shushing Hollis when they received a few sideways glances.

"The *right* card will give you a performance assignment for night three. Assuming you make it that far." Ophelia's words turned sour at the end. "So, choose wisely because your chosen envelope could seal your fate."

Seal our fate? Copper wondered as she looked for a hint of where the cards might be hidden. *Is that what happened to Ezlyn and The Knight?* It dawned on her then that she'd never learned his name.

"Oh, and one more thing," Ophelia mentioned. "You'll be doing this…in the dark." She said, and the lights all went out with the loud clatter of a switch. "But…perhaps this can light your path," she said, and a bucket of glow sticks appeared under a small sign with a blinking arrow.

"And Remember Dear Rebels," they all waited with bated breath for her to say the final key phrase that officially started night four. "Play fearlessly."

Immediately, all five players leaped into action, grabbing glow sticks and breaking them to initiate the illuminating qualities captured inside. There was an urgency to the task that spurred them all on.

The glow sticks varied in size, color, and flexibility. Some were large with neon green fluid and could be used as a flashlight, scanning the ground and surrounding surfaces with a sickly hue. Others were thin, with fasteners on the ends that could secure them around a neck or wrist in a stacked pattern, giving them a prismatic, rainbow effect.

"Here," Raleigh took a handful and gave a few to Copper. She could feel the crunching in her hands as she fastened several around her body with her eyes on climbing the Ferris wheel.

"Don't go for the easy one," Raleigh subtly directed. "This is a game of skill. You must prove that you are willing to go above and beyond…"

"I kind of figured…" Copper nodded, fastening a long glow stick around her head; its contents glowed a soft teal with tiny butterfly pieces floating around inside.

"Doesn't seem so bad," Lord Hypnos sniffed, using the largest glow stick available to point at things both near and far.

"Yes…well dear," Lady Illuminae waved both hands in an arching motion to levitate the glow sticks, fanning them out before her to light her way. "may the brightest competitor win…"

The Huntress seized the first glow stick she saw and crushed it between her teeth, the glowing fluids running over her lips like a rabid, salivating dog. "I intend to," she snarled, glowing dribbles flying from her lips.

That's one way to free up your hands, I guess. Copper grimaced.

"Gross," Hollis Roux murmured from the sidelines, able to see the mixture of saliva and luminescent fluid splatter from where she stood.

When Copper turned around, she noted that the Huntress took the smallest light possible and slipped around the nearest corner. She said that woman was not someone she wanted to meet in a back alley. Making a mental note of her path, Copper went in the opposite direction.

Copper surveyed the street level, noticing one or two pieces of parchment at various games and recognizing that those would take a fair amount of illusion skills. There was another carved into the core of the carousel, but that also could take more time than she'd care to spend retrieving it.

She needed something fast but also something that wasn't so…obvious?

Copper decided she needed to seek out an envelope that would put her in a performance she could master with ease. Thinking of Pharaoh, an idea dawned on her, causing Copper to lift her face toward the sky and the heavy metal circle of the giant Ferris Wheel.

There, spinning on clear pieces of wire, were several envelopes.

Could it really be that easy? Would the more challenging envelopes be more difficult initially, only to bear a sweeter prize upon retrieving them?

"Only one way to find out," Copper muttered with a shake of her head.

When she reached the base of the Ferris wheel, there was already a lilac-colored glow stick scaling the side ladder leading toward the top. Copper knew there was more than one envelope up there, but when she saw Raleigh climbing some sort of tower ride nearby, she knew she was on the right path.

Copper climbed straight up the pedestal that held the Ferris Wheel in place, using the inner bars as a ladder. Once she reached the core, she looked at the arms that extended in a dozen or more directions. Approaching the main bars before her like a jungle gym, Copper began to climb again, her arms and back beginning to burn.

Quickly gauging the progress of the others, Copper blinked twice, then squinted when she noticed a hazy section on the ground behind Lord Hypnos that devoured all light.

"You," Copper frowned, recognizing the demented shadow for what and who it was.

And it appeared to have the ear of Lord Hypnos.

CHAPTER THIRTY-NINE

Peril

WHEN COPPER REACHED FOR a bracket a little further up than her survival instincts would have liked, Lord Hypnos contorted the wheel at its base using the bejeweled cane she received at the opening ceremony, even though he'd already collected the nearest envelope to him.

"What are you doing?" Copper shouted to him, all her glow sticks shifting to one side as the structure swayed.

"Playing the game, Love!" Lord Hypnos gave an oversized laugh.

Copper made a strangled sound when the Ferris wheel lurched. Looking up, she noticed that the first envelope was just outside the upper cap of the encased ladder, forcing her to squeeze between the bars and leave her protective climbing apparatus.

Dodging debris and twisting metal, Copper finally reached the top of the Ferris wheel where the Huntress already stood on the upper curve. She tiptoed on the cool metal surface with a catlike grace that Copper knew she wouldn't have when she finally swung her body up and over onto the beam that jutted out from the top, leading to a series of envelopes.

Planting her feet firmly in the wedge of two bars, Copper took a long moment to eyeball precisely where she could approach the envelope in the safest capacity when the whole structure began to shake.

A savage sound came from her left as the Huntress charged at Copper. With wide eyes, Copper dropped down, gripping the underside of the top bar as the Huntress skidded to a halt.

"What are you doing?" She cried, heaving herself up. She found her footing again as the wheel continued to turn.

"Hey!" Raleigh roared from his place on one of the tallest rides in the area; he got her attention just before he tossed a long stick with wide buffers on either end.

Copper caught the item and turned on her heel just in time to block a blow from the Huntress.

"This event is mine, Vagabond!" The Huntress snarled, shoving Copper back before she ran toward the external panel. "I will not die so the likes of you can win. I have no more bloodshed on my hands than you! Heir killer!"

"Heir killer!" Copper growled, barely maintaining her balance as she lurched forward, shoving the Huntress down and into one of the ride baskets. Doing her best to balance as they made a full circle and came back up toward the top, Copper walked out to grab her envelope, trying to ignore how her head spun at the sheer height.

She could hear the creak of the metal as the Huntress came up behind her.

"I wouldn't," Copper warned.

It was slight when the Huntress's balance suddenly shifted, but it was just enough that she began to waver in her footing when the wheel turned a few feet. She tried her best to steady herself, but years of practice did her no good when her platform trembled at its base.

Copper jumped forward, grabbing the Huntress's arm before she fell, but to her surprise, when she laid over the bar and stared down into the young woman's face, it was not the ravenous Rebel who had sunk her teeth into the glow stick who looked up at her.

"Who are you?" Copper wheezed, confused.

"Let…me go," the albino woman's dark wig shifted as she struggled against her, legs dangling in the air.

"You'll…fall!" Copper recognized her as the performer she'd seen Raleigh sniffing around during the off hours of the game.

"Her name is Xerxes," Raleigh had confided in her. "I don't know if it's anything…but I'm not bored."

"Trust me," Xerxes eyeballed the top of the cliff, a fair distance from them, with a palpable unease. "I know how to fall."

Copper lifted her head, realizing they had been watched the entire time as a pensive crowd of onlookers sat on the multi-level deck patio of a cliff-top restaurant. The whole place was practically brimming with patrons who watched the Rebels struggle through night four while enjoying their dinner.

Of course, Copper thought, feeling foolish for ever believing that this was anything more than a source of entertainment that the Extravaganza could capitalize on. She was sure the venue had even sold tickets:

Watch the next episode of The Red Game from the comfort of our cliff-top lounge. Indulge in our most expensive delicacies as the Rebels risk their lives solely for your rapt entertainment!

"You're sure?" Copper returned to the present when she heard Xerxes struggle under her tight grip, her fingernails unintentionally pricking Xerxes's skin.

"You're in danger, Copper James," Xerxes ground out. "If we don't put on a show, you'll all be picked off one by one, and then we'll all be stuck here…" she struggled again. "forever!"

"I don't…" Copper shook her head.

"Do it now, before that old man and his cane change the rules of physics again!" Xerxes snarled, glaring down at Lord Hypnos, who stood in the street, continuing to cause chaos for the others. Raleigh was nearly pulled from his perch thanks to a flag wrapped around his head. "They already got to Ezlyn…"

"I saw a shadow."

"I'd keep that to myself," Xerxes frowned.

"Is it…" Copper tried to ask when

"Cassian isn't who we thought he was," Xerxes's face slackened into weariness. "It'll be a miracle if any of us make it out of here alive."

Copper felt the Ferris Wheel come to a complete halt. Visually judging the length between where they were and where Xerxes would land, she let go.

Xerxes adjusted to gravity with the grace of a seasoned tightrope walker. She climbed over a lesser rung with catlike agility and seized the nearest card. She'd been exposed and needed to finish that portion of the game quickly to flee the scene.

What had happened to the real Huntress?

Copper looked down through the geometric order of the interwoven bars that made up the wheel's structure and watched as Xerxes descended the ride with incredible accuracy. Her gaze then flitted to Lady Illuminae as she strolled up to the starting point with her envelope like the family cat who'd just eaten the pet canary. All of that, paired with the noticeable magical ability of Lady Illuminae and Lord Hypnos, made Copper realize that she would have to work that much harder to win. Copper snatched the floating card from just above the highest point of the Ferris wheel, the red triangular flag at the top whipping her relentlessly.

Giant spotlights flashed on with an audible shudder, revealing the remaining four rebels at various points from Copper at the top, trickling all the way down to Lord Hypnos on the ground.

Xerxes had disappeared into the shadows, and The Huntress was nowhere to be found.

"Congratulations, Rebels…" Ophelia's voice came on over a loudspeaker. "On completing tonight's event."

Flower-shaped lights, glowing in shades of honey, violet, and indigo, bloomed over the restaurant, and the onlookers rose to their feet, cheering.

Awkwardly, Copper waved her envelope.

She was used to physically demanding maneuvers in her smuggling life. What she wasn't used to was an audience.

"Yes, yes…" Copper said through gritted teeth and a sarcastic note to her words as she sat on the upper curve of the bar. "I'm glad you're entertained."

A not-so-subtle shift happened then. Copper looked straight down to see a shadow at the base of the Ferris Wheel tip its hat to her before the base crumbled with the groan and whine of bending steel.

"No…" she whispered, frozen under the wobble of the entire structure.

Most of the rebels had cleared the area, but Copper was still planted at the top and regretted that immensely.

A series of engineers flooded the place in noticeably plain work clothing, as did The Black Gate with their neatly disguised weapons. Ophelia looked around, listening to what looked to be livid shouts from the head engineer.

But, all the rushed efforts in the world couldn't stop one of the supportive legs of the Ferris wheel from breaking it two and setting the entire structure at an angle with bone-jarring force.

"Copper!" Raleigh yelled as the entire area fell silent after the looming structure. "Get down from there!"

Everyone else had managed to escape, and as the restaurant was frantically cleared, the entire wheel leaned.

And Copper James fell with it.

CHAPTER FORTY

A Long Way Down

Hollis Roux's scream could be heard for miles around, echoing a cry of terror that was deep and raw; the hollow screech made sure that no one could've missed her unfolding horror. Tanith pulled her still-screaming form toward the edge of the fairway and away from danger. Their escape was the last thing Copper saw before the Ferris Wheel fell forward in one long, roaring groan of crashing metal as it shattered the top floor of the cliff-top restaurant.

Tucking inward with the descent of the wheel, Copper ricocheted off the internal framework of the Ferris Wheel as it began to tip, a sudden jerking sending her tumbling sideways until she fell into a ride car. Pressing into the corner of the bucket, Copper watched the world turn as the ground rose swiftly to greet her.

Don't fall, don't fall, don't fall! Copper cringed until she realized the entire structure was easing to a stop. Her chest heaving, she opened one eye, then the other, looking around with a surprised expression as the wheel halted in midair.

"Pull!" she heard a voice from below shouting.

Shifting upward, Copper turned around and saw a series of men decorated in Black Gate and engineer clothing holding a series of ropes.

What kind of rope does that? Copper thought as the ropes appeared to have securely fastened themselves unassisted. *And where can I get my own?*

Copper moved to climb down, needing to get out of harm's way, but just as she made it to the outer part of the car, it was as though invisible scissors were cutting one rope at a time, causing the wheel to twist at an awkward angle. Seeing the collision before it happened, Copper tried to outrun the worst of them by leaping and pulling herself up from one car to another.

But she hadn't moved fast enough.

#

The breaking of the Ferris Wheel into multiple fractures of twisted metal sounded like the distant roar of an ancient dinosaur. The unexpected decline of the event had drawn Pharaoh out of the Big Top, Ellis close on his heels. He watched in shock when the fairway sparked with the bent structure as it twisted over several tents and rides and took down several strings of lights in its path.

"What happened here?" Ellis stopped Akos as he sprinted past; Pharaoh stopped a few steps closer to the scene.

"The Red Game happened; what else?" He barked, clearly in a hurry. "We've got casualties at the restaurant, hazards in eight different spots on the fairway, and Copper James was on top of the wheel when it fell!"

Pharaoh's charismatic mask shattered. Stumbling backward until he was near where Ellis found Tanith and Hollis had sought refuge, he tried to get a better look at the damage. His eyes roamed the fairway, visually calculating the trajectory and desperately searching for her in the night.

"Are you ok?" Ellis asked them, but Tanith just looked at her in wary silence.

"I can't find her!" Raleigh joined them, shouting over the chaos that ensued as people screamed, running in every direction when the smaller tents in the area began to collapse.

Hollis bobbed around. Stooping low, her eyes narrowed when she peered

"There!" Hollis Roux stooped under a fallen canopy and pointed at a ride car wedged between the twisted metal and broken canvas. "She's there!"

A single word cascaded over them, pointed and pleading. The word wasn't 'help.'

It was a name.

#

"Raleigh!" Copper screamed his name as she dangled from the open door of a Ferris Wheel buggy.

When the ride had begun to topple, Copper had maneuvered her way down the side and held on for dear life, but the impact of the wheel with the side of the cliff had jarred her free along with a slew of rocks and dirt. She'd barely caught herself on the latch of a door, and her fingers paled under the pressure of holding them in place. Her muscles were burning from the exertion of holding herself up after all the climbing she'd just done.

You've got to hang on, she told herself. Because Copper knew if she slipped, even in the slightest?

She would fall.

#

"The Wheel of Death," Raleigh shouted, his eyes immediately going to Pharaoh as he pointed to a ride nearly as old as the circus.

"Are you insane," Tanith balked. "You can't go up there! Let the Black Gate take care of this!"

"They won't get to her in time," Pharaoh mentally mapped out the path Raleigh pointed to.

"Up, over, and down," Raleigh gestured, suggesting they use the tandem wheel as a catapult to get Pharaoh up into the air, over the debris, and down onto parts of the Ferris Wheel that remained intact.

"Go," Ellis urged them. "Go now!"

"Let's go," Pharaoh nodded sharply, accepting the dangerous endeavor.

Raleigh and Pharaoh leaped into action.

Scaling the sides of rides and stumbling over sagging tent roofs, Raleigh and Pharaoh wound separate paths toward the second tallest structure in the fairway.

"Raleigh!" Copper called out again, her voice frantic.

"Hang on!" Raleigh jumped over a fallen game tent.

"They're coming!" Hollis Roux bounced on her feet, a physical manifestation of the nervous energy crackling in everyone's blood. "Just…hang on! They're coming!"

Together Raleigh and Pharaoh got the tandem wheel of death swinging end over end. It was a sandless hourglass of metal mesh spinning faster and faster until Pharaoh was able to slip into the inner part of the rapidly passing ring. Raleigh continued to keep the momentum going as Pharaoh made one, two, then three cycles around as he climbed from inside the ring to the outside. Plotting his landing point amongst the wreckage, he waited until he was nearly level with the spot and let it pass him by, leaving him a little room to fall into the spot and eyeball his landing.

Not knowing if the portion of the intact metal would fully bear his weight, Pharaoh flung himself into the air and stuck his landing perfectly. Barefoot, he scaled the sturdier piece of metal, relieved that he had not crashed through the tent below.

"Don't!" Copper screamed, the jolt of his landing nearly knocking her free from her lifeline.

"I'm here!" Pharaoh shouted, climbing through pieces of buggy and tent, lowering himself down onto the still intact car above the one she hung from. "Just don't let go!"

Raleigh quickly joined them, but he must have jumped too soon, as Pharaoh heard him land in the sloping canopy of one of the taller tents. But there was no time to check whether his suspicions were correct.

Get to her. Get to her now, or she dies. Pharaoh's inner voice urged as his footing slipped on the smooth surface of the domed buggy. Gripping the bar overhead, he straddled the roof, as there weren't enough bars for him to climb between the car and where Copper hung. Flipping forward into the car, he leaned out and over the seat. Hooking his toes between the cushions, Pharaoh dangled his entire body over the side of the car until he was able to grasp the structures below and descend through the metal framework.

He could reach her. He could reach her and save her and…

Copper looked up at him, and the fear in her eyes, the way it lined her face, brought him right back to the night his performing partner had died.

Ellis, when she had been alive and beautiful and thriving, had given him the same look just before she'd fallen to her death.

Not another Ellis…

His eyes fell to where the projection of his grief had been standing. Where Ellis had been watching with Tanith and Hollis.

But she was gone.

And she had been for a long time.

Ellis gave him a single nod before he reeled in the magic he'd used for years to keep a version of her with him and focused it all on the moment at hand. He couldn't let another woman die by the hands of the circus.

The car Copper hung from was damaged, making Pharaoh believe that any more weight on its fastens would break it free from its already precarious angle. He threw an item forward, and though no one could see what it was, it secured Copper's grip to the edge of the car as she held onto the flailing tiny door for dear life.

Using a rope made from torn banners that once decorated the sky over the fairway, Raleigh slung his way up and over a broken portion of the mangled tent and ride.

Copper's limbs visibly trembled when Raleigh stood diagonally below her and Pharaoh hung above. Her whole body shook as the wheel began to slip from where it was pinned against the cliff.

"Here," Raleigh shouted over the sickening sound of grinding metal, casting the banner over Copper's head to Pharaoh.

Pharaoh caught it with ease, manipulating the fabric to create a sling that settled under Copper, with Pharaoh holding one end and Raleigh pulling the other side taught.

"Let go," Pharaoh instructed, focusing sharply on her as he did one final visual sweep of the makeshift slide.

"No," Copper grimaced, too afraid to look down and see her obvious rescue but clearly too tired to hold on.

"Come here to me," Raleigh coaxed.

With a muted squeal, Copper slipped as the car she held to broke away from its final fasten.

Pharaoh muttered a curse under his breath; releasing his feet from the curve of the seat, he plunged head first toward her.

Raleigh lurched forward, still holding tight to the fabric as the car pulled him down.

Pharaoh snagged Copper by the crisscrossed straps of her jumpsuit that lined her back, using the magic he'd reserved for Ellis to summon tattoos off his skin, projecting wide bands of aerial fabric to keep them from falling as the car passed them by.

"Hold on," Pharaoh grimaced. The magic seared through his skin as he wrapped an arm and leg around the remaining metal of the fallen Ferris Wheel. The awkward impact jarred him so hard that his ears rang, and his jaw stung from clenching his teeth. "I've got you!" He ground out, his fist tightly gripping that fabric that had engulfed Copper, safely cocooning her from a fatal descent.

But, this time, it was Raleigh's turn to fall.

And Copper's scream rivaled Hollis Roux's as it followed Raleigh Danger all the way down to the cold, hard ground below.

CHAPTER FORTY-ONE

Interview

IN THE AFTERMATH OF night four, an inquiry was immediately enacted by the Black Gate into the death of Raleigh Danger, Supernatural Detective known during The Red Game as The Rogue.

By the time his body had been removed from the playing field, only three of the remaining Rebels could be found.

Copper James, The Vagabond, was not available for comment.

CHAPTER FORTY-TWO

Peril repeated

"I STILL DON'T KNOW how it happened," Lady Illuminae whispered.

Separated from her husband, she was quiet, possibly still in shock. One for lofty hats and soft fabrics; she hadn't wanted to participate in the game.

But her husband had other ideas.

Fame.

Greed.

Power.

All of it had been his intention to play and win the game. Consigning both their names had just been another chance at entering.

"I didn't think they'd take us both..." she murmured. "And no one was supposed to die. That wasn't how the game was played when I was younger..." She dabbed at her eyes with a lace-trimmed handkerchief. "Oh, and the way his body was...mangled and twisted. Saints help him...he was just trying to save her!" A fresh wave of tears rolled down her face, dotting the bare table before her.

Lady Illuminae provided little in terms of investigatory facts in the death of Raleigh Danger and was excused shortly after her interview.

#

In a dimly lit interrogation room, Lord Hypnos sat with his hand folded in front of his mouth, his eyes shut tightly.

"Take me back to the moment you approached the Ferris Wheel," Akos prodded.

His elbows propped on the gray table, Lord Hypnos opened steely eyes full of turmoil and stared back at Akos.

"I'd received a magic-endowed walking stick to replace the one I use regularly at the opening ceremony."

"Yes, we were all there," Akos replied when the older man didn't continue.

"I'm accustomed to handling magical objects, you see, being that my position to the empress is…"

"We're aware of who you were before you entered the game."

Lord Hypnos ran a finger or two along his collar in a feeble attempt to loosen it. "I just…something happened. Something went wrong. It was as though some dark power came over me and…"

"You tried to kill one of your fellow players."

"I did no such thing," the rotund man harrumphed. "Yes, I…we…the cane…bent the Wheel…but I am not a homicidal man! I'd never even heard of the Smuggler…Vagabond, whatever it is she calls herself these days…before the game!"

Akos sat back in his chair. "As a man self-proclaimed to be accustomed to handling magical objects, are you saying you lost control of your item?"

Lord Hypnos' face deepened to a ruddy, red color. "Had I know that your kind used a vile sort of magic…"

"What happened after you bent the metal and tried to end Copper James?"

Lord Hypnos fell silent. His angry eyes were still on Akos. "It fell."

"And Detective Danger?"

"He attempted to save the woman on the Wheel."

"And then he fell?"

"Yes," Lord Hypnos nodded grimly, a sour grimace marring his face. "And then…he fell."

#

The Huntress glowered at the member of the black gate from her side of the table. She didn't know his name, though she was sure he had told her. She wouldn't have even cared enough to know what he was, occupation or otherwise, had he not been wearing the uniform of the many members of the circus who had stopped her from hunting her opponents in the night.

"He fell," The Huntress stated in a cold, matter-of-fact tone, refusing to have a seat at the table. "What else do you want me to say?"

#

In the aftermath of the night's events, Copper quickly left the fairway and tucked herself and Hollis Roux within the safety of their new little apartment inside the mountain that faced the sea.

They did not enjoy whatever festivities remained in the aftermath of the accident.

They did not help clean up the fairway.

They hid away together, and no one saw them for the rest of the night.

When Hollis Roux finally fell asleep, it was Copper's turn to cry.

Because Raleigh Danger was dead, and they were now, truly undeniably alone.

Chapter Forty-Three

Escaping the Obsidian Hall

WHEN THE EVENING MIST clung to the edge of The Grand Aurora Hotel, something woke on floor thirteen that none of the guests on any other floor could have possibly imagined. Then Copper James had burst through a doorway in the southeast corridor, and everything changed.

He'd spent so long in the Obsidian Hall that he was more shadow than man. Dragging one foot in front of the other, he had trudged through a sickness that plagued the prison floor day after miserable day. The place was a hollow, lifeless thing that bound you in your worst nightmares, suffocating even the brightest burning ember of hope.

"Out," he rasped as the darkness clung to him. His hair was filthy and sticking to his face with the exertion of just trying to put one foot in front of the other. There was no help coming for him.

He was brought here to die.

That was their first mistake.

The clock struck midnight, chanting out twelve tones over the seemingly endless floor and reminding the inhabitants that another night of misery had only begun.

One…

His eyes flickered from gleaming crystal blue to a brown so dark it was nearly black. The look on his face continually shifted from determined to eerily elated and back again.

Two...

The ground seized up around him. Sword in hand, he hacked away as the thick branches of thorns wound up and around the hall, trying to block his path.

Three...

The pull of a thousand icy hands weighed on him, dragging him down to the ground before he clawed his way back up again. It was a seemingly endless cycle that he was determined to break.

Four...

A bodiless wailing surged throughout the floor. The sound blistered his skin and infiltrated his senses with a wash of excruciating force.

Five...

Blood seeped from his eyes, from his mouth, and pooled in his ears. He was forced to gasp for every breath as though he were being strangled by imaginary hands but continued his struggle to move forward.

Six...

The foul stench of rot filled the air.

Seven...

He stepped around wide-mouthed holes that began to fall open in the floor, lined with vibrating razor edges, eagerly trembling for their next meal.

Eight...

Blackbirds swarmed him as he stepped into a high-ceilinged corridor. The moon shone on their glossy coats. He grabbed one and then another until they warped into a cloak made of black feathers. Clothed in cackling midnight, The Raven King pressed on.

Nine...

Water flooded the halls, a wild roar of a flash flood sweeping him off his feet. A desperate hand emerged, grabbing onto the broken molding until he could swing himself up and over into the neighboring hall because the flood only ran in one direction.

Ten…

He lifted his face toward the metal door, heavily inscribed with dozens of languages, all warning the same thing: Do not pass.

Eleven…

Taking a fistful of the wall, he dug his gloved fingers into it, leeching something dark and terrible from deep within the Obsidian Hall. The shadows seeped into his nostrils as he took a steadying breath, teeth ground into an angry line as he pushed forward.

Twelve.

"Open," he cast a hand forward and smiled when the door before him did just that.

Act V
Performance

And then there were four.

My most sincerest of condolences on the tragic loss of another Rebel at the hand of The Red Game.
But as they say, the show must go on!
To better understand your role, find a partner in our sea of performers and, for one night only, soar through the skies, breathe flames, or simply master the sleight of hand.
Become one with The Extravaganza, and you will find the next item that you seek. Just remember to be careful, because...four will play.
One will remain.

And as always,
Play fearlessly. For only the bravest of souls will win.

Welcome to the Season of Shimmering Souls
Act V

The Grand Master of the Red Rebel Extravaganza

CHAPTER FORTY-FOUR

The Love Language of Wildflower Scones

THE INVESTIGATION HALTED THE game for an entire day.

Which was good because sometime in the night, Copper's grief had turned to rage.

Rage for the loss of another life.

Rage over her severe lack of control in the game.

Rage that made her want to cut Lord Hypnos' throat.

In the surge and ebb of her raw emotions was the scorching, bitter sensation of being wronged by an unseeable force. So, she'd gone down to the cavern and screamed all her hate and hurt at Cassian's doorway until she'd grown hoarse.

"You left me!" The accusation ricocheted off the walls, a hand coming to her mouth when she heard her voice blame Raleigh for his own death. It gave her pause and brought a fresh wave of tears as she collapsed to the floor.

Until she was found.

"Feel better?" Pharoah had asked from the opening of the room.

Copper whirled on him, a sneer curling her upper lip. "What do you want?"

At that moment, she was the wild magic of the circus filtered through the lens of the agony she felt every time she closed her eyes and saw the expression on Raleigh's face as he'd fallen. All the hurt that had welled up inside her had been poured out, and all that was left was the need to fix it. To make it all go away.

Pharaoh watched her for a long moment as though deciding if it was worth continuing the conversation. "Not here." He said finally, extending a hand to her.

Copper gave him a disgusted look. "I'm not going anywhere with you." She wiped her face with her sleeve and turned her back to him.

"Okay," Pharoah grumbled, clearly not having the patience to deal with her. "The way I see it, you can either stay down here and cry, or you can help me do something about all of this."

"Why would I help *you*?"

"Because *I* helped *you*." The depth of Pharaoh's voice rattled something inside her when he crouched down behind her. "And I lost a friend in the process."

Copper tucked her chin against her chest, turning her ear toward him. "What can we possibly do against a monster like that?" She gestured toward the locked doorway.

"Oh," Pharoah groaned as though he was sore as he rose to his feet. "You'd be surprised."

Copper hugged her knees and closed her eyes, unable to bear the weight of taking one more step forward in life, let alone the game.

"Come on," he toed her hip. "I need to talk to you about something. And you need good food and a hot cup of something caffeinated. You look like death."

"You really are lovely." Copper dropped her shoulders in exasperation, "Really, it's a wonder you're not more popular…" she grumbled, but after a long moment, Copper scooted to her feet and followed the sound of his chuckle.

#

The morning shed a new light on the shores of Cape Solaera. Copper had spent more nights than she could count, slinking around under the halo of the street lamps and glows of Extravaganza shows, followed by sleeping during the day, that the daylight almost felt foreign as she squinted at the light.

Not just foreign but *wrong*.

To be walking out in usually crisp air.

Breathing that air.

It felt wrong.

You should be here; her heart reached out to Raleigh and was found wanting.

The soft fabric of Copper's plain shoes paired well with the gray of her cotton gown. The long hem flirted with the ground, and the almost too-long sleeves were bunched in anxious fists when the gentle scent of lilacs filled her nose. Pharaoh had encouraged her to freshen up a bit, and for that, she was grateful.

Her freshly washed hair was tied into a messy bun atop her head, a few stray beads of water slipping down her neck as she walked down the cobblestones leading into a curving avenue. There, Copper found a little cafe framed in large lilac bushes and crowned with a shining roof that, when the sun hit it just right, the place resonated in a warm glow.

Copper surveyed the small groupings of outdoor tables, separated by large potted plants, paired with a series of booths tucked up against the stained glass windows. Even in street clothes, Pharaoh was unmistakable.

"You look more human already!" Pharaoh verbally poked at her, rising to his feet when their eyes met.

Copper hesitated; the raw depth of emptiness that overwhelmed her clouded her judgment. Her reactions were slower than usual. He approached her gently as he guided her to a booth.

Although he had made it clear that he was not there to help her when they'd first met in the market, Copper somehow found herself seated across from Pharaoh, unsure why she'd been summoned. But after what had happened with Raleigh, Copper assumed that the initial facade had very little to do with his true intentions.

"This isn't right," Copper shivered. "People can't just…die…not for a game. Not for something like this." her emotions presented in a series of awkward hand gestures, including rubbing her face and smoothing her clothing.

"It's not right." Pharaoh agreed as he watched her from behind a steaming cup of coffee. "Do you have time to talk?"

Copper nodded, staring blankly as a woman dressed in the color of sunshine set a mug of spiced tea before her. The steam on her face softened some of the tension she held there, paired with the welcome aroma of sweet vanilla cream, cinnamon, and cardamom reached her.

"Hollis, my ward. She was sleeping when I left. Tanith said she'd wait with her until I returned."

It had been an awful experience to bring Hollis Roux down off the proverbial ceiling. And while Copper knew that death couldn't be foreign for Hollis, having been raised on a pirate ship, the shock of it all, paired with the lateness of the hour, had struck an almost obsessive cord with her until she'd finally collapsed into a fitful sleep.

In the still hours of the morning, the magic and adrenaline of the night had begun to bruise into submission, allowing everyone a chance to settle into a moment lacking in chaos. The breeze was sweet as it flowed through the little silent streets until it reached the outdoor cafe.

"Are you…all right?" The depth of Pharaoh's voice at that early hour reminded her of a rumbling thunderstorm on the horizon.

"No, I'm not," Copper tried to hide her grief in a miserable laugh. "But what choice do I have?"

"It's not the first time someone has died in The Red Game," Pharaoh admitted, setting down his red clay coffee mug.

"I feel like there's a 'but' in there somewhere," Copper coaxed, running her thumb along the inner curve of her pearl and opal mug handle.

"*But* it was a breach of contract, and I think you and I can work with that." Pharaoh quirked his mouth. "It doesn't usually happen like…that. There are safeguards, rules in place that you, as Rebels, will probably never see."

"Tanith made it sound like the Red Game was notorious for nefarious acts."

He visually weighed the options with a subtle shifting of his head. "Maybe in the past, but the safeguards…"

"Failed."

"What?"

"Your safeguards? They failed. And now a man is dead." Copper went on, her voice taking on a bitter quality. "A man I have known almost my entire life…died."

Pharaoh stilled. "I'm sorry for your loss."

She scratched the side of her neck, sighing deeply as her head throbbed, probably from dehydration. If Pharaoh was right, and there were traditional measures set in place to prevent things like that from happening…then what had gone wrong?

"I was told there wasn't a protection clause…" She murmured, trying to figure out what he was getting at.

"There wasn't, and it was a breach of contract."

"How can a new contract be in breach before it's signed?"

"Not *your* contract, Copper…but *mine.*"

"You're contracted into the circus?"

"We all are, in varying levels," He took another long drink from his mug. "Mine is…an unusual one."

There was a familiar swagger to the way Pharaoh spoke. The persuasive nature of his voice and that confident posture.

Where have we met before? Copper wondered at the familiarity of him.

"What does that have to do with me?"

"Raleigh's death is in direct breach of my contract, and I believe we can fight it."

Copper sat back, feeling dazed. "*Fight* it?"

"If you win this game and draw Cassian out, I can challenge the magic of the game and potentially fix this."

"Fix…death?" Copper's expression flattened.

"You'd be surprised what's written into the magic that holds this place together."He eyed her, a sparkle of mischief in his eyes. "But I am as equally bound by my contract as I am aware of its loopholes."

"So you need my help," Copper sighed. "I feel like I've been having this conversation on repeat."

"You're a talented woman with a blossoming reputation. Are you surprised that people seek out your skills?"

Again, such a familiar note in the way he flattered her.

"Honestly, I'm surprised that I wake up every morning after everything that's happened to me in the last few years."

There was a pause between them then.

Copper closed her eyes against her own words, feeling the raw sensation of oversharing.

"It's Cassian…he's the one doing this then?" Copper said before she opened her eyes and found a distant look on him.

"It's always Cassian." His voice was tainted with the haunted twinge of a life lived in the shadow of something terrible.

"I saw him…before I came here."

Pharaoh's attention was razor sharp at those words. "What did you say?"

"I mean…" Copper pinched the bridge of her nose, feeling a headache coming on as she tried to gauge how much was too much to share with a complete stranger.

Someone who saved your life isn't exactly a stranger.

"I agreed to do a job for him. I tried to steal a necklace from Clarke & Wylder, the oddity shop?"

"I'm…familiar with it." Pharaoh swallowed further unspoken words.

Copper paused, making a mental note of his reaction.

"The job went…south."

Pharaoh's shoulders slumped as he sat back against his side of the booth, his head falling back as he let what she said sink in. "And then Raleigh came along to save you."

"Yes," Copper nodded, noting that he had connected dots that had remained unseen for her. "We came here because the ringmaster set me up for failure, and I wanted to make him pay. He followed me here probably so I didn't get myself killed and…well." She gestured with her mug in the direction of the fairway. "We all know how that ended."

Pharaoh tipped his head back up to look at her, an unreadable expression on his face.

Copper dropped her gaze to her cup again. "I don't know why I'm telling you all of this. I don't even know you."

Pharaoh leaned in a little, a small smirk tugging at one side of his mouth. "So get to know me."

Copper held his stare. "Pharaoh," she said his name smoothly in a thoughtful way, as though trying to wrap her mind around the world itself.

"Hm?"

"Is that your given name?" she asked, "For all I know, that could be some kind of stage name."

"It *is* my given name," he said after swallowing another drink from his steaming cup. "Does that surprise you…Copper." he pointed out her equally less-than-conventional name.

"Touché," she scoffed, drinking deeply before resurfacing in the conversation; she listened to the rich sound of Pharaoh's laughter.

It was then that the waitress brought out their food. The meal Pharaoh had ordered them was divine. Copper couldn't remember the last time she'd eaten.

Piping hot eggs of their choosing, paired with perfectly seasoned potatoes and a thick sauce that could only be described as heavenly. She'd forgone the toast in favor of a sweet, wildflower scone slathered with honey and current jam after reading a small sign posted on the table about the unique love language of wildflowers in Rovernaum.

Pharaoh had eaten something similar, though instead of the scone, he had gotten a side dish of grilled pair stuffed with goat cheese wrapped in bacon. The fresh melon salad had been little more than a garnish, but it was gone just the same.

"Do they really speak to each other, the wildflowers?" she asked him.

Pharaoh took her in for a long moment. "There's an entire festival centered around it, actually."

A gentle mending took place in the potentially false hope he'd give her about Raleigh and the time they'd spent in the upscale corner of the eating district. It was warming and quiet that she couldn't bring herself to leave the slight reprieve. But something was gnawing at the back of her mind.

"Can I see him?"

"Raleigh?"

Copper nodded.

"No."

"No?"

Pharaoh appeared to be no more than a handful of years her senior, just in how he spoke and carried himself. He didn't have the telltale signs of traditional aging, but there was a depth to his soul that was so…inviting. However, something so vile rose inside her when he denied her request that she had to tamp down the urge to reach across the table and slap him.

"Why not?" Copper insisted.

Who do you think you are? Her temper screamed.

The cockiness, the challenge that he presented to her, and this slow hunger that had burned in his eyes as he watched her drink made him…something else in her mind's eye. Again, Copper returned his dark gaze for a moment too long and found herself saying something she hadn't meant to.

"I don't think I ever got around to thanking you for saving me," she said so quietly that the sound of her cup settling against the table seemed loud.

"I didn't expect you to," he shrugged, leaning forward on his folded forearms on the table. "And really, I wouldn't thank me until we've won because you have a hard few days ahead of you, and I'd hate to have to return such hard-won gratitude."

Copper shook her head at him. "Do you really think we can do this?"

"I wouldn't have invited you here if I didn't."

Chapter Forty-Five

Of Diamond Descent

No matter how many times a person joined in the festivities under the big top of the Extravaganza, there was always such a breathtaking quality of magic and wonder that swept over patrons that it was nearly indescribable. It was as though any performers, past or present, had left behind a small part of themselves to dance about the room with each note of music played, every dazzling smile garnered, and any act carried out with expert skill.

A man, who had not been there in quite some time, had quietly joined those seated on the benches and waited for the show to start. The main tent's flaps were drawn tight, and a crowd filled the entire arena. As the show began, the lights were dimmed, and soon, only the faintest glimmer of twinkling light drew the eye to the next act overhead.

As the crowd hushed, tucked somewhere in the shadows, a twisted smirk filled the lower half of a man's face, like a lion knowing its prey was about to step into view. "Let the games begin," he purred with malicious delight as dozens of stars lit up the tent's ceiling.

A pensive melody played, one set in motion with a few strokes on the keys of a single piano. Joined with the siren call of a haunted violin, all attention was drawn to two illuminated eyes, rimmed in molten orange, moved in a swaying motion as though freed from the confines of a body.

In a flash, the spotlight whirled around, revealing the curve of Xerxes' bare legs. The tail of her waistcoat curled like a cat's tail, lifting and turning in its own accord, splitting to reveal a tiny pair of black shorts and a navel ring with a crescent moon dangling from it.

Xerxes inhaled sharply when the magic hit her; a surge of a midnight galaxy overtook her, starting from the farthest reaches of her limbs and surging up her body. A sea of fireflies fluttered to her, illuminating every strand on her head in a brilliant sky of stars. The wide slits on either side of her jacket reached past her wild mane of hair tumbling down around her waist.

"You really are something..." The man murmured, watching the galaxies spin around Xerxes like they had always been together, swirling in the heavens.

As though she was of a cosmic, diamond descent.

The beat of the drums kicked in then, pounding on as Xerxes made it to the middle of the tightrope, and two hoops ignited around her arms.

Once upon a time, the tightrope walkers had been trained to perform without a secured tightrope. This forced them to keep their minds sharp and their rope levitating and maintain their balance.

Then Cassian disappeared, and a lot of the magic went with him. Xerxes had only performed on a static rope, never having enough magic to suspend her platforms and rope in midair.

The man saw the tethers of Xerxes's rope as an insult. "No more training wheels." He lifted a hand, and chaos entered the tent with a single motion.

#

Xerxes was fully immersed in her small portion of magic allowed her during each performance. So much so that she almost missed the crackle of the rope fasten wearing away. But it was a crackle nonetheless, and she knew from experience what that meant, though it should not have been happening when she was in the middle of a performance.

In a split-moment decision, her eyes scanned the crowd, spotting a dark figure where one should not have been. At the climax of her act, Xerxes tumbled forward, expertly slipping an opal spike from the binding at her ankle and plunging it toward the dark figure.

Unable to see if her weapon had found its mark, Xerxes returned to her platform just before the entire rope burst into flames, searing from one end to the other with a spray of sparks. The rope fell to the floor, no more than a pile of ashes.

The crowd erupted into a chorus of applause, and while Xerxes smiled and waved, her eyes fell on a face that shouldn't have been there.

The opal spike sunk into the center of a support pole on the far wall, wiggling back and forth under the force of the throw and collision.

The perpetrator, if they were ever there at all, had vanished.

#

A light had ignited in Copper when she and Pharaoh parted ways. She wasn't foolish enough to blindly believe the Extravaganza could bring Raleigh back to life, but she could root herself in the semblance of a plan they'd worked out together.

She could keep going until the game was over.

Until she saw his body, dead or alive, for herself.

"He just…flew in the window!" Hollis marveled as Aloysius tucked himself into the curve of Copper's neck when she entered their living quarters.

He gave her a distressed squeal, his little claws grazing her skin as he tried to get closer than physically possible.

Because he had lost Raleigh too.

"I was wondering where you'd run off to," Copper mused, pulling him from her shoulder to tuck the grieving creature against her chest and pet him slowly. "It's okay. It will be okay." She repeated, partially for her own sake.

And something inside her believed it.

"Can we keep him?" Hollis bounced up and down excitedly.

"I think so," Copper answered as she passed the small creature to her. "Why don't you see if you can find him something to eat?"

As Hollis danced around the large room, offering Aloysius this treat and that, Copper looked to Tanith, who was openly amused by the entire scene.

"Ah, to be so…resilient," Tanith said, one eye still on Hollis as she gathered her things. "I take it your meeting went well?"

Don't think yourself the only one aware of Cassian's moves. Xerxes's words echoed in the back of her mind.

Copper thought about her answer. "It went as well as could be expected."

Tanith waited expectantly but was not given any further details. "I'll be back this afternoon to dress you both," she said quietly and excused herself without further prying.

I'm sorry, Copper thought as she watched Tanith go. *I just don't know who to trust right now.*

But she kept her regrets to herself, and when the door to their lodging was closed, Copper slipped down to where she kept The Tome of Fable and settled in with Addy to do a little research into the binding powers of the wards surrounding the Extravaganza.

"Tell me everything you know about the Extravaganza contracts," she told the book, thumbing her way through several pages as they illuminated throughout the book.

"Now you're onto something," Addy's voice was rife with triumph. "It is good to see you finally using your head."

"Thanks," Copper answered dryly. "Now, Let's see what kind of damage we can do before tonight, hm?"

#

Xerxes found Copper James in deep caverns even *she* didn't know about. Found was probably the wrong word as she'd followed Copper the moment she'd slipped the hood of that cursed cloak over her head and believed herself to be invisible.

But not everyone turned a blind eye to that sort of magic.

Xerxes hadn't known what she would do or say when she cornered the Rebel, but between Raleigh falling to his death and her own near-terrifying experience, there had to be an outlet for all the pain she was feeling.

Because Xerxes didn't *do* feelings.

It's why she'd cut ties with everyone and everything to become a performer in the circus.

But Raleigh was something else. Something different.

The sickly glow of the cavern only soured Xerxes' intent. Raleigh was dead, and Copper James was down there playing with…bugs?

"Why did you bring him here," Xerxes sobbed the second she saw the hem of Copper's cloak pooling on the ground. She hadn't meant to cry. She was white-hot rage, and the tears made her even more mad.

"Excuse me?" Copper turned a wicked glare in her direction.

"He was safe in the capitol!"

Copper's eyes became glassy as she stared forward. "None of us are safe. Not there and certainly not here."

"Don't be stupid."

"What do you care?" Copper sneered. "You met the man a few days ago!"

"Because I loved him!" Xerxes screamed. "And I didn't just meet him. I wear so many faces and have shared a lot of experiences with him…you can't possibly understand."

Copper rubbed her face with both hands. "Why did you follow me here? Do you want an apology? Do you want me to say it was my fault because I don't need someone else to tell me how deeply at fault I am."

"I saw him the day after you made your deal with the devil."

"How could you possibly know…"

"Don't think yourself the only one aware of Cassian's moves."

"It was his choice to come here…" Copper climbed to her feet, her face tight with anger.

"Did you know that Raleigh gave me red powder in exchange for information on you?"

Copper blinked. "Am I supposed to be impressed?"

"You are not the end all on information about him. Do you still believe you were his greatest ally?"

"I understand you are grieving for whatever perceived relationship you believe you had with him, but now is not the time to let your emotions get the best of you."

Xerxes' vision turned red and hazed around the edges. "He protected you. He loved you. And you let him die!"

Copper stomped over to Xerxes, grabbed her by the collar of her shirt, and shoved her around the edge of the stone that blocked her line of sight from what Copper had been staring at. "Do you see this doorway? It's…"

"Cassian's doorway," Xerxes said around residual sobs. "It was how he came and went without anyone knowing…"

Copper released her. "Before you decided to become my own personal stalker and accuse me of Raleigh's death, instead of coping with your own emotions, Pharaoh came to me about the ringmaster and what would happen if we don't stop him from getting free!"

Xerxes panted, starting to regain control.

"So, don't you think we have bigger problems than your *feelings*?" Copper pointed to where the sealed doorway once was and how it laid not only open but also ripped off its hinges.

"What do we do now?" Xerxes sniffled. "I mean…is there…a plan?"

"Of course, there's a plan." Copper walked away from her. "Come with me," she gestured when Xerxes didn't immediately follow. "And hurry up because I have a game to play."

CHAPTER FORTY-SIX

How to Steal a Show

COPPER PASSED THROUGH ONE interconnected tunnel after another, light coming and going as they went through the series of pathways hidden from view as far as the rest of the circus was concerned. Her shoes shuffled along the stone walkway once so frequently traveled that it was worn smooth.

"How do you know about this place?" Xerxes followed along, appearing comfortable enough that she must have known of the older, deeper passages herself.

Copper didn't falter in her unhurried walking, waving the open tome in her hand in response as though it was a flapping bird. "It's amazing what you can find in a book."

"Bringing her along may not be the best of ideas," Addy warned.

Copper squinted as a shard of daylight fell across her eyes. Eyes that had spent too many hours reading in the dim lighting of the cavern that held Cassian's doorway. Her body ached with a stiffness that came from an extended time sitting on a cave floor, but her mind was sharp, focused, and curious.

Leaving Xerxes behind might bring its own kind of trouble.

She knew what it was to be that unhinged after someone she cared about died. Knew what kind of trouble Xerxes could cause if left to her own pain and longings to stifle that by any means necessary.

Copper had experienced the broken shards the waves of grief could rain down on a body, on the mind, in the wake of Raleigh's passing, but with the hope Pharaoh had given her, it didn't compare to the agony she'd experienced a few years ago…

"This is different," Copper chirped at the map in the book as it unfolded before her, pausing briefly when it stopped at a wall of stone.

"Where exactly are you taking us?" Xerxes crossed her arms with a huff. The golden cuffs around her wrists sent glimmers of metallic light swirling around the hall with the gesture.

Everywhere but in the corner.

As though the light had been swallowed up.

Copper turned her attention away from the book. A tinkling melody similar to windchimes breathed across her skin. It was faint, but she knew the sound of a glamor anywhere. Careful to manage her balance in case she was wrong, Copper brought her left foot forward and down, passing right through the wall and down onto a hidden staircase. The loose leg of her swishing pants swirled around her legs as the sudden stop.

Xerxes paused, blinking once, then twice at the optical illusion. "Wait, this hasn't always been here?"

I'm sure it hasn't…for you. Copper made it a few steps down the spiral stone stairs before Xerxes passed through the not-wall and followed.

A meeting was about to occur in a forgotten cavern dotted with bioluminescent creatures. The once swollen underground lake had borne a series of water circus events when the Extravaganza was young, and the ringmaster wasn't so corrupt. The walls were painted with glimmering fish and people alike in various states of performance. Some swam with creatures Copper didn't recognize, and others dangled and flipped from high places.

But that was then, and as the dark gave way to the sultry glow of the blue and teal waters, others filtered in from different halls and passages until they stood in the echoing chamber around the residual shallows of the underground lake.

"I didn't know this place still existed," Xerxes murmured.

"I think there's a lot about Cape Solaera that's remained hidden for a very long time," Copper answered, running a thumb over her book as she took in the space.

Pharaoh was waiting on the far side of the cavern in a dark tunic slung over tight performance pants. His hair was tied back, and the unlaced strings of his collar dangled over the paint on his chest as though he'd been in the middle of preparing for a performance later that night. Ophelia entered just behind him. The canary yellow of her sundress brought a levity to the room.

A small woman, twisted and wrinkled with time, stood on the lake's edge, her trembling hands swirling and summoning the water to stand in a shining wall formation with unseen magic. She was draped in a colorful garment, her head wrapped in a similar fabric.

The wall solidified, and in it was an image of the wild man Copper recognized from her first night in the circus. The one who reminded her of the swagger of a lion stalking through the grounds, but he looked much more refined this time. His wild mane of red hair was slicked back, the tan of his tunic and pants framed in a forest green cloak as he sat in a reclined, careless position.

"That's...August," Xerxes said under her breath, still unsure of what was happening.

August. The name was a cool caress along the back of Copper's mind that pulled her toward something that felt forgotten. *You,* an echo inside her, reached out to him. *I remember you.* But was it her or the magic of the tome that was drawn to him?

"You were going to include *Momma Lou* but not me?" Xerxes snarled, pushing past Copper and toward Ophelia, even if there were rocks, water, and an expansive cavern between them.

"What are you doing here," Ophelia's voice took on a lethal quality. "*You* shouldn't be here."

"None of us should be!" Xerxes stopped, frustration binding her body in tension.

"You're right," Momma Lou agreed, a salty purse to her lips still lingering at Xerxes's insinuation as she waddled back from the brink of the waters and seated herself on a small boulder. "This meeting is being held amongst ancient shadows of the forgotten," she gestured a tremorous hand in the general directions of the walls. "Even the echoes that assault us from every angle whisper of the past and of a group of people that should never have met."

Copper watched in silence and noted that what she said held some truth. None of them should have crossed paths. But the magic had touched all of their lives in one way or another, and it had led them all to that place, in that time, with one goal in mind.

To survive Cassian September.

Anything else they might feel was secondary to the fact that no one was safe so long as Cassian went unseen and anything but held responsible for his actions.

"Why are we here," August's voice reverberated throughout the cavern, similar to the rumbled echo of a lion's roar.

Copper was the last to join them, head held high, her cloak billowing in her wake. Standing in a staggered circle, she met each of their gazes.

"It's come to my attention that this circus is cursed, and no one thought to tell us as Rebels before we signed up for what very well could be our final act," Copper announced as she snapped into view, having dropped the hood of her cloak.

"Well, no one said you make a boring entrance," Addy sighed.

"We believe that Cassian is lying in wait to make an entrance," Pharaoh explained, unsurprised by her arrival as he was the one who had suggested she come. "He is biding his time to regain his strength and either break free of his bindings or reclaim control of the game."

"And do what? Torture us all with his theatrics?" August said dryly.

"How vain you are, sitting in your pretty perch outside this cursed place…" Addy verbally sneered at August for Copper's ears only.

"Your freedom from this place has made your tongue dangerously loose," Momma Lou warned him with a pointed gesture from her cane.

"I was there," August sat up. "I visited Cape Solaera during your little opening ceremony, and I found it lacking any profound insinuation that Cassian had broken free from the Obsidian Hall."

Copper's stomach dropped at the mention of the prison floor.

He had been there.

Cassian had been trapped in the Obsidian Hall.

And was supposedly still there.

She tried and failed to wrap her mind around what that meant. Her gaze fell.

"I saw him," Copper said, her voice sounding far off even to her ears as she questioned her memory.

Her own ability to recognize foreign magic.

"Where?" August pushed, his brows furrowing.

"Mere weeks ago," Pharaoh added. "In Aerimora."

"An illusion," August dismissed the idea with a careless wave of his hand.

"Which is it," Ophelia took a few steps forward. "Do you think he castrated to the extent that he is unable to break free or capable of projecting an illusion of himself through the layers upon layers of wards in the capital city?"

"Perhaps you assisted him," August boldly suggested. "As Momma Lou projects my presence now. You who blindly followed him for…"

"A man is dead," Momma Lou smacked her cane against the ground, and a wave of magic-bright light pushed out from her in every direction. All eyes turned to her. "Now we can bicker all we want about the plausibility of Cassian's ability to escape the prison floor…or we can do something before he succeeds in whatever he has planned!"

The cavern fell silent.

"You would do well to remember that I am the one who sacrificed the most to see him bound all those years ago," Ophelia said with grave calm.

He touched me, Copper reminded herself. Cassian had touched her. She'd felt his breath on her face.

It was real.

He was real.

"Pharaoh, you called this gathering together. What is it that you intend to do?" Momma Lou shifted a little on her stone seat in order to see him better.

"We plan to use this." Pharaoh pulled out a necklace, and from it dangled a small moonstone vial reflecting the glow from the lake and a shining amulet the color of death, blood, and magic that shouldn't be used lightly.

Copper's free hand went to her throat, this vision of the necklace forcing bile to rise there. It was such a visceral reaction to an item that previously meant nothing to her.

"What does a replica of the empress' necklace have to do with any-thing?" August frowned. "He won't think it's real."

"But what if he does," Ophelia passed her hand over the necklace. When she pulled her back, the necklace glowed with a radiance that the costume piece had lacked before.

So easy, Copper thought. It was so *easy* for them to wield magic in the Extravaganza. *No conduits, no powders or tokens.*

Everything she knew about magic changed daily.

"You think you can draw him out with a few party tricks and a piece of costume jewelry?" August's words were laced with cruel amusement as he clasped his hands before him.

"I know I can summon him with the one thing he wants most," Copper stepped forward and set the book on a stone projection. "I've been studying the rules no one bothered to tell us, and this is the only chance to break this curse."

And bring Raleigh back.

She couldn't say it, but the idea lingered in the silence between them.

Ophelia made a comment then that it was only for Pharaoh's ears. Copper wouldn't have even noticed it had he not turned to look at her over his shoulder.

But Xerxes certainly did.

"And why should they trust you? Why should any of us, *ringmaster.*" Xerxes sneered. "You, of all people, should know what is going on in this place, and yet you stand among us acting as lost and uncertain as the rest of us."

"You think I would choose to let Ezlyn suffer? To watch others *die?*"

"And what if you're wrong?" The prowling mystery of August from night one was gone. In its place was a glowering man with golden skin and elongated canines that flashed in the glimmers of light in the cavern when he growled his displeasure. "How many more of you am I going to have to drag off to the Asylum the way I did, Ezlyn?"

Ezlyn. The Fae. So that's what happened to her?

"Is that what you've been doing? Smuggling out the players one by one?"

August neglected to meet her stare. "No."

"Ezlyn was removed after she came in contact with a questionable item. The Blue Giraffe Asylum is part of August's territory. Only the monks there could help her now." Momma Lou informed them all.

"What do you suggest?" Xerxes' face glowed blue as she approached the lake.

Copper grabbed a swath of glimmering fabric and gave them a feline grin. "We steal the show right out from under the ringmaster's nose."

CHAPTER FORTY-SEVEN

The Man Made of Stars

S CURRYING TOWARD THE OPENING ceremony of night five, Hollis Roux was very aware of how upset Tanith would be for not having the time to appropriately dress her.

"It's Copper's fault for leaving me behind!" She practiced her excuse. "If she'd taken me to training, I wouldn't have had a chance to wander off!"

It was weak in the way of excuses, but she'd just had enough of Tanith, her rules, and the tasks she found monotonous. Plus, when they'd returned to prepare for the evening's events, Copper was still missing, and the Tome of Fable had been grumbling away in its locked chest.

"You're all I need," Hollis told Aloysius when he perched himself on her slender shoulder. She'd affectionately started calling him 'Wishy,' and he'd quickly gotten over the humiliation of the nickname when Hollis had wandered into a mess hall called 'The Sun Basket' where he'd been fed and fawned over by performers for the remaining part of the afternoon.

The sun had all but gone down, and Hollis had removed him from his glory in favor of finding her seat for the show that was about to take place.

Maybe Tanith wouldn't be *so* mad if she...

Blinded by the series of spotlights swirling about the place, Hollis Roux was oblivious to the world around her as she basked in the joy of her newfound pet.

But then she tripped.

Her mouth fell open when she rolled onto her back and saw what had unexpectedly halted her. An impossible man in a dark suit stood over her with pieces of starlight delicately warming the outline of his form.

Looking to the left and right, Hollis found that no one was disturbed by his presence. In fact, they didn't notice either of them as she stared blankly at the man who stood over Hollis.

"Here, let's get you up," he offered, helping Hollis to her feet and dusting her off.

In that moment, Hollis Roux regretted so many things.

But mostly, she genuinely regretted wandering off. She needed to run, to get back to Copper.

To where it was safe.

But for the life of her, all Hollis could do was watch him. She was wholly enraptured by his presence and the way the light framed his face. From the airy sheen to his hair to the glimmering constellation of freckles on his face. The man made of stars looked at her with a familiar smile and burning eyes that flickered back and forth between the deepest brown and striking silver.

But that wasn't the thing that kept her rooted in place. The way he simply *lived* took her breath away.

I saw.

Her mind all but accused him.

Because he was…alive?

She had watched him fall.

The sound of his body hitting the pavement still haunted her nightmares.

"Detective Danger?" she asked, sure her eyes had deceived her.

Chapter Forty-Eight

The Living Carousel

IN THE FINAL MOMENTS before the performance events of night five, Copper stood in one of the dressing rooms, painted from head to toe like some sort of human canvas. Tanith had been replaced as her dresser by a different woman from the costume department, as she was more of an art piece than a player in an outfit.

When the final dusting of holographic highlighter was swept across her cheeks, Pharaoh appeared in the doorway, waiting to drape the glamoured necklace over her head.

"Ready?" He asked her when she looked at him in the mirror.

"Sure," Copper answered casually, taking the box they'd tucked the necklace into from him. Her hands trembled slightly when she held the piece in her hands.

I wouldn't risk my spot in The Grand Aurora for my own family, let alone the likes of you. Saul's voice swelled in her mind. Reminding her over and over that there was just as much at risk, if not more if their plan didn't work.

"Here," Pharaoh offered to help. "Let me."

Copper watched as he pulled her hair aside, the calluses on his hands brushing against the sensitive skin of her neck as he maneuvered the necklace until it slid over her collarbones.

The weight of the amulet and vial pairing was heavier in her mind than it was on her body.

"I can't imagine your performing partner is too happy about this," Copper said casually, noting his blonde companion was nowhere to be found.

Pharaoh hesitated, and for just a moment, Copper could have sworn a shadow passed over his face. He'd warned her about the magic's effect on his personality during his contracted performance periods, but this was something else.

"Ellis was a showpiece, nothing more."

Was, Copper noted the word and wondered what it meant. But before she could push the subject further, she was being herded by stagehands toward her starting point for the show.

After their meeting in the cavern, Copper had spent the rest of the afternoon playing the game. She'd entered the tent hesitantly, card in hand, ready to practice for her performance.

And, of course, she'd been assigned to Pharaoh.

Whether that was just the luck of the card, she'd won from night four, or interference from Ophelia was something she didn't have an answer to.

She was prepared as she could be and ready to perform with the entire aerialist wing of the troupe. They'd gone over the entire show until she could probably do her part in her sleep.

But as they raised her up on a platform in the shadows, Copper was brutally aware of not only how high up she was but that they'd she'd practiced with a training harness, and that was nowhere in sight as the show began.

#

A hush fell over the audience as the lights dimmed and color washed from the world. A plucky circus tune swelled inside the tent.

Copper forced herself to take the challenge head-on, letting her fear wash through her, replaced by a forced sense of calm. Looking around, feeling exhilarated, her eyes caught a movement on a distant platform.

And reeled backward, surprised by what she saw.

A ghost stood on a solitary platform, tall and dark, with hair as black as night. It felt as though her heart had stopped in her chest. It was Raleigh, watching in the shadows.

Or was it Cassian?

It has to be Cassian. But recognizing that didn't make her feel any better.

Copper's nails dug into the sturdy fabric that secured her to her platform. She did a double take; he was there, gone, and there again, his gaze never faltering.

A door appeared on the amethyst floor. Cold and gray on one side, it rotated on its own, revealing behind its threshold a colorfully painted fairway with rides and balloons laid out in chalky pastels. The door rotated once more, and in a flash of light, Xerxes dressed as Ellis appeared atop the frame, her legs crossed and clad in jewel-tone tights.

"Music and laughter, dreams and magic," her words echoed over a series of several speakers. "The aerialist troupe of The Red Rebel Extravaganza welcomes you to step through the doorway of your childhood and into a night immersed in imagination. Take a seat and join us in a ride made of dreams on the living carousel!"

Xerxes spread her arms outward, and the door opened wide, revealing several crimson bolts of fabric drawn taught in a diagonal, overlapping pattern that aligned with the far curve of the floor. Her torso was clad in a leotard made of white peacock feathers dotted with teal and indigo gems in the center of each feather.

Pharaoh stepped out from the shadows under the accentuation of a bold spotlight. The crowd cheered as he walked into the arena in his famous black pants. With his hair tied up, his entire torso was decorated in splashes of foreign galaxies of black, white, and the deepest of purples.

Taking one of the red silks, Pharaoh wrapped it around his dominant arm, and with a running start, he launched himself up into the air, swinging around the entire circle of the tent. Seven others dressed in costumes reminiscent of old-fashioned carousel horses joined him as he gracefully swung through the air, the tail of his silk rippling behind him.

As another set of performers joined them, dressed in ivory jeweled bodysuits, intermingling with the others giving them a visually varied effect, Pharaoh found the center of the circle they created and wrapped his legs in the twin to his fabric. His body stretched; Pharaoh lowered himself swiftly in a dynamic drop as four matching carriage seats lowered from the circle, coming to the ground as he flipped over and landed on his feet.

Copper stepped out onto a thin metal platform. Dressed in a midnight-themed leotard of night sky blue paired with shards of stark white fabric and a sea of iridescent stars. A train of tulle flowed behind her, matching the shimmer that coated her legs. Her left eye was painted in a deep blue splash and speckled with lemon stars that swept down the side of her neck.

The music swelled and surged. Swift and ethereal, the melody of the stars rained down upon them.

Pharaoh climbed upward as the platforms around Copper dispersed, and another dozen performers stepped out, leaping onto various trapeze apparatuses, sending them soaring and tumbling in the air.

Come and get me, she thought with a smirk. To the uninformed eye, that might have appeared to be for Pharaoh, and perhaps a small part of it was.

But she'd caught a second glimpse of Cassian and knew their plan was working.

Pharaoh launched at Copper as she slipped her foot into a loop under another performer's rope and swung out of his reach. She gave him a dazzling grin as she swooshed through the air, her long blonde hair and sparkling skirt rippling behind her. Together, they played a game of cat and mouse, loftily sprinting across the lit platforms as the others swung and flipped in a pattern of organized chaos around them. As Pharaoh came closer and closer to catching Copper, he was finally a breath's distance from her, the audience fervently cheering for them to be reunited, only for her to laugh when she was pulled in a different direction. The necklace she wore caught the light and swung freely on its too-loose chain.

With each flash of the lights, one by one, the performers of grouped costume styles began to fill in the circular pattern from all directions. First, the horses, then the sea animals, the large cats, exotic birds, and then the fantastical creatures unique to the empire. A rainbow of colors fell into place as costumed performers swung around the core of the carousel like children around a maypole.

The fun of the moment halted when Copper noticed a panicked Tanith standing off to the side instead of being in the seats set aside for her and Hollis.

"Stop," she whispered, her eyes straining as Cassian sat in the front row, flipping the rose gold coin Hollis kept amongst her few personal possessions.

Hollis…Hollis! Her mind cried the name over and over, and she realized how vulnerable she had left her ward.

Pharaoh waited at Copper's eye level and offered his hand to her as thirteen other pairs did the same.

"What is it?" Pharaoh tried to ask over the chaos of music and sounds.

"I…" Copper panted. "Something is wrong…"

Each woman was guided to their matching seats, decorated with crescent moons and swimming mermaid figurines. Fifty-Four performers moved around the circle, fourteen of which were stationary items and carriage benches.

An elegant metal dome of scarlet and gold panels with flashing lights and oval mirrors descended as the seats raised high into the air to meet the twisted core bringing the carousel into complete formation, creating the living carousel. The audience cheered as the performers bobbed up and down to the timing of the music, mimicking the carnival ride.

Copper tried and failed to visualize Hollis as she rode in the circle. Her moment of aerial effort was over.

In one of the final rotations, Xerxes descended from the bottom with her hoop and four other performers. Together, they created a star formation arching in unison just as Pharaoh slipped onto the bench beside Copper, wrapping his arm around her.

"What happened? What did you see?" He asked her.

"He's here," Copper told him frantically. "He's here, and I think he has Hollis."

A wicked laugh echoed in the arena, stirring the audience from their enamored expressions of awe from observing the show up to that point.

"What is that?"

"Where is it coming from?"

"Is this some kind of joke?"

And still, the laughing increased. Deep and rich and resonating in the arena.

"We'll find her," Pharaoh assured her. "Just stick to the plan."

Copper's skin crawled. She couldn't look at Pharaoh, couldn't look back at any of the platforms because everywhere she looked, she saw Raleigh.

I never thought I'd wish for a time when Ellis was the only ghost that haunted the circus.

A whining creak splintered the chaos as a piece of overhead rigging shifted before it fell, taking a few performers with it.

"No!" Pharaoh boomed, launching forward as the piece of mettle cracked the amethyst flooring.

A sickly haze filled the air as the laughing continued.

"Where are you?" He roared, relieved to see his team members had been snatched out of the air by others before they could plunge to their doom with the rigging. "Show yourself!"

A proud, lazy voice sighed around a final laugh. The disembodied voice rose to Pharaoh's challenge.

"Come find me, brother."

Chapter Forty-Nine

Pandemonium in Bloom

THE GLORY OF THEIR performance faded the moment Copper's feet touched the floor. She'd sprinted to Tanith and then outside the tent when Hollis was nowhere to be found. Met with the dusky hues of the harbor after sunset, Copper saw overdressed patrons and vendors capitalizing on the draw of a rebel performance.

Everything but what she was looking for.

"Why didn't you tell me you'd *lost* her?" Copper whirled on Tanith as she tried to see reason, tried to spot the cherry red braid in the crowd.

"I gave her a little more free rein to explore. The circus is mostly safe and…"

"Mostly?" Copper snorted. "*Nothing* here is safe!"

"Where is she?" Pharaoh tried to ask but was overshadowed by Copper's wrath.

"Please, Copper. Calm down. Let us help," Tanith pleaded as Pharaoh finally made his way through the crowds to them.

Calm down?

All she could feel was panic.

And betrayal.

Of course, she'd lost the only innocent thing in her life.

Of course, she'd trusted someone from *The Extravaganza.*

"Who are you to tell me *anything?*" Copper sneered at Tanith, jerking the woman's hand off her arm. "You might have deluded yourself into thinking you are *safe* tucked away inside your cursed seaside oasis. But let's not forget that I have been fighting for my life since the moment I met your *ringmaster.*"

The Extravaganza is a place that will toy with your every sense. Raleigh had told her when they'd been preparing for the game. *Trust nothing but what you know for yourself.*

What Copper knew was that Hollis trusted people even less than she did.

What Copper knew was that child wouldn't have missed that show had she not been…distracted.

Copper had left her book and Addy behind when she prepared for night five. Momma Lou had recommended the absence of any other magic when they tried to capture Cassian to avoid him using it in his favor.

"How could I have been so *stupid…*" She turned to Pharaoh. "Was this the plan the whole time? Trick me into trusting you so your brother could escape?"

Copper spotted Aloysius panic-swooping above them, and it might as well have been a white, fluffy banner that screamed *Here, she's over here!*

"No, I would never. *He* wouldn't…" Pharaoh stopped talking when he saw Cassian wearing Raleigh's face. There was a wicked gleam in his eyes when he spotted them over the top of Hollis Roux's head.

Copper pushed through the crowds toward a decorative fountain in the street, and there, the tiny ginger and the towering silhouette made of shadow and stars, waited quietly.

"How?" Hollis stared up at him, an innocent picture of awe.

Copper stopped short, feeling the necklace shift around her throat.

The last time she let her emotions get the better of her, Cassian won. He preyed upon her weakness. Her desperation to be anyone, anywhere else.

Revenge, Raleigh. I want revenge. It's what she'd told him moments after he'd saved her from the Obsidian Hall. She'd promised herself, Raleigh, the universe, and anything else that listened in that hallway outside the cursed prison.

If the ringmaster wants to play a game, then so be it.

And what if you're wrong? August had been against the idea from the very beginning.

And maybe she was. Maybe she was a fool for not snatching Hollis up and running as far as her feet could carry them. But in the same breath, Copper slowed her pace to something more casual.

"There you are," Copper crooned, the picture of serene bliss; she forced the glow and satisfaction of another night won into her face.

"Miss me?" Raleigh's eyes glimmered with mischief as she approached.

Copper's stomach dropped to her feet when he met her gaze and winked. She'd expected Cassian.

Not Raleigh.

Copper's mind went in a million different directions, finally honing in on what she knew he'd *want* her to do.

A game. A game. This is all just a game to him. If he wanted to play, then Copper would put on a show that had even the ringmaster eating out of her hand.

"How are you here," Copper murmured, her voice cracking a little as she subtly guided Hollis away from him.

"I thought you'd be happy to see me." Raleigh smiled at her with his fine suit and not a single hair out of place.

"I don't understand." Hollis shook her head.

"I watched you die." Copper forced tears to her eyes, the tremble in her voice though? That ache she couldn't hide? It might have come across as grief and loss and disbelief, but there was a monster forming inside her that desperately wanted out.

Wanted to claw the stolen face off until Cassian revealed himself.

"It's not the first time," Raleigh shrugged, taking in those tears as though they were his life's work. "Probably won't be the last."

Copper crossed her arms and tilted her head to the side. "Is this funny to you? You come back from the dead, and you give me…what? Riddles?"

"What did you expect?" Raleigh asked, his words flippant and borderline mocking as he leaned in to whisper. "You came here to play. Remember?"

His gaze fell to the necklace.

Yes, the word unfolded in Copper's mind like a lover's caress. *Did you see your prize? Of course, I have the necklace. You sent me for it, remember?*

Copper touched the too-long chain. "It's a good thing the ringmaster sent me for this. I don't think the game would have gone as well as it has without it, don't you agree?"

The steel that overtook his gaze betrayed everything he was and everything Raleigh was not. "Where did you get that?"

Copper summoned a look of confusion for him. "What do you mean?" Her voice was sweetness and springtime and utter innocence. "I was wearing it when you saved me from the Obsidian Hall."

"No," his wicked gaze flickered from Raleigh's silver eyes to Cassian's brown and back. "You weren't." A rumble of thunder and Raleigh's face melted away, revealing Cassian, the intense focus never faltering. "Because I was there."

A blink of an eye.

A second's worth of distraction and Cassian struck.

"Beautiful, isn't it?" He purred into her ear, suddenly behind her, as he slipped a finger under the chain of the necklace around her throat.

Copper jerked forward, and the necklace snapped.

The necklace that was historically on an unbreakable chain…broke.

"That's enough," Pharaoh stepped forward, an outstretched arm warning him to move back. "I don't know what you think you've accomplished here…but this ends now."

Cassian stood there in satisfied silence until the glamor burned off and the piece of costume jewelry deteriorated into sand that blew away on a fantom wind. "I've already achieved everything I've wanted here," he said absently as the final grains of sand flitted from his fingers.

"Step away from her," Pharaoh bore his teeth, slowly approaching them.

Cassian casually glanced to his left and right as Ophelia and Momma Lou flanked him with visible magic glowing from the staff in Ophelia's hands, and the amulet set into Momma Lou's head wrap. His bored expression snapped back into place. "Aren't you bound by the circus…you couldn't touch me if you…"

"We're done here," Copper said bitterly, taking Hollis Roux by the hand and leading her away. "This game is over."

"Don't," he shouted, "walk away from me."

"Funny thing about sleight of hand," Copper palmed the small vial that she'd been given at the opening ceremony. In one smooth movement, she ripped the stopper from the rose-shaped glass and showered him in the pink liquid inside. "You never see it coming."

Momma Lou, Ophelia, and Pharaoh encircled him. The section of stone beneath his feet began to glow.

"Clever." Cassian laughed. He gave them a slow, thoughtful nod as he took in the scene.

"You dared to wear his face?" Copper snarled.

"Come a little closer, and I'll tell you exactly what I did to get that face."

Copper crossed her arms. "If you wanted me dead?" She looked him up and down. "You should have killed me yourself."

There was no challenge, no occasion to rise to. "You can rot in whatever prison they put you in next for the crimes you've committed against me and everyone else trapped here."

"Trapped here," Cassian repeated, unhinged amusement in his voice. "Hardly."

But Copper didn't bite.

In her mind's eye, he'd been dismissed.

"I warned you," he called after her and Hollis. "*Don't* walk away from me."

"Let's talk about this, Cass," Pharaoh coaxed, clearly seeing what Copper could not.

But the time for negotiation had passed.

"I wouldn't do that," Momma Lou warned, her hands raised, and glowing blue orbs appeared with them.

Cassian gripped his fists tightly against his sides, anger marring his features.

And then simply let go.

He let go of every safeguard. Every plan and scheme to get what he wanted out of the Red Game. Cassian let go of the foothold he had in reality, and a blue light bathed the square as a sea of orange fish swam over every surface.

It was beautiful.

This delicate display took coordination and effort. That release of power that hadn't been seen in ten years surged forward and crashed into Copper's back.

"No!" Pharaoh roared from somewhere in the distance, but he was too late.

"Thanks for playing," Cassian breathed the goodbye, and just like that…Copper was gone.

CHAPTER FIFTY

ENCHANTED fire RAGED THROUGH Copper's veins.

She'd cried out as she tumbled headfirst into the long, waving reeds. The sensation of white-hot pain piercing through her rocked her to her very core as though she'd been struck from behind.

It had only taken a few moments for her to regain her bearings. As quickly as she'd been hit, the connection to that power had been severed.

"Hollis?" Copper sat up, her fingers digging into the rich soil. All around her, she saw the thin stalks of grass dancing. It would have been beautiful how this ordinary-looking grass responded to her had she not felt the acute absence of the small hand that had been grasped tightly in her own.

"Hollis!" Copper could only manage to come to a kneeling position before the pain wracked her once again. A wicked ripple of aftershocks raked over her crispy nerves. Copper choked out a sob, the pain and the fear overwhelming her. A torrent of thoughts rained down upon her as she tried to come to terms with her situation.

What had happened?

How had she gotten here?

And where was Hollis?

"I'm here!" Hollis Roux's voice rang out, loud and clear, not too far in the distance.

The grasses parted under the swooshing steps of someone much larger than her ward. The grass was so dense that Copper imagined it would be like wading through chest-high water.

But then a man crouched down beside her, a large staff and a dark fur mantle strewn over his broad shoulders and chest.

"So I take it your little 'heist' didn't exactly go in your favor," August gloated as Copper sat before him on the ground.

"Not yet," Copper gave him a sneer masked in a fake smile.

"You too, huh?"

"You…" Copper blinked up at the Knight. "You're alive!"

"He is," August offered her a helping hand. "And from what I've heard, you're lucky to be alive."

Copper rose to her feet with his help and saw several others standing around them.

Hollis fought her way through the grass, batting and grunting her frustration as she went. "What happened!" She threw her arms forward.

"Are you hurt?" Copper reached for Hollis but swayed on her feet, earning her another steadying grasp of August's large hands.

The grass danced and glowed in response to his touch as he smoothed out a small circle around Hollis, allowing her to move freely.

"I…don't understand what happened." Copper shook her head, still feeling drowsy.

"You were cast out of the game." The Knight explained. "We've been waiting for you."

"Where are we?" Hollis wrinkled her nose at their foreign surroundings.

Copper drew a ragged breath as she took in the grasses that seemed to go on for miles. Beneath the sparkling night sky, the grasses lit up in a torrent of red, yellows, and oranges as though they burned with every sway and touch.

"It's beautiful," Copper marveled.

A dark man in a pristine uniform stepped forward.

"Warden Montgomery," August looked to the other man. "I believe our next step is yours."

"Of course, your Majesty," the man dipped his head in a show of respect.

"Your Majesty?" Copper couldn't help but frown up at him.

"You're a King?" Hollis chirped.

A deep purr of a laugh rumbled through him. "Something like that."

"Then that means…" Copper looked around, blinking slowly as she took it all in. "This…this is the actual kingdom. The Sacred Grasslands of Rovernaum?"

August nodded. "And the magic you need to return to the game is on the other side of the kingdom."

Copper's face slackened. "Shepherd, take me now…"

August answered with a broad grin, revealing those elongated canines. "Copper James and Hollis Roux," he addressed them with a measure of pride. "Welcome to the Fields of Fire and Starlight."

Acknowledgments

I want to thank my mom, Donna, for teaching me how to dream. Your imagination is beautiful, and you are one of the most talented people I know. (If you don't know it.) She and my dad, Jerry, showed me what it meant to work hard and honor God with your life. Thank you to Ashley Weaver, Kallyn Lagro, Liz LaFrance, Katrina Hough, and Lauren Hoskins for being my rocks during the hard parts, my sounding boards when I didn't know if any idea made sense and that random texts like: "If you were a magical, carnivorous plant…what would you look like?" It was never at a respectable hour, but someone always answered. I found my tribe of adventurous writers and enthusiastic readers in them; they are more than I could have asked for. Thank you to Aaron P. (You know who you are.) You helped me find myself again, and I will never forget the hours you put in to help me figure out what that looked like and how to even get there at all. Thanks to my editor, Fiona, who wasn't afraid to ask the hard questions that made me look at parts of this book in a new light. And to you. If you, as the reader, have made it this far, thank you for starting this journey with me. Buckle up. It's going to be a TRIP.

Note from the Author

The Red Rebel Extravaganza started in mid-summer 2019. What began as this circus obsession paired with the idea of a game gone wrong developed into this life-consuming project of telling the story of Copper James. I've spent the last 3+ years developing this world, and this is just the first book of many I have planned for this series.
Welcome to The Empire of Aerimora, where The Red Game is about to take the shore of Cape Solaera by storm!

www.ingramcontent.com/pod-product-compliance
Lightning Source LLC
Chambersburg PA
CBHW070557300726
48975CB00006B/1619